Mia Sheridan is a *New York Times*, *USA Today*, and *Wall Street Journal* bestselling author. Her passion is weaving true love stories about people destined to be together. Mia lives in Cincinnati, Ohio, with her husband. They have four children here on earth and one in heaven.

Mia can be found online at:
MiaSheridan.com
Instagram: @MiaSheridanAuthor
Facebook: MiaSheridanAuthor

Also by Mia Sheridan

Falling for Gage
Grayson's Vow
Kyland
Stinger
Travis

MEN AND MONSTERS
Unwanted
Unnatural

ACADIA DUOLOGY
Becoming Calder
Finding Eden

Unnatural

MIA SHERIDAN

PIATKUS

PIATKUS

First published in the US in 2025 by Bloom Books,
An imprint of Sourcebooks
Published in Great Britain in 2025 by Piatkus

1 3 5 7 9 10 8 6 4 2

Copyright © 2025 by Mia Sheridan

The moral right of the author has been asserted.

*All characters and events in this publication, other than those
clearly in the public domain, are fictitious and any resemblance
to real persons, living or dead, is purely coincidental.*

All rights reserved.
No part of this publication may be reproduced, stored in a
retrieval system, or transmitted in any form or by any means, without
the prior permission in writing of the publisher, nor be otherwise circulated
in any form of binding or cover other than that in which it is published
and without a similar condition including this condition being
imposed on the subsequent purchaser.

A CIP catalogue record for this book
is available from the British Library.

ISBN 978-0-349-44424-6

Printed and bound in Great Britain by Clays Ltd, Elcograf S.p.A.

Papers used by Piatkus are from well-managed forests
and other responsible sources.

Piatkus	The authorised representative
An imprint of	in the EEA is
Little, Brown Book Group	Hachette Ireland
Carmelite House	8 Castlecourt Centre,
50 Victoria Embankment	Dublin 15, D15 XTP3, Ireland
London EC4Y 0DZ	(email: info@hbgi.ie)

An Hachette UK Company
www.hachette.co.uk

www.littlebrown.co.uk

Primum non nocere.

> First, do no harm.
> —HIPPOCRATES

PROLOGUE

Present Day

The answers to every burning question Autumn had ever had about her history might be sitting in one of the four file cabinets across the room.

She leaned forward in her chair, craning her neck until she could see her social worker, Chantelle. The older woman was standing on the other side of the hall just outside her office. Her back faced the partially open door as she spoke to the coworker who'd interrupted her meeting with Autumn to have a stack of—apparently urgent—forms signed.

Autumn had come there begging for information and clarification from one of the only people who could give it to her, but it'd quickly become clear that Chantelle was only going to continue to stonewall. The same way everyone had, all her life. If Autumn wanted answers, she was going to have to steal them.

It's now or it's never.

With a deep inhale, Autumn pushed herself off the chair, rounded the desk, and slipped quickly past the door, cringing as she waited to hear her name called in a warning tone. But the only sounds were the continued noise of a busy office and the murmurings of Chantelle and the man she was conversing with as she signed his forms.

Autumn blew out a slow breath as she put her hand on the nearest file cabinet and pulled the handle of the top drawer. Her heart pounded as she prepared for a squeak, but it glided open noiselessly. *Thank the heavens.* Autumn's gaze flew over the labeled tabs, attempting to quickly ascertain Chantelle's filing system.

Years. She has them organized by year. These are the most recent.

Chantelle's laugh rang out, and Autumn jerked, her breath hitching. *Just another minute. I'm so close.*

She was all in now. She couldn't fathom leaving this office with nothing.

Nothing about her childhood.

Nothing about her moonlight boy.

No. The thought of *him* bolstered her courage, and she took a step to the right, making a guess about where her own file might be. She'd entered the system twenty-three years before as a newborn baby. It had to be in one of the two farthest cabinets.

Autumn squatted down and pulled the bottom drawer of the third cabinet open, but this time, a squeak emerged from the older hardware. She froze, her heart pounding so hard she felt mildly dizzy. She caught a few words from the man speaking to Chantelle that sounded like "…court-ordered hearing, and…" It was only a snippet but enough to tell her they were still talking business and were otherwise occupied. For now. She pulled the drawer open a little more, just enough to see the dates.

Not this one. But very close. Hurry!

Autumn sprang to her feet, pulling open the top drawer on the final cabinet. The blood whooshing in her head slightly muffled the surrounding sounds, but she didn't think even the smallest squeak emerged.

"Hey, thanks for taking the time…" the man outside was saying. *They're wrapping it up. Oh God.*

Again, her gaze flew over the tabs separating the file folders within. *Yes! There.* The year she was born. Autumn's shaking hands went to the dated section, riffling through the files, eyes landing on what she'd been looking for.

Mercy Hospital for Children.

"Good luck today," Chantelle called. Her voice was closer. And Autumn heard her approaching footsteps as she shuffled through the paperwork.

My name. There's my name.

She pulled her file out, several more coming with it. She didn't have time to put the others back, instead sticking the short stack under the front of her shirt and then wrapping her large, bulky sweater around herself. She hit the open drawer with her shoulder, and it slid back into place just as Autumn took a giant step away from the cabinets and Chantelle reentered the office.

"Sorry to keep you—" Chantelle stopped, words halting as her brows raised, obviously surprised to see Autumn standing instead of seated like she'd been.

Autumn struggled not to visibly swallow, tried desperately not to appear as though she'd just done something unscrupulous. And illegal.

"Are you leaving?" her social worker asked. Her gaze

moved to the purse on the floor next to the chair where Autumn had sat begging Chantelle for information she wouldn't give. She obviously knew something was off.

Autumn needed to go before the older woman worked it out and demanded that she turn over what she'd stolen. She moved quickly, grabbing her purse and heading toward the door. "Yes. I just remembered I'm late for another appointment. Thank you for your time, Chantelle."

Chantelle stepped in front of Autumn, taking her by her upper arms and causing Autumn's heart to jolt. *Oh God. Don't make me fight for these files. I will.*

But Chantelle sighed, her face melting into what looked like empathy. "Listen, Autumn, I know it's hard to accept that you lost fourteen years of your life."

Autumn stayed still, afraid to move lest the sound of rustling papers come from beneath her clothing, but she was relieved to see that Chantelle wasn't a total bureaucrat. She still possessed some humanity.

"I'm sorry you suffered. I truly am. But you still have your whole life ahead of you. Take it and make it count."

Autumn nodded. She intended to do just that. She pulled away from Chantelle, the unmistakable sound of the files shifting under her sweater causing Chantelle's eyes to widen. Autumn dipped away from her and raced out of the room.

"Autumn!"

She heard Chantelle's voice from behind her and picked up her pace, rounding a corner and then another, practically flying down the stairs and then running for the main door.

She ran as if her life depended on it, her painful past and her bewildering connection to her moonlight boy clutched firmly to her chest.

CHAPTER ONE

Nine Years Ago—Mercy Hospital for Children

The dream was always the same.

She was running through the woods as quickly as her frail body was able, something—*no someone*—fast on her trail. The moon was high and full, a glowing orb in the sky above the trees, casting the dense forest in fluctuating streaks of pearly light. Her breath came heavy, lungs aching, heart hammering. Whoever had given chase meant her terrible harm. She could smell his intention, enveloping her far before his arms were able.

Hide. Her head whipped back and forth, searching for a suitable location but finding nothing. There were only thin tree trunks and a carpet of pine needles.

She tripped then and went sprawling, fear and frustration clashing inside her, an internal gong of soul-crushing defeat, as she rolled to her back, ready to face her attacker. She was certain she'd be no match for the person in pursuit. She'd be no match for a young child if he or she had an ounce of strength, and that unfortunate truth didn't change in her dreams. But she refused to die unaware. She'd face what was coming. She'd look death in the eye as he overwhelmed her, her *spirit* the muscle her body lacked.

The blur of a fast-approaching figure. A flash of silvery white. A gasp of breath. Hers.

And then the dream…changed. Always before, she'd hidden, rolling herself into the smallest ball she could inside a fallen tree trunk or behind a large enough rock.

Her pursuer skidded to a stop, and his face came into view. Her heart lurched, staggered breath pluming in the chilly air. Autumn blinked, lifting her head as far as she was able from her reclining position. A breeze blew, the boughs of the trees taking command from the wind and leaning aside in tandem. Moonglow glittered through the created opening and fell over the man…no, *boy.*

He's a boy, no older than me. But…

Her gaze danced over him once and then again before she met his eyes. The trees swayed, the shaft of moonlight fading to sterling tinted night. But in that moment, she'd seen him. All of him.

He was a boy, yes, but he was larger than any adolescent or teen she'd ever seen and unusually muscular, his chest bare, a large, jagged scar running from his throat to his navel.

And his hair. His hair was stark white and bone straight, hanging over his ears and in front of his eyes, a striking contrast to his smooth, light brown skin. He gave his head a small jerk, his choppy bangs shifting from his forehead to reveal midnight eyes, dark and fathomless.

And there was something protruding from his hair on his right temple. It looked curiously like a bolt.

What are you?
What are you going to do to me?

Her heart quickened, the forest wavering. This was a dream, of course, brought on by the medication, but it was the most vivid dream she'd ever had. And the only time she'd been caught.

She felt the bite of the cold, the hardness of the earth under her, and the burn of her weakened muscles, crying out from her efforts. She couldn't explain it, but in this bizarre hallucination where her brain was somehow registering her senses, it only stood to reason she'd feel whatever he did to her as well. Fear quaked inside.

She lifted her chin, drawing her shoulders back.

"Do your worst." Her voice quivered, but her gaze did not.

His heavy brow lowered as he leaned forward, peering at her more closely. His fists were clenched, but she no longer sensed that violent intention rolling off him the way she had before.

He took a step forward, then another, looming over her now, seeming to want to get a closer look.

He was...something. His hair...it...sparkled. His dark eyes were an endless universe.

"How did my mind come up with *you*?" she wondered aloud.

His head twitched again, gaze narrowing. Light shifted, tree branches swayed, and still, they stared. She saw now that his eyes were a deep twilight blue, the shade of the sky mere moments before it dimmed to black. Her breath released. She wasn't scared anymore. It seemed like years that she'd been running from him, *hiding*, and now that she'd come face-to-face with her nightmare, she was no longer frightened. *Funny.* His pale brows twitched.

"You're...magnificent." The word was whispered. It didn't seem quite right. Not that he wasn't magnificent. He was. But he was more than that. "Are you made of nighttime itself?" she asked the boy, eyes like twilight, hair like moonglow, a fanciful collaboration of all that was mysterious and nocturnal.

Something about the thought delighted her. Her mind was a more interesting place than she'd given herself credit for. She'd created *him*. With the help of narcotics, true, but even so... She let out a slight laugh, and the boy reared back like she'd slapped him with the faint, breathy sound.

Behind her, a scream rang out, high-pitched and filled with terror. The boy looked sharply in that direction, his fists rising as though readying for a fight. His hands were so large, veins protruding in his muscled forearms. He looked back, hesitated, then before she knew what was happening, he scooped her up as though she were a mere feather, deposited her behind a nearby tree, and then dumped an armful of pine needles over her. He leaned in, putting his finger over his full lips. *Shh*. He even *smelled* like the night—wind and fire.

He backed away, fading before her. The dream became misty again, the forest blinking, twisting, the boy made of night growing faint. He seemed to hesitate before turning and ducking away out of sight.

He hadn't attacked her at all.

He'd...saved her.

Autumn let her head fall back to the earth, her lips tipping, eyes shutting as the dream world around her glittered to dust.

She woke with a smile. But her smile faded as her eyes opened, the mint-green hospital walls greeting her just as they did each morning. Autumn sighed as she sat up, stretching her back and trying not to catalogue her aches and pains. What was the point? Everything hurt. Everything *always* hurt. Gingerly, she swung her legs over the side of the bed to sit up, waiting as the head rush subsided.

"Sleep well, sunshine?"

"Better than usual." She paused as Genie, the morning shift nurse, wrapped the blood pressure cuff around her arm and pressed a button as the cuff tightened. Autumn focused on breathing as what she knew was a slight tightening to anyone else made her grimace in pain. "I had the dream," Autumn said, her breath releasing along with the machine-induced grip.

Genie looked from the numbers on the machine to Autumn. "Did you manage to escape again?" she asked.

Autumn shook her head, the smile creeping over her face. "No. I got caught this time."

Genie's expression registered confusion before she let out a short laugh, removing the cuff and tossing it aside, apparently satisfied with whatever the number read. "And that was a good thing?"

Autumn nodded. "I was caught by moonlight himself." She stepped down from the bed, wincing as her hips took her slight weight, the flare of pain soon subsiding so she could move.

"Ah. Well, who doesn't want to be caught by moonlight himself? He was very handsome I'm assuming?" Genie asked, shooting Autumn a smile.

"Handsome?" Autumn frowned, conjuring the boy's face. "No, he was much more than handsome. He was…"

She *still* couldn't think of the right word. "Fascinating," she settled on, picturing him again. She wished she knew how to draw well. She'd sketch him now while he was still fresh in her mind, before he faded away as all dreams tended to do with time. Even very vivid ones. But she didn't know how to sketch well. Still, she'd take her journal to class and do the best she could. *Those eyes, that hair, that scar...* Of *course* her mind had added a scar. That was almost to be expected. She was *surrounded* by scars. By sickness. By surgery. It only stood to reason that her unconscious thoughts had hung on to that aspect of her life, even in sleep.

She looked at her arm, where scratch marks stood out. She'd done it before, scratched herself in the night and woken with bloody skin. This time wasn't so bad.

"Do you need help in the bathroom?" Genie asked. Autumn had almost passed out the day before when she'd leaned over the sink and stood too fast.

"No, but will you stay close by?"

"I'll be right here, changing your bedding. Autumn—"

Autumn turned, her questioning look turning into a frown when she saw Genie's suddenly troubled expression. She took a few steps away from the bathroom door she'd been about to enter. "What is it?"

Genie's shoulders lowered. "Zoey died in her sleep last night."

Autumn's stomach plummeted to her feet, and bile burned her throat. She brought her hand to her mouth, giving herself a moment before speaking. "Zoey? No. She was doing so well."

"We all thought she was too. You know how it goes though. This damn disease...things can deteriorate rapidly." *This damn disease.* Genie paused, gazing at Autumn with concern. "They're going to make the announcement at breakfast, but I thought…I thought you'd like to take a little time…"

To cry alone. The words went unsaid, but she saw them in Genie's eyes. *Zoey.* Autumn's heart constricted, chest aching as a steady buzz took up in her head. She pictured the tiny twelve-year-old girl with dark curls and a heart of pure gold. She'd dreamed of being a ballerina. An impossible wish that could never come true no matter how long she'd lived. She'd done slow pirouettes down the hall just three days before…

Dance, sweet Zoey. You're well now. There is no sickness where you are.

Autumn had suffered this same clawing grief and uncertainty so many times before—this familiar tipping feeling that made her want to grab on to something solid and the terrifying knowledge that there was nothing there that would hold her steady. It never got easier. It never demolished her any less. She could only ride it out.

"Thank you, Genie." Autumn did want to cry. Where no one could hear her. Where she could be alone with her grief. Where she could mourn again when she'd already mourned so many times before. Yet each loss cut just as deep, the scars she carried internally far deeper than any that marred her skin.

CHAPTER TWO

The small form was dwarfed by the large hospital bed, machines blinking and beeping softly from behind her. So much equipment for one tiny girl.

Autumn dropped her school bag from the class she'd attended in the south wing and sat down at Mara's bedside, taking her friend's skeletal hand in hers. Mara's eyes blinked open, and she gave Autumn the slip of a smile. "How are you feeling?" Autumn asked.

"About as good as I look."

Autumn squeezed one eye shut, wrinkling her nose. "That bad, huh?"

Mara laughed, though it was shallow. "Worse." She adjusted her body, wincing. "There's not much more they can cut out before I'm all out of the necessary organs," she said, and though her tone was matter-of-fact, her bottom lip quivered slightly.

Autumn gave her hand a squeeze even as she felt tears burn the backs of her eyes. "If the surgeon removed enough, the Mesmivir will take care of the rest."

But Mara shook her head. "You're always optimistic, Autumn. But…it hasn't so far. And…I don't know if I want to do this anymore."

A slice of fear cut through Autumn. "Do what?"

"Live like this. What kind of life is it? Constant suffering? Unending surgeries." Mara gestured to her body, the wound from her most recent operation covered in gauze. Autumn knew that beneath Mara's white nightgown, there were numerous scars from previous surgeries, the ones that had attempted to remove tumors so her body could overcome the cancer.

"What's the alternative, Mara? We have to fight. If we don't, what is there?"

"Peace."

Peace.

The yearning that one-syllable word brought produced a physical pang that rose above her myriad other aches. *Peace.* Others felt that. Others woke in the morning and sprang out of bed with healthy bodies, their minds focused on classes, meetings, or maybe the date they had planned that weekend. Did they stop to consider the peace they possessed? The peace that enabled them to hum distractedly as they listened to music or scrolled through social media? Autumn could only wonder.

What she *was* certain of was that she'd give anything not to wonder but to *know*.

"That's what we fight for," she told Mara. "No matter the improbability." And they had to address the improbability that Mara would heal, didn't they? Because truth mattered too, and if Mara couldn't count on it from her other sick friends who carried the same burden as she did, regardless of scale, then who could she trust to provide honesty?

Fight, but not blindly.

Yet Autumn didn't tell her about Zoey. Not today. Not when Mara was still so fragile. She hadn't been able to attend breakfast in the cafeteria, so she wouldn't have heard the announcement.

Autumn squeezed Mara's hand. "You just had surgery, and you're feeling especially ill. But you'll be up walking the halls soon, and you'll get that fighting spirit back."

"Walking the halls." Mara sighed. "Great. Really something to look forward to." But she gave Autumn a faint smile and squeezed her hand back, even if weakly. *There it is. That glimmer. That fight.* Autumn would be there to help her friend lace up her armor when she was ready.

For a flash, Autumn thought about her dream, and something strange blossomed in her chest. She'd almost call it excitement, but that seemed too strong a word for something only in her imagination.

"You must look at me and worry," Mara said, taking Autumn's momentary silence for concern.

"Of course I worry—"

"No, I mean, you must worry that you'll be me in a few years."

The door opened, Mara's nurse bustling in and chirping an overly cheery good morning. Autumn let go of Mara's hand as the nurse she believed was named Cheryl took Mara's vitals and asked her questions about how she felt.

You must worry that you'll be me in a few years. Autumn turned her head, staring unseeing out the window to the wide stretch of emerald-green lawn and paths where a few early morning walkers strolled, arms linked with nurses, children and teens who moved slowly and hunched over as though they were ninety. A wheelchair went by, the occupant's head hung low, lank flaxen hair covering her face.

You must worry that you'll be me in a few years.

A buzz of guilt vibrated through her. Of course she did. And perhaps more than others because she was one of the ones who hadn't yet developed any tumors. That *yet* loomed large, and rarely did a day go by when she didn't fear that the next scan would show what was practically inevitable.

Her fate.

She was an ADHM baby, the chemical name a long chain of consonants she'd known once and would recognize on paper but couldn't spell unless she thought long and hard about it. And she had no interest in doing that. The acronym told the tale, and there wasn't anyone in the Northern Hemisphere who hadn't heard of it at this point.

ADHM, a street drug that had hit the market sixteen years before and addicted hundreds of thousands of people, was known by other names too: satellite, blue lightning, blind man's vision, Lucy in the Sky (and the simpler offshoot, Lucy), among the more popular and well-known. The users of ADHM who had gotten pregnant while taking it had had babies riddled with cancerous tumors, and if they weren't born with tumors, they developed them soon after. There were a rare few, like her, who remained tumor-free longer, thanks to the medication all ADHM babies were put on at birth. But they were the exceptions. Her body had responded amazingly well, but like all of them, she was a ticking time bomb. Her clock simply held a few more digits. The oldest ADHM baby had lived until sixteen. His name had been Logan, and he'd lived in the room down the hall. He'd loved classical music and read philosophy books. The nurses had called him an old soul, and Autumn had hoped that was true and he'd lived a hundred lifetimes, because this one had been far too short. Logan had died five days after his sixteenth birthday.

Autumn was fourteen and three months.

And her last scan, while tumor-free, had shown a concerning thickening of her stomach walls and swelling of her uterus.

She was scheduled for a full hysterectomy in three months. Most female ADHM babies had them earlier to avoid the tumors that would inevitably grow there, but Autumn had been a late bloomer, her periods had been light and absent of the severe pain often associated with their disease, so the surgeon had put it off, opting to keep a close eye on any changes.

Because many if not most of those who had given birth to ADHM babies were chronic addicts, often living on the street, and diagnosed with one or several mental illnesses, a large swath of the kids were wards of the state and lived in government-run facilities like Mercy Hospital for Children. It served as a home, a hospital, and a school. Most had never met or known their birth mothers.

Autumn stretched her back as the nurse took Mara's temperature. She felt especially sore this morning. The Mesmivir was their only hope of keeping the tumors under control or, in her lucky case, away entirely for as long as possible, but it also came with a long list of side effects ranging from unpleasant to horrible. It made them sick and achy. It gave them severe rashes and stomach issues, which often necessitated feeding tubes. It brought on migraines and cognitive disorders. But it was the sleep medication, designed and manufactured specifically for their bodies, that gave them vivid dreams so realistic they engaged all their senses.

Autumn had hated those dreams. Until last night. Before, she'd dreaded them because she'd woken disoriented and afraid. But this time, she'd opened her eyes with this sense of wonder and a feeling that the dreams were not at all what they seemed.

Cheryl patted Mara's hand. "The pain meds should kick in shortly." She shot Autumn a look. "You have ten minutes, and then this young lady needs to rest." Then the nurse bustled out of the room, the soft-close door shutting silently behind her.

Mara adjusted herself again, wincing. "You'll feel better in a few minutes," Autumn told her.

Mara nodded, but her expression remained pained.

"I had one of the running dreams last night," Autumn said, the words spilling out quickly, attempting to distract Mara from her obvious discomfort until the medication started working. *If* it started working. Because they'd been on every drug imaginable since birth, their tolerance was sky-high. Finding the right dose that would ease their pain without putting them in a coma was a challenge the doctors sometimes failed.

"Oh, I'm sorry," Mara said.

Mara knew the dream too. They'd all had a version of it. Likely because they were all highly suggestible and had no personal knowledge of regular life. The only things they knew intimately were each other, the hospital and its grounds, and the woods beyond. They seized on the experiences spoken of by others, even dreaming similar dreams. Certain materials were banned at Mercy because they brought on terrible nightmares that felt far too real to ADHM kids—horror movies, ghost stories, even tearjerkers. Once, a girl named Gracie, who was new at Mercy, had told them how she'd found her mother dead in the bathtub, and that night, they'd all dreamed about it in some form. Autumn's dream had featured a creature with hanging skin emerging from a murky lake.

"No. That's the thing. It was the same dream, only... different. *Better.*"

"Better?" Mara's eyes lit with a small spark of interest. "What do you mean?"

"I got *caught.*"

Mara blinked, her mouth forming a small O. "And that was...better?"

"Yes. Because of who caught me."

Mara pulled herself up on her pillow, and though she flinched, the expression was slight, and it smoothed out as she lay back down. "Tell me."

Autumn described the incredible way he looked.

"He sounds like a monster!"

Autumn laughed, but it faded quickly, her brow wrinkling. "Yes...but no."

"What did he do?"

"He just *stared* at me like he didn't know what to do."

Mara's eyes began to droop, her shoulders lowering as her body relaxed into the mattress.

Autumn exhaled a sigh of relief. *Sleep, Mara. Heal.*

"If that's all that happens, then we should all stop running in our sleep." Mara's eyes fluttered once and then fell shut. "Maybe I'll dream of the monster too. And if I do, I'll take your lead," she murmured, the words floating away as her hand went limp.

Autumn moved a piece of hair off Mara's cheek. The blanket had slipped aside, and she saw the heavy surgical bandages. She also saw the lumps beneath her gown she knew were tumors. Hopelessness descended. Mara would need a miracle to survive. So it was with less hope that Autumn took her next breath, knowing that it was only a matter of time before she'd have to say goodbye to another friend.

Autumn stood slowly, allowing her body to adjust to the change in position, and then made her way to the door. A nurse guided an old woman toward the elevator. Someone's grandmother—a few of those visited occasionally. She was weeping. She'd just received bad news. There was no lack of that at Mercy.

Autumn grasped her hands together, her head tilting as she caught sight of something on the side of her thumbnail. She brought it closer, frowning, using the nail of her index finger to remove the dark substance embedded. She stared at it, then rubbed it between her fingers, feeling its gritty texture. *Dirt*. She'd had dirt under her thumbnail. Dirt that had been deep enough under her nail that she'd missed it when she washed up that morning.

How was that possible when she lived in what could only be described as one of the most sanitized "homes" there was? She lived in a hospital where not even a speck of dirt existed.

CHAPTER THREE

Autumn lay in her bed, staring upward, the large, dropped ceiling morphing into the nighttime sky. She blinked it away, the bright, full moon disappearing, the outline of the fluorescent lights coming into focus. *Reality.* She sighed. The medication helped, but she was a *natural* at merging fantasy—dreams—with reality. No wonder she felt as if she'd been sleepwalking through most of her life.

She turned to the side, uncomfortable. She was so skinny that her bones poked at her skin from the inside and hurt. *Stop complaining, Autumn. You have it far better than most around here.*

True. Not that that said anything great.

Her gaze hung on her journal, still sitting on the window seat where she'd been writing in it earlier. Carefully, she got out of bed, walking to where it lay open. She read over the words she'd written.

Does my birth mother ever miss me, I wonder? Does she

think of the day I was born? Was it dewy that October morning? Did she name me Autumn, or did someone else? Maybe it was her favorite season. Perhaps she once jumped in piles of leaves and ate caramel apples. Maybe those happy memories surfaced when she looked into my eyes. Did she first ask to hold me as my cry filled the room? Does she hear that phantom sound sometimes when she comes awake suddenly in the dark of the night? Does she think of me when the leaves change color and fall to the ground? Does the memory smell like firelight and taste like apples? Does she feel a reaching inside? Does she cry? Does she wonder? Or is it only me?

Pain pierced her, emotional more than physical, but it only added to her overall feeling of sickness, and she decided against writing any more. She returned to her bed, climbing in and lying gingerly against the pillows.

She lifted her hand, stretching her fingers, and it wavered in front of her, skeletal. God, she really did feel especially nauseated tonight. She could tolerate most of the side effects, but she hated the nausea. She hated it.

She turned her hand, peering at her thumb, the corner of her nail completely clean now. She was troubled by the dirt. Just a tiny smudge that had come from beneath her fingernail, yet combined with the dream...

What are you thinking, Autumn?

She didn't know. Only that equal parts fear and excitement sparkled inside her and the feeling was unfamiliar... overwhelming.

What could it mean?

Either the dirt was a mere coincidence but one she couldn't explain, or she'd actually been out in those woods.

Impossible. She looked at the scratches on her arms, the ones she'd assumed she herself had made. The medication made them sleep very deeply, and that, combined with the skin conditions so many of the ADHM kids faced, often resulted in them scratching themselves in the middle of the night. It was one reason their nails were constantly trimmed. But the scratches on her arms—though not deep—looked razor thin. *Something that might happen if one fell on a bed of pine needles.*

"Stop it," she muttered to herself. She didn't want to feel *crazy* on top of all the other ailments she suffered. Her body belonged to the disease she'd been born with. To the choices her mother had made. It belonged to the doctors who tried to keep her comfortable. It belonged to the medication that had to keep her sick in order to keep her well, the ultimate unfair trade-off. But her mind? Her mind belonged to her. As did her will. Her spirit. Her heart. Those precious treasures were *hers*, and no person, no drug, no disease could ever, ever touch them or make them less without her permission.

She turned again, gritting her teeth at the discomfort, settling, and staring at the strip of dim light coming from beneath the door to her room. Was it possible that she'd slipped out of bed and into the forest? Had she been sleepwalking and actually *gone* there? It wasn't as if the Mercy Hospital for Children was a prison. There was very little security. She could have slipped out, unnoticed. She pictured herself, walking like a zombie out of her room, past the temporarily empty nurses' station, down the elevator, and out the front door. Perhaps she'd run through the woods from the monster of her imagination, the one who'd turned out to be a dreamy, fascinating boy. Of course, she'd made him up too, dreamed him, even if her body had traveled to the place where she'd picked up a speck of dirt that had lodged beneath her fingernail.

But what if you didn't?

Her heart gave a sudden gallop, and for the breath of a moment, the thought itself made her feel fully alive instead of half-dead. As always, the heavenly moment was extremely short-lived.

But the thought remained.

How did I dream him up? Autumn had thought initially that he was a culmination of that which she knew from experience and that which she believed about herself. And he was. The nasty-looking scar, long but straight, obviously made by a surgical blade. The bolt, which might represent the idea that she was being held together precariously in some fashion bound to fail, or maybe the feeling that she was part machine. Part *thing*.

Or even that her body would work far better than it did if her various diseased parts were replaced by metal and steel.

Yes, that all made sense. But what about his hair? His eyes? The curiosity and flash of...hope she'd seen in his gaze? Those things felt foreign. They felt as if they'd come from outside herself.

Which might mean he did too.

Autumn had no earthly idea how to explain that suspicion, yet it persisted all the same.

A small knock sounded on the door, and it was pushed open. The night nurse, Salma, came in with a warm smile and a tray in her hand. Autumn pulled herself to a sitting position, giving Salma a smile in return.

"You didn't eat much dinner," Salma said, glancing at Autumn's chart and setting the tray containing her nightly cocktail of medicine on the bedside table. "The nausea again?"

Autumn placed her hand on her concave stomach. "It's bad tonight."

Salma's eyes filled with sympathy. "I'm sorry, sweetheart." She put her hand on Autumn's forehead the way a mother would do. A few of the nurses were like that. Others relied solely on equipment and readings to ascertain the patients' health status. Autumn had been tended to by enough nurses to know that that was what separated the good ones from the wonderful ones. The *wonderful* ones, like Salma, made you feel as if you were being cared for in the same way they would care for their very own child. And to motherless children like Autumn, it made all the difference. *All* the difference.

Not only that, but other than their friends who suffered with the same condition, their doctors and nurses were the only ones who *touched* them. The tenderness of an embrace, the warmth of another hand in theirs, was deeply longed for but mostly nonexistent. Autumn and others who were well enough sometimes took day trips to museums and science centers in New York City and sometimes the movies. Autumn saw the way people looked at them with their oxygen tanks and wheelchairs and various other medical apparatus and shrunk away as if they might catch whatever they had with a mere brush of skin.

Salma sat down on the side of Autumn's bed, taking her hands. Autumn gripped her. Salma's hands were warm and soft. She turned Autumn's arms over and gazed down worriedly at the scratches. "You haven't suffered from rashes in months. What are you scratching yourself for?"

Autumn shrugged. "How do I know? I did it in my sleep."

Salma pressed her lips together, her expression showing

displeasure. But Autumn didn't get the feeling Salma was displeased with her. Maybe just the situation. The unfairness of it all. "Do you want me to bandage you up so you won't accidentally make it worse tonight?"

"No. I think it was just a one-time thing."

Salma stared at Autumn's arms for a few moments longer. "There seemed to be a lot of scratching going on last night," she murmured before giving Autumn's hands one final squeeze and letting go.

"What do you mean?"

But Salma shook her head. "Oh nothing. Just the full moon I guess."

The full moon.

"Did you know that more babies are born during full moons?" Salma asked.

"No. Why is that?"

"No scientific reason, but it's true even so. Not everything can be measured, at least not by us. My mother used to say that the full moon brings on all manner of strange behavior. It influences things."

"Like dreams?" Now that Autumn thought about it, the dreams of running and the one of *him* had all come during the full moon. *Is that why I made him of moonlight?*

"Definitely dreams." Salma leaned in conspiratorially. "If the moon is powerful enough to move the tides, just imagine what else it can sway."

Can it bring dreams to life?

Autumn's lips curved, but she didn't speak of the boy with Salma. She'd been ruminating on it, and she wanted to clear it from her mind for at least a little while.

"Will you tell me about your mother, Salma?" *If I can't know my own, then let me know yours.* Salma was so sweet—Autumn figured only someone good and kind could have raised a woman like Salma. "Did everyone love her?"

A wistful smile crossed Salma's lips, and she let out a fluttery laugh. "Oh no. She wasn't like you, sent here to tend to others' hearts. She'd say it just like it was, whether it hurt your feelings or not." But despite what sounded a bit like criticism, love was shining from her eyes.

"What's better?" Autumn wondered. To forever be mindful of harsh words or overly honest opinions or to lay it out there, come what may?

Salma laughed. "Well, it's *best* to be just who you were made to be. And my mother, God rest her soul, felt plenty comfortable sitting you straight down, looking you in the eye, and saying, 'Girl, those pants don't do a thing for you, and neither does that wreck of a boyfriend.'"

Autumn laughed. "Did she say that to you?"

"That and many other things." Salma rolled her eyes but then smiled, the wistful one again. "But then she'd hug you so hard you'd know there was always a place for you in her arms. I miss her terribly. I miss that I always knew I could count on her to tell me exactly how she saw things. And then she'd accept it without judgment if I respectfully disagreed." She smiled again. "Despite her brand of delivery, which wasn't always appreciated, she was usually right in the end." She paused. "She was fiercely loyal and passionately dedicated to truth. She always did the *right* thing, regardless of whether it made others like her and whether or not it was popular…or safe." A worried frown tilted her mouth. "And she encouraged me to do the same." Her eyes met Autumn's, and then she looked away. She appeared troubled, thoughtful for a few moments.

Autumn yawned. Talking to Salma had served to ease

her body and her mind. She glanced at the cup of meds. She'd always welcomed the absence of pain the medication provided, but now...*now* she had questions that would only be answered if she could pull herself from the dark depths of slumber where the medication delivered her. "Salma, do you think...do you think instead of bandaging my arms, I might cut down on the sleep medication?" She didn't want to stop taking it completely. She suddenly *wanted* the dreams it brought. She just didn't want to be practically comatose.

Salma picked up the cup, but at Autumn's question, she hesitated, the cup halfway between the tray and Autumn. Her eyes tilted downward, and an expression came over her face Autumn didn't know how to read. "Dr. Heathrow won't approve of that," she said almost woodenly. "He's very, very insistent on the cocktail protocol, and the sleep medication is a part of that. I've requested tweaks based on specific cases, but the answer has always been absolutely no."

Salma's gaze lifted slowly, meeting Autumn's, and Autumn stilled. She swore the look in her favorite nurse's eyes was grief. Then a flash of anger that melted into something that appeared to be resolve before she looked away.

Autumn blinked, wondering if she'd read far more in Salma's gaze than had actually been there. Or misinterpreted it. "Do you...do you think a different drug protocol might be better for me, Salma?"

Salma hesitated, but then shook her head. "Dr. Heathrow's an expert, sweetheart. I'm just a nurse." *Just a nurse.* Salma apparently didn't understand how big the word *just* was in that particular sentence.

Autumn thought of Dr. Heathrow with his cold eyes and distant expression, the way he seemed to look through the Mercy kids rather than at them. The way his lips moved silently as though he was forever calculating things in his mind. Yes, she supposed he was an expert—a *genius* she'd been told—and one who kept many of them alive far longer than life alone would have allowed, but she was forever thankful that *Salma* and the other nurses were the dispensers of his drug cocktail rather than him. She'd prefer he stay locked in his lab, far away from her.

"Anyway," Salma said, handing the paper cup of medication to Autumn. "These are your sleep medications. You definitely wouldn't want to halve the dose for a week and then halve it again for another week before doing away with them entirely. That would be against protocol."

Autumn blinked as Salma stood, taking the few steps to the sink against the wall and turning on the faucet. She began humming as she washed her hands.

Autumn looked down at the tablets. There were two of each. *Halve the dose.* She quickly removed one of each type and shoved them under her bony hip. Then she tipped the cup to her mouth, reaching for the glass of water on her bedside table and swallowing them just as Salma grabbed a paper towel and turned around. Autumn handed her the empty cup.

"Good girl," Salma said, taking it and tossing it into the trash near the sink. She picked up the second paper cup, this one filled with six pills and capsules, and handed it to Autumn. "And you definitely, definitely don't want to stop taking the yellow and blue capsules. Those make up the Mesmivir. The other ones are simply medications that expedite its delivery. Alone, they're harmless."

Harmless.

Which meant the other ones caused harm. But she already knew that. It was part of the trade-off she'd so recently considered.

Salma handed her that cup and turned away, walking to the sink and washing her hands *again*. Autumn's heart gave a jolt. The sleep meds had been one thing. She'd inquired about cutting down on those but...was her nurse giving her instructions on how to wean herself completely off her medication? *Why?* Why would she do that? The medication was keeping her tumor-free. The medication was keeping her alive.

But it was also keeping her half-dead.

And Salma loved her. Autumn knew she did.

Do it. Live. No matter how long.

You have that ability where others don't.

Mara flashed in her mind, her friend's scarred and tumor-riddled body. *What would she give to feel healthy, even for one day?* A wild thrill moved through Autumn, and it practically made her gasp. *That* was within her reach. She could have that if she wanted it.

Autumn removed the Mesmivir from the cup, stuffing that under her hip where half the sleep meds had gone and downing the *useless, harmless* pills that remained, swallowing them with water.

Salma turned back again, taking the cup, and Autumn saw that her hands were shaking. "Good girl," she repeated, and this time, she sounded slightly breathless.

She's scared. For herself or for me? Or maybe both. Autumn was scared too. Scared but...strangely elated.

Salma leaned forward and took Autumn's face in her hands, kissing her forehead. When she leaned back, there were tears shining in her eyes. "My special, beautiful girl," she said. "Grow strong." And with that, she picked up the tray, turned, and hurried out of the room.

CHAPTER FOUR

Autumn's morning nurse was a thin-lipped shrew, ironically named Joy, who had only been at Mercy for a few months. Thankfully, she was rarely on Autumn's floor, and her type of unpleasant personality was the exception rather than the rule when it came to the staff. Autumn took the offered paper cup of morning meds and feigned a minor coughing fit as she palmed the same ones she'd slipped under her hip the night before. Thankfully, joyless Joy looked away as she fake hacked and didn't notice the—unpracticed—sleight of hand.

Autumn showered, tossing the pills down the drain, and then once dry, she dressed distractedly, her heart beating more swiftly than usual. She was scared, anxious. *What if you're wrong and the price you pay for this comes quickly?* She had a scan in about a month. *What if they find a tumor or three or six? Will it be worth it?* The way her blood raced and her breath came short—not because she felt ill but because she felt a shiver of *life* move through her sickly body—offered up the answer: *yes*.

Yes, yes, yes.

The mere idea of feeling unmedicated and experiencing physical normalcy was suddenly a draw too strong to deny. She'd only considered going off her pharmaceuticals because Salma had all but instructed her how to do so, but now that the promise of strength—no matter how momentary—was shimmering before her, Autumn could not let go. She gazed at her sallow, sunken face in the mirror, feeling slightly surreal. She was certain of her choice, yet it'd happened so quickly, with nothing more than an off-the-cuff question and the unexpected instructions from her favorite nurse.

Maybe that's the only way it could have happened. If you'd considered it too much, you'd have chickened out.

She was glad she hadn't chickened out. She turned away from the mirror.

She'd only skipped two doses, but already she felt better, stronger. The nausea had gone completely, and she ate all her breakfast for the first time in months.

Over the next several days, her stomach pains diminished and then disappeared. When she looked in the mirror one night before bed, there was color in her cheeks, and her lips had taken on a subtle rosy hue where before they'd been practically bloodless.

Her muscles ceased aching, and one day as she headed to dinner, she came to a stop right outside the cafeteria, realizing suddenly that the ceaseless ringing in her ears had stopped. She blinked, bringing her fingertips to her ears in wonder and almost laughing out loud. The tinnitus—yet another side effect of the medication—had been ongoing and aggravating, but she'd learned to live with it as if it was just part of existing. As she stood there, the realization that it in fact was not almost brought tears to her eyes. Her head felt clear, the fogginess that had been a constant companion had lifted, and she felt bright and alert. *Alive.*

Autumn palmed the pills for the next week and then the next, her strength doubling by the day.

Yes, but there will be a price.

She pushed the thought aside. She was willing to pay it, she knew that much. She just didn't want to consider it too closely and risk her fear taking over. So far, she hadn't dreamed of her monster. But again, those running dreams—or, more specifically, *hiding* dreams—had come during the full moon. The more she'd thought about it, the more certain she was. There was a possibility she'd never dream of him again, the possibility that *all* the medication she'd been taking, not just the sleep aids, and that inexplicable pull of the moon Salma had spoken of had worked in perfect combination somehow to bring on that particular vivid dream. So on the night of the full moon, she'd take a dose of the sleep medication. A singular dose would wear off the next morning. But she wouldn't take the others. She refused to feel hopelessly ill again when she'd just begun to really *live.* Even he wasn't worth giving that up for. She pulled her shoulders back. *Will it work?* There was only one way to know. There was still a little less than two weeks until the next full moon.

A week to get *strong.*

She wanted Salma to see her. She wouldn't tell her what she'd been doing, but she would certainly know. She wanted to share her happiness, brief though it might be, with someone. But Salma hadn't been to her room since Autumn had started palming the pills. Was she on vacation?

She walked to the nurses' station where Ian was sitting in front of a computer. He smiled as she approached. "Hey, good lookin'."

Autumn smiled back, leaning on the desk. "Hey, Ian. I haven't seen Salma this week or last."

His smile slipped. "They didn't tell you? She was let go."

Autumn's breath stalled. "What? Why?" *No, no, that can't be right. Salma was the best of the best.*

And though Ian looked sad to deliver the news, he merely shrugged. "I don't know."

"Is there any way to get in touch with her?"

"Not that I know of, and I doubt they'd give out her personal information anyway."

Woodenly, Autumn pushed off the counter, muttering a thank you to Ian and walking away. Loss twisted through her, but she steeled her shoulders. She was no stranger to loss. In fact, one might say she was intimate with it. So why did it still hurt so badly? *I need you, Salma.*

She was let go.

Why?

Did she do something wrong? Did they find out she'd all but spelled out how Autumn might wean off her medication? No...no, it couldn't be that. If they'd found out, someone would have confronted Autumn about it and made her resume her treatment.

My special, beautiful girl. Grow strong.

Autumn looked over her shoulder, but the hallway behind her was empty. Instead of heading down the hall that led to her room, she made a sharp right, bypassing the elevators and pushing the door to the stairwell open. If she was going to get strong, she needed to exercise. And this was one of the only places where no one could see her. She stared over the railing to the floors below. There were three, with two flights of stairs separating each landing. Six flights. She walked slowly down all six flights, and despite her pace, her heart sped, her chest rising and falling as a light sweat broke out on her forehead. Autumn turned, peering up, inhaling deeply. "Mount Everest," she muttered.

She glanced behind her at the door that led to the lobby and the elevator bank that would take her back up to her floor. She should use it. She'd just descended six flights of stairs, an impossibility just weeks before. It was enough for one day.

Yet she stood there, staring up at that faraway door.

There had been a maintenance man named Joel who'd worked at the hospital when she was seven or eight. He'd retired years before, but she still remembered him. He'd been nice. He'd whistled while he worked, and if Autumn was feeling well enough, she'd chitchat with him while he fixed this or that. One time, there had been some damage to a whole section of penny tile, and he'd started to replace it when she sat down to watch. She'd remarked on the tiny tiles and the large space and that it looked like it would take him a hundred years to finish it. But he'd only smiled and said, "Well, Miss Autumn, how do you eat an elephant?" She'd laughed and wrinkled her nose, no idea how to answer. But Joel had winked and answered for her. "One bite at a time," he'd said.

She looked up at that door again, putting her hand on the rail and lifting her foot, beginning the climb.

"How do you climb Mount Everest?" she murmured, setting her foot down. *One step at a time.*

She climbed those six flights of stairs that day, resting on each landing before gearing up for the next. When she took that final step to the top, she nearly wept with victory. She might even have clapped for herself if she'd had the strength to lift her hands. Instead, she shuffled back to her bed and slept for hours. But not the sleep of the sick and the drugged. The rest of one whose muscles ached with growth and whose spirit soared with accomplishment, even while in peaceful slumber.

Autumn tackled those six flights of stairs every day after classes and lunch were over, when she'd normally be resting or reading or, if she felt strong enough, sitting outside in the sun. She pushed herself mercilessly, ever aware of the possibility that her time was dwindling. Down, then up, until she could walk the stairs in both directions without breaking a sweat.

Next, she began jogging. Only down at first, but then she jogged one flight and walked the rest, then two, then three. Over and over and over.

Her muscles burned, her vision blurred, and still, she powered on. There was something utterly addictive about feeling in control of pushing the boundaries of her body. The medication had set the limits of her capabilities. Now it was *her*. She was giddy with the feeling.

She began doing her stairwell exercises not only in the afternoons but in the mornings as well.

On the eve of the full moon, Autumn jogged down the stairs, turned, and began jogging straight back up. She doubted herself on the fourth flight but kept going anyway. By the time she leaped onto the top landing, tears were stinging her eyes, and sweat was rolling down her back and dotting her forehead as she panted for breath.

The door from the hallway opened suddenly, making her jump and step backward against the railing.

"Autumn?" It was Genie.

Autumn couldn't even catch her breath enough to greet her.

Genie stepped forward, her surprised expression transforming into concern. She took her in, clearly seeing her jackhammering pulse, bright red and sweaty face, and her staggering breath. "Autumn. Oh dear, you shouldn't try walking up the stairs. What are you thinking?" She took her arm. She'd assumed Autumn had just climbed the two flights from the floor below, even if incredibly slowly. The truth was she would have looked just like this weeks before after what was now an easy task. "Take the elevator. None of you are in any condition to climb stairs. Come with me. I'll help you back to bed."

Autumn nodded and allowed Genie to lead her back to her room. "Genie," Autumn asked when she could manage a few words. "Do you know why they let Salma go?"

Genie shot her a glance, pressing her lips together for a moment. Autumn could see that she was considering whether to say something. But Autumn knew Genie enjoyed gossiping, and if she knew something, she'd say so. "Well," she started, glancing around. "I heard she got caught stealing from the hospital."

"Stealing?" That didn't sound like Salma. Autumn didn't believe it. "Stealing what?"

"I don't know. Medication maybe. But that's all I heard. Now, lie down for a while, and don't let me catch you on those stairs again," Genie scolded, though there was affection in her voice.

Autumn sat on the window seat in her room, tracing a raindrop down the glass and gazing out at the woods beyond. She pulled out her journal and drew a large, round circle in the middle of a blank page, her lips curving into a smile. Tomorrow night, she'd take the sleep medication they gave her. She had to recreate the circumstances that had caused her to dream of him. Nerves skittered along her spine as she gazed at the moon just coming into sight in a darkening sky, a mere slip away from being full.

CHAPTER FIVE

A moan rose around her as her eyelids slowly opened. *Groggy. Hazy.* The groan had come from her own lips. She blinked, trying desperately to bring the world into focus. *The dream. I'm in the dream.* Despite the jolt of excitement, her limbs felt so heavy, and she didn't want to move. But she heard rustling in the trees around her, and her skin prickled, her heart picking up speed. *Run. Hide.*

She cried out softly as she pulled herself to her knees, head swimming, world tilting. *Oh God,* she hated this feeling. She felt sick again as the drugs swirled in her system, weighing her down, making her feel bleary and foggy and *weak*.

You wanted to be here, didn't you?

Yes. No. Not like this.

In only a short time, she'd become used to feeling in control of her body, and suddenly she was not. She felt scared and frustrated, completely and utterly out of sorts. And she was sitting in a bed of pine needles in the middle of the woods. *I want to be back in my bed.*

She had a flash of memory, or what she thought was memory. Movement. The squeak of wheels. *Was I in a wheelchair?*

She reached behind her back, feeling the lump of her soft-covered journal. She'd put on a tight pair of shorts beneath her nightgown and stuck it in the waistband before bed. If she had been moved by wheelchair, whoever had done the moving hadn't felt it. It remained where she'd hidden it just before she'd slipped under. She could hardly remember why she'd done it now. *To sketch your surroundings. To write things down you might not remember when you wake. Yes, right.* It'd seemed a good idea at the time. She squinted, trying to focus her foggy mind, but before she could attempt to dredge up anything else about possibly being dumped out here in these woods, she heard something large coming through the foliage. Something that was making no effort to disguise the noise of its arrival.

The sudden gallop of her heart spurred Autumn to her feet, and then she leaned on the trunk of a tree for a moment as the world stopped spinning and she got her bearings.

This is the part where you run. Where you hide.

She pulled in a breath and turned her head as she searched her surroundings. She was still groggy, and it took her a minute to take stock. A few skinny trees, a small rock. *Nothing.* Adrenaline pumped through her veins and brought her more clearly into the present. She was still drugged, but she didn't feel like she'd always felt in this dream before.

This dream that is no dream.

The sound of movement drew closer, a branch snapping, feet hitting the ground.

With a small huff of breath, Autumn sank back to her knees, picking up a nearby stick and using it to dig in the soft, damp earth. Her breath came harshly, sweat breaking out on her skin as she dug as long as she dared before coming to her knees and pulling a pile of leaves and pine needles into her hole.

The *thing* approaching drew closer, louder. That was no animal.

Was it *him*?

Who else could it possibly be?

With a quick sweep of her arm to make the ground look as undisturbed as possible, Autumn came to her feet. Her breath sawed in and out of her chest as she waited…waited, until the person appeared through the trees. *Tall. Muscular. Moonlight hair.*

Both fear and excitement tumbled through her, and with a small squeal born of the intoxicating mix of emotions, Autumn turned and ran, sprinting like she never had before.

There was a moment's pause, and then she heard him give chase.

She dipped behind a tree and swerved around another, finding her coordination, her legs pumping with her newfound strength, muscles burning, but deliciously this time. Miraculously.

She raced through the forest as she'd done so many times before, the moon full and bright above. *Before*, she'd only had the energy to hide, barely crawling into a log or behind a tree, curling into the fetal position, and waiting to die.

But she was strong now. She could run! And even after she'd taken a small amount of medication just hours before. She laughed with delight, rounding a rock and doubling back. She plastered her back to the large expanse of stone, waiting for a beat, two, until she could hear that he was almost upon her where she "hid," and then with a cry of triumph, she sprang out.

Her moonlight boy let out a raspy sound of surprise and skidded, flailing his arms to right himself and coming to a jerky stop. His expression was half shock, half rage, solid white teeth bared, one brow raised, and one brow lowered in a way that was almost comical.

Almost.

They stood mere feet apart, his bare, scarred chest rising and falling in tandem with hers. The bolt in his head was gone, but in its place was a shaved patch of hair, the skin there red and raw. Their gazes locked, and Autumn suddenly felt angry too. All this time, he'd been chasing her to terrify her. Her, in a drugged, half-awake state! How *dare* he? Wasn't her life hard enough as it was?

Her gaze narrowed, lip curling. The boy cocked his head, a wary light entering his dark eyes as he watched her. She lunged at him and then away. Startled, he stepped back, a surprised bark of laughter coming from his throat. A low growl that she had to admit sounded less fierce than she'd gone for emanated from her chest. Despite the lack of menace in the sound, his laughter fizzled, and then she lunged for real as he stumbled backward, an expression that was purely incredulous on his face before he turned and ran.

She chased him this time, and she swore she heard his laughter floating back to her on the wind. She was still a little groggy, but she also felt fearless, because *why not?* What on earth did she really have to lose? Her life? Ha! That would be gone soon enough. She leaped over a rock, skidding on a patch of soggy leaves, grabbing hold of a tree trunk, and coming to a sudden though slippery stop as he turned this time, amusement dancing over his features as he lunged at her and then away as she'd done to him. Indignation exploded within her. He wanted to toy with her? Okay then. She bounced once on the balls of her heavy, sock-clad feet before pushing off the tree, turning and running again. He gave chase, and even though she was pushing her body to its limits, sweat dripping down her forehead and stinging her eyes, her lips curved in a satisfied smile before a puff of breath disturbed it.

She tried to orient herself, worked to remember where she'd started, and led him back that way.

Her lungs were burning, muscles *screaming*. She was infinitely stronger than she'd been just a month ago, but she was still weak by most standards. And certainly much weaker than the boy hot on her heels. *There.* She spotted it ahead. The formation of the trees she'd woken to, the ones that had been right in front of her as she'd sat up, rubbing her head groggily, feeling for the journal she'd hidden in the back of her shorts. *My journal!* She started to reach for it, but she could feel it wasn't there. *No!* She didn't have time to worry about that right now though. Her gaze shot to the ground. *Is that the spot? I think so. Yes.* He'd sped up, and she felt the warmth of his body directly behind her, heard his exhale, the brush of his fingers...

With her final burst of effort, she leaped over the hole she'd dug and covered, crying out as she hit the ground but twisting around and watching as he stepped right into it, his ankle twisting as he pitched forward. She squealed, falling backward, raising her hands defensively as he fell. He let out a monstrous grunt and caught himself with his arms just before his full weight slammed on top of her.

Okay, so maybe it hadn't been the most well-thought-out plan.

Their faces were mere inches apart, exhales mingling as they breathed harshly together, eyes wide and staring. He looked utterly shocked. Time slowed and seemed to stop. His indigo eyes were a hint lighter in the center and almost black around the outside, and from this close vantage point, she could see tiny gold flecks. *Fascinating*. He shifted minutely, and she became aware of the size and weight of him. Eyes still held, she reached up and plucked a hair from his head.

He let out a confused grunt but remained where he was, raising his chin minutely and taking in a small inhale with his nose. "You're better," he said, his voice raspy.

Her eyes widened, and so did his, his gaze flicking toward her mouth and then away.

He speaks. Had she thought he didn't? Well, yes... because she'd thought him nothing but a dream. But he was no dream. She was sure of it now. She could see him, feel him, smell his nighttime-scented skin. He could smother her beneath him if he wanted. But she didn't think he wanted to do that because...well, he *wasn't* doing that.

"You protected me last time," she said. "From what? You could have hurt me, and you didn't."

Her words seemed to pull him from some hypnotic state, and he shivered slightly, pushing up off her. "Them," he murmured. "The others."

She sat up, looking at the silvery hair held between her fingers. "Others? Who are you?"

He was turned halfway away, looking into the woods. She twisted the hair around her index finger and then stuck it under her tongue, the only place she could think to hide it if in fact someone was cleaning her, redressing her, and returning her to her bed as she suspected they were.

A loud scream pierced the still night, and she jerked in

the direction from which it came, opening her mouth to ask if he knew what was happening, when she saw a blur between the trees, moving swiftly toward her.

She leaped to her feet, stretching her arms out defensively as the human shape barreled forward. She heard a growl and a yell. She thought she screamed before the impact. Before all went dark.

Autumn woke in her bed, the "dream" rushing back. She blinked, swallowed, tried to organize her thoughts as she sat up.

The door opened, and a humming Genie walked in. "Good morning. You slept in."

Autumn glanced at the clock. *Nine a.m.* She never slept that late. Of course, her aching body had always woken her before, not just in the morning but all through the night. She tested her limbs. Slightly achy, but in the same way they were after she'd run the stairs.

"Good thing it's Saturday," Genie said, smiling and handing her the first cup of medication.

Autumn glanced down. She was in her blue-and-pink-striped nightgown, the same one she'd gone to sleep in. And she still wore the thick, white socks with treads on the bottom that kept her perpetually cold feet warm. She tilted her head and sniffed. Her nightgown smelled like laundry detergent, and she could detect the clean scent of soap on her skin. It was amazing how much sharper all her senses were since she'd stopped taking the pills.

She turned her hand over, peering at her fingernails. No dirt. Not a speck. They hadn't missed any this time. *Who are they?* She worked to keep the suspicion from her gaze as she looked at Genie, turning her thoughts away from the onslaught of questions attempting to invade her mind. For now. Just for now.

Indigo eyes with gold flecks. A voice like sandpaper and silk.

Autumn palmed the pills and then the others, faking the sip of water.

"Oh dear," Genie said, frowning as she pulled the neckline of Autumn's nightgown aside. She reached for her chart and jotted something down. "You're bruising again. I thought the switch in brands of blood thinner got that under control." She set the chart down on Autumn's bedside table. "Well, we'll see if he wants to revisit things, because that's a nasty bruise," she said, giving Autumn's collarbone another glance. Genie's gaze shifted away. "Autumn," she started.

"No," Autumn whispered, shaking her head, denying what she knew was coming. She'd heard that tone in Genie's voice. Too many times. Far too many times.

"Mara passed last night, love. I'm so sorry."

Autumn squeezed her eyes shut. *Oh, Mara.*

Genie put her hand on Autumn's leg, giving it a small pat before she stood. "Would you like me to stay while you get washed up?"

Autumn gave her head a small shake, attempting to muster the semblance of a smile for Genie. "No," she said, "I'll be okay."

Genie hesitated another moment, her expression sad and a little worried but not overly. They'd traveled this road before. They'd all be all right. And then they'd go down it again. Before it was Autumn's turn.

Genie went into the bathroom, and Autumn heard her refilling some items. Autumn focused on her breath for a few moments, saying a silent prayer for sweet Mara. "Run,

Mara," she said, picturing her friend racing on strong, healthy legs toward the pearly gates.

Recalling the impact in the woods, the one that had slammed into her shoulder, knocking her to the ground, she gingerly touched the back of her head. It felt tender to the touch, and there was a small lump under her hair.

If her body had ached the way it once had, she wouldn't have even noticed such a thing among so many other pains, some of which were far greater.

Genie came out of the bathroom, giving her a gentle smile. "Just buzz if you need me for anything, okay?"

"I will. Thank you, Genie."

As soon as the door had shut behind her, Autumn reached in her mouth, swiping her finger under her tongue. There it sat on the tip of her finger: a wet, balled piece of silvery hair.

CHAPTER SIX

The show swam before Samael's eyes, his mind removed from what he was watching, the vision of her face the only thing he saw. *The girl.* That was what he called her. *The.* As if she was the only one when there were many others. He didn't know her name. He didn't know any of their names. Only that he'd been given permission to kill her if he wanted.

It wasn't wrong, Dr. Heathrow said, because they were sick—dying a slow, painful death—and sick things must be put out of their misery. It was humane, yet others made excuses for doing what was right, not because it wasn't but because they were scared. *Weak.* Certain things were difficult for ordinary men because they didn't have the physical power or mental strength to carry out that which was necessary.

Samael understood. He'd been sick. So sick and in so much anguish that he'd wished to be put out of his misery. And his pain hadn't even been a death sentence. He'd known that he would heal. With time. *How does she live, knowing she's going to die?*

And why does she fight for her life with such fire?

From what he'd heard, they all did in the end.

Instinct, Dr. Heathrow had said. Nothing more than that. Deep down, we were all lizards, followers of our instincts above all else.

One of the men on the screen plunged a hammer into another man's head. Beside him, Amon gave a short laugh, leaning forward, his hand fisting as if he was the one holding the weapon.

Sam brought forth the girl's face again. He liked to use the time they were given to watch TV to think about her, wonder about her.

He thought about the soft, red velvet book with the ribbon around it that she'd dropped in the woods, that he'd found after he'd fought Fenris off. He'd snuck it here in the back waistband of his pants. He'd first put it to his nose, hoping to inhale her scent, but it had smelled like a hospital. It smelled the same as the hallways of the place he called home. He'd let out a disappointed sigh and hidden it under his mattress. He hadn't dared look at the book last night. He'd open it later and see what it was. Discover what the girl had brought with her.

Last night, she'd been stronger. She'd run faster. She'd dug a hole in the ground with her bare hands. She'd tricked him! He let out a disbelieving laugh at the memory alone, and Amon joined him, looking away from something that spurted blood on the screen that Sam had missed and then back at the show.

And she hadn't smelled like poison. Not even the hint of it.

Why?

What did it mean?

Instead, she'd smelled like... Sam squinted his eyes, trying to remember her scent. Kind of like the red Jell-O they were served as a treat after surgery. *Sweet*. He massaged his temple, the one that was just bone, no metal plate beneath his skin. No...no, not like Jell-O. But *sort of* like that. *Good. Happy. Relieved.*

He didn't have words to describe what she smelled like. All he knew was how it made him feel.

There was a shift in his peripheral vision, and he turned to see Zagan lean forward as something exploded on the screen, followed by Amon's laughter again. Sam's gaze moved to Morana. She wasn't looking at the television. She was staring straight at him. The way she stared, paired with the intense expression she wore, unnerved him. Morana didn't usually make eye contact. Her gaze was most often fixed on a computer screen. Not games though— numbers and columns of data. Sometimes she sat there and watched it scroll by for hours, jotting things down. He'd heard the doctors say her aptitude for numbers and patterns was impressive. He'd heard them say they might be able to amplify it. Sam wasn't sure what that meant, but in any case, her stare continued to make him feel odd, like she was analyzing something about *him*, so he looked away, moving his mind back to the girl.

Her cheeks had been flushed with health, not with sickness, and her black waves were shiny. *None of their hair was ever shiny.* He'd wanted to touch it. He'd wanted to run his fingers through her hair and put his mouth on hers. But not like in the movies they watched. He didn't want her to scream and cry. What would it be like to feel her lips curve beneath his own? Because he didn't want to kiss her once but twice, and then maybe again.

No, no, don't think that way. Anything more than temporary desire is weakness.

Amon stood up, dancing around with his head lowered, jabbing at the air as the final credits began to roll. "That was awesome!" he declared.

Sam gave a half-hearted nod. He couldn't really remember much of what they'd watched. He'd been thinking of her. Picturing her. Wondering about her.

The door opened, and the nurse named Delia entered. "Sam, Dr. Heathrow would like to see you."

A hollow feeling began in the spot right beneath his ribs. He'd been expecting this, and now he'd have to explain. *Lie.*

He wasn't good at lying.

He'd promised never to lie to Dr. Heathrow. And he knew Dr. Heathrow would never lie to him.

Amon was slamming his fists into the punching bag that hung in the corner now, so without a goodbye, Sam followed Delia out of the room, walking down the familiar hall toward Dr. Heathrow's office.

"Come in," the doctor called when Sam rapped.

His office was tidy and clean, just like the doctor, who always smelled of soap and disinfectant. He was short and trim, and when the doctor was standing, Sam towered over him. They all did, even the few girls in the program.

Sam sat down in the chair in front of his desk. Dr. Heathrow laced his hands, studying him. Sam didn't like it, but he didn't look away.

"What happened last night, Sam?"

Sam resisted the urge to run his clammy palms over his thighs. That would be a giveaway that he was nervous.

"You attacked Fenris. His nose is broken. He said you went after him instead of the girl."

"I wanted her for myself," he said. *True*. But not all the way true.

Dr. Heathrow studied him a moment longer, unlacing his fingers and sitting back in his chair. "Why that one?"

"She's stronger than the others. A challenge." Again, true.

The corner of Dr. Heathrow's lip tilted. "Ah. A challenge. Hmm." He paused. "When you say she's strong, what do you mean?"

Sam twitched very subtly, but Dr. Heathrow's eyes narrowed. He'd caught it. *Breathe. Slowly. Lower your pulse rate*. Boom. Boom…boom…boom. His heart slowed as he commanded it to. "She has more fight than the others. Maybe she's not as sick."

Dr. Heathrow tilted his head. "Maybe. Some of them… have more time." He appeared thoughtful. "I'll inquire," he murmured, and a buzz of alarm made Sam's heart fall back into the quickened rhythm of moments before. But what else could he have done other than answer Dr. Heathrow's questions?

"Am I in trouble?" he asked.

"No, no, of course not. Like I've told you and the others, do as you please in the woods. There's no one to see you, no rules to abide by. If you desire a specific girl, then have her. Just…don't drag it out. That's not wise."

"Or merciful."

The doctor's expression changed minutely, and Sam got the impression he was annoyed. "No, it's not." Dr. Heathrow looked at him for a beat and then stood, coming around his desk and taking the seat next to Sam. He turned toward him. "Your sense of integrity is noble." But the way he said the word *noble* made Sam think he meant something else.

He cares for you. He's the only one who does.

He patted Sam's knee lightly with his fist. "Just don't let it get the best of you," Dr. Heathrow said. "Don't let it make you second-guess your mission."

"Yes, sir," Sam said as he stood.

"Sam."

He had started to turn but now stopped.

"It's time to do the next surgery."

Despair made him jolt. "No. You said—"

"I know what I said, but I've changed my mind. I consulted with Dr. Swift and…it's for the best. I've considered your age and your current vital stats. Your youth and other physical requirements are optimal now, and I don't want to risk that changing."

He was shocked by the unfamiliar desire to cry. He hadn't experienced that sensation of weakness for a long time. Years. He couldn't remember the last time he'd felt tears on his face, regardless of what he'd endured.

Tears were useless anyway. He'd only be punished for them.

Still. One plea. Just one. Maybe it was Dr. Swift, the program head he only knew by name, that was pushing for another surgery. Maybe Dr. Heathrow could be convinced. Sam fell to his knees. "Please, *please,* I—"

"There will be no discussion." Still, Dr. Heathrow nudged Sam's head so that it lay on his lap. He stroked Sam's hair the way a father would, his voice softening. "You're sixteen now, young, but old enough to understand that my decisions always have your best interests at heart, right? You're like a son to me, Sam. My own child. I don't take my decisions regarding your health lightly. Never."

Sam's heart had slowed. It'd slowed so much, Sam

wondered if it would stop beating altogether. Almost hoped. He closed his eyes. He both hated Dr. Heathrow's hand on his head and craved it. *Touch.* Comfort and pain.

He'd dared to dream the surgeries were finished. He'd endured so many already. Too many to count. *Oh God, the pain. The pain, the pain.*

"Now then," Dr. Heathrow said, giving Sam a slight push so that he sat up. The doctor wiped his hands together, done with the conversation.

Sam came slowly to his feet, his legs shaky.

The doctor glanced at his watch and then stood as well, giving Sam the ghost of a smile. "Go lose yourself in a video game, eh? Have some fun. There's always a game to join."

Yes, there always was. The other boys loved games. The girls did too, but mostly the boys. Sometimes Sam did. Sometimes they bored him. Sometimes they even disturbed him, but he'd never tell Dr. Heathrow that. He didn't know why they disturbed him. They were only games on a screen. "I'd rather read, if that's okay." There were comic books and a few other titles on the tables in the lounge, but those weren't the books Sam intended to read. "I'd like to be alone for a while. To prepare my mind."

Dr. Heathrow smiled proudly. "Prepare your mind. Yes. Good. All strength begins in the mind." He tapped his own skull. "But the body is what we use to fight. The body must be strong too. See you soon, Sam."

Sam nodded once and headed toward the door.

He didn't cry out loud. But inside, he roared.

CHAPTER SEVEN

The nurse pushing the wheelchair carrying a small, bony boy who was staring straight ahead stoically turned the corner and went out of sight.

Autumn waited a moment and then moved from behind the tall hydrangea bush where she was standing, half-obscured. She hardly dared a glance as she rushed past the path where the nurse had turned, ducking into the doorway just beyond. She stood there for a moment, catching her breath as she listened. There was only the gust of the wind and the call of a distant bird.

She leaned out, turning her head in both directions before once again stepping onto the path that led to the newer section of Mercy Hospital, the one she'd been told was mostly used for research and development and the occasional surgery when the other operating rooms were all in use.

She reached the high fence that she'd only seen from afar, gripping the wires as she peered through. The building was much newer than the brick and stone structure used for the children's home and mostly devoid of windows. *Odd.* Researchers and scientists weren't known for their conventionality necessarily, but surely, even they liked a ray of sunshine now and again. Or maybe they developed products whose ingredients fared better in very specific conditions. What did she know about any of that anyway?

There were KEEP OUT signs along the fence, but clearly, the warnings didn't possess teeth as there was no barbed wire at the top. Her eyes moved to her hands on the links. *And it's not going to shock you if you touch it.* She was glad she hadn't considered that before she'd gripped it, or she might not have tried. Then again…why should there be barbed wire or any other physical deterrent? It wasn't as if the kids at Mercy had the strength to scale a fence anyway, even if they wanted to.

Well…except her.

A spiral of pride wound through her, making her feel slightly delirious. What a dizzyingly delightful thought it was that she was now strong enough to scale a fence! The realization gave her courage, and she let go of the wire, stepping back and looking at the entirety of the chain-link fence, deciding on the best place to climb. Only the side of the older building was visible. There was no window view to this area.

A spear of indecision poked at her, but she brought *his* face to mind, remembering the motivation that had led her to this fence in the first place. He was real. The hair she'd plucked from his head and placed beneath her tongue proved it.

And if he was real, he lived somewhere nearby. *Where though?* He obviously didn't live on one of the floors above or below her. The only place she could think of was *this* place. This windowless laboratory. And though she was afraid, the monster with the soul shining from his midnight eyes was too much of a lure. *I have to know.*

She gripped the fence, beginning her climb before she could talk herself out of it. *Grip, pull, find a foothold. Grip, pull, find a foothold.* Halfway up, she made the mistake of looking down. A small whimper escaped her throat. *What are you actually doing, Autumn? Have you lost your mind?*

That question gave her fortitude, because she was clear on the answer, and she turned back, continuing on. *Grip, pull, find a foothold.*

No. I have not *lost my mind.*

I might have just found it.

The *reality* she thought she'd been living might actually be part dream. *Or deception.* But she couldn't think too much about that just now. She needed at least a few answers first, and this was her chance to get some.

She threw her leg gingerly over the top of the fence and started her descent. *Grip, release, find a foothold*, only much, much faster this time.

When her feet hit the soft earth, she allowed herself a small shimmy of victory before turning, ducking, and moving behind the foliage that lined the chain-link obstruction between the old and new buildings.

She moved down the slight incline to the edge of what looked like a power station or generator or who knew, a tall fenced-in area containing enclosed boxes and heavy corded wires twisting from one row to the next. There were stickers on the gate and the boxes warning of electrocution. As she walked to the edge, she could see there was a path beyond. She hesitated. *Should I follow it?*

Yes. Autumn tiptoed slowly down the path toward the

large windowless building. She squinted at it, and from this close distance, she could see several doors along the side, all with what looked like keypads. The portion of Mercy where she lived didn't have any such thing. Of course, they had some basic security, but not like this.

Maybe there's just very expensive equipment here that requires a different level of protection.

When she was almost at the place where the path broke off in either direction, she heard voices and what sounded like wheels on pavement. With a sharp intake of breath, she pressed her body against a nearby tree, clenching her eyes shut as the voices approached. The squeak of the wheels grew louder, covering what she now thought was a...pained groan.

Autumn's breath stalled, her heart rate increasing as she pressed her lips together, attempting to become as small as possible. There were two voices. *Women. Serious tones.* The squeak of the wheels pierced her ears, echoing inside. They passed by the place where she stood, their conversation continuing. She caught a few words of medical jargon but not enough to interpret or understand.

When they had moved a short distance away, Autumn peeled herself from the tree, moving around its side. The nurses' backs were to her now, one pushing the gurney, the other walking beside her coworker. Autumn leaned out as far as she dared, her eyes widening as they turned along the path, the white sheet covering the person on the gurney shifting slightly to expose half of a human face, purple and swollen grotesquely, one eye staring directly at her.

Autumn clamped her hand over her mouth to keep herself from screaming, her heart slamming in her chest. The flash of a tiny red light under the eaves of the building across from her caught her eye, causing her panic to ratchet higher. *A camera? Was it a security camera? Oh God.*

The second the nurses turned out of sight, Autumn booked it back the way she'd come, scurrying up the incline, tripping and cursing herself for her clumsiness. She ducked, running along the short row of bushes to the place where she'd climbed the fence and ascended rapidly as though someone—*or something*—might reach up, grab her leg, and pull her back down.

CHAPTER EIGHT

"You look good, Autumn, and your vital signs are wonderful."

Autumn's nerves fluttered. They'd run tests on her heart and her lungs a few days before. They'd done an ultrasound and a CAT scan. All the diagnostics were performed by machines. Today, they were going to take her blood. Test her urine. Would they know? Would they realize she'd been off her medication for a month now? Of course they would. They were medical professionals. How would they not? The machines might not show it, but her bodily fluids most definitely would.

She couldn't be put back on the medicine yet. Not yet. *I need time. Just a little more time where I have the strength to figure out what's going on here. To determine what to do.*

To find out what in the hell is going on at the fenced-in building next to this one where I saw a very real human monster.

"That's nice to hear, Dr. Murphy. I feel good." She feigned a small cough. "Not great but...I don't expect to with my condition." She'd limped in and taken a seat gingerly, wincing when she made contact with the chair, even though cushioned for their frail bones. But she couldn't do much to hide the weight she'd put on nor to diminish the glow of her skin or the clarity that had taken over her eyes. She cast her gaze to the side. "I was wondering though if I might put off any more tests for another few weeks. The needle is always the worst for me." Which wasn't a lie. Often because of her collapsed veins, it took even the most experienced nurse poke after poke after poke to find a vein. She wrapped her sweater around her. Surely they'd notice how plump her veins were now. "I'd like to...enjoy this...reprieve while it lasts."

Dr. Murphy smiled, leaning forward. "I have one better than that, Autumn."

"Better?"

"Much better." His smile grew wider. "You're being released. We believe you're cured."

Her body jolted. Her *world* jolted. Her mouth fell open. "*Cured?*" The word came out in a croak, sounding strange and foreign. "That's...that's not possible. There's no cure." *What is happening?*

The doctor's smile slipped just a hair. "Perhaps *cured* isn't the right word." His brows knitted. "Because you're correct, there's no cure for the disease associated with ADHM. But we, the other doctors and I, have looked at your test results, and those, in combination with the fact that you have thus far remained tumor-free, indicate that you have responded well to the Mesmivir and other medications. We'd like to conclude that it's something to do with your DNA, but we don't have enough empirical evidence yet."

Autumn stared, dumbfounded.

The doctor pushed his glasses up on his nose. "There are

things we're still learning about this disease, and while your case is rare, we've been hypothesizing, and it's the only thing we can come up with."

How could this be? She hadn't been *taking* her medication. It felt as if cymbals were clanging in her head, and she couldn't determine if they were warning bells or sounds of far-off celebration. She was too afraid to strain her eyes in search of a victory parade, too fearful it wouldn't really be there. Yet at the same time, panic and confusion consumed her. Why was this happening so quickly? No process? No preparation? She didn't understand. "What if you're wrong?" Her voice was still a mere croak.

Dr. Murphy's gaze shifted slightly to the side, and a troubled expression crossed his face. "Well, I've asked that question too, Autumn...er, expressed my concern...but Dr. Heathrow is very certain and believes we should be too. He's spent the last sixteen years studying every angle of this disease and believes wholeheartedly you will not begin to show signs with your history thus far and your current numbers." He paused, that troubled expression returning before he very obviously rearranged his face into a false-looking smile. "However, an off-site doctor will see you regularly. Every couple weeks to begin with and then once a month. You'll be run through a battery of tests every six months to make sure your numbers remain stable and your scans are clear."

Doctor visits every couple weeks? And then tests every six months? She'd seen nurses daily since birth, been tested and run through machines, and had fluid drawn at least once a month all her life. She'd couldn't fathom anything different. She was...cured? She was...leaving? But this was her home. Where was she supposed to go?

Autumn burst into tears, raising her hands and covering

her face, panic and fear and joy and disbelief all warring for center stage. In the end, the disbelief won the battle. "Is this a *dream*?" she wailed.

She heard the creak of Dr. Murphy's chair as he stood and felt his hand on her shoulder, patting. "No, no. I can assure you it's no dream. Speaking of vivid dreams though, we'll begin weaning you off your medication. It's what causes them, as you know. You'll be given instructions before you leave for your foster home."

She shuddered, sniffed, wiped at her face. *Weaning off?* Just like that? It didn't make any sense. They didn't know she'd stopped taking the Mesmivir. As far as they knew, it was the medication that was keeping her well. Wouldn't they want to determine that before they sent her away to a… "Foster home?" she choked out.

Dr. Murphy stepped back. "Yes. You leave today. I… well…" He thinned his lips momentarily in what appeared to be disapproval, and she sensed somehow that the doctor had conveyed all the same questions she was now asking herself but hadn't been given answers that satisfied. That tiny red light from the security camera in the other facility flashed in her mind for some reason she couldn't quite determine at that moment. But why would they send her away because of that rather than confronting or even punishing her? "Dr. Heathrow was quite insistent. He's made all the arrangements." Dr. Murphy made that expression again but added a smile, slightly happy but mostly perplexed, the look of a man delivering good news even he hadn't expected. And she supposed that was accurate. How could *anyone* have predicted *this*? "It's soon, I know. But this disease has taken enough of your life. It's time to live, Autumn. It's time to be a normal teenage girl."

Normal? What did that mean? How could she ever be normal? Her head began whirling, thoughts tumbling. *Leave? Today?* "Where am I going?"

"A small town about an hour and a half north from New York City in the Shawangunk Mountains." Dr. Murphy sat down at his desk and pulled a pad forward and began writing on it.

"So far away from the hospital?" Autumn asked. "How will I visit my friends?"

Dr. Murphy stopped writing, adjusting his glasses again and meeting her eyes. "The truth is, Autumn, that it's not the easiest task to find available housing for teenagers in the system. We were lucky to find a gentleman willing and also up-to-date on all his inspections and paperwork."

A gentleman? They were sending a teenage girl to live on her own with a *man*? Would anyone be checking to see if she felt safe? The walls of Mercy were all Autumn had ever known. She had no clue how she'd survive out there…with a *gentleman*.

Dr. Murphy paused and then began writing again before speaking. "It's also probably better, as far as a clean slate, to put some distance between yourself and this hospital." He stopped writing, placing the pen down and offering her a thin smile. "Perhaps even necessary."

Her stomach dropped. "But everyone I know is here." *And something bad is happening. Something I'm still trying to figure out.* And *him. He* was here. Somewhere very close by. Maybe even in the building next door.

There were so many confusing concerns and a hundred questions barreling full speed through her mind. She wanted to begin shouting them, demanding answers, pleading for someone to make this make sense.

"What about my books?" was all she managed to whisper. They'd been donated to the hospital by a charity, and each child had been allowed to pick a few to keep as their own. She had so little else that only belonged to her.

"I'm afraid you'll have to leave those behind as there's only time to pack the essentials. But books can be replaced, and the other children will enjoy them."

The door burst open. Autumn was startled as a group of nurses entered, Genie, who was in front, holding a cake lit with candles, her smile glowing as tears shimmered in her eyes. The nurse behind her blew a paper party horn, further startling Autumn as they all began singing "Walking on Sunshine," the song that had become the unofficial anthem of celebration at Mercy many years before. She hadn't heard it in a long while. There weren't many opportunities for celebration there.

Genie took her hand and pulled her to her feet as another nurse held the brightly lit cake. Genie pulled her into her arms, squeezing tightly and whispering, "So happy for you, kiddo. We're all going to miss you." She let go and nodded to the cake.

Autumn's head spun, and she used what breath she had to blow out the candles as the nurses applauded and exclaimed words of happiness and celebration, bouncing Autumn from person to person.

It felt surreal, and for a moment, she believed she was *in* one of those vivid dreams Dr. Murphy had just spoken of. Only, as he'd said, the medication caused those. And Autumn no longer had it in her system.

Tears flowed as she hugged the women who had served as surrogate mothers to her, all in one way or another. And her heart mourned again that Salma wasn't there. *I need you, Salma. Where are you?*

She was offered cake, but she couldn't eat a bite, so the nurses hugged her again, offering well-wishes and filing out, off to the lounge, she supposed, where they'd celebrate her but mostly the fact that every great once in a while, there was good news within the walls of Mercy Hospital.

Dr. Murphy glanced at his watch and grabbed a slip of paper off his desk, handing it to her. She'd collapsed back into her chair once the last nurse left. He offered her his hand, and she took it as he helped her to her feet. She didn't have to feign weakness. She felt half out of her body, shaky and unsteady. "A nurse has packed your things, and a car is waiting in front. You have about fifteen minutes to say a quick goodbye to a few friends, and then you have to be off. Time to leave Mercy Hospital far behind and begin your new life. We wish you godspeed, Autumn."

CHAPTER NINE

He ran his hand over the soft red velvet cover, pulling on the satin ribbon that held it closed. The book fell open, its pages filled with what he knew must be her handwriting. It was small and surprisingly loopy. He wasn't sure *why* that surprised him, but it did. She just didn't seem like a loopy person. He'd have expected her handwriting to be bold. His eyes ran over the words, finding the uppercase *S*'s and the *a*'s and the *m*'s. *That's what it would look like if she wrote my name.*

He read a few lines near the top of a middle page. *How do you build a temple that takes a hundred years to build? How do you conquer time? How do you overcome death? How do you eat an elephant?*

His brow dipped. He didn't know what any of her questions meant, but he was especially confused by the last one. Why would anyone want to eat an elephant? He'd never heard of such a thing. He wanted to ask her why she would wonder about eating an elephant.

He squinted, mulling it over in his mind. You couldn't

eat an elephant, even if you tried. Some of it would be disgusting, and you'd throw it back up.

Maybe you could cut it into pieces so small, you could swallow them whole. You wouldn't even have to taste them.

He frowned, thinking about that. *No, because if you did that, it would take decades. The meat would be rotted by then, and you'd die of food poisoning.*

He gave his head a small shake, feeling mildly ridiculous for pondering such a thing, reaching up to massage his temple but letting his hand drop before it made contact. He didn't like the way the metal felt beneath his skin. It gave him the oddest sense of sadness. He told himself it shouldn't. It'd been very necessary.

Sam turned the page, moving on from the elephant eating question, looking at the drawings next to the words. She'd sketched things. She wasn't good. It made him smile because he saw the effort in it and also her frustration in the renderings she'd scribbled over. But next to each scribble was another attempt. *She never gives up.* That did not surprise him.

He turned another page and another. He'd start over from the beginning and read through every word, but first, he wanted to flip through and take it all in, see exactly what it was. Had she written stories? Poems? Cartoons? *Private thoughts?* His heartbeat quickened. He flipped a few more pages, stopping suddenly when he came to a drawing. He tilted his head, bringing the journal closer, his breath stalling. Was it...*him*? She'd drawn a full moon shining down on a person—a man with hair falling over his eyes, his chest bare, a long scar running from throat to navel. Sam lifted his hand, running it over the twin scar on his own abdomen.

A buzz of *something* lifted the hairs on his arms, and he felt like laughing out loud. Joy. He felt…*joy*. She'd drawn him! She'd thought of him when she went back to her room, and she'd picked up a pen and this book and sketched him from memory. His body and his face. He closed his eyes, picturing it, wanting to be in that moment with her, if only in his head. The features she'd drawn were blunt and unskilled, but he thought he saw himself in them anyway.

That buzz grew, making him feel happy and alive. His eyes moved to the words beneath the drawing, reading each line and then again, this time more slowly.

I made a boy of moonlight,
Skin of dusk and starlit eyes.
Waxing, waning, or in between,
A wish, a miracle, or just a dream?

He blinked, reading it for the third time. *I made a boy of moonlight. Him?* He'd never read anything so…beautiful. He'd never read anything beautiful at all. *A boy.* The girl saw him as…human? Sam lifted his hand slowly, waving it in the air in front of him, bending his fingers. Was he? Sometimes he didn't feel that way. He felt created, yes, but not by moonlight or miracles. He felt made of nuts and bolts and steel and things that invaded his mind whether he gave them permission to or not. Visions that circulated in his brain even as he tried to sleep.

His thoughts of the girl belonged to him though. There was no way anyone could know, and because of that, they could not be taken away. The thought felt odd, secret, and victorious in a way nothing else he'd been *told* was a victory ever had. The tests. The completion of surgeries. The successful experiments performed on his body. All the things Dr. Heathrow and the others had celebrated.

He heard a noise outside his door and closed the book quickly, sliding it under his mattress. His treasure. His only one. The person outside passed by his room, but Sam stood anyway. He'd look at the book more later when everyone else was sleeping.

He made his way down the hall, passing by the game room where he heard blasts and booms and yells and whoops of victory. Outside, the air was cold, the electric wires close by tingeing the early afternoon with a slight metallic scent. It was better than the heavy pheromones and disinfectant smells that filled his nostrils inside the building though. He stood there for a few moments, staring at the old hospital building beyond. It was where she lived. He wanted to see her. Talk to her. *Know* her.

Possibilities—*fantasies*—wound through his head, leaving only feelings and imprints. He didn't know how to clarify them, and he was too scared to do that anyway, so he left them as they were, a blurry silhouette in the back of his mind that he *felt* but refused to define.

A car moving up the hill caught his attention, and he watched it as it drove toward the hospital gates. He saw a head of dark, silken waves through the back window. Was it her? Where was she going? Alarm ricocheted through him, and he moved quickly to the chain-link fence separating this facility from the other one, grasping it with his fingers, staring out, watching as that car drove through the gates and turned out of sight.

Gone.

CHAPTER TEN

The mailbox in front of the small yellow house that backed up to thick, fall-hued woods spelled out the name Clancy in peel-off reflective letters.

Bill Clancy. That was the name the social worker who had driven her here had said belonged to the man who'd agreed to foster her.

Autumn liked to consider herself at least moderately brave. Life had dealt her a crap hand, and she'd accepted it with as much grace and fortitude as she'd been able. She'd suffered pain, both emotional and physical. She'd been lonely, mourned people she'd loved, and endured circumstances that most others, even if they lived to the ripe age of ninety, never would. But now? Now she was terrified.

"Here we are, Ms. Sterling," the social worker said cheerily.

What's her name again? Before attempting to remember, Autumn dismissed it. *What does it matter? She only drove me here. I won't see her again after this.* A deep shiver went through

Autumn as the car came to a stop and she waited as the social worker got out of the vehicle, coming around and opening the back door as though she were a child.

I feel like a child. A child who's about to be abandoned. Again. She'd had less than two hours to adjust as her entire world was flipped upside down. Fifteen minutes to hug those who meant the most to her, to try to manage the slew of emotions rising and falling inside as her friends both cried and celebrated, squeezing her as tightly as their weak, emaciated bodies allowed and then standing in the hospital doorway, waving as her car drove away, leaving behind everything familiar to her.

The social worker had had the emotional awareness not to attempt small talk. Either that or she really didn't care to have a conversation with a fourteen-year-old girl. Autumn wouldn't have been able to manage it anyway, her throat clogged with tears, her mind spinning with thoughts and fears and too many questions to attempt to arrange or put into coherent language.

She stepped from the car. The air smelled clean and fresh, with the slight bite of woodsy chill. Mercy Hospital was right outside New York City, but even removed, it hadn't smelled like this. The hint of city exhaust from cars and factories and people living right on top of one another was always there. She hadn't realized that until now.

A man appeared in the doorway, stepping out onto the porch and stuffing his hands in his pockets. He wore a pair of jeans and a red-and-black flannel shirt. He had to be at least fifty, with a short graying beard. He watched as the social worker guided Autumn up the gravel pathway to the base of the short porch.

The man smiled, but only slightly. He appeared nervous,

uncertain, and for whatever reason, that impression allowed Autumn to take a full breath. "Hi, Autumn. I'm Bill."

She stepped slowly up the two steps but stayed at the edge of the porch. "Hi," she said, and she was proud that her voice didn't tremble.

The woman behind her cleared her throat. "Well, I wish I could stay as you two get acquainted, but unfortunately, I have a long drive back."

She bustled up the stairs and there was some hand shaking, fleeting smiles, and wishes for luck. And then she was right back down the stairs and heading to the car seemingly as quickly as possible, hopping inside and backing out of the driveway. Autumn watched as the woman's brake lights disappeared around the bend, her mind surely moving swiftly from the skinny orphan girl she'd just dropped off on to her own lists and plans and other personal worries.

Autumn was well and truly alone. With…the *gentleman*.

She turned back toward Bill. He gave her an awkward smile, moving from one foot to the other. "You must be hungry," he said.

She shook her head. She'd throw up if she ate anything right now. "No. Thank you."

He frowned, smoothing his mustache, looking confused as though his one solid plan had just crumbled to dust and he didn't have another.

"I could drink something," she offered.

His face lit up. He smiled, and Autumn could see that he was handsome. *For an old man*. "Great. Yes. I have drinks." He waved his hand, indicating she should enter the house, and picked up the suitcase containing all her worldly possessions. Now minus the thing most dear to her, her journal—her thoughts and fears set to words—which had been lost in the woods.

It's okay. You can get another. The thought caused a zap of panic, and for a moment, she felt like the blank page that would sit at the front of a new journal. She wondered if, without her old one, she'd even remember who she'd been. Before.

She walked through the doorway hesitantly, taking in the large open room she'd entered. There was a cozy living room area to the right, a fire burning in the fireplace, a dining area to the left, and a kitchen at the rear. Large windows across the back wall looked out to the woods.

It was homey and lovely, and something about it made her want to cry. She didn't know if they were happy or sad tears and was still too emotionally discombobulated to figure it out.

Bill moved around her, placing her bag near a hallway just beyond the living room that must lead to the bedrooms, and walked toward the kitchen. "I bought a few different kinds of soda and juice. And I have sweet tea. Water of course." He turned near the refrigerator, looking at her hopefully.

"Water would be great."

He went about getting two glasses and pouring from a pitcher in the refrigerator. He placed them on the butcher block island in the middle, and Autumn climbed up on one of the wooden stools across from where he stood. She took a small sip of the water, waiting to make sure it settled. When she set the glass back down, she saw that he was studying her, an expression on his rugged face that seemed unsure but also a bit sad.

"You must feel..." He shook his head. "I can't even imagine what you must feel, Autumn. So I'll tell you how

I feel. I feel nervous. I feel worried. And maybe like I'm in over my head here. My wife, Allie, died two years ago." He paused, and she saw him swallow, recognized the tremor in the words and knew he still grieved. "She was younger than me. I must look very old to you." A small fleeting smile. "I met her later in life, but she was my every dream come true. She was worth the wait. We planned to end our days together sitting on the rockers on the porch out front." Another pause, another shimmer of grief in his eyes. He leaned back against the counter behind him, crossing his arms. "Anyway, the baby thing…it didn't work out right away, and we knew time wasn't on our side. Allie, she…she was so sure God had a plan for us. But she said sometimes you have to explore all your options and see where God meets you. We became foster parents. We requested a newborn, but that newborn never came. Allie got sick and, well…priorities shifted."

A newborn. He'd wanted a newborn. He'd pictured his wife holding a baby, and instead he was alone, a strange teenager standing in front of him, dropped off to share his home. She supposed maybe he felt as lost as she did.

Yet he'd obviously kept up his foster parent status. "Were you planning on raising a baby…alone?" she asked.

He met her eyes, seeming surprised that she'd spoken so many words. He ran a hand through his brown hair with gray at his temples and stared at her for a moment, obviously working out why she'd asked. He looked away and scratched the back of his neck. "I don't know. I stayed current with the paperwork, the inspections…I don't even know why." He sighed, looking off out the window. "Maybe because Allie'd wanted it, and to let it lapse felt like…" He pressed his lips together obviously at a loss.

"Letting her down?" Autumn asked quietly.

His eyes widened, and she saw a glint of gratitude in his expression. "Yeah. Yeah, that's it. I couldn't do that. I wasn't ready."

I wasn't ready. It'd been two years, and still, he hadn't been ready to let his dead wife's dream die along with her. Autumn felt a catch in her heart.

"Truth is," he said on a small chuckle that was short-lived, "I suppose I didn't expect anything—any*one*—to come of it at all." His features contorted slightly into a wince, and his eyes moved over her face, maybe wondering if he'd insulted her. But he hadn't. Autumn found she felt more comfortable in his presence with every honest word. "There's not much use in the foster care system for a fifty-one-year-old single man who works odd hours."

"What do you do?" she asked.

"I build furniture."

Autumn glanced around, looking more closely at all the beautiful furniture she'd noticed on the way in. "Did you—" She used her finger to gesture from one piece to another.

"Most of it," he said. "I built the things Allie wanted. I'd never really built furniture for my own home before."

"Why?"

"Oh, you know, the cobbler's children syndrome, I guess." When she stared at him blankly, he chuckled. "It's a proverb that just means people don't usually benefit from the product of their own trade." He looked behind her and tipped his chin. "It looks like there's quite a sunset happening out there. Do you want to check it out?"

She turned around, giving it a brief glance. "Sure," she said, getting up and walking with him to the front porch. The sky in front of them blazed deep pink and fiery red.

They stood there for a moment before Bill looked away

from the sky and turned to her. "I figure we're both out of our element here, Autumn. And we're both searching for solid footing. What I'd like to start with is this: in that search, we tell each other how we feel, because neither of us is a mind reader. At least I'm assuming you're not."

Autumn managed a small laugh and felt a loosening inside. "I'm not." She held out her hand, and he took it. "Deal."

He smiled as they shook. "Deal." They both let go, Bill turning back to the sky.

Autumn ran her hand along the rocker next to her, glancing at the one beside it. They were beautiful, just like the things inside. Bill had made these. She knew without even asking. She took a few steps and then sat down in it, moving it back and forth. The sun lowered. The earth felt still and peaceful.

Could this feel like my home too?
Home. A real one.

She pushed the question aside. She didn't dare answer it. Not yet. Still, she'd enjoy the feel of sitting on this porch with this man who was obviously kind, watching the setting sun. Moments. It was all she'd ever had. If anything good had come from being sick all her life, Autumn knew how to enjoy them.

As she sat there, the picture of *him*, her moonlight monster, flashed in her mind's eye. She'd lost him too, hadn't she? She'd lost the opportunity to find out more about what was going on at Mercy Hospital. *No, I won't let it go. I'll figure something out. Maybe this man will even help me.* But that remained to be seen.

Bill took the seat next to her. She looked over at him, and he met her gaze, his eyes moving from her to the rocker he'd built for his wife with his own two hands, giving a small, sad smile and a nod. "Okay then," he said quietly as though accepting the fate he'd been handed rather than the one he had planned.

CHAPTER ELEVEN

Nine Years Later

Autumn smiled as she stepped from the car, the sun streaming through the trees and hitting her face. The leaves crunched beneath her feet as she headed toward the small blue house, rapping twice on the door.

It was only a minute before it was pulled open, the old woman standing there in a faded red robe, her hair in tight curlers. "Autumn."

"Hello, Ms. Hastings," Autumn greeted, stepping forward and giving the dour old woman a quick hug. Ms. Hastings appeared momentarily stunned, and Autumn used the opportunity to breeze past her into the tidy house with the paisley sofa and a fireplace mantel full of framed photographs, none of which were current.

"They didn't tell me the house calls were going to continue indefinitely," Ms. Hastings mumbled as she followed Autumn's lead to the porch at the back of the house where the

TV was still on, a panel of highly made-up, coiffed women drinking their coffee and solving the world's problems, or at least the "problems" of those who carried thousand-dollar purses and made weekly visits to the spa. Autumn switched it off. Ms. Hastings took her customary seat in the well-worn velvet recliner, sighing as she sank down into it.

"Not indefinitely," Autumn said. "Only as long as it's determined you need them." Autumn dropped her purse and medical bag, shrugging out of her sweater and grabbing the instruments she needed.

"Determined by whom?" Ms. Hastings grumped.

"Determined by me, your nurse and healthcare professional."

"Humph."

Autumn placed the stethoscope in her ears and put the chest piece on Ms. Hastings's warm, wrinkled skin. "It's a beautiful day out," she said, satisfied with the sound of the woman's heart, removing the earpieces and hanging the stethoscope around her neck. "We should sit in the sun for a bit," she said, nodding to the small patio out the window where a wooden bench sat directly in a puddle of sunlight.

"I'm just fine in here."

"Vitamin D is good for you."

"What's good for me is my fanny parked in this chair watching my shows."

Her shows. Autumn wrapped the blood pressure cuff around Ms. Hastings's arm and pressed the button. The soft purr of the tightening cuff sounded as Autumn tipped her chin toward the dark TV. "That stuff rots your brain. Those fake *people* rot your brain."

"They're not fake—"

"They *are* fake. They live in a box."

The machine let out a whistling sound as the pressure released, the cuff deflating. "You sound like my mother."

I sound like your daughter should sound if she cared about you and had anything to do with your life, Autumn thought, picturing the dusty picture on the mantel of the high school graduation photo of the girl, now a woman, who had called once after her mother's surgery, been told she had made it through, replied with a terse word that reeked of disappointment, and not called back again. *Nor* visited, though she only lived an hour away. Autumn didn't know all the ins and outs of their relationship, so she supposed she shouldn't judge. All she knew was that the grief of loneliness hung on Ms. Hastings, and her body wasn't going to heal as quickly if her soul was withering away. "I'm wise beyond my years," Autumn said, giving the woman a cheeky grin and holding out her hand.

Ms. Hastings grumbled a little bit more but let Autumn pull her to her feet and walk her out the back door and onto the sun-drenched patio.

They sat down on the bench, and Autumn scooted close, taking the woman's hand in hers and patting it. "Doesn't that feel good?"

"I know these visits aren't necessary," Ms. Hastings said, and there was a small tremor in her voice. Fear maybe. Sadness.

"They're necessary to me," Autumn said, patting her hand again and holding it tighter.

"For how long?" the old woman asked, and the tremor that time was definitely fear.

"A while, Ms. Hastings. Quite a while."

Ms. Hastings's shoulders lowered, a breath releasing.

"What's sun got to do with medicine?" she murmured.

Autumn squinted up at the sky, breathing deep. "Everything, Ms. Hastings. Feel that vitamin D soaking into your skin?" she asked. "It's invisible but it *heals*. It's sort of like magic, isn't it?"

"Magic, humph. You're some kind of nurse, Autumn Clancy." But Ms. Hastings tipped her face, closing her eyes, a very slight smile gracing her lips. The warmth of the sun. Human contact. Not things listed in medical books but medicine all the same.

Who knows that better than me?

"Bill?" Autumn called, dropping her sweater on the back of the couch and walking to the hall that led to his bedroom. The door was open, and she didn't hear him puttering around inside, so she turned, leaving the house, walking around the side to the large shed at the edge of the trees. She heard the momentary buzz of the saw, and when she opened the door, Bill looked up from where he stood at the counter, a piece of freshly cut wood in his hand.

His smile was instantaneous. He took off his safety glasses and set what looked like a table leg aside. "Hey, darlin'. I didn't know you were stopping by."

Autumn smiled too, walking forward and squeezing him tightly. "Do I need an appointment?"

"Never. This is your home. But I would have had some tea made and been a tad less dusty."

"I don't need tea, and I'm used to you dusty," she said on a laugh.

He grabbed a nearby rag and wiped his hands off. "And," he said, "I would have hidden this because it's not quite done."

Autumn's eyes widened as she caught sight of the rocking chair right next to him, the stained wood dark and rich. Her breath caught. It was an exact replica of the two on his front porch. "You made me a rocking chair?" she breathed, tears gathering at the backs of her eyes. "But... but my chair is *here*."

He smiled, shrugged, looking as pleased as could be. "And it always will be. But I figured you needed one at your place too. I've been meaning to make you one since you moved out and finally got around to it."

She moved her hand along the curved, butter-smooth wood of the back. "It's beautiful. It's the best gift I've ever received," she said, meeting his eyes. *You're the best gift I ever received.* She reached up and hugged his neck. "Thank you, Bill."

"You're welcome, darlin'."

She gave the chair one last admiring look. "Do you have a few minutes to visit?"

"There will never be a time when I don't have at least a few minutes for my favorite girl."

Love and warmth enveloped her. She smiled, and together they walked toward the front porch, taking their usual seats in those old rocking chairs. The ones where they'd first established the rules of their newfound, unexpected father-daughter relationship, the ones they'd sat in as Autumn had later complained about teachers, shed a few tears about bad dates and breakups, talked about plans and dreams. She'd confided that she wanted to be a nurse as they'd sat in these chairs, and she'd later opened the letter that had told her she'd been accepted into the nursing program at a nearby college. He'd brought out a bottle of champagne that she hadn't seen next to his rocker because he believed in her so wholeheartedly and popped the cork, and she'd laughed and cried and hugged him hard. "What would you have done if I hadn't gotten in?" They clinked glasses, hers very small. And he'd grinned and said he would have very covertly used his foot to slide the bottle under his chair. She'd laughed and then cried again. And now here she was, an RN who loved her job every bit as much as she'd dreamed.

It was in this very spot where she'd told him about the first fourteen years of her life and then later haltingly confided in him about waking in the woods, about the dream that was no dream, and about the boy made of moonlight. She'd expected Bill's disbelief. But he had believed her. He'd asked questions, tried to puzzle it out with her, and though she hadn't cried in that instance, she almost had. It was the first time she'd put her experience to words. And talking about it had brought it back to life. She'd needed time to adjust to her new life, her new home, her newfound health, and in that time, she'd almost begun to believe that the experience *had* been a dream… or…something misty and inexplicable, brought on by the medication. But telling Bill had brought back the *feeling* of what had happened while she'd supposedly slept in her bed and of *him*, the specifics of his eyes, the silken shine of his hair, and the particular scent of his skin. He was *real*. And though easier, though far away and removed from her current life, she would not forget him.

There hadn't even been time for an inquiry. The Mercy Hospital for Children had mysteriously closed a year after she'd arrived on Bill's doorstep, two months before she'd worked up the nerve to spill all her secrets to him. She'd been crushed when she'd found out, not only because she had no idea how to find her friends or potentially the boy from the woods but because there was now no way to prove what she'd experienced had been very real.

She'd seen doctors every few weeks at first, and they'd done extensive testing that showed she was generally healthy if underweight, anemic, and deficient in several vitamins and minerals. They'd given her instructions on how to wean off the pharmaceuticals she was on, which was easy considering she'd already gone off those medications. Her health hadn't only remained stable, it'd improved vastly, so she'd been cleared for checkups every month, then every six months, and finally once a year like any other ordinary person. *Ordinary.* One of the most beautiful words in the English language to Autumn. She was ordinary. Not only of body but of mind. She'd told her doctor about the dreams she'd once had, though not all the particulars—not about the dirt under her fingernail or the singular pale hair hidden under her tongue—and he'd nodded and said, yes, that was very typical for those prescribed the medications she'd taken.

She'd had a life to live, classes to attend, goals to achieve. Still, she hadn't given up. She'd spent her spare hours attempting to track down the kids she'd once lived with and the nurses too, particularly Salma. But she'd run into one dead end after another. And she'd been an hour and a half out of the city, only able to do her investigative work by phone.

Bill had done what he could, but he too had been brushed off by social workers, blatantly told to cease encouraging Autumn that her dreams were reality or that the hallucinations she'd experienced had been real. Side effects. Merely side effects, and common ones at that. It wasn't helpful to humor her, they said. He owed it to his new charge to make it possible for her to settle into her new life, and she could see in his eyes that though he believed Autumn, he also didn't disagree with that part of their advice. There was really no tangible proof of what she'd told him, only the claims of a once highly medicated girl. There might be other explanations, right? There was plentiful information on the internet about not only the dreams that came along with the medication Autumn had been on all her life but the fact that in some children, it also caused the hallucinations the doctors had spoken of. What if she'd sleepwalked? What if her experience was something *other* than what it seemed? Not nefarious but...explainable? Was it likely, or even possible, that the hospital where she'd once lived had been purposely putting their patients in danger...offering them up as...what? Prey to be hunted by...human monsters? The more Autumn tried to make sense of it and the further away in years she moved, the more it *felt* like a hallucination...a fever dream...distant and separate from reality. She didn't even have her journal anymore, the chronicle of her time at Mercy Hospital and the whisperings of her soul as she'd trudged through a valley of shadows toward what she assumed was an almost certain death.

Yet despite the somewhat bleary nature of the first part of her life, and even though her new existence was filled with stability, with friends, with ordinary problems and mundane days, she couldn't escape the vision of *him* that still filled her mind when she closed her eyes. Her moonlight boy.

And because of him, she hadn't stopped searching. She hadn't ceased going down avenues that might eventually bring her some kind of clarity.

Her tenacity finally paid off when she was seventeen and managed to locate Genie, who had been working at a hospital in another town outside New York City. She'd seemed surprised and delighted to hear from Autumn and had invited her to her apartment. Bill had taken the day off and driven her there, and she'd tearfully reunited with the nurse who had been a constant in her life for so many years. But though she'd probed, Genie had appeared confused by Autumn's questions about the dreams and repeated what she'd been told so many times before: it was the medication and only that. The bruises, the scratches, all explained by the disease. She'd seemed sincere, and on one hand, Autumn wanted to believe that *Genie* believed what she said. Because though Autumn was desperate for answers, to know that women she'd thought of as mothers had intentionally and knowingly allowed her to be put in harm's way would have been devastating.

Genie had been able to clear up one mystery, however, and it was a crushing one. The reason Mercy Hospital had closed so abruptly was simple really: the clientele had drastically reduced. That meant, of course, that so many of Autumn's friends had died, and there had simply been no reason to keep such a large establishment open.

She'd feared as much.

Still, she powered on.

And now she was there to tell Bill what more her digging had accomplished.

"I might have found my mother," she said softly. "Or at least…her name."

Bill's head turned. "Your mother?" He paused, digesting that information. "After all this time?" He let out a soft chuckle. "My tireless girl! How? Where?"

She gave him a slight smile. *My tireless girl*. So why, inside, when it came to her unending personal investigation, did she feel so beaten down? "New York City. It might not be her, but I'm going to pay the woman a visit and find out."

"Do you want me to go with you?"

Autumn thought about that for a moment. "No. I think I'd like to do this alone." Bill was her safe place. Her living proof that good things could—and *did*—come to those who waited. She wanted to keep her two worlds—the one she'd come from and the one where she belonged—separate, at least temporarily. She wasn't even sure exactly why. It just felt right to her.

"Okay," he said after a moment. "Just promise you'll be careful. And, Autumn, whatever happens…" He reached over, taking her hand and squeezing it, seeming unable to have the right words to finish that sentence. She saw it in his eyes though.

"I know, Bill," she said. "I know."

Autumn breezed through the door to the jail, greeting Patty the receptionist, who had the phone to her ear, with a wave and heading toward the sheriff's office. Sheriff Monroe wasn't in his office, but she found him standing in the kitchen, perusing a box of doughnuts on the table in front of him. She pushed it to the side and set down the Ziploc baggie of muffins she'd brought with her.

"What's that?" he asked, raising a suspicious brow.

"What it's not," she said, "is an overload of sugar and simple carbs. No seed oils either."

"Oh God, it's fiber, isn't it?"

"It's good for you."

He grumbled before taking a muffin from the baggie and biting into it. Autumn waited as he chewed and swallowed.

"Not Krispy Kreme," he said. "But not half-bad." He took another bite.

Autumn grinned. "Remember, your body is a temple. Treat it like one."

"Yes, Nurse Ratched."

Autumn laughed. "Cell one?"

"Yup."

She walked through the small building to the cell areas near the back where she found the man slumped on the bench. She pulled the unlocked cell door open. "Hi, Seymour."

He looked up, eyes bleary and rimmed in red. "You again?"

She sat down next to him. "*You* again? We've gotta stop meeting like this, Seymour. It isn't at all proper."

"Proper? I don't know nothin' about proper."

"Sure you do. You've just forgotten temporarily. I'm here to remind you."

In answer, he tipped his head back, letting it hit the wall behind him.

"Also, you smell terrible," she told him. "And you look like death warmed over."

"Where's my pep talk?"

"That *was* a pep talk."

He mustered a small humor-filled snort but then closed his eyes and sighed. "Give me the seal of approval so I can get out of here, wouldja?"

She put her hands on her knees, staring at him for a moment. He was thirty-six years old, and he looked like he was fifty-six. She kept hoping this would be the last time she'd see him sitting in a cell detoxing on Monday morning, and he kept disappointing her. "You've gotta stop drinking, Seymour. Didn't I tell you Franklin Brown said he'd accompany you to meetings at the church on Springhaven? They meet every Friday night. They'd welcome you with open arms."

"Yeah, yeah," he said, not opening his eyes.

"You have to make the choice though. It's up to you." She thought of the kids she'd grown up with, the ones who would have given their right arm to be able to stop waking up sick. "Do you know how many people would give anything to have a choice between feeling well and feeling half-dead?"

"Don't put a guilt trip on me."

"I'm not. I'm trying to inspire you to recognize the gifts you've already been given. Accept them now before it's too late. No guilt. Just...hope. Belief." She patted his knee. "This is no way to live, Seymour. Waking up in a drunk tank every Monday morning. Constantly feeling sick and miserable. You can do better than this."

"Can I?"

"Yes. *Yes.* Leagues better."

He spared her a glance and then was silent for a moment as she waited for him to blow her off. Again. What she'd said was true. She continued to hold out hope. But ultimately, his life was up to him.

"Fine. Friday night," he mumbled.

For a moment, his words didn't register. "Really?" she breathed. "Really?" She grabbed his hand.

He made a groaning sound as though the jostling movement was enough to make him want to toss his cookies, and looking at him, it probably was. She let go.

"I'll text Franklin and he'll pick you up. Friday. Be ready. The meeting starts at six thirty." Despite his stench, she leaned forward and kissed his cheek.

He smiled but didn't open his eyes.

She found the sheriff back in his office. "Seymour is cleared to go."

"You realize I don't need your clearance to send him on his pitiful way."

She sat down in the chair in front of his desk. "I know. But I appreciate you letting me have a few words with him before kicking him out. He's agreed to go to an AA meeting this Friday."

The sheriff stopped what he was writing and looked up at her. "Do you think he'll follow through?"

"I hope so. But if not, it's a step closer than I've gotten with him before."

The sheriff gave a terse nod. "You put too much faith in people, Autumn."

"No," she said. "I like to think I have a good handle on human nature. But when life has given you a second chance, you can't help wanting to help others reach for theirs too. It just feels like a"—she searched for the right word—"duty."

"You're going to be disappointed more often than not."

"Maybe. But still."

"But still." His smile was filled with affection. She'd started working as the on-call nurse for the sheriff's department a year before, but she'd known Ralph Monroe since she'd moved to town. He was a childhood friend of Bill's, and he'd made it a point to keep an eye on her, make sure she was settling in well and that everyone knew that if they messed with her, they messed with the town sheriff and all its deputies. When she was a teenager, that had been both a blessing and a curse, but now she was only grateful for the way so many had stepped forward to make her feel welcome, both because they were kindhearted and because they loved Bill, who was a lifelong resident.

Ralph's wife, Veronica, and daughter, Caitlin, had also become part mother/aunt and cousin. Caitlin was only a year older than Autumn, so she'd been a lifesaver on many occasions when Bill didn't quite know how to mentor her. And Veronica had modeled what a wonderful mother could look like. Autumn hoped someday she'd become a mother herself, and if she did, she'd try her best to be just like Veronica.

She cleared her throat, looking away for a moment. "I might have found my mother," she said softly for the second time that day. "I'm making the drive to New York City tomorrow morning."

She'd told the sheriff about her suspicions regarding the hospital. She'd even told him about the boy in the woods and asked if there was anything he could do in an official capacity to look into the facility. He'd tried to help her as much as he could, but he didn't get far. He was in a different city, and her records were sealed, as were those of the other patients who'd lived at Mercy Hospital. He could help her report a crime if she had even a shred of evidence, but she didn't, and she knew as well as anyone else that they'd all say she had had hallucinations or dreams so vivid she still thought they were real.

Now she shifted her eyes, waiting for him to tell her she was crazy for continuing to search for answers, but when he didn't say anything at all, she looked back.

The sheriff regarded her. "I don't suppose I could talk you out of it."

She shook her head.

"Didn't think so. You're sweet as sugar, Autumn. But stubborn as a damn mule."

She grinned. "Thanks."

"You have to make me a promise though. Put some pepper spray in your purse. And, Autumn…hope for the best but expect the worst."

"Promise." She left the office, making her way to her car. *Hope for the best but expect the worst.* She knew what he meant. Her mother had been an addict when she'd gotten pregnant with her and given her up to the system. That was all she knew about the woman. And that was if it was even her. Autumn had managed to come up with a list of names via the hospital where she was born and a few social workers and clerks who had given her information they maybe weren't supposed to because she was so persistent, but there was no guarantee this woman was the same one who had birthed her. Even more than that, there was no guarantee that if it was, the woman would acknowledge it or even agree to speak to Autumn. This was a crapshoot, but in all reality, her whole life had been a crapshoot. The thing was though, she'd *won* too many times not to keep trying. If there was a possibility this woman could provide answers that might lead to more, then she had to try. She had to.

Impulsively, she turned into a parking lot near the edge of a cliff that looked out over the Hudson River. The wind whipped her dark hair as she exited her vehicle and walked slowly toward the lookout point. Water lapped the rocks below, the deep blue water winding in front of her as far as her eyes could see. She pulled in a big breath of cool, pine-tinged air, an odd feeling moving through her that she was drawing closer and closer to some inevitable something that would change everything for her. *Again.*

CHAPTER TWELVE

Autumn didn't necessarily want to think about why a person would rent a room for an hour, but that was what the sign in the window advertised. But it also offered longer-term stays apparently, because the woman she was looking for lived here. She stepped into the dank lobby, the smell of cigarettes and mildew hitting her nose, waiting a moment for her eyes to adjust to the low lighting. An old man sat, hunched over at a desk against the far wall, reading a magazine, a cigarette hanging from his lip.

"Hi," she said as she approached. She waited a moment, but he didn't look up. "Um, I'm here to see a…resident."

"Name?" His voice was hoarse, and he reached up, removing the cigarette and stubbing it out in an ashtray in front of him that was already full of old butts. His fingers were dry and yellowed, and though she didn't know the man, it pained her to see a human being who was so obviously unhealthy and probably unhappy if the way he'd barked the singular "greeting" at her was any indication.

She smiled, trying to catch his eye and, at the very least, offer some kindness. "Deborah Dunne."

He used his yellowed finger to travel down a list of names written in handwriting that was indecipherable to Autumn's eyes, landing on one and picking up the phone. He pressed a couple of buttons and, a moment later, told the feminine voice on the other end that there was a girl there to see her. Autumn's heart pumped harder. The man hung up the phone and pointed toward the singular elevator at the back of the lobby. "Room four twelve," he said, picking up the pack of cigarettes next to him and tapping one out.

Autumn took the elevator that smelled like urine and disinfectant to the fourth floor, careful not to touch anything inside the small, dingy car. For a moment, the scent reminded her of being back in the hospital, only unlike there, here the urine odor was far and away winning the war over whatever cleaner had been used at some point.

The hallway leading to room 412 was dim, the lights buzzing and lowering intermittently. Autumn pulled her purse closer to her body, drawing comfort from the pepper spray she kept inside, mindful that defective wiring was probably the least of any danger she'd confront in this sketchy hall.

She rapped on the door when she came to it, not allowing herself time to back out. She was here, and she was going to see this through, come what may.

The door was pulled open by a bony woman with sharp cheekbones and lank brown hair.

Autumn pulled in a breath, immediately overwhelmed by emotion. *Deborah Dunne.* She'd never shared her mother's name. The hospital had assigned Autumn a surname when she'd become their ward, and she'd been a Sterling before she was a Clancy. But although this woman's eyes were dull and lackluster, Autumn recognized them immediately: she stared at the same ones in the mirror each day. Autumn's heart simultaneously rejoiced and grieved. This human shell of a person was her mother. She was certain of it. "You're Deborah Dunne."

The woman gave Autumn a suspicious once-over. "I am. What do you want?"

Autumn mustered what she hoped was a disarming smile. The woman's eyes narrowed with even deeper suspicion. *Fail*. Well, she was already off to a crummy start, might as well dive right in. "Hi, I'm Autumn Clancy. I believe I'm your daughter."

Deborah's face did a number of things, none of which gave Autumn the impression the news delighted her, but then she leaned forward, peering more closely at Autumn. "What do you want?" The news, apparently, made that moment no different from the previous one, given she repeated the exact same question.

"To ask you a few questions," Autumn said. "That's all." She might have given an alternate answer had the question been asked differently, but it wasn't. *To know you*. She gave herself a heartbeat, two, of disappointment, not delving into the depth of it right then. That was for later, perhaps to process with Bill or maybe alone. But she acknowledged it so she could temporarily tuck it away.

The woman gave one long-suffering sigh but stepped back, opening the door wider and allowing Autumn entrance. The room was just as neat and tidy as she'd expected it to be based on the woman's appearance, which was to say it was an abysmal wreck. Autumn gingerly picked up some form of undergarment on the back of the wooden chair near the bed, started to wipe at the crustiness on the seat, thought better of touching it with her bare skin, and sat down.

Deborah sat on the bed, drawing one leg beneath her and peering at Autumn again for several long moments as Autumn peered back. Upon closer inspection, she recognized her own cheekbones and the shape of her top lip. Perhaps Deborah did too, because her next comment was, "Huh. Yeah. I see it. Hold on." She stood, walking to a dresser and opening the top drawer. She took a pile of papers out, riffling through them, all the while mumbling what sounded like, "Thought it was in here." After searching deeply in another drawer, she paused and looked at whatever was in her hand. She walked back toward Autumn, holding out what looked like an old, weathered picture. "That's me."

Autumn took it from her and stared at it as Deborah sat back on the bed. It was Deborah, only much younger, a brightness in her eyes that definitely wasn't there now, her skin smooth and flawless, hair half up and half down, coincidentally the same way Autumn was wearing her hair now. She looked even more like Autumn in this picture, and a part of her wanted to ask if she could keep it, but some deeper part knew instinctively that it meant more to this person than Autumn herself did. The tangible reminder, perhaps, that she hadn't always been an emotionally void old shrew. She handed it back. Deborah stared at it with a wistful look, reinforcing Autumn's assumption from a moment before.

"I spent my first fourteen years at Mercy Hospital with all the other ADHM babies," Autumn said, though Deborah hadn't asked and likely wasn't all too interested. She wasn't sure of another way to start the conversation though, so she started there.

Deborah bit at her nail for a moment but then shook her head. "No. I didn't take any Lucy in the Sky. I almost did, but he slapped me right before I was about to inject it." She shrugged. "It was his stash, the dude I was with at the time, and he flipped when he saw me about to use it. He smacked me good and hard, and I was seeing stars for the next few days. I went to the free clinic about it. They told me I had a concussion, and I was pregnant too."

Confusion overtook Autumn. "Wait...you didn't take it. Ever?"

"Not the hard stuff. Not while I was pregnant." Deborah looked away as though considering. "Just the thought of it made me feel like pukin'. It was the damnedest thing. Maybe I should have kept on getting pregnant. Maybe I wouldn't have ended up here." She waved her arm around the sad, dingy room with stains on the exposed bedding Autumn refused to consider.

"How is that possible though? I was diagnosed as an ADHM baby." *I was sick for the first fourteen years of my life.*

"Couldn't tell you. Maybe the hospital staff looked at me and assumed."

Autumn's gaze flitted over her. The sores on her pallid skin, the old track marks on her arms. The way she kept itching and twitching. If she looked even remotely like this twenty-four years before, Autumn might have assumed the same thing. "The man who slapped you, he was...my father?"

Deborah shrugged. "Who knows." She tilted her head, studying her again. "You look a little like him in the chin. Pointy little thing. Stubborn." She paused, her shoulders dropping. "Mean. But suppose he woulda been that with any kinda chin, because you don't seem mean."

They were both quiet for a minute. Deborah's eyes kept flickering toward the dresser as she scratched at her arms, making Autumn think there was something in it beckoning to her. Autumn waited for the woman to ask her something. Anything. But she remained distracted by the drawer.

She stood shakily, giving Deborah the only smile she could muster. "Do you, um, need some food? I could—"

"Money would be good."

"For food?"

"Mm-hmm." More scratching. A twitch and then another.

Autumn dug in her purse, taking out two twenties and placing them on the table. She knew this money wouldn't be used for food, but maybe even a small amount of generosity—kindness—would change...something. Deborah just stared.

"I appreciate the time. I...ah, I'll check in from time to time?" Autumn offered awkwardly.

Deborah waved her hand in the air, dismissive. "Don't bother. But if you want to drop some money in the mail now and again, I won't say no."

"Oh. Ah, well, I'll see what I can do," Autumn mumbled. The last thing she wanted was to support this woman's bad habits, but she was also her mother. *A mother who doesn't give a damn that you exist and never did.* She wanted to lecture the woman. She wanted to spit at least a few ugly words at her, but as she stood there looking at the sad shell of a human, she had a feeling more than anything, the woman needed...a hug. Whether she realized it or not. And though she had hurt her, Autumn stepped around the side of the bed, bending down and taking Deborah in her arms.

Her birth mother tensed and then went kind of slack but didn't move as Autumn held the embrace. When she stepped back, Deborah was looking up at her, blinking with surprise.

Autumn headed for the door. Still, she couldn't help it; she turned back. She might not see her mother again, and she had to know the answer to the question that had stayed with her as long as she could remember. "Did you name me? Did you pick out the name Autumn?"

Deborah stared at her for a moment as though she'd forgotten Autumn's name entirely, that look of surprise still clear on her face. But for the moment at least, she seemed to have forgotten the drawer. "Uh, no. Nurse did."

Well. Another mystery solved. No, her birth mother had not named her. A bureaucrat had given her a surname, and some unknown nurse had chosen Autumn. Maybe she could at least try to pretend that that person had tried to think of something beautiful for the sick, unwanted baby girl who would float by her, as fleeting as the falling leaves outside the nursery window. Or maybe it was random.

The truth is good. Even when it hurts.

"Thank you again. And…have a nice day." Deborah remained seated, and Autumn pulled the door closed behind her. She called for the elevator, but when it didn't come immediately, she opened the door to the stairwell, jogging down all four flights as quickly as her feet would carry her, the same way she'd done so long ago at Mercy Children's Hospital, working her muscles strenuously for the first time in her life. When she made it to the lobby, she was winded, but the bout of exercise had mostly helped her recover from the exchange with Deborah Dunne. *My mother.*

No, the woman who birthed me.

I didn't take any Lucy in the Sky. I almost did, but he slapped me right before I was about to inject it.

The woman's words came back to her as she breezed out the front door of the building, turning the corner and stopping, pressing her back against the bricks. She closed her eyes, a few tears escaping and, along with them, the dream, the longing to believe that she'd been wanted. The scratchy surface abraded her palms as she dragged them along the wall, helping to keep her grounded. The hot tears continued to stream down Autumn's cheeks for several minutes. She'd spent her life wondering…hoping, and the reality she'd just been faced with was a harsh slap to the face. *The soul.* She took a deep, shuddery breath, raising her head, wiping the tears, and standing tall. Grief was a barren land of shadowy what-ifs. She'd allowed herself to go there, but she wouldn't allow herself to stay.

Autumn walked back onto the main street, her gaze pulled upward. Even though it was just past midday, she could see a translucent sliver of moon in the pale, sterling sky. Whether it was full or not, the moon always made her think of him, and she welcomed that now. The boy she'd once believed to be nothing but a dream. Her moonlight monster. The name seemed silly now, but in that moment, the thought of him brought her an odd comfort she couldn't explain.

She looked back to the street, raising her hand to hail the cab coming toward her and then stepping toward the curb.

As the city streets streaked by, Autumn gazed out the window, unseeing. She pictured that slap from decades before and the faceless man who'd delivered it. In her mind's eye, she saw Deborah flying backward, the needle in her hand dropping to the floor.

How could you be thankful for something like that? Yet she was. She was thankful that man had slapped her mother, even if it had been done in cruelty. Because it was the slap that had saved Autumn's life.

But now, more than ever, Autumn wanted answers. She wanted to know why she'd been placed at Mercy Hospital if she'd never been sick. There was only one person she could think of that might be able to offer clarity, and she worked a few miles away.

"Hi, Autumn, come on in," Chantelle Rogers said, not even attempting to hide the weary note in her voice.

Autumn entered the social worker's office and took a seat in the chair she'd sat in so many times.

"Autumn, I've told you over and over that I can't give out information about the whereabouts of—"

"I'm not here looking for my friends this time," she said. She'd already tried in vain to find the others she'd known well at that hospital, not only to reunite with them but to see if they could offer more in the way of the shared dreams they'd had…and to find out if they were even still alive. Genie had crushed most of that hope with the information she'd given about Mercy's closing, and the few friends Autumn had found on her own had annihilated the last of it, because the place she'd found them was on grave markers. She was one of the lucky ones. Only it wasn't luck, and that was what she was here about this time. "I found my mother," she said. "She said that I shouldn't have ever been at Mercy Hospital. She never took the drug. So…*I was never an ADHM baby.*"

Chantelle's face registered surprise. "How did you find your mother?"

Autumn waved the question away. She'd cajoled the information that had helped her find her mother from a few kind clerks and newly hired social workers. She wasn't going to rat them out. "I just got lucky. Anyway, it was her. I was already pretty sure, and then I went to see her. She's my mother."

Chantelle studied her for a moment, sitting back. Chantelle wasn't unkind. She was just overworked and underpaid and couldn't understand why Autumn wouldn't just leave things well enough alone when she'd found such happiness in her life. The woman was never going to be able to put herself in Autumn's shoes because she wasn't interested in doing that. And to be fair, Autumn supposed that that was as much a coping mechanism as anything when working the type of job Chantelle worked. If she constantly put herself in the shoes of the kids she placed, she'd surely end up emotionally devastated. "This woman you're sure is your mother, she could have been lying about not taking the drug. It's what junkies do. They lie."

"Yet I'm one of the only ADHM kids who made it past sixteen?"

"There are others."

"Three percent," Autumn said quietly. "Three percent of ADHM babies survived." There were only a handful of them across the country. And because the drug had been a new phenomenon that swept in unexpectedly and created a horrible epidemic, it had taken time to realize the effects and then banish it completely. There were still cases, but by and large, they were in poor, urban areas where drug abuse, in general, remained a problem that ruined lives.

"You're among that three percent," Chantelle said.

"Don't you think it's a coincidence that I'm one of the rare few who made it past sixteen and my mother told me from her own mouth that she never took the drug? The woman couldn't have cared any less about impressing me, trust me."

Chantelle sighed. "Listen, Autumn, I hope you're right, okay? I hope that there was a misdiagnosis or some other error in paperwork and that you in fact weren't born with ADHM in your system, because even for those who make it past sixteen, we don't know the long-term effects, if any." What she was saying was, *Great for you for making it to sixteen and then beyond, but I can't say for sure that the three percent of you won't all be dead by the time you're thirty.*

"But how does a misdiagnosis of that degree happen?" Autumn asked, raising her arms and dropping them in frustration. "Fourteen years of my life, Chantelle. I was deathly sick, not from the disease but from the medication!"

I thought my death was all but imminent for fourteen years. Do you have any idea what that does to a person's soul? And although she hadn't had much time to process what her mother had said, she felt anger brewing, her entire life flashing before her eyes through a completely different lens. *Who misdiagnosed my blood results at birth? Who signed off on committing me to years at Mercy Hospital?*

And who the hell began shoveling the cocktail of drugs down her throat? Drugs that she'd never needed at all.

A knock sounded, and Autumn looked up to see a man peeking into Chantelle's partially open door. He pushed it open a bit more, and Chantelle turned in her chair.

"Er, Ms. Rogers, sorry to interrupt. Can I get your signature on some forms? It will only take a few minutes, and I need them before court in an hour."

"Sure. Excuse me for a minute, Autumn," Chantelle said, standing and following the man from the room.

Autumn sat back in her chair with a frustrated sigh, her gaze moving to the file cabinets across the room.

The file cabinets that might contain the answers she'd just been denied.

CHAPTER THIRTEEN

Sam lifted the last bale of hay, placed it on top of the neat pile he'd formed, and then used his arm to wipe the drops of sweat from his forehead.

A shaft of light filtered through the hayloft window, trickling down to where Sam stood, and he raised his face, closing his eyes as he felt the touch of warmth.

What happened in Macau, Sam?

Despite the sun, a chill wafted through him—an internal freeze—and he opened his eyes, stepping from the light and then taking off his gloves and tossing them aside.

He'd failed. He'd failed a mission, and because of it, Dr. Heathrow had removed him. Banished him. Thrown him away. *When you're dismissed, you die. Your purpose has ended.* His guts still twisted when he thought of the moment the doctor had pointed at the door, sadness and disappointment in his eyes as he told Sam to pack his bag and go.

So he'd left to die as he'd been trained to do. It was his final mission. What other choice did he have anyway? He had no skills other than those he'd been trained in. *Hunting. Killing.*

When you're dismissed, you die. What the order really meant was when you're dismissed, you kill yourself. Which was for the best. He wouldn't survive on his own, because he had no idea where to even *start*, nowhere to go. But…he hadn't gone about the killing of himself right away. After all, the last mission didn't exactly spell out a time frame. So for a while, he'd used the only skills he'd had to keep himself alive. He'd hunted. Animals this time. He'd built campfires. He'd kept himself warm and fed. He'd taken weeks to consider the best way to die. He had a weapon, of course; he'd packed it in his bag when he'd left. Which was what was expected, considering he was on a suicide mission.

When you're dismissed, you die.

On his other missions, they'd given him a cyanide pill to take in the event of capture. But Dr. Heathrow didn't give him a cyanide pill when he banished him. Sam wondered why and figured maybe it would make authorities suspicious if they found a man dead by cyanide on a nature trail somewhere.

Yes, he'd planned to die. He still did. And he was mostly fine with it because he *deserved* to die. But then he'd stumbled across the old man, lost in the trees at the edge of his own property. The man hadn't been afraid of him, even though he knew he looked like the monster he was—his hair darkened with dirt, beard ratty and unkempt, military-style clothes, and a gun in his waistband. He was filthy. After all, he'd been living in the woods. But the old man had smiled and sounded relieved to come upon another person, and then he'd reached his hand out to Sam, mostly in the right direction. It was then Sam realized the man was blind.

No wonder he wasn't afraid of him. *Him*, the large, muscular stranger with exposed scars, *young* but with a head full of dirty hair that was strangely as pale as the moon. They'd made him cut it short and dye it when he went on missions.

I made a boy of moonlight.

He'd said her words over and over as he'd sat at the edge of the stream or the base of a tree, lying in the sun and planning the best way to die.

Were her words what kept him alive longer than he'd meant? Maybe. But they were only a temporary stall for what he knew was necessary. Inevitable.

He had no place in this world.

He didn't *want* a place in this world.

Life was only pain and suffering and ugliness and loneliness too terrible to bear.

The only beautiful thing he'd ever known in his miserable life was her. *A momentary light. A small taste of what beauty meant.* But she was long gone, somewhere far away, living a better life.

Or so he hoped.

But despite his appearance and the way his voice croaked the first words he'd spoken in weeks, the old man had smiled at him, happy and relieved by his presence, and he'd led the blind man back to the path he'd wandered from. The man had offered him a meal and then later a job working on his apple farm, and he'd accepted though he had no idea why.

You are supposed to be dead, Sam.

The other workers there did look at Sam strangely, but only at first. They all had stories. The old man, apparently, liked to collect unwanted souls. Outcasts. Throwaways. Criminals and misfits. And now those who were supposed to be dead but weren't.

Some of them robbed the old man or collected a paycheck without having done any work. He stood on his porch each Friday, grinning broadly and handing out money, even to those who didn't deserve it. The old blind fool.

Sam did work though. Sam did the work of five men because it helped him forget his pain and kept his memories at bay.

He climbed ladders and picked bushels of apples. A bushel, he'd learned, was equal to sixty-four U.S. pints. Sam hadn't known that before. His education was limited. He'd taken classes. He'd learned to read and write and do basic math. He'd studied some science and geography. But mostly, his education had been on fighting techniques, war tactics, and weaponry. He'd been taught only what he needed to know. Sam piled hay and mucked out stalls. He fed goats and cows and chickens and pigs. He repaired fencing, thinned brush, and did many other small chores.

He didn't talk to anyone except the old blind man occasionally. The other workers all thought he was a big dumb idiot who could barely form words, and that was what Sam preferred.

Sometimes in the evenings, Sam sat perched on the fence at the edge of the yard, eating an apple and watching the sun as it fizzled, glittered, and faded to dust.

He could see in the old man's window then, and he watched as his family, who visited often, sat down to dinner, laughing and talking and passing dishes of steaming food. He thought of her words.

If life were an apple, I'd sink my teeth into it and take a big bite. I'd let the juice drip down my chin and grin as the sweetness burst across my tongue.

And then I'd find someone and give them the other half.

She'd been sick and wanted to know what it was like to *live*. But she'd wanted to share it too.

Sam's eyes moved around the table through the window. He wondered what it would feel like to meet someone's eyes over a basket of rolls and have them smile at him and laugh at his joke. The whole concept seemed so alien that the wondering alone made him feel ludicrous. *What kind of joke would you tell, Sam? You're the joke. Even thinking about a scenario like that is the joke.* And if he couldn't even picture it—couldn't begin to imagine—why did the vague notion bring him pain? He wanted it, he supposed, and he had no right to such a longing.

He was who he was. Some had been created to laugh with family around dinner tables, and some had been created to sit alone on fences, looking in. Always looking in.

He thought of her as he worked. He pictured her face and remembered the way her eyes had sparked with enough fire that he still felt the warmth. He'd taken that glow with him to Chennai and Lagos and other destinations he didn't remember the names of.

He'd taken her with him to each and every forgotten place, and he'd carried her words, as much a part of him now as his organs or his skin but even more so. Because her words and her ideas were hidden away, tucked deeply into the only parts of him that had never been touched. Not muscle or bone but something deeper, something far more essential. Her words reminded him that despite it all, there were still parts of himself that were only his and could not be prodded or poked or sliced into.

And that very idea was his downfall, perhaps.

And his saving grace.

But again, he didn't want to be saved. Yet he could not let her go. Would not. So he suffered. And he lived on.

Because to die would be to kill off a piece of her as well. And that, he realized, he could not yet do.

Soon, but not yet.

"Sam," the old man, Adam, called.

Sam turned, grunting in response.

"I need you to pick up a new generator for the barn. It's going to be a cold winter, and I can't risk the power going off out there. I have an old friend in the city who gives me great deals." When Sam didn't answer, the man cocked his head as though listening for something Sam wasn't saying. "You do drive, don't you?"

"Yes. I drive," he said. He didn't have a license because he didn't have an identity, but he knew how to drive.

Adam lifted his hand, and a pair of keys sailed through the air. Sam reached out and caught them easily.

"Take the pickup," Adam said, turning and tapping his cane on the dirt path that Sam had brushed free of tiny pebbles and debris that morning so the old fool didn't trip and smash his head open.

"These paths need to be paved," Sam noted.

Adam waved his hand behind him, dismissing Sam's words. "I like the feel of dirt under my feet. And I expect someone will help me if I injure my foot on a rock."

Sam scratched the back of his neck. "Why would you expect anything when so many people let you down?" *Lie to you. Cheat you. Steal your things.*

Adam's smile only widened. "People do let me down a lot," he said. "But sometimes they don't."

Sam sighed. *Sometimes* didn't seem like something to stand around grinning about. He shrugged and looked over at the red pickup near the fence next to the long driveway that let out on the main road. Sam didn't want to drive. He didn't want to go into New York City. He didn't want to be around people and buildings and noise.

"Hey, Sam," Adam said, turning around, his milky eyes strangely trained directly on him. "Who hurt you?"

Who hurt you? The question confused Sam. Especially because Adam couldn't see all the scars that littered Sam's skin. Maybe someone had told him about those. Maybe someone had seen him washing himself off under the faucet behind the barn and noticed that the scars weren't only on his face and his arms but on his back and the biggest one of all trailing from his throat to his stomach. Still, those scars weren't the reason he was alone. Shamed. Discarded. That had been his doing.

"Me," Sam answered. "I hurt myself."

Adam seemed to stare at him for several moments, finally nodding. The old man looked sad but also understanding. "That's the worst kind of hurt." The old man paused. "Do you think I'm lucky, Sam?"

Again, Sam was confused. "Lucky?"

"Yes. Do you see me as a lucky man?"

Sam stared at him. He was old and blind and relatively ugly too—though who was Sam to talk?—with bare, dirty feet and employees who regularly stole from him. But he owned an apple farm and sat around the dinner table while people laughed and talked. People who kissed him on his cheek when they stood up to leave. "Yes," Sam answered. "I think you're a lucky man."

Adam nodded once. Then he unbuttoned his shirt-sleeves, rolling them up slightly and holding the undersides of his wrists out to Sam. There were two long scars up the middle of each arm. "I agree," Adam said solemnly. "I am a lucky man. But I didn't always think so." He dropped his arms. "Things are always changing, Sam. Life is moving all around us, even when it seems to be standing still. Have faith." Then he turned, tapping his stick on the dirt again and heading toward his house.

Sam stood there for a moment, watching him walk away. *Life is moving all around us.* Sam had no idea what the old blind fool had meant. Maybe he was foolish and crazy too. *Have faith.* In what? That someday Sam might feel lucky too based on some circumstances he couldn't picture or imagine? He'd had faith once, faith in the missions.

But did you? Did you really?

Maybe not if his current situation was any indication.

Sam went inside the small room in the back of the barn where Adam let him sleep. The other workers slept in a barracks-type room in a building closer to the orchard, but Adam, for some reason, had given him his own, with a door and a lock. Maybe the other men had told Adam they were worried the giant with the scars, white hair, and strange eyes who barely talked would murder them in their sleep.

Or worse.

Who knew better than he did that there were worse things than dying?

Sam sighed as he looked at himself in the mirror. He wondered what he might have looked like without all the surgeries, physically altering medications, and other procedures that hadn't been explained to him. He'd probably look normal. People probably wouldn't stare at him with a mixture of fear and fascination.

But he wasn't normal. And he never would be.

He picked up the razor on the small sink in the corner.

Maybe he should use it to cut his wrists. He'd bleed out. It'd be a quick-ish death. He turned the razor over, considering it. It was pretty dull, but it'd still do the job if he pressed hard enough. He pictured the long scars on Adam's arms. He pictured the old man's face. He glanced down at the floor. If he did use the razor, then his blood would soak into the wood of the floorboards, and they'd probably have to be replaced, and what kind of way was that to thank Adam for giving him a job, a roof over his head, three meals a day, and all the apples he could eat?

Instead of killing himself with the dull razor, he retrieved the metal scissors from the toolbox he'd been given to make repairs on the farm. They were large and rusty, but he used them to trim his beard into something more manageable and then shaved it off completely with the razor, the tufts of white falling to the floor. Then he picked up the scissors again and used them to cut his hair, the silvery chunks mixing with the tufts of beard and contrasting with the dark stained wood. In the end, his hair was very short and choppy, but Sam figured it was less alarming than the mass of white he'd been pulling into a ponytail at the nape of his neck for the last few months. People *would* stare at him on the streets of New York City, where the crowds weren't only made up of criminals and misfits but rather everyday, ordinary civilians. Sam didn't like to be stared at, but he'd also been trained to *blend in* as much as he was able, and apparently, he was still the creature they'd trained him to be. At least in some ways.

He felt his smooth chin with his fingers, turning his face left and right, noting how much sharper his jaw was than it'd been before, realizing how much weight he'd lost. If he'd had some hair dye, he might have colored his hair, but he didn't, so Sam grabbed a ball cap on his way out the door.

He made the drive into New York City, the back roads becoming highways, the highways filling with congestion, the noise increasing along with the smell of exhaust and factory smoke. The traffic slowed to a crawl, and Sam felt the eyes of people who pulled up in cars next to him, but he kept his gaze straight ahead.

Adam had left the name of the store where he'd bought the generator in the truck, including directions, and Sam drove there, pulling up to the dock out back, where a man loaded the item into the truck bed, barely sparing him a glance. The errand was done in record time, and Sam headed toward the entrance to the highway that would take him back to the farm.

But just as he was about to take the turn, he veered the opposite way instead. "What are you doing, Sam?" he murmured to himself. Except he knew very well what he was doing. There was an apartment in the heart of the city that he and the others used between missions.

He knew it was a bad idea, the same way he'd known it was a bad idea to help the little girl. Save her.

What happened in Macau, Sam?

The same way he'd known, all those years ago, that it'd been a bad idea to protect the other girl. Autumn.

I made a boy of moonlight.

He didn't feel quite as incapable of resisting this time, but he *did* feel pulled.

So Sam parked the truck, locking the covered flatbed where the generator was tied down, pulled on his ball cap, and headed toward the subway where he jogged down the stairs and was swallowed by the ground.

CHAPTER FOURTEEN

Sam wasn't the only monster on the New York subway, even if, that particular day, he was the largest, so he barely received a glance. He kept his head down, cap pulled low, and sat near the back, disembarking when the train pulled into the familiar station. Sam came up out of the ground and walked the six blocks to the door situated between the Vietnamese restaurant and the dry-cleaning shop, the one he'd stayed at before leaving for his last job in Macau. Although he was nervous, he worked to keep his heart rate steady, his training kicking in the way it was meant to do. He rapped twice, paused, and then gave four quick knocks and a light kick to the bottom of the door. A moment later, in response to the specific signal, the door was pulled open.

Amon stared at him indifferently. He had training too. Sam had had no idea if anyone would be at the apartment, and he was no happier to see Amon than he'd be to see anyone else.

"Sam. What are you doing here?"

Sam knew he meant *here*, at this apartment, as well as he meant *here*, on this earth, but Sam only answered for the former. "I was in the area. I thought I'd see if anyone was home." *Home* wasn't the right word for a place so transitory, but he couldn't think of another. *Why did you come here, Sam?*

Amon stepped back, allowing Sam to enter. "Doc won't be happy about this."

"I know." *Doc* wasn't happy about a lot of things when it came to Sam. Hence the fact that he was living in a barn and considering when he was going to kill himself.

"We thought you were dead," Amon said, and Sam knew that by "we," he meant himself and the others he'd been trained with. If they'd been "team members" once by virtue of the fact that they'd trained together, they weren't any longer. Their work was solitary. And for that, Sam was grateful. At least he had been the only one affected by his own weakness.

Sam just shrugged.

Amon stared at him. "Do you need assistance?"

Sam let out a short laugh. He knew Amon was asking if he needed help killing himself, and a part of Sam was strangely touched by the offer. And a part of him wanted to take him up on it because he knew Amon would do a much better job than he had done himself, which was to say he'd definitely end up dead. "No."

Amon had always been different from Sam. He'd not only taken to the training, he'd seemed to relish it. It was why he was sent on the most dangerous missions, the ones where violence was likely and hands-on combat might very well be necessary. If he was here in the city apartment, he was being sent on another job. It was where they stayed prior to departing for the location of their next assignment.

He knew the location of this apartment had been chosen for the lack of cameras in the area, at least for the time being. If that changed, new technology was installed nearby, or any other number of reasons, the location would be moved. Sometimes two members stayed at the current temporary apartment, but rarely more than that. Their work was intermittent, and they had a whole group to divide it among.

Sam took off the ball cap and ran a hand over his choppy hair before putting it back into place. "Something unexpected came up," he said in answer to Amon's quizzical look about what Sam wanted if it wasn't help with offing himself. "I'm dealing with it first." *There are apples to be picked, fences to repair, and I can't seem to let go of a girl I barely knew once a decade ago. I can't seem to let go of this world that she's still in. Somewhere.*

Amon's eyes narrowed slightly, but he tipped his chin anyway. "I won't call Doc and tell him you were here."

Sam nodded, even if he was vaguely surprised. Amon was as committed to their mission as any of them were, and perhaps even more so. A buzz of suspicion vibrated very subtly somewhere inside Sam. Why was he willing to break rules now?

"Anyway," Amon said, "I have to go because I have a job today." He walked to the table near where Sam was standing and grabbed a piece of paper. Sam caught the word *Deercroft* and the number 1358. Before he read anything else, Amon crumpled the piece of paper, walked to the sink, brought out a lighter, and set it on fire. He watched it burn for a moment before dropping it in the sink, running water over the ashes and rinsing them down the drain.

Amon went to the bookcase and pulled out a drawer, loading a pistol into the holster at his side and pulling his jacket closed. He turned and looked at Sam. There was something in his expression that Sam had never seen before. A stark resoluteness that caused that buzz to intensify.

"A job," Sam repeated.

Amon looked away, and Sam saw the very slight sheen of perspiration on Amon's forehead. "Yes. A job." He met Sam's eyes. "We have to do what's necessary. The mission is what matters. The mission is all that matters." He moved toward the door, and Sam walked with him. "Goodbye, Sam," Amon said, and Sam could tell he meant it as a permanent one.

Sam looked at the man he'd known for as long as he had memory. He had a sudden, vivid glimpse of Amon as a boy, maybe nine or ten, laughing at Sam who had slipped on a patch of ice and sprawled gracelessly yet unhurt. Sam had seen him laugh many times after that day, but there had always been an edge of menace in it, the shine—subtle at first and then distinct—of violence. That late winter day was the last time Amon had laughed with joyful abandon.

"Goodbye, Amon." Sam didn't shake his hand. Truthfully, though his gut instincts were telling him something was going on under the surface that Sam wasn't quite grasping, he wasn't worried for Amon, nor was he going to miss him. Sam was a monster, but so was Amon. They'd both been raised to be. Amon had just taken to it very naturally. And with more commitment.

A door behind him opened, and Sam turned, surprised to see Morana emerge from one of the bedrooms. Behind her, the sheets were rumpled, and Sam spotted some blood. Morana and Amon had obviously used each other. It was common. Those in the program all knew what to expect from each other, and many of them enjoyed being hurt.

And doing the hurting. Sam had never participated. Sam had never touched any woman's naked body. He'd been aroused before, but he'd attended to it himself. He didn't like the feel of hands on his naked skin. But even more than that, he didn't want to risk unleashing the monster inside him. He didn't want to risk losing control.

Amon looked over his shoulder, hesitating when Sam didn't close the door and follow, but then he glanced at Morana, obviously deciding she could make sure the door was locked behind Sam. Amon headed down the hall and out of sight.

Sam stood awkwardly at the doorway but still inside the apartment. "Morana," he greeted.

"Hi, Sam." There was something on her face he couldn't quite read. Surprise, but maybe…gladness too. As though, opposite of Amon, she'd expected that he was dead and wasn't disappointed to see that he was actually still alive. "What are you doing here?"

"Just stopping by. Are you…leaving on a job too?"

Morana's eyes were glued to Sam as she moved even closer. Her robe slipped a tad, and he saw that there were bruises on her collarbone. She pulled the silken material back in place, covering the marks, and when Sam met her eyes again, he swore he saw shame there. Her gaze darted away momentarily. "Yes. I leave in a few hours." She reached out her arm, and Sam stilled as she touched him tentatively. *What are you doing?* Morana had never touched him before. Morana had rarely talked to him before. "Do you ever think…do you ever think there's some other version of yourself living a different life somewhere?"

He stared, waiting for her to say more, to explain the question or the reason for it so he knew how to answer. "No."

A smile played across her lips, and that surprised Sam too. He didn't think he'd ever seen Morana smile. He'd grown up with her, yet he couldn't have described anything about her teeth. Did one stick out in front? Was the bottom row crooked? Were they bright white, or did they have a yellowish cast like Amon's? Sam had no idea.

"I think about that, another life I might have lived," she said. "I think about that a lot. Especially right before a mission. I hope there are other versions of me out there."

Sam didn't know what to say. He had no idea what she was talking about. He thought about asking about her mission. Was this one particularly dangerous? Did she expect to die? Was that why she was talking like this? About some alternate existence? He was confused. He didn't think Morana was sent on dangerous assignments. She was short and skinny, and she had a slight limp from a surgery that hadn't gone quite right. But she was a genius with computers and was assigned jobs that required that expertise, both in the field and virtually. He didn't know all of what the others did, but he knew that was her skill. That had always been her skill. And it was one the rest of them did not possess.

"I'm glad you came here, Sam, and that I got to see you. I'm glad you still could."

He'd read her right then. Amon might not have been glad to see him alive. Amon would have helped him follow through with being dead if Sam had simply said the word. But Morana was glad he was not. He felt a…lukewarmth, at least, in his chest, and he recognized it as what might have been a friendship. *If.*

And maybe that was part of what she meant by another version of her living a different life. *If.* So many ifs. But what was the point of that?

Sam dipped his chin. He almost said thank you, but that wasn't right because frankly, he was planning on following through with the final command. He just hadn't done it yet.

"They named us after monsters," she said. "Did you know that?"

"Monsters?"

"I looked it up. All our names are so unusual, you know?" She went to the kitchen island. After taking a sip, she said, "Amon comes from a Greek spell book that lists seventy-two demons. Amon is the Marquis of Hell." She set the water down and leaned back against the counter. "Morana is a Slavic goddess of death. And in the Talmud, Samael is an archangel." She paused, her lips tipping the barest bit. "The goddess and the angel. Almost like we were made for each other, right, Samael? Anyway, I could go on. All the others from the program are named similarly. All monster inspired."

Sam considered her, thought about how he felt like a monster and looked like one too. "Fitting, I guess," he finally said.

"Do you think? Do you think they meant to make us monsters? Or do you think we already were?"

A cell phone rang in the back room, startling Sam slightly. This whole conversation felt…surreal.

Morana glanced back. "That's my call," she said.

For a few beats, they simply stared at each other. Sam felt troubled and odd, like he should say something but also like he didn't know this woman well enough to know what that might be. "Good luck, Morana," he finally said. "I hope it goes well."

"By whose definition?" she asked. But then she smiled and waved her hand as if to disregard her statement. "Good luck to you too, Samael."

Sam left the apartment. Back out on the street, he pulled his ball cap low again, stuffing his hands in his pockets and hunching his shoulders, trying to make himself as indistinct as possible as he walked back toward the subway station. *Why did you come here? What was the purpose?*

But Sam had no purpose. Not small or large nor anything in between. *I am nothing alone. I am a tool for the greater good.* That's what they'd told him at least.

The thought had always brought both comfort and despair. But now there was only despair because his one purpose had been taken from him.

They named us after monsters.

Half an hour later or so, he was back in the red pickup truck. He sat there, still feeling off-kilter about his visit to the apartment. Morana had confused him. But he was more concerned about what he'd seen on the paper that Amon had burned. The instructions for his job, Sam knew, because he'd received similar instructions before.

Deercroft.

1358.

Military time: one fifty-eight. *What time was it now?* Sam wasn't sure. He didn't have a phone. That had been taken from him. But he knew it was somewhere around one o'clock.

Deercroft.

They named us after monsters.

Sam turned the key in the ignition and then shut the truck off again, letting out a soft growl, directed toward himself. *How many more bad ideas are you going to have before you die, Sam?*

More importantly, how many more are you going to follow?

There was a café just up the block that had a sign

advertising internet, and he jumped from the truck, heading in that direction. He paid the woman at the counter for thirty minutes, her gaze lingering on him as he turned away.

He sat down in the plastic chair, far too small for his large frame, clicked on the browser, and typed in *Deercroft, New York*.

A list of hits came up, and he clicked on the first one. *A private school*. Deercroft Academy was a private elementary school in the city.

Sam's hand fell from the mouse, and he sat there for a moment, picturing the sheen of perspiration on Amon's forehead, the man who had been trained not to sweat.

We have to do what's necessary. The mission is what matters. The mission is all that matters.

Sam couldn't stop a mission. Missions were happening all over the world. The other program members were carrying out *missions* everywhere, some perhaps right that second. He didn't know where. He didn't know why.

You know this time though, his mind whispered. *Deercroft. One fifty-eight.*

Each mission is for the greater good.

The greater good.

What did that mean though? No one had ever defined it for him.

Sam glanced at the time on the computer. One twenty-seven.

He hesitated only a moment before scooting back, the chair falling to the floor with a loud clatter. Sam didn't bother to pick it up. He turned and headed for the door.

CHAPTER FIFTEEN

Autumn slowed to a walk, breath coming quickly as she melded with the other New Yorkers moving through the crowded streets. She'd rolled up the stolen files and stuffed them in her mostly empty purse and secured it around her body. Now she gave one final glance over her shoulder, secure in the belief that no one was on her tail. If Chantelle had called the authorities present in the building and they'd attempted to follow and detain her for stealing official, sealed documents, she'd successfully evaded them.

For now.

Would they pay a visit to her home? Maybe. She'd deal with that when the time came. She'd even give the files back. After she'd scoured every piece of information.

She turned the corner toward the sign for the subway that would deliver her to the bus she'd taken into the city. She'd read her file as soon as she was safely seated in the back and headed home. Would it contain anything she didn't already know? Something worth noting that no doctor had ever mentioned to her?

And what if there isn't?

She'd been so fearful as she'd stolen her file, but now she was even more afraid the theft had been pointless.

She patted her bag as she hurried toward the subway stairs at the end of the block. *If there's nothing here, will you give up your search for answers? For the meaning behind your suffering?*

Could she?

Is it time?

She picked up her pace, practically running again.

No.

No, I could not. It's not in my makeup.

She thrust her shoulders back, determination filling her. No, she would not give up no matter what, because not doing so was important. She felt that. She knew it with every fiber of her being.

A sudden wind whipped up, causing her to turn her head. Across the street and up a ways, a man's ball cap flew off, and Autumn's heart nearly stopped. She gasped and turned, her neck craning as she watched him rush ahead and then scoop it off the ground where it'd landed before replacing it on his head.

His head of silvery-white hair, the color of moonlight.

It can't be. It can't be. Oh my God!

The world took up spinning again, the first two rotations overly fast and erratic, making Autumn feel as if she should grab something stable. She noted his size, a full head above the other men on the street, and the bronze tone of his skin. *The world isn't spinning, Autumn. You are. Now pick up your feet and* move.

She did, running across the street as a car stopped short

of hitting her, its brakes squealing. She leaped for the curb, losing sight of him in the bustling crowd, weaving between people, and then stepping out into the street again—being mindful of cars this time—to get a better view.

She didn't see him anywhere.

Her heart pounded, panic making her feel like screaming his name. But she didn't know his name. She didn't even know if it was *him*.

How could it be? *It's impossible.*

You're standing here on a street corner in New York, twenty-three years old and healthy. Nothing *is impossible.*

She pushed back into the crowd, again moving in the direction he'd gone, jumping sporadically in an effort to see above the people in front of her, some of whom were much taller.

She came to a four-way intersection, her heart sinking when she saw neither hide nor hair of the very large man with the red ball cap.

No, wait. There he is.

She squinted, heading toward a less busy neighborhood. The groups of people walking that way were much sparser, the larger crowd continuing on in the direction of the subways and the lines of taxi cabs, the office buildings, and the restaurants.

She saw a tall head far down the block, second-guessing herself when she began to move toward it. How could he have possibly gotten that far away in such a short amount of time?

Because he has legs twice as long as yours, that's how.

The light turned green, and Autumn hurried across the intersection. There were smaller retail shops on this street and a large church up ahead. Now that the crowd had thinned,

Autumn picked up her pace, jogging in the direction where she thought she'd seen his head. *Even if it's not him, which it's probably not, you'll never forgive yourself if you don't find out.*

She heard the sounds of children playing, laughter and joyful shouts, and realized that what she'd thought was a church was actually a school. She looked up at the name on the front of the building: *Deercroft Academy.*

Her breath became short as she stopped for another moment, peering up the street where there were very few people and the shops turned into row homes. Had he gone inside one of them?

Deep disappointment descended. *I've lost him. Again.*

She walked past the school, unhurried now, stopping at the corner of the grand, stone building and looking to her right.

It felt like her heart did a strange dip and swerve. There he was, standing at the fence, watching the children play.

The world seemed to grow brighter, then everything faded except for him and the patch of ground he was standing on. She opened her mouth to call to him, to say what, she wasn't sure.

I'm here.
Don't disappear.
Wait.
It's me.

The words crowded her mind, all of them seeming wrong yet right.

Then she heard a number of distant pops before an alarm suddenly rang out. Autumn turned toward the building where the sound was coming from. *A fire drill?* A teacher called calmly to the children on the playground, and the children began walking toward her. *Yes, a drill.*

But before she could form another thought, the sharp sound of unmistakable gunfire split the air, the laughter of the children turning instantaneously to screams.

The white-haired man bolted toward the schoolyard and ran along the fence. He kicked open a gate and sprinted inside. It all happened in less than thirty seconds.

Autumn ran too, toward the children in navy-blue uniforms, scattering in terror as the gunfire continued, popping loudly, coming from somewhere just beyond. She saw a woman near the swings, who was ushering children toward her, go down, the children around her grabbing their heads and ducking as the screams grew louder.

The man with the moonlight hair stepped in front of several running children, pushing the first one so that he flew backward into the others. The wall directly behind the spot where they would have been erupted in concrete craters as bullets hit.

Autumn pressed herself to the fence, her gaze flying around, trying to make sense of what was happening, attempting to figure out what to do.

"Amon!" the man yelled. His ball cap had come off, and now she could clearly see that dazzling shock of silvery blond hair she'd seen only briefly on the street.

The crowd of children were converging on an outdoor stairwell as another man appeared from around the corner of the building. Autumn stared, her breath coming in sharp pants, sweat dripping down her cheek. There was an adult body next to the slide. The teacher who'd fallen near the swings remained unmoving, and Autumn could see the puddle of blood pooling around her body.

She heard the sounds of little feet running up the mostly obscured stairs, a line of them at the base still fully exposed.

Oh God, run! The moonlight man had moved quickly toward them and was now the only obstruction in the front of those children pushing and clamoring for cover.

"Get out of my way," the man with the gun gritted out.

"No," the man with the white hair grated back. His voice was hoarse, guttural, deeper than she remembered it, no longer that of a boy.

The face of the man with the gun morphed from cold resolve to indecision as the sound of sirens rose in the distance. The gunman glanced toward the place where the stairwell was enclosed by an outside wall, that coldness blossoming again but now overlaid with what Autumn could only call violent yearning. *Bloodlust.* He raised his weapon toward the still-exposed children at the base, and the man with the moonlight hair spread his arms wide, acting as a human shield. The gunman fired repeatedly, the blast of gunfire mixing with the piercing screams. Her moonlight boy jerked back, righting himself and then jerking again and again—performing a horrifying dance—as the bullets ripped into his flesh. The children pushed forward, the last one finally making it around the concrete barrier and into the covered stairwell just as the man who'd shielded them crumpled to the ground.

Autumn, who'd been mute with shock, screamed then—a sound of horror—and the gunman's head whipped toward her as he raised the gun again. *Oh God. Oh no. Brace.* Autumn turned her head and clenched her eyes shut, hearing the weapon fire and waiting for the slam of a bullet that didn't come.

With another terror-filled cry, she opened her eyes to see the gunman lying still on the ground, a spray of blood surrounding him, blood trickling from the gunshot wound at his head.

Autumn brought her hands to her mouth, giving herself three breaths to get hold of herself before springing into action. She ran from one wounded teacher to the second, tears trickling down her cheeks as she put two shaking fingers to their still pulses. A wail rose inside her, and she tried desperately to hold it back, or she'd lose it completely.

Save the ones you can, Autumn.

If there was anyone to save.

She moved to a third teacher. She was gone as well. *No children were shot. Not out here at least.* Autumn's shoulders shook as she moved past the dead gunman, kicking his weapon aside irrationally. He was no danger anymore. She then ran to the man with the moonlight hair. The sirens were drawing closer. How far away? Fifteen blocks? Ten? *Hurry. Please hurry.* She knelt beside the man she'd followed here and looked at his face. It was him, there was no doubt. She brought her fingers to the scars at his temple, the place where she'd once seen the bolt-like object embedded in his skin.

She looked up and around, searching for what, she wasn't sure. Someone else who might help? Someone to call to? But there was no one. Only her. All the others were safely hidden inside, waiting for the cavalry to arrive. *They're coming. Hold tight. They're coming.* Her gaze darted to the still form of the gunman again, as if he might rise from the dead at any moment and continue on some form of weaponless killing spree. Autumn looked back at the man, once her moonlight boy. There was blood soaking his shirt and more on the thighs of his black jeans. He'd been shot in the chest at least twice, maybe three times, and in the legs as well. Horror coursed through her, making her feel heavy and numb.

A sound came from his throat. A moan.

Autumn jolted. *You're alive.*

She brought her trembling fingers to his throat, feeling the fluttery pump of his pulse. Yes, he was alive, but likely not for long.

"Help me," he said, and her eyes flew to his face. "Please," he breathed. "Please. Get me out of here."

Autumn blinked. "Get you out of here? I... You're very, very hurt. You'll be okay. Help is coming."

He grabbed her sweater, giving a small yank, and Autumn let out a yelp. His grip loosened. "They won't help me," he said. His eyes met hers, so beseeching, so filled with fathomless pain. His head dropped back to the pavement. "They'll hurt me."

The words moved through her, or rather the feeling, the deep despair with which he'd uttered them, rattled her bones. *They'll hurt me.* Her gaze moved from the scars on his face to the beginning of the one at his throat that she knew sliced all the way to his navel. Yes, someone had hurt him, again and again, and though she didn't know who or how or why, she did know that once upon a time, he had saved her. He was inexorably woven into her past and maybe even her soul.

Because he had not only saved her, but he'd been the catalyst that had helped her save herself.

She also knew that he had saved at least a dozen children that, if not for him, would have been shot on the playground or before they escaped around the corner of the stairwell and into the building. She'd seen it with her own eyes.

"You won't be able to walk," she said, glancing down at the blood on his thighs. His femurs were likely broken, if not demolished by bullets.

"I can," he said. "I can walk." And as if to prove it, he moved his legs, bending them as he prepared to stand.

She hesitated, confused and stunned. Maybe his legs had only been grazed. Still, he'd been shot many other places. And he was far too big for her to carry him.

"Okay," she said shakily. "But you'll have to help me help you. I can't do it alone."

His gaze met hers, such immense relief shining from his eyes that it boosted her impulsive decision and gave her the burst of strength she needed to stand and attempt to haul him to his feet.

With a roar of pain and anguish, he lifted himself, stumbling slightly, panting as he came to his feet. *His legs hadn't been hit directly*. If they had been, he wouldn't have been able to support his weight at all.

"This way," she said, wrapping her arm around his waist as they moved toward the spot in the fence where they'd both entered what seemed like ten million years ago. His ball cap was lying on the ground, and she scooped it up. They ran/stumbled, him grunting with pain and effort as she did what she could to support his massive weight. He had to be six foot six and weigh twice what she did. At least.

They exited the schoolyard, moving in the opposite direction from which they'd come, away from the approaching sirens, ducking behind a row of hedges and moving as swiftly as possible toward an alleyway just beyond.

He sagged against the brick wall, his eyes clenched shut as he breathed for a moment. He was doing everything he could to stay conscious. Most people would have been flat on the ground. Most people would have been dead from injuries like his. She took the opportunity to lift his shirt and quickly assess his wounds more closely. He'd been hit twice, once in the side and once just underneath his heart. He was lucky to be alive. And she still couldn't comprehend how he was standing. His shirt was already soaked through with blood, and she removed her purse still strapped around her and then took off the sweater she was wearing over her long-sleeved shirt. She pressed the thick, absorbent piece of clothing against his wounds to stanch the flow.

"Stay still," she instructed, pulling the navy zip-up sweatshirt he was wearing closed around her sweater. "You need to press on your wounds so you don't lose any more blood. And here." She grabbed the ball cap she'd folded and stuffed in her back pocket and handed it to him.

He stuck it on his head, and then he brought his hands to his abdomen, applying pressure before giving a small grunt and a nod, letting her know he was ready to continue.

She strapped her purse back around her chest, and then they started walking again, down the alley toward the street it opened out to ahead. Autumn wondered how long they had before someone inside the school told them about the large, white-haired man who'd been there. *And you. Someone probably saw you too. Even in the mayhem. Please don't let there be security cameras catching our exit.*

They stepped out onto the residential street, turning toward the business district that would likely be even more congested as rush hour approached. She glanced over at the man who had his arms wrapped around his abdomen, her arm around his waist as she worked to support him as best she could, given—if he toppled over—he'd easily take them both down.

"I don't know where to go," she said, and even she could hear the panic in her voice. The shock was wearing off, leaving her cold and shaky. Devastated.

Two young women and a young man were dead, maybe children too. A sob moved up her throat, and she swallowed to hold it back.

"I have a truck," he grunted.

A truck. A truck. For a moment, the words didn't compute, there was so much static in her brain. *A truck. A vehicle. A getaway vehicle. Oh my God. Autumn. What are you doing?*

"Take me there," she said. She could still change her mind. She could still drive him to a hospital. He could barely remain upright, so she knew he was little threat to her or anyone else.

They turned onto the busier main street, becoming part of the foot traffic. She leaned into the man, wrapping both arms around him, and made herself smile and then laugh. It sounded tinny and unnatural, but no one around them seemed to notice. They were just any ordinary couple, him cold, his arms wrapped around his middle, and her seeking his warmth as they snuggled, laughing and enjoying the nippy fall day.

Several police cars, ambulances, and fire trucks raced by them on the street, the pedestrians gasping and turning their heads. She heard a few voices raised in alarm, their phones held in front of their faces as they gasped about a school shooting that had happened a few blocks away. None of them looked up from their phones as they said it though. None of them even gave Autumn and the huge man clutching his stomach a second look.

"Here," he said after they'd walked what felt like a thousand miles and they staggered around a corner. There was a red flatbed truck with a white covering near the middle of the block, and the man reached in his jean pockets and removed a singular key. His hand was shaking so badly that

Autumn took it from him and opened the passenger door. The moan he made as he lifted himself into the seat pierced Autumn's heart. He sounded like a wounded animal.

Take him to a hospital, Autumn. If you don't, he'll probably die, and it will be your fault.

She ran around the truck, opened the door, got in quickly, and then sat there for a minute, trying to get hold of her racing heart and inability to draw a full breath. "Did you know that man?" she asked when she'd found her voice. "The shooter?"

The man adjusted himself, letting out a small whimper and then another groan. His naturally tan complexion had lost most of its color. He was going into shock. He met her eyes. "Yes."

"Were you a part of what happened there?" She saw the young woman's face, the one by the slide, her expression peaceful as if she'd merely fallen asleep. Autumn's stomach knotted, and she felt vomit moving up her throat again. She clenched her eyes shut, blocking the vision from her mind. *Breathe. In. Out.*

"No," he said, his voice fading. His eyes fluttered, and his hands dropped from where they were still placed on his abdomen. "I tried...I tried to stop it."

I tried to stop it. He had. She'd seen it. Not only had he tried to stop it, but he'd also taken a spray of bullets in that effort.

There was a drugstore on the corner, and Autumn glanced at the man whose eyes were only half-open. "I'll be right back," she said, jumping out of the truck again and jogging to the store. Inside, she bought an over-the-counter sleep medication and the strongest pain pills they had. She couldn't risk buying bandages and other supplies in the quantity she needed, not here. Her sweater would have to do for now. Thankfully, the man who rung her up barely looked up from his phone.

Back in the truck, she shook the pills into her shaking hand and then roused him enough to get him to swallow them despite having no water. He did so without complaint, and then she put the keys in the ignition, the truck coming to life with a soft rumble. She only had one more question. "What's your name?"

His eyes didn't come open, and for a moment, she thought he'd lost consciousness. "Sam," he slurred. And then he did black out, his body going limp, head lolling on his massive shoulders.

CHAPTER SIXTEEN

Autumn slammed on the brakes, the truck jerking to a stop in Bill's driveway. "Shit," she hissed, glancing over at Sam. The jolt of the vehicle hadn't disturbed him though. He still sat hunched over, his neck bent, head almost resting on his shoulder. Panic spiked, zigzagging through her system. Again, she reached over and felt his pulse. Not strong, but he was a fighter; she'd give him that. *Please keep fighting. I'm putting everything on the line here.*

She barely remembered anything about their race out of the city, except that she'd gone between glancing in the rearview mirror for the flashing lights she expected behind her at any moment and putting her fingers on his pulse every few minutes, making sure his heart was still beating. *If he dies, you'll go to prison.* She might anyway for…what was she doing? Harboring a criminal? Aiding and abetting a crime? He'd been there for some reason. He'd known the shooter. Oh God, she couldn't consider all the ramifications because she'd lose her nerve about whatever it was she was already too far into. She still couldn't believe she was taking this risk. She was gambling with everything she had. *Everything.*

With New York City far behind them, she'd finally pulled off at a rest stop and examined his wounds. The bleeding had mostly stopped, which was a good sign. She was pretty sure she could see one of the bullets right beneath his flesh. She'd need to remove it. The other one appeared to have gone straight through his side, but she couldn't be sure. His rib was likely broken, and he'd lost so much blood, he was in shock. Not to mention medicated, even if only by over-the-counter products. She'd given him a lot, but his wounds were extensive, and he was a very large man.

Her sweater was saturated with his blood, so she folded it and placed it on the floor. *They'll have his DNA at the crime scene. They'll test it.* Was he in any public databases? She had no idea, but she'd know soon enough. If they were able to identify him, his picture would be all over the news.

Autumn jumped from the truck and ran for the house but pivoted when she saw Bill walking from his shop. She skidded, reversing course as he rounded the corner, his face breaking into a smile that immediately dropped when he took in her face.

"Darlin'? What's wrong?" he asked, rushing forward. His gaze went to the truck in his driveway momentarily, his brow creasing before he looked back to her, eyes traveling from her face to her feet quickly and then back again. "Are you okay?"

She took in a gulp of air, nodded, and then shook her head. "Yes. No. I mean, Bill, I need your help."

"With what, honey? What's going on?"

Autumn pointed over her shoulder at the truck, parked

so that Bill couldn't see the giant, wounded man sitting in the passenger seat. "There's a man in there, Bill. *The* man."

"The man? Autumn, slow down. What man?"

"The man from the woods. His name is Sam." *Sam. His name is Sam. My moonlight boy has a name!*

Bill froze, his gaze darting to the truck again and then back to Autumn. "What? How?"

"I don't have time to get into all the details. He's been shot and he needs medical attention. Bill, I need to use the lake house."

Bill had bought a lake house—really more of a fishing cottage—the year after Allie died. He went in the summers to fish and the fall and winter to walk in the woods and bask in the utter solitude. To seek healing only nature could provide. Of course, just a short time later, Autumn herself had arrived at his door, and his life had been flipped upside down, so he didn't use the cottage regularly.

Bill's eyes were as wide as saucers. "The lake house? Wa-wa-wait. You're going to take a wounded stranger—"

"He's not a stranger," she insisted, casting her eyes to the side momentarily. "Exactly. I mean he is, but—"

"I can't allow it. He needs to go to a hospital."

Autumn set her shoulders back. "I don't have time to argue, Bill. I love you more than life, but I'm going to help this man whether you let me use the lake cottage or not. I'm already in deep. I fled the scene of a crime—"

"The scene of a crime!" He gripped his hair, spinning around and then back. "What is happening here?"

"I'm on the run is what's happening. I might be a fugitive. I'll explain everything later. But right now, I need medical supplies, and I need a place to hide him. I'm sorry to drag you into this, but…Bill, I need you. Please help me."

She beseeched him with her eyes, and he looked at her for a moment before setting his jaw, looking away, and then giving one curt nod.

"What's mine is yours, Autumn. You know that."

Autumn let out a breath of relief. "Thank you."

Bill still had a mildly shell-shocked expression on his face, but she could relate. And she was the one who was going to have to do her best to dig bullets out of a man twice her size with whatever supplies Bill could obtain and the things she had at her apartment in her medical bag that she'd have to ask Bill to pick up. "Let me see this man."

"I don't have time. I'm heading to the cottage, and I need you to gather everything you can from the list I'm going to make for you and meet me there. And, Bill, I need you to *hurry*."

Before he could respond, Autumn raced inside the house, grabbed a piece of paper and a pen from the kitchen junk drawer, and scrawled a list she hoped was legible. Then she ran back outside, grabbed Bill's hand, and stuck the list in it before racing to the truck, jumping in, and backing out of the driveway. Bill watched, his mouth open slightly, not having moved from the place where he stood, as if he needed a minute or two to let the events fully catch up to him.

Autumn let out another relieved breath when she glanced in her rearview mirror and saw that he was walking quickly to his car. His unending faith in her brought tears to her eyes. *Thank you, God, for Bill.*

Autumn used a poker to move one of the logs closer to the center of the blaze and then, satisfied, stood, returning the tool to its stand next to the stone fireplace.

Her shoulders lifted and fell as she released a breath that felt as if it'd been lodged in her throat for the last few hours, if not longer. For several moments, she stood staring into the crackling flames, allowing her mind to go blank. *Relief.* So much was made of emotions like joy and ecstasy, but no one gave enough credit to the moment after you feared the worst would happen and realized that you'd avoided disaster.

Sweet relief.

Even if she still wasn't out of the woods just yet. Literally and figuratively.

And neither was he.

She turned, heading back to his bedside. She'd somehow managed to rouse him just enough that he'd helped her assist him down from the truck where she'd gotten a blanket beneath him and dragged him, inch by painful inch, inside the house. He hadn't so much as stirred. Thank the good Lord there weren't stairs at the fishing cottage, because she'd have had to leave him lying in the dirt. By the time Bill had arrived with the supplies, she'd had Sam stripped from the waist up and washed, his wounds cleaned with the few supplies in the first aid kit in the bathroom cabinet.

"We should call Ralph. He'll know what to do. We can still explain this. If this man dies—"

"I'm not going to let him die." Confident words for a girl who was scared to death. Yet she was going to do as her moonlight boy had asked her. She was committed. In her mind, there was no turning back now. *Help me. Please get me out of here.*

She'd met Bill's worried gaze, tenderness engulfing her. *We,* he had said. *We* should. *We* can. Who would she have become had she been placed with someone else all those years ago? He'd believed in her from the very first day. A gift more priceless than a pirate chest of gold. Yet she had to do this without him.

"I need you to leave, Bill."

His eyes had widened, and he shook his head. "No way—"

"Bill. I need to focus. I have to do this alone."

"I'll stay outside."

"No," she had told him, adding firmness to her tone. She was going to give this everything she had, but if the worst did happen, she didn't want Bill involved. He had looked momentarily hurt but then sighed, and she could see that he was going to honor her request.

"He could hurt you," Bill had said, a final try, but his assertion held little passion. Autumn had looked back at Sam, lying still and bloody and all but helpless on the bed Bill had helped her move from the bedroom into the main room and lift him onto.

"I'll tie him to the bed."

"Promise?"

No. "Yes."

Still, he'd obviously been struggling. He was trusting her, but it was costing him to set aside his protective instincts. *I love you, Bill.*

"If anything goes wrong, you have to drive home."

She'd nodded. "I will. I'm going to shut my phone off. I can't risk it being pinged out here." *Just in case.*

"I'll bring you a burner phone," he'd said before gathering her in his arms in a sudden bear hug and then letting go just as quickly. He'd exited the house, and a moment later, she had heard his car start up outside and the crunching of gravel as he drove away.

She'd taken in a large breath, and then before she could

overthink things, she'd gathered her supplies. Thankfully she had some prescription pain medication for a patient whose chronic pain she managed. She'd be as sparing as possible and deal with any fallout from the missing doses later. But Sam needed it now if he was going to remain unconscious as she operated on him. So Autumn administered the medication, scrubbed her hands, and began the task of removing the bullets from his body.

He'd moaned and seemed to attempt to thrash, but he hadn't come fully awake. She'd felt terrible for his pain but remained focused. There had been several bullets embedded in him after all. But they'd all come out clean, and as far as she could tell, there was no internal damage. *A miracle.* She'd frowned in confusion, however, when the bullets had come out bent, one nearly flattened. Something about Sam was very unusual—wrong even—and a deeper spike of worry caused an uncomfortable twinge inside.

The things she'd seen—and felt—inside his body would need to be explained.

Autumn had stitched his wounds, bandaged him, and then collapsed in the chair next to his bed. She'd closed her eyes and let the floodgates open, tears rolling. *Adrenaline.* She'd held her emotion back so she could get the job done, but it engulfed her then, draining and overwhelming. *I did it. I did it.* Once she had gotten hold of herself, she'd checked his vitals, made a cup of tea, and sat on the small deck, allowing the clean air to fill her lungs and soothe her soul.

Now infection was their worry. But Bill had brought her antibiotics, and she'd monitor his vitals for any sign that infection was setting in.

Autumn moved away from the fire, going to Sam and checking his pulse. *Stronger. Better.* She put her hand on his forehead. It was warm but not overly so, and his breathing was even and steady. She'd wait an hour and then give him another dose of pain meds to keep him sleeping. It was best for him. Sleep healed.

She positioned her chair so that she could lay her head against the wall and also watch him. She still couldn't believe he was there, right in front of her. Part of her felt as if she'd fallen down a rabbit hole. It had been just that morning that she'd woken and showered and headed to New York City, yet it felt like a lifetime ago. *It was*, something inside whispered. *That was a different lifetime. This is a new one. Don't you feel it? The intangible divider that separated* that *Autumn from this one?*

Yes, she did. The same way she'd felt when she'd been declared healed and been driven away from the hospital toward a life she couldn't picture nor prepare for. Maybe all lives were separated into sections, the crossing of some lines jolting, others barely a blip on the radar, each only fully discernible later, when the bigger picture could be seen, when questions became answers, when turmoil became clarity.

The last rays of sunlight wavered, mixing with the coming night, casting a milky glow on his face. "Sam," she murmured, still disbelieving that she knew his name after all this time, all these years. The sun shifted, brightening, fighting to stay for just a moment longer. *Sam.* She'd only ever seen him in moonlight. *I made a boy of moonlight.* Those long-ago words wove through her mind. Maybe she'd been wrong. Maybe he was a strange combination of both the sun and the moon. Dark and light. Reality and fantasy. She'd thought him a dream once, only he was very real. Despite her fear and the precarious situation at hand, a wash of something akin to joy trickled through her. Effervescent. Glittery. *He's here, right within my reach.* How? *How?*

Her eyes moved over his features. He was as she remembered: strangely beautiful. Under the filtered sunlight, she could see that his unusual hair was a thousand different shades of white, pale yellow, and a bare scattering of gold. She reached over and felt it under her fingertips. Coarse and silken, an odd contrast, just like the silvery shade in relation to his skin tone. She'd never seen anything like it. *Like him.*

His skin was bronze and smooth, except for the scars on his temples, another one traveling from his ear to his chin, and several marring his throat. Then there was the one she'd remembered that went from his neck to his navel and several more on his abdomen. His legs were littered with scars as well, matching ones on his knees and thighs. She frowned, wondering *why* he'd been operated on again and again. Someone—or many someones—had taken a knife to him so many times. And they'd replaced whole parts of him. She'd gotten a glimpse of it when she'd been digging for those embedded bullets. It hurt her to know he'd felt so much pain. That he'd had to heal, over and over and over. Yet he had. And she prayed that he would again.

He was obviously strong. *Mighty* was probably a better word.

His jaw was square, but his cheeks were thin, hollows beneath his bones, and though his frame was large and muscular, his ribs could be seen easily above his bandages. It appeared he hadn't been eating much recently.

Where have you been?

She kept watching him, cataloguing his features,

committing him to memory in a way that felt almost desperate, a secret fear that her time was limited, her fight to hold on to him as hopeless as that of the waning light.

His brow was heavy, but his lips. Ah, his lips were full and lush, the only softness to his otherwise inordinately masculine face, even if they were set in what appeared to be a perpetual frown. Broody. Suspicious. Something about it made tenderness rise inside like a wave. Something about those lips was a challenge to Autumn. *Make me smile*, they said. *I dare you to try.*

At that moment, she made it her goal. How beautiful those lips would be curved in joy.

His eyelashes were long, in the darker shade of gold randomly flecked through his hair. And she could see the same pale speckles under his dusky skin. Not only unusual but unnatural. Almost fantastical. *But what does that mean exactly?* In a way, it was as though he glowed from the inside.

He was a strange combination of colors and features that didn't seem to go together in any traditional way, yet he was undeniably attractive to her.

Was it because she felt a curious connection? Still, after all these years? Was it because something about this man still felt…magical? A dream come to life? A walking fantasy?

Maybe. Or maybe it had nothing to do with any of that. Maybe it just *was*.

Autumn couldn't help herself. She ran a hand over his cheek. He moaned, shifting away, whimpering and tensing, as though anticipating some sort of pain. Cruelty when he was too weak to fend it off. Sadness swept through her, a rushing river of compassion, full of sharp rocks that snagged her heart.

Autumn sat back, considering the whole of him, casting her gaze over his myriad scars once more and again wondering what brutalities he'd suffered and why.

"What did they do to you?" she asked, her heart aching. Sam's eyelashes fluttered as he dreamed. She would have to wait for an answer.

Her gaze went to the blanket she'd spread over his lower half. She'd had to cut his jeans off but hadn't removed the blue boxer shorts he'd been wearing even though the waistband was soaked in his blood, and it'd dried stiff and crusty. She wanted to respect his privacy. Yet she could clearly see that at least one part of his anatomy was working just fine, and though he might be different from other men in several noteworthy ways, what was going on down south was very usual. *Your eyes lingering on the bulge beneath the blanket isn't exactly respecting his privacy, Autumn.*

Still, her gaze remained glued. He was a large man, and all his...various parts were obviously sized as such. She saw him twitch, the blanket rising slightly as at least one part of him regained consciousness.

Well, that was a measure of health, wasn't it? And as a professional...*oh, quit it. Your justification is pitiful. You just want to stare.*

She resisted rolling her eyes at herself but averted her gaze from Sam's nether regions, feeling ashamed but not *overly* ashamed. It wasn't like he *knew* she was staring at his ample package.

Autumn stretched. She was exhausted. She stood and walked to the sofa near the window. She'd set her alarm and get at least a couple hours of sleep. Her purse was on the coffee table where she'd tossed it after dragging Sam inside and retrieving the things from the truck. She suddenly remembered the files she'd stolen from Chantelle's office and dug them out of her purse.

She hadn't had time to fully explore her emotions with regard to her birth mother. She'd all but shut it out since leaving the ratty hotel room where she lived, and then, well, life had flipped on its dang axis. She'd have to deal with that eventually, but did she really have to deal with whatever other upsetting facts might be laid out in her social services file?

Autumn pulled her legs beneath her, spread a blanket on her lap, and smoothed out her file on top. She was going to ask Sam for answers when he—God willing—woke up and was strong enough to talk. She may as well start the conversation knowing as much as possible about her beginnings and all that had happened—whether immaterial or not—prior to her meeting him in the woods in the dark of night.

She stifled another yawn, setting the other folders aside and opening hers. There was no copy of her birth certificate contained within—apparently, Chantelle had been honest when she'd told her that information, specifically her birth mother's name, was sealed.

She flipped through the forms that had been filled out by social workers preparing to place her at Mercy Hospital for Children where a large population of other state-ward ADHM babies were being cared for. Her eyes caught and held on a small line near the bottom of one of the pages, inquiring on the date of ADHM diagnosis. The date listed was her birthday, but written next to that was the phrase, "Suspected ADHM."

Suspected?

Across the room, Sam made a grunting sound in his sleep as though responding to her distress. She watched him for a moment, but he appeared to simply be dreaming, which was good because it meant he was sleeping deeply.

Autumn looked back at the paper, a frisson of confusion buzzing beneath her skin. *Suspected ADHM*.

They hadn't been sure she was ADHM positive when she was born. Because her mother had told them the same thing she'd told Autumn? They'd doubted her perhaps. Another lying junkie. Par for the course when it came to addicts. But still, they'd listed her as *suspected*.

But there were tests that would indicate whether a mother had taken ADHM, even in small amounts, during pregnancy. They were in-depth, and results could take weeks from what she knew. But they'd performed those tests later when she was at Mercy Hospital, and they'd come up positive...right?

She set her file aside and picked up the other three in the stack. The names on the folders were for children she didn't know and had either lived somewhere other than Mercy Hospital or been on a different floor than her, and their paths hadn't crossed. She flipped through each file, going directly to that same line. Two of them simply had a date of diagnosis, but the third one, a boy, said the same thing as hers: "Suspected ADHM."

Autumn set them all aside, massaging her aching head. She felt disturbed. Deeply worried. Yet without her medical records, she had no way to confirm that the *suspected* ADHM diagnosis had become a *definite* ADHM diagnosis.

And if it hadn't?

Autumn stood, heading to the bedroom where there was a second twin bed, suddenly so weary she could hardly stand. Or think. Yet even as she dropped into sleep, the incredulity remained. She'd *found* him. She'd *saved* him. Her moonlight boy. Sam.

CHAPTER SEVENTEEN

Agent Mark Gallagher assessed the scene. The emergency vehicles were long gone, as were the first responders. *And so are the victims. And the survivors who will spend the rest of their lives* surviving *what was experienced here, in ways both big and small.* Tragedies like this one were never over, not after the crime scene had been cleaned up and processed. Not after the funerals. Not even after the worst of the grief had begun to diminish and the rest of the world got back on the merry-go-round of life.

His gaze went to one of the outlines. It was smaller, likely one of the young women who had lost their lives out here. There were another two nearby and one more in the building. In addition, two children and another adult had been shot, but as of now, it looked like they'd all survive. *Thank God.* A madman had fired at little children and the adults protecting them.

Mark had survived his own tragic loss—continued to survive it—when his daughter, Abbi, passed from cancer, but she hadn't been that small. He and his wife had received twenty blessed years with their precious girl. As he thought about how close two sets of parents had come to losing their little ones, it struck him that he'd been lucky. And as God was his witness, he never thought he'd feel lucky again. Especially not where Abbi was concerned. But he was. Standing there, he was so grateful for what he'd gotten, even if it wasn't close to enough.

"Agent Gallagher?" The lead detective on the case, a potbellied man in his sixties with a bald head and a mustache, approached him, a thin young woman with a ponytail next to him. The woman looked shaken, her eyes wide, skin ashen. *Lord help her.* She'd never unsee what had happened that day. "This is Ms. Maples. She was in that classroom right there," he said in his thick New York accent, pointing to a room that had a direct view to the playground. "She saw everything."

Mark stepped forward, reaching out and taking the woman's hand in his. "Ms. Maples. Thank you for meeting me here today. I'm sure it's the last place you wanted to come after what you witnessed yesterday. After the losses you suffered." He dropped her hand, and she pulled it back, stretching her fingers, not seeming to know what to do with her arms, finally dropping them by her sides.

"It's okay, Agent," she said, her voice clear and remarkably steady. "I'll do whatever I can to…" Her lip did tremble then, but only minutely, and she quickly got hold of her emotions. "I'll do whatever I can to help." She lifted her chin, and despite her obvious distress and the fact that she might be suffering from an understandable case of PTSD, he saw that she contained grit too. He was good at recognizing that quality because it was rare, especially in the wake of a very recent trauma. "One of those kids who's fighting for her life in the hospital was mine," she said, her lip trembling again. "I don't mean mine as in she was my daughter but... she was in my class, and when you're a teacher, well, they're all yours. Twenty-three sets of parents entrusted them to me."

"What happened was not your fault, Ms. Maples. You could not have done any better."

"I don't blame myself, Agent. I followed protocol and locked down the classroom as soon as the warning signal went off. Erica was in the bathroom though, and he shot her as she came out."

Jesus. From what he understood from the initial briefing, the gunman had initially entered the building through the front door, shot a teacher near the entrance immediately, and then begun shooting anyone he encountered in the hallways. Luckily, the school had a good plan in place for such an event—a tragedy in itself that one was needed—and had implemented it to perfection. It'd saved lives. The gunman had attempted to enter a couple rooms, but when he was unsuccessful, he'd exited through a side door and gone around back to the playground. The kids on the playground had begun lining up to hunker down in the open stairwell, but the gunman had arrived before the stragglers near the back of the playground had made it to safety.

It'd all happened in six and a half minutes.

"Can you tell me about the other man? The one who you said shielded the children? Walk me through it if you can."

Ms. Maples pointed to the spot outside the exposed staircase. "The teachers who were outside with the kids started calling them to the designated spot when the siren went off over the loudspeaker. They seemed calm, as they might have thought it was a drill. I considered pounding on the window but then thought better of it. It might have wasted time, them looking around for the source of the noise, me signaling, them trying to read my lips from above..." She waved her hand around.

Good, Mark thought. A clear thinker in a moment of extreme stress. And she'd likely been right not to distract them and waste precious seconds. Precious lives.

"Anyway, all the kids were gathering. I was praying that the gunman had left the property, that he'd given up, but then he emerged from right there"—she pointed to a spot just beyond the jungle gym—"and he began shooting." Ms. Maples gulped back what was obviously a sob of grief.

"Where was the other man?" he asked.

"The blond man... No, it wasn't blond so much as white. A silvery sort of white, hard to explain—"

"Wait, he had white hair? Was he old?" That surprised Mark. He hadn't waited for the full description of either the gunman or anyone else involved before hopping on a plane. But when he'd heard about a second man who'd acted as a Good Samaritan of sorts but then disappeared, he hadn't pictured him being old—because he'd taken a slew of gunfire to the midsection and the legs and then walked away.

But Ms. Maples shook her head. "No, quite young actually. I know, strange. And he didn't have albinism, because his skin was tan."

Mark's brow furrowed. "Could his hair have been dyed?" The good thing about the description was a man like that wouldn't be difficult to spot.

Ms. Maples shrugged. "I guess that could be it. Anyway, he was over there," she said, pointing to a spot by the gate. "And when the gunman appeared, he yelled something at him. It sounded like Damon maybe. Or Aiden. I don't know. The window was shut, and there was lots of shouting from both inside and out. I was watching but also trying to keep the kids away from the window. But his voice was deep, and he yelled as if he knew the gunman. The gunman seemed to know the white-haired man too, because he yelled something back that I didn't catch. He was angry, and I don't know…I got the impression the white-haired man was there to stop the gunman. And then…he just threw his arms out wide and…well, he jumped in front of the children, shielding them." She closed her eyes, no doubt imagining it. Then she whispered, "It looked like he took a dozen hits before he fell." She grimaced. "It was awful. But it was enough time for those kids to get to safety."

"Is that when the gunman brought the weapon to his own head?"

"Yes, but first he pointed it at a woman standing by the fence."

"A woman?" No one had mentioned a woman.

"Yes. I just remembered her actually." She shook her head. "Sorry, in all the confusion, I didn't remember her. Yes, there was a woman, and she wasn't a teacher here, because she was outside the gate at first. She was…wearing jeans and a bulky sweater." She furrowed her brow. "Red maybe? Or pink? Anyway, the gunman raised the gun and pointed it at her, and she seemed to brace, but then he brought it to his head instead and fired. I guess the shock of seeing that…what happened right before it sort of disappeared from my mind temporarily."

"That's not unusual, Ms. Maples." It was why he liked to interview witnesses right after the event and then after some time. "Where did the woman go after the gunman shot himself?"

"I don't know. The police cars arrived out front, and

I ushered all the kids to the door. I knew from watching that the gunman was no longer a threat. Even so, we waited behind the door for help to arrive. When they did, we exited out the front door. I didn't see the white-haired man or the woman in the sweater after that."

"Can you tell me anything else about what the woman looked like?"

Ms. Maples rubbed her temple, obviously straining to recollect. After a moment, she shook her head. "I'm sorry. I see her outline in my mind and that sweater, but...I just can't remember anything else about her."

"Okay. You've been a big help. Thank you, Ms. Maples. You're meeting with the sketch artist now?"

"Yes."

"Will you see if you can remember anything more specific about the woman too, and if so, have a sketch drawn up for the team of investigators?"

"Of course."

Mark removed a card from his wallet and handed it to her. "If you think of anything else, please give me a call."

She glanced at it and nodded. "I will, Agent."

A deputy escorted her back through the crime scene where techs still worked collecting evidence from the pavement, and the lead detective turned back toward Mark. "My boss told me the FBI wasn't going to arrive for a couple days. Some holdup or another. Can I ask why you came alone, Agent? And all the way from Montana?"

Mark looked at the detective. There was a holdup in the FBI getting there? That was concerning. And familiar. And made him all the more certain that his instincts were correct regarding this event. He cleared his throat. "I'm here because this might be connected to a larger case."

The detective considered him for a moment. "What makes you think that?"

"Some similarities." Mark couldn't say much more than that, not on that point anyway. He might be wildly off base anyway. But his gut told him he wasn't. Especially in light of the second man who'd been there, the one who'd tried to stop the gunman and then disappeared. The shooter was dead and could no longer provide answers, but the white-haired man was not. And that man hadn't fled the scene for no reason. Mark did not believe he'd been there randomly. "Are you collecting camera footage from the surrounding area?"

"Yup. There's a business district that way," the detective said, pointing in front of Mark. "So there's a lot. Unfortunately, there aren't any good views of the back of the school, but we're scouring the surrounding streets. It will be a lot of tape to go through, but at least we have the timing to narrow things down. And in the meantime, we've got an APB out for the man with the white hair. It's just too bad we don't have more than that one descriptor to go on. Hopefully the sketch provided by that teacher helps."

Mark nodded. "Detective…I need to ask you not to release a sketch to the public just yet."

The detective looked momentarily taken aback. "Someone might be able to identify him. It might not be a lot to go on, but a head of white hair on a young man is quite a descriptor."

"I think it's important that we identify him first. Let's go back to your office, and I can explain more." *Not everything, but some.*

The detective considered him for a moment, stroking his mustache before giving a nod. "I can give you a lift."

Mark followed the detective from the schoolyard, glancing at the spot where the man with the white hair's blood had soaked into the concrete after he'd taken a slew of bullets and then evidently walked away. *Or been helped.*

The man with the white hair.

Was he one of the lost?

And if he wasn't, who the hell was he?

CHAPTER EIGHTEEN

Sam was back in the hospital, about to go under the knife. *Again.* His soul wailed, body flailing as the pain enveloped him. Hot. Scalding. *Crushing.* The pain not only made his nerve endings sizzle torturously, but it also made him feel so lonely. Forgotten. He bellowed, the sound of a trapped animal. Misery.

Shh, my moonlight boy. You're okay. Stop moving, and you won't keep ripping out your stitches.

A tiny prick in his arm, small and painless. He calmed, the silkiness of her voice wrapping him like a cocoon. *Safety.* Beauty. So many times, he'd recited her words in his mind, but he'd never been able to conjure the sound of her voice. Maybe he'd finally lost his mind. It was a relief. How often he'd prayed to find relief in the void of insanity, but his prayers had never been answered. Now they finally had been. God did see him. He'd gifted Sam madness, and even sweeter, *she* still remained. He hadn't been asked to leave her behind. *Mercy.* He finally knew what it felt like.

He heard a man's voice briefly, and he didn't like it, but then he was gone, and it was only her.

"What can I do?" she asked.

"Whisper in my ear," he begged. He wanted her to touch him, but he couldn't bear the feel of human hands, so he asked for her voice, the touch of her breath.

"What would you have me whisper?"

"Tell me that I'm human." *Tell me that I haven't been drained of the last bit of it.* He wanted to hear it from her, even if it wasn't true.

A pause. Had she left him already as he plunged lower into the depths of insanity? "You're very human," she said. "Do you know how I know?"

No, he didn't know, and he suddenly couldn't remember how to speak. He felt a very light weight on his chest, the warmth of flesh. She'd placed her hand on his heart. He felt a gust of breath at his ear.

"I *know*," she whispered, "because your heart is beating beneath my palm. And I know because you cared enough to save me once. And now I'm going to save you."

If saving me means I have to leave this place—leave you—*then I don't want to be saved.*

He drifted, and when he came to, there was a slight weight on his shoulder, and he felt the tickle of hair. A faint snore, breath on his skin. She'd fallen asleep on his shoulder. His heart sang. He inhaled her hair. Not strawberry Jell-O. It made him want to laugh that he had once thought that. She smelled nothing like a strawberry. And definitely not the gelatin variety. "Madagascar," he murmured.

He felt her stir. "What?"

"In Madagascar," he slurred. "There was a boy in the street...selling...vanilla beans from a basket." He saw it, pictured it as if he'd floated there and was again standing in that street. "There was a flower box filled with...white flowers in a window." He swallowed. His throat burned. "I could smell their scent mixed with the...vanilla." He inhaled again. *Heaven.* "That's what you smell like." *A peaceful street in Madagascar, under an orange sky.*

"Why were you in Madagascar?"

To kill a man. Someone's enemy. But he kept that to himself. He didn't want her to know. He didn't want to say that he had no idea *whose* enemy and that it hadn't mattered anyway. But it did, didn't it? In his sane life, it was *all* that mattered. The mission—whatever mission that might be—and his role in carrying it out. He'd spent his life being taught that the mission mattered: the individual missions and the overall mission. His purpose. His only purpose. No wonder they'd cast him aside. He was worthless and weak. So why didn't he care? Why didn't he want to try to be better at the missions? Why would he rather die than be brought back again?

What happened in Macau, Sam?

He moaned. He felt pain, but not the physical kind. He didn't want to think about missions or Macau. He only wanted to think about baskets of vanilla beans cast in a citrus glow. And her. Always her. He didn't like the way his thoughts were clearing, taking shape. He wanted to drop back into the abyss of insanity where only good memories lived.

Her sweet-smelling hair tickled his shoulder again.

He drifted once more, further this time, that cocoon drawing tighter, the silkiness cradling him. He felt warm. Happy maybe, though he couldn't well remember the feeling or if this was it. He liked it though, whatever it was. Here he could let go of missions and enemies and Macau. *Yes,* he thought. *I enjoy madness very much.*

The pain was back. He bellowed again, swatting at the fiery brand running across his skin.

"Stop it now," she said. "Lie still, and you'll be fine."

Her voice. He stilled as she told him to, the pain lessening. Not unbearable, just...uncomfortable. And itchy. And hot. Strange. But not painful.

"Shh." Her breath against his ear. He sighed. "Trust me."

Something tugged at his lips, and if he could have lifted his arms, he'd have batted it away.

"Well, look at that," she said. "A *smile*. Goal attained. I wasn't sure you were capable."

Whatever hot thing was on his skin was uncomfortable and...wet. He started to raise his hand to bat it away, but she caught it, pressed it down.

"You need a bath. A proper one," she mumbled, and he heard the sound of water hitting water. "But this will have to do for now."

The warmth again. Her voice as she hummed. He liked being crazy. He liked it very much. *Thank you, God.* He felt that tug once more. He believed in God now? He even talked to him? Yes, being crazy was very nice. He would definitely stay here.

The moaning sound filled his brain, and he had an odd *rising* sensation as though he was floating upward. Only not floating...exactly because whatever he was immersed in was sludgy and dark.

Where am I?

His thoughts scrambled as his mind searched for something that would anchor him. Her. Her voice. *Where is she?*

A feeling of panic took over. Was he emerging from the safety of insanity? Was she gone? The moaning again.

Me. It's me.

He tried desperately to sink back down into oblivion, but his panicked thoughts had only worked to bring him more fully awake.

Awake? Am I asleep?

This did feel slightly familiar. *Drugged. I'm drugged.*

Oh God. Am I waking from another surgery?

No, no. Please no. He struggled to remember, to orient himself.

Amon. The schoolyard. The gun. The children. The pain.

"Help me. Please. Get me out of here."

Her. She'd been there. She'd been *there*.

He lifted his heavy lids, blinking at the scene before him, trying to make sense of it.

It was a cabin, the walls and ceiling made of planks. There was a fire blazing in the fireplace directly across from him, snapping and crackling. He could smell the barest hint of smoke. His gaze shot from one side of the cozy room to the other. There were uncovered windows on each wall, and he could see that it was dim outside but not dark. Early morning or early evening? He didn't know. He could see the tops of trees and the cloud-filled sky but nothing else.

Sam attempted to pull himself upright, but the pain in his abdomen stopped him. He collapsed with a grunt, looking down at himself. There was a red-and-black-checkered blanket covering his bottom half, and extensive bandaging covered where he'd been shot in his chest.

It was steadily trickling in now. The memories, the

screams. *Who? Who could have possibly been the enemy Amon had been sent to kill?* Sam had heard of others sent to kill children in foreign lands as reprisal for the sins of the father. Reprisals the details of which they weren't meant to question or understand. But Amon had fired randomly at a schoolyard of children. *Why?*

Sam let his eyes fall shut for a moment, but now that his memory had returned, the visions were more vivid behind his lids. So he opened his eyes once more.

The door squeaked, and he tensed. *She* entered, and his heart nearly stopped. *Her.* In the flesh. He'd *seen* her there, on the playground, but he'd thought it was some sort of vision or hallucination brought on by shock. He'd kept her there with him, guiding him to his truck, because he was so weak, he couldn't do it alone. He wouldn't have made it otherwise. So he'd pretended. He'd brought her forth to help him cope as he'd done so many times before. Yes, she'd seemed brighter, more vivid, but he'd been very, very hurt. He'd expected to die. And that would have been okay. He was supposed to be dead anyway.

Maybe I am.

She had a small pile of firewood in her arms, and she put it down next to the fire, humming as she added a piece. She hadn't looked at him yet.

Am I in heaven?

But that couldn't be it, because if there was a heaven, *he* certainly wouldn't have been sent there.

Her hair was dark and wavy, and she had it twisted up on the top of her head. She was wearing jeans and a green-and-gray flannel shirt that looked far too big for her.

She was still *her*, but she was a woman. He watched her, trying to orient himself, attempting to merge the girl she'd been with the woman she was, even while disbelief and fear and wonder overwhelmed him.

She stood, brushing her hands together and turning. She did look at him then, and her eyes widened in surprise. Her cheeks were rosy from what must be the cold outside, and for several beats, they simply stared. Wide eyes, narrow chin, the most perfectly shaped mouth he'd ever seen. *Autumn*.

She's beautiful. More beautiful even than he remembered. He'd tried so hard to keep her features vivid in his mind over all the years since he'd last been face-to-face with her in the woods, but he realized now he hadn't even come close.

Then she smiled, and there was the strangest pressure—an expanding—just under his ribs. An angel—*his* angel—was looking at him and smiling.

"Well, hello." She walked slowly toward him but stopped a few feet from where he lay. "How do you feel?"

"It's you," he said, and the words came out as little more than a whisper. He cleared his throat and tried to put some force behind his words. "It's you," he repeated.

She nodded solemnly. "Yes, it's me. And it's you. Sam."

"You know my name." He was wondrous. He didn't know where he was or even who he was or if this was reality or some version of insanity or a fever dream or a medication he'd been given. But whatever it was, he didn't want it to end.

"Yes, you told me your name. Do you remember?"

He cast his mind back, wincing from the pain in his head. "No."

She took a step closer. "That's not surprising. You've been very sick."

He glanced down at his chest. "You helped me."

She bit at her lip, a worried look coming into her eyes.

"Yes. I'm a registered nurse. I removed the bullets. It didn't appear they'd hit anything vital. I stitched you up. I administered antibiotics, and I've been here monitoring you. It was a risk, Sam. I thought you might die, and if you had…"

"Thank you," he said, a whisper again. "Thank you." He felt strange. Something he couldn't identify. *Like crying.* He felt like crying. It was unusual. He didn't think he knew what crying felt like anymore. "Autumn," he said. "Your name is Autumn." It had been written at the front of the book with the red velvet cover, the one he'd been forced to leave behind when he was banished. His treasure. His only treasure. Yet he'd carried it with him anyway, secure in the vault of his mind.

She nodded slowly, taking another step toward him. "Yes. Did they tell you my name?"

"They?"

Her forehead dipped. "The people at the hospital all those years ago? The ones who sent you out into the woods?"

"No. It was in the front of your book."

She looked confused for a moment, and then understanding dawned, and she released a short breath. "My journal," she said. "So *you're* the one who stole it?"

"I didn't steal it. I found it."

"Did you read it?"

He cast his eyes down. "Yes." *A thousand times, and then again.*

She set her hands on her hips. "Hmm. You shouldn't have done that. Those were my private thoughts."

He felt embarrassed. Ashamed. Mostly because her words had meant so much to him, and she hadn't wanted him to read them. He felt a quivering inside, a different sort of hurt than he'd experienced before. "Sorry," he mumbled.

The words he'd cherished so much had been stolen words, not meant for him at all. He'd known that, of course. But to hear it out loud from her created a piercing pain.

In his peripheral vision, she took a step toward him. She was within arm's reach now. "It's okay. Listen...we're at my father's lake cottage right now. Sam, he's worried about me helping you. About me being alone out here with you."

His gaze flew to hers. "I won't hurt you," he said. Could he if he wanted to? Even wounded like he was? Yes. But he had no desire to hurt Autumn.

She watched him for several moments, and he felt his face heat. It surprised him. He didn't usually get embarrassed, but he felt exposed under her stare. Because he cared what she thought of him. Down deep in a hidden place where he stored the few valuables that mattered to him. He knew she must be thinking that he looked like a freak and a monster, even while he was so stunned by her beauty he could barely speak.

"My father believed I'd tie you up," she said.

His stomach lurched. He'd been tied up before—strapped down—while they'd done horrific things to his body...as he'd screamed and begged them to stop. He wouldn't hurt Autumn, and he wouldn't beg, but he'd turn this house upside down before he'd let her tie him down.

But before he could respond, she said, "I didn't tie you down. Not even when you were unconscious. And I'm not going to attempt it now." She gave him the side-eye. "I have a feeling you'd try to leave if I did. But I'm going to trust you, Sam, because I have good reason to believe you're kind and that you won't hurt me even if you could."

"I'm not kind," he said, because he wasn't, and though

it hurt and embarrassed him to know she saw him as the monster he was, he also didn't want to lie or mislead.

She looked thoughtful for a moment. "Decent then."

"No, I'm not that either."

She let out a small laugh that quickly died. "Well, honest anyway."

He considered that. "Yes. I'm honest." Or rather he'd never had much reason to lie. His job had not required words meant to deceive. Only brute force action had been necessary.

"Good. Can I trust you?"

He opened his mouth and then closed it. He wasn't sure how to answer that. Trust was an odd thing to ask about. There were a dozen reasons he could have said *no*. But... this was *Autumn* asking him. "Not to hurt you?" he clarified.

"Yes."

"Yes, you can trust me not to hurt you."

"Good." She stepped all the way to his bedside. "I'm going to take your temperature and look at your wounds, okay?"

He nodded, and she pulled a chair up, sitting down and gently peeling the bandages away. He had so many questions, but he hardly knew where to start. "Why were you there?" he asked after a moment. "At that school."

She paused, her hands stilling. "I followed you."

She'd *followed* him?

"I was in New York City trying to find more information about my past." Something almost dreamy moved across her pretty features. "I saw you on the street," she murmured. "And I followed you." She met his eyes. "We have a lot to talk about, Sam."

CHAPTER NINETEEN

The man who'd entered Deercroft Academy with a firearm, ultimately killing four teachers, wounding two children and a custodian, and finally shooting himself, was named Jason Leads, and he'd lived alone in a studio apartment in Queens. He was a loner, apparently, and his neighbors reported that they'd only seen him on occasion, either coming or going. He'd barely responded to attempts at conversation, only giving terse, one-word replies to neighborly greetings.

Mark used his gloved hand to pick up a photo on the desk in the small main room. It was the suspect, along with an old woman with a head of tight gray curls. The woman had an oxygen tube in her nose but was offering a weak smile. Leads's grandmother, Shirlene, who had died ten years before. Other than her, the suspect had no family and no friends who'd come forward. A *complete* loner.

Just like the others.

The suspect worked as a website designer from home. The computer was gone now, being looked over by techs, but Mark didn't expect that anything of any consequence would come from it. The police had ID'd the suspect after a wallet and a Deercroft Academy brochure were randomly found wrapped in a jacket and stuffed behind some shrubbery near the front of the school the day after the tragedy occurred and hours after Mark had surveilled the schoolyard. *Convenient.* It looked as though the gunman had intended on returning for the personal items he'd brought. The authorities had gone to the man's apartment and found ample evidence that he was in fact the shooter, and techs had finished up that morning.

"Do you see anything unusual, Agent?" the cop who'd accompanied him here asked.

"No," Mark answered. The bed was unmade, covers thrown back. He expected the DNA found on the sheets and elsewhere would be a match to the body in the morgue. He'd also bet that the body had been left unattended long enough that he couldn't be sure it was even the same man who'd been transported from Deercroft Academy.

But of course, he had no way to prove that, and he'd sound like a lunatic if he voiced such a thought.

"The diagram was found over there?" he asked the man who had been one of the first responders to arrive at the apartment and seal it off after Jason Leads had been identified.

"Yeah," the officer said. "On the bedside table, along with another brochure from the school. The shooting was definitely not random or spontaneous. How long he was planning it though is hard to say. Any clue to motive?"

"That aspect's out of my purview," Mark said. But he anticipated that a motive would not be found. *Crazy* was the conclusion they'd have to come to. *Just plain crazy.*

Which was very legitimate in plenty of crimes, even if

crazy could be defined in more technical terms. But not this one. At least he didn't think so.

"Oh right, you're working on a separate case." The officer opened his mouth as though to ask about that, then realized Mark wouldn't be able to answer and sighed. "At least he made it easy for us to identify him. And then he left all his plans behind."

Mark made a sound of agreement. *Yes, too easy.*

Then again, he didn't want to jump to conclusions based on what was in large part a gut instinct. He had to consider the possibility that Jason Leads was not connected to the lost, even if the man with the white hair was. Perhaps it was easy to identify Jason Leads because he hadn't planned on getting caught, hadn't planned on someone stepping in, and had adjusted plans at the last minute with a bullet to the head.

Why had he considered that drastic option necessary though? Why hadn't he tried to get away? The white-haired man was down, and the police were still blocks away.

There was time. After all, the white-haired man and the unknown woman had managed to evade police. Then again, they'd had some time. When the police had arrived, the gunman was dead, and they hadn't immediately known about the other man and woman.

Some interesting things had come out from forensics the day before though regarding the white-haired man, things they were having a hard time explaining. Notably, several of the bullets they'd found had appeared to *hit* him but then been stopped and ended up on the schoolyard, the heads blunted. Almost as if he wore armor.

The forensics team had appeared stumped. Mark had only become more certain the white-haired man was someone it was imperative he find, and quickly.

Mark looked around for a few more minutes and then left with the officer, parting ways in the downstairs lobby. Mark walked to his rental car parked just down the block and sat in it, tapping the wheel for a moment as he considered what he knew and what Jason Leads's apartment had confirmed for him.

He took his phone from his pocket and pulled up several different news pages and scrolled back a few days on each.

A married senator from the East Coast had been caught soliciting sex from a sex-trafficking victim in DC. The lawmaker had run his campaign on a platform of old-fashioned family values, so the scandal was particularly damaging. He claimed a sex addiction. Mark sighed. When caught with your pants down—literally—claim an addiction. Become the victim. Cast those accusing you of indecency as the indecent ones for their lack of compassion and understanding. The senator had done exactly that, and then he'd gotten his wife to make a teary statement about how she was sticking by her husband and attempting to understand his addiction. Even so, there were calls for him to resign, and the calls were getting louder. His party leaders were sure to step in any moment and press him on stepping down.

The other story that caught Mark's attention was about money said to be missing from the Department of Development and Urban Housing in New York. Some officials were calling for an investigation, though those being accused were claiming the discrepancy was a simple case of human error and that nothing untoward had happened. To make matters more suspicious, however, the accounting data drives had gone missing, so the accountants were having to recreate the records from what data was available. Mark read through a few statements of various officials, some calling the whole situation outrageous and corrupt, others saying that an explainable situation was being blown out of proportion by windbags looking for a crime that wasn't there.

He scrolled forward on all three sites he'd brought up, noting that neither story had been mentioned since the school shooting had occurred.

"Well, aren't you all lucky?" Mark muttered, thinking of those involved in the scandals that had been front-page stories two days ago and now weren't even back-page news.

Only he had a very strong feeling there was more than luck involved. *And four young teachers paid the price.*

Mark closed the browser and opened his phone, dialing his wife's number. She picked up on the second ring. "Hi! I didn't expect to hear from you until tonight."

Mark smiled, leaning his head back on the headrest. Just the sound of her voice brought him the calm he sought. Humans could be so damn wicked, and though it was his job to hunt them down and capture them, he was human too, and sometimes the evil he uncovered plain depressed him. He let the gratitude for his wife, Laurie, wash through him. He never took it for granted. He'd almost lost her, and he never let himself forget it. Not to death but to heartbreak and misunderstanding, doubt and despair. They'd made it though, and because they'd walked through that valley and emerged *together*, they were stronger than ever.

"I had a minute and thought I'd call."

"I'm glad you did."

"What are you up to?" he asked her, needing to hear about some normalcy.

"I just got home from Jak and Harper's. They had some

errands they wanted to run together, and I watched Eddie for them. That boy never stops, I swear. I'm worn out." But the way she said it made Mark smile too.

Mark had played a part in solving not only the crime Jak was wrongly accused of but the mystery of the young man's parentage and background after he'd been discovered having lived alone in the wilderness for much of his life. Mark and Laurie had grown very close to Jak and his wife, Harper, in the aftermath. And now, their four-year-old little boy was as much their grandson as their flesh and blood would have been if their daughter, Abbi, had lived and had children. They adored little Edmond Fairbanks and loved nothing more than spoiling him rotten. Mark didn't feel an ounce of guilt about it either. Eddie's parents kept him grounded and enforced the rules. *Grandfathers'* boundaries were different, and he pushed each and every one. The balance worked.

"Tell them all I said hi."

"I will. Jak thought…you might have some news for him."

"Not yet. I'm confirming a few things first. But it looks…similar."

Laurie let out a breath. "Oh." A lot was contained in that little word, and Mark heard it all. She paused for a moment. "I read that the suspect took his own life."

"Yes," Mark confirmed. "But there's someone else…of interest. Like I said, I'm still trying to confirm a few things." He scrubbed his hand down his face. Damn, he was tired. He hadn't slept well the night before, tossing and turning and trying to put things together from the little he had. "Or at least draw the outlines of a picture, if there's one to draw."

"Let your gut point the way," she said.

The fact that she still trusted his gut—and maybe now

more than ever—was another small miracle. He'd turned away from what he knew to be true once in an effort to avoid his pain. He'd figured things out in the nick of time. But he *had*, and that was the important thing. That gratitude again. That she was on the other line, and she was his.

"I will," he said. "I love you."

"I love you too."

Mark disconnected the call and sat there for another minute, staring at the nondescript apartment building where Jason Leads had lived. He thought of the photo again, of the guy and his dead grandmother, picturing the man's hefty build. The witnesses had described the gunman as very muscular, though eyewitness descriptions were notoriously faulty, especially in high-stress situations.

But where were all his other guns? A shooter rarely had only one.

Let your gut point the way.

His *gut* told him this was exactly what he thought it was.

Which meant he had to find the white-haired man, who'd somehow gotten away despite being shot several times, and the woman in the coral sweater, who still hadn't come forward.

CHAPTER TWENTY

"Here, hold on to me," Autumn said, bending her knees and leaning toward Sam so he could grasp her shoulder as he stood.

He grunted and gave her a look he hoped told her that was a bad idea.

Autumn shook her head and stood straight, her expression aggravated. "Fine then, do it yourself."

Sam pushed himself off the bed, wincing as he came to a slow stand, unbending his large frame inch by inch. When he'd straightened to his full height, he released a breath. Things seemed to be in order. And he hadn't felt anything tear.

"Okay?" Autumn asked.

"Yeah. Okay."

"Good," she said. "Mere mortals wouldn't have survived."

He frowned. He wasn't sure what she meant by that, except that he was…inhuman. Different. Which was true, but he didn't like to hear her point it out. Didn't like what she now knew about him, the things she obviously must have seen.

She paused, her eyes moving over his features and then to his frowning lips. Her mouth curved downward too as if responding to his. "I just meant…you're very strong, Sam."

He followed Autumn to the bathroom.

"I put a new toothbrush on the sink for you, and anything else you might need should be in there as well. I'll be right outside," she said. "Just yell if you need me."

Sam closed the door behind him, going about his business slowly, like an old, decrepit man. Like Adam. He felt an odd sensation in his chest and…did he miss the old fool? Yeah, he did. He didn't know *why* exactly, but he did. And he hadn't returned his truck or the generator he'd been sent to pick up. Adam likely thought he'd stolen it. He probably wasn't surprised. He let people steal things from him more often than not.

So why did Sam feel guilty about it? Especially considering all the other things he should be worrying about?

He shuffled to the small sink, bending enough that he could splash water on his face and use the toothbrush Autumn had set out for him. He brushed his teeth and then stood upright even more easily this time. He'd experienced this part many times before. He'd heal. He'd get better quickly. He couldn't do more than hobble yet, but once he was able to get around well enough on his own, the worst would be over.

"Everything okay in there?" Her voice came from directly on the other side of the door.

That tugging at his lips. He looked up at the mirror in front of him and realized he was smiling. He reached up, running his fingers over the unfamiliar shape of his mouth.

"Hello? Sam?"

"Yes. Uh, yeah, I'm fine. I'm going to take a shower."

"Are you sure you don't need..." She was quiet for a moment, and he felt one brow raise as he waited for her to finish that sentence. *Are you sure you don't need me to help you?*

The vision appeared in his mind, bright and vibrant, her arms around him from behind as he stood under the spray of water. Skin on skin. He shut it down. The picture made him feel too many sensations and all at once. Desire. Fear. Confusion. Shame.

"Er, I mean, are you sure you can manage it?"

"Yes. I can manage it," he told her through the door.

"You'll have to be careful with your bandages. Try not to get them wet, but I'll redress your wounds when you get out."

"Okay." He waited for a moment until he heard the soft creak of the wooden floor under her footsteps before getting undressed. She'd helped him pull on a pair of sweatpants the day before, and he removed them now, and then the ruined boxers, soiled with his blood, balling them up and tossing them in the small trash can near the sink. For a moment, he stood looking at himself in the mirror, all the scars more obvious against his sickly pallor. They jumped out at him, making him feel nauseated and ashamed. Autumn had seen them all up close. He wondered if she'd been horrified when she undressed him, and he cast his mind from visualizing that moment. Had she drawn away from his ugliness? Winced? *Gagged?*

He turned from the mirror, making the shower water run cold. The stall was small, but he fit inside, even if he had to bend to wet his hair. As he washed himself gingerly, he thought back to that schoolyard. He couldn't get the sounds out of his head. It was always the sounds that haunted him. The visions hurt, but the noises shook him...the gunshots, and worse, the cries. There were so many cries that mingled in his mind. Sad cries. Terrified ones.

The hopeless ones were the worst, yet he wasn't sure why.

Sam thought of Amon, of the look on his face as he raised his hand and shot at Sam. His eyes had held anger, but he'd seen the hopelessness there too. And the resolve.

What Sam still couldn't understand was what the job had been and why Amon had seemingly shot at random children. Had he fouled up the job on purpose? Because what he'd done could not have been a mistake. *Get out of my way.*

Sam had been sent to kill too, but not like that. His targets had always been singular and precise. And never young children.

It's not for you to understand. Follow orders, and do not question.

How often had those instructions been reiterated?

The program would send someone to kill him now. He'd questioned. He'd failed to follow orders. But most unacceptable, he'd intervened in an operation, whether it was one the program member had botched or not.

They don't know where you are.

Even if his description was being broadcast on the news, he was only *here* by total happenstance.

No one else on earth would have helped him. Only her.

She'd followed him. She'd recognized him. *Remembered* him.

Only because *she* was there, at that schoolyard, was he safe.

There was something...astonishing about that. He couldn't wrap his mind around it. But Sam wasn't good at wrapping his mind around things anyway. He hadn't been taught to be a *thinker*. He'd been taught to be a doer. He'd been taught to follow orders.

He shut the water off, stepping from the shower and using the towel hung on the bar to dry himself off.

"Are you okay?"

His gaze went to the door, and his lips tugged again. She was attentive, he'd give her that. *Because it's her job.*

No, it's not. She did this willingly.

She'd put herself at great risk. He wasn't worth it, so he'd leave as soon as he was able to travel and allow her to go back to her life. *Away from the mess she unwittingly fell into because she followed you.*

Out of habit, Sam had parked on a side street unlikely to have cameras and tried his best to travel down the streets in a way that would avoid most public surveillance on the way to the location of Amon's job, Deercroft Academy. But for obvious reasons, he hadn't been able to be as mindful on the way back. He had to hope, though, that if they'd been caught on camera, it was only briefly, and there was no way for the authorities to identify either of them.

Do you trust her? Do you trust her not to turn you in? He paused, thinking about that for a moment, because it was an important consideration. If the police captured him, he'd go to prison. Not only because of the shooting he'd run from but because he'd done terrible things...yes, at the direction of other people, but that wouldn't matter to the authorities. They'd convict him. They'd study him, which he could not allow. That would be even worse than being killed by the program. Because "studying him" meant hospitals. It meant doctors and labs. Maybe surgeries against his wishes. Sam would rather die.

He'd enjoyed his first taste of freedom working on the apple farm, and he wasn't sure that he'd found happiness...exactly...but whatever it was, it was as close as he'd ever known. As far as Autumn though...yes, yes, he did trust her. Not only because she'd also been involved in helping him escape the scene of a crime but because he'd lived in her mind almost half of his life. He'd breathed her thoughts. He'd used the words from her journal to ease his suffering. He'd pondered the gentleness of her heart perhaps even more than she had. She was wrapped around every beautiful thing he'd ever noticed in the world. And for a man who'd been trained to commit ugly, gruesome acts and who'd seen so much depravity, that was magic to him. *She* was magic. And if it turned out he was wrong about trusting her, then he wouldn't need to kill himself, nor would the program. That realization would do it for him.

He wrapped the towel around his hips. It was too small, and he tugged it as best he could, tucking the small available portion of corner into the waist before exiting the bathroom.

She was standing a few feet from the door, and she rushed forward, obviously meaning to help him. But he raised his arm to let her know he was capable of walking back to the bed. However, the movement caused the corner of his towel to come untucked, the too-small piece of terry cloth falling to the floor.

Autumn came up short, and for several beats, they stared at each other across the very small distance before her eyes drifted downward, her gaze halted between his legs before Sam had even thought to cover himself.

He froze, watching her watch him, her eyes widening,

then blinking, but still held on the one part of him that had not undergone experimentation, well, not that he could remember anyway. It seemed to work as it should, though no woman had ever confirmed that for him.

Sam wasn't embarrassed by nudity, his or anyone else's. In a way, he felt detached from his skin and his various parts. His body belonged to the program, to doctors. To others. He'd never been consulted about what happened to him or what did not. But Autumn's eyes on his naked skin, his naked *sex*, caused an odd prickle of…something to begin at the base of his spine. She seemed…unable to look away. But her expression was not filled with disgust or fear or the other emotions he might expect. Autumn was obviously interested, and from what he could tell, it was of the good variety.

He felt a loosening, something he hadn't even known he held tight until that very moment. He'd kept his eyes averted for so much of his life, not wanting to be seen. Knowing that he was ugly. He'd noticed women look at *other* men the way Autumn was looking at him. He'd never imagined a woman would look at him that way, much less the one woman on earth he held above all others. And for the very first time in his life, he felt like a whole man.

Tell me I'm human.

She'd confirmed his question with her words.

But now she was confirming it with her eyes. And it meant infinitely more, because he didn't think this woman's eyes could lie.

Nor her nipples, pebbling under the fabric of her shirt.

He wanted to stand there forever, watching her watch him. Feeling the thing he was feeling. It must have a very specific name, a word that perfectly described it, but he didn't know what that might be.

Wonder?

Joy?

Rebirth?

She jolted as if she'd just realized she was staring, let out a small laugh, which sounded like it was filled with bubbles, and rushed forward, grabbing the towel puddled at his feet. When she stood, her head grazed his manhood, and he sucked in a small breath that ended in an even smaller groan. She sprang away, almost tripping and falling, dropping the towel again. He watched her, amused and…interested. Her touch…it had been unexpected and arousing, yet not…bad.

"Oh my God, I'm so sorry." Her cheeks had turned bright pink, and she brought her hands to them, looking positively mortified.

Sam laughed.

Autumn froze, staring, then blinked, her eyes widening before she too laughed and then clapped a hand over her mouth. "Oh my God," she said again. She scooped the towel up off the floor and then tossed it to him and turned away, her laugh dwindling to a groan.

Sam caught the towel and held it in front of him.

"Note to self: get bigger towels," she murmured.

He felt…happy? He didn't know. He wanted her to look at him again.

Autumn grabbed a pair of sweatpants and threw them his way too. He pulled them on gingerly, and she must have seen from her peripheral vision, because she turned back to him. Her cheeks were less pink, and she seemed to have moved past her momentary embarrassment. "Let's get those bandages changed."

"Yes, nurse."

Her gaze flew to his, and she looked mildly surprised,

pausing for a moment but then nodding, taking the towel from him, and walking to the bathroom door where she hung it over the shower. "It usually steams up in here," she said. "Were you not able to get hot water? I wonder if the water heater is—"

"I used cold water."

She came out of the bathroom. "Cold! Why?"

Why? He scratched at the back of his neck. Why did he shower with cold water? *Habit?* "We didn't have hot water in the hospital. I guess I'm just used to it."

She stared at him, her mind obviously going over something. He could see it in her eyes. "Tell me about the hospital, Sam," she finally said. "Tell me about it while I dress your wounds."

A spear of worry made his back arch slightly, and he stepped forward, walking to the bed where she'd changed the bedding and propped the pillows against the wall. He sat down slowly, stiffly, scooting back to relax against the pillows. When he looked up at her, she was still watching him expectantly. He wasn't supposed to talk about the program or the missions or those he'd been sent to kill. But he also wasn't supposed to talk about the hospital. Because it all started there.

He considered her for a moment. *You owe her.* And he trusted her. If not for her, he'd be sitting in a prison cell right now. But also...she was unlike anyone else on earth who might have asked him about *the hospital*. Because she'd *been* there. Even if they lived in different buildings. Even if their experiences there had only been remotely similar. The hospital was part of her past as well as his, even if in different ways. So he would tell her what he could. "The part of the hospital where I lived was like yours. We were sick, and they helped us."

"Were you an ADHM baby too?"

"Yes, but they cured us early of that."

She approached him slowly, sitting on the edge of the bed. "Cured you? There's no cure."

"The cure they used on us had too many side effects. They discontinued it. It cured us, but it caused many other problems."

She reached for the kit of supplies on the floor before speaking. "Yes, the medication I took was the same. But it kept us alive longer, so the effects were deemed worth it." Autumn carefully removed the old bandages he'd kept mostly dry in the shower. Her gaze was focused on her work, and it was easier to talk to her about this while her gaze was averted. "Why did they have you chase us?" She speared him with her gaze suddenly.

He couldn't look away from those dark, soulful eyes, the ones connected to the beautiful mind that had come up with so many beautiful words and ideas.

"Because they were trying to make us strong." *Vicious.* "And you were weak and dying anyway."

He saw the pain in her eyes before she moved her gaze back to her work. Even so, her hands remained gentle. He realized that she could tell someone what he'd just disclosed to her if she wanted to. But no one would believe her. Most of the kids she'd lived with were probably dead. The ones who'd been out in those woods were certainly dead. He'd seen the ground staff removing some of the bodies. Of course, he wouldn't tell her that. He couldn't. The hospital was closed. So what did it matter if she knew the basics of *why*?

"They were trying to make you strong," she repeated. "How so?"

"We'd survived a disease that most didn't. But that and the medication that cured us caused a lot of damage. Some things had to be replaced, so we underwent many surgeries. Dr. Heathrow believed that he could not only heal us but make us better and stronger than ordinary people."

She was silent as she worked, clearly processing, clearly troubled. "So they used us as...what? Bait?"

He thought about that. It didn't seem like quite the right word. They'd never been told precisely what to do with the kids they left in the woods, except to wait for them to wake. Then they could capture them and do as they pleased. Anything they wanted. Sam didn't know *all* of what pleased the others, only that they came back with a shine in their eyes and blood splashed on the front of their clothes. And he'd heard the screams. Yes, he had at least some idea of what *pleased* the others, but he chose not to consider it too closely. "No," he said finally. "As practice. As training."

Her hands, applying ointment to his wounds, stilled. "Practice? Training?" Her voice cracked on the second word. "For *what*?"

He couldn't tell her more than that. He wouldn't. He had been created to be a monster, and she could see that from looking at him, but she didn't have to know the extent of his purpose. The gruesome details. She didn't have to know that he was even more monstrous on the inside. *And*, he told himself, *it's dangerous for her if she does.* "Practice hunting, chasing." He looked away.

"To what end?" she asked.

"So that we could join militaries and be special forces with unusual and superior skills," he said, which was sort of true but not the whole story. He tensed, grimacing as though she'd hurt him, and she focused her attention back on applying the bandages and tape. *Gentle hands. So gentle.* The world wasn't made for gentleness like hers. Who knew that better than he did? She still seemed troubled but mostly sad.

"So the military was involved?"

"It was mostly research work. I don't know the specifics of who funded it. What I do know is that I'm not supposed to talk about it. The program or the research." *Plausible deniability,* they called it. If he was captured before he could take the cyanide pill, it was better that he not know any details. The only name he knew was Dr. Swift, but he'd never seen so much as a photo of him.

Autumn's brow dipped again. "Research. On kids."

He heard the distaste in her voice, and he didn't disagree entirely, yet for some reason, he felt compelled to defend the program. "They saved us first. We had a special mission because we had strength others never would. Never could."

She was quiet for a few minutes. "Did you want that, Sam? To be in the special forces?"

"Want?" He'd never thought about what he *wanted*. And no one had ever asked him. He'd been lucky, he was told. *Lucky* to be one of the chosen. Lucky to have survived and then to have the opportunity to become more than any other man. *More* special. *More* important. *More* purposeful. They were called for the greater mission because they were greater men. And women. "It wasn't a matter of want. It was a matter of gratitude. And of duty."

She looked up, her hands stilling as her gaze washed over his face. Sunshine. Her eyes on him felt like sunshine, and each time she cast it upon him, something inside seemed to grow. Something that, without her light, had lain dormant in the dark. Waiting.

"How often did you chase us?" she asked.

"Once a month, during the full moon."

"Why the full moon?"

He gave a slight shrug. "I don't know. To make it more exciting maybe? To provide more light? They didn't say. You weren't always there. Sometimes it was others. Most of them never woke up."

"What did you do with them, Sam?" He saw that she was suddenly holding herself very still, waiting for his answer.

"I hid them. You were the first one that ran from me. You were stronger than the others."

She was quiet again for several long moments as she secured the tape. "They told us we were dreaming," she said. "About being in the woods. They told us the medication brought on dreams so vivid they seemed real. And sometimes hallucinations. They told us we were imagining things."

"You weren't."

She tossed the roll of gauze down. "Yes, I know. I know." She covered her face for a moment, her shoulders rising and falling as though she was attempting to rein in her emotions. "I know," she said again, and this time it sounded more like a sigh. She dropped her hands and stood. The scissors she'd used fell from her lap and clattered to the floor. "They were supposed to care for us, and they used us. They threw us to the wolves."

She wasn't wrong.

"But they were supposed to care for you too, Sam. And I know you say they did, but..." She shook her head. She turned away and then turned back. "The ADHM, the medication...is that why your ribs were replaced, Sam? I thought the bullet would have shattered them, but it didn't. Because they're made of steel. You have other steel parts too." Her gaze moved to his bandaged legs and then back to his eyes. "Your kneecaps. Your femurs. They were hit, but the bullets were deflected. The wounds on your legs were direct hits, but they're merely flesh wounds."

Sam looked away even as he nodded. He felt shame creep through him, casting a shadow over the sunshine. He felt exposed in a way he hadn't before. *Much* of him was made of various metals. His ribs, his knees, his thigh bones, his shoulders, and his temples. Any person on the street could see what had been done to his hair and his face and the scars that might show beyond his clothes, but no one had ever looked inside him. No one knew the ways in which he'd been carved out and replaced.

He'd been a mere shell, and Dr. Heathrow had created a human where one had not existed before. Yet *human* felt like a misnomer to Sam. Monster felt more accurate. So it was how he defined himself.

"The man who... The shooter, he was one of the kids in the hospital with you? In the same program?"

"Yes."

"That day...when you said *they* wouldn't help you, that they'd hurt you, you meant the heads of the program you were in?"

That day. In the schoolyard. "I wasn't supposed to be there," he murmured. He felt her gaze on his face but didn't look her way.

"Did you have any idea what he was going to do?" She seemed afraid to ask the question, her words soft and hesitant.

Kill children. "No," Sam said, meeting her eyes. "I visited him an hour before. He seemed off. Something was wrong. I saw an address at his apartment. I went there. It was the school. It was too late. I tried..." He closed his eyes briefly. If he'd only been ten minutes earlier. Just ten measly minutes, and everything would have been different.

"Why did he do it? Do you know why? Did he…go rogue? Or…go *crazy*?"

"Maybe. I don't know the why."

She looked away worriedly. "They obviously will have recovered his body. They'll begin an investigation."

"They won't trace him back to the program," Sam said. They'd do whatever necessary to avoid that.

Autumn bit at her lip for a minute. "I called my job and took a leave of absence. But that only gives me about four weeks. You have to tell someone what happened to us, Sam. Not just with the shooting but with the hospital. The training. The *woods*. It wasn't *right*, Sam, no matter how they justified it."

"I can't tell anyone about the program, Autumn. I meant it when I said they won't help me, they'll hurt me. And as far as the training, they'll say we were both sick and delusional. No one will believe us. No one will back us up." He caught her eye. "You've tried, haven't you?" Because she was not one to let that go. She'd told him she was in New York City looking for answers about her past. But more than that, he'd read her journal—he knew her, or at least he knew she was a fighter. She would have fought. It would have gotten her nowhere.

Her frustrated groan was confirmation. "Finding answers is more important than ever now though, Sam, because this program, it's obviously capable of great evil." She gazed upward. "Yet I have no internet out here, no way to look into…anything. Even if I knew what that anything might be." She brought her gaze to him. "What are we going to do?"

We. No one had ever used that word with Sam before, and it brought him a measure of joy, but it also brought fear. *We* weren't going to do anything. *He* had to ensure she wasn't permanently caught up in his mess. "I'm going to get better," he said. "And then I'll go."

She stared at him. "Where will you go?"

Sam shrugged. He wondered if the old man would take him back. If he took his truck to him and made up a story about... *What, Sam? Will you tell him you got abducted by aliens who finally returned you to Earth?* There was no place in the world for him. Once he left here, he'd have to follow through with the final mission. He really had no other choice.

Sam watched her as she set her supplies down, his gaze following the line of her profile...her body, attempting to commit her physical self to memory, the way he'd catalogued her thoughts and her dreams. Her body was as beautiful as her mind and as mesmerizing.

Finally, she turned, releasing a sigh. "Do you have any questions for me?"

He studied her. He had a million questions for her. He wanted to talk about all the things she'd written, the questions she had. He wanted to know if all the dreams she'd dreamt had come true. But he couldn't do that. And he didn't know how to anyway. But he did have a request.

"Is there paper here?"

"Paper? Um, yes." She headed to the kitchen area where she removed a pad of white paper from a drawer. She took it over to him and set it next to the bed, along with a pen.

"Thank you."

"What do you need it for?"

"I owe someone something," he said. "It's going to take a while, but...how do you eat an elephant?"

One brow went up and one brow went down, and she gave a soft laugh. "What?"

"One bite at a time."

She kept looking at him like he was partially crazy.

"You wrote that in your journal," he reminded her.

She stepped back to the bed and sat down again, and without her medical supplies in her hand, her closeness felt more intimate. His body tensed, and he didn't know if he liked it or not. She cast her eyes away for a moment. "Yes," she said as if just remembering. "How do you eat an elephant."

He'd looked up the confusing phrase many years before, one of the few times he'd opened the internet for purely personal use. "It's a parable," he told her, though she probably knew that. There was a princess in it and a king. He'd laughed when he read it, something he thought had no answer, suddenly making sense through the use of a story.

"Yes," she said, smiling.

Her teeth were so pretty. And there was a very small dimple at the corner of her mouth that was pretty too. Her top lip looked like a bow. He wished he could stop time and stare at her for as long as he wanted to. Which might be forever, and he couldn't think of a better way to spend it.

Her eyes lit up as if with memory. "A parable that means even seemingly impossible tasks become doable if you break them down into small bites."

He laughed softly, and her smile expanded, gaze moving over his face. Something came into her eyes, and for a moment, they simply stared at each other, both of their mouths curved into smiles. She glanced away first, her hand fluttering to her throat where her finger ran along the delicate silver necklace she wore.

"I couldn't find the answers to the other questions though," he said.

She looked back at him, her hand dropping. "Other questions?"

"How do you build a temple that takes a hundred years to build? How do you conquer time? How do you overcome death?"

Her eyes widened. "Oh," she breathed, and her shoulders dropped slightly. "Well. Those are deeper questions that I still haven't found the answers to."

She glanced at him through her lashes, and he got the odd sense that she felt shy. He didn't think anyone had ever felt shy around him before. Scared, yes. Horrified, probably. But shy? *This is new.* It made him feel strange. But not bad strange.

"Thank you for reminding me that I once asked those meaningful yet perhaps unanswerable questions," she said with a smile. "I'm going to ponder them again and see what I can come up with." She patted his knee and then looked alarmed, her face blanching. "Sorry. Did that hurt?"

"Not anymore," he said.

"Not anymore," she repeated, and her voice was slightly breathless. She stood. "I should…get dinner started," she said, her finger moving over that chain again. Their eyes met again, held, before she turned away and then scurried to the kitchen.

He lay back on the pillows, grimacing as his body adjusted and his wounds pulled. But despite his physical aches and all the reasons he had to feel worried and upset, his lips tipped into a small smile. He was *here*, under the same roof with his precious Autumn, and he had no idea how it had happened, but it was real, and it was true. And he found he was thankful he'd put off the final mission. Because although he hadn't been able to save those teachers, he'd been given some time with *her*—however long it lasted—some time in heaven before the lights blinked out.

CHAPTER TWENTY-ONE

Mark opened the door to a smiling delivery girl. "Agent Mark Gallagher?"

"Yes," he said, taking the package she was holding out to him and signing for it on her digital pad. "Thank you," he said, handing her a tip.

"Thanks! Have a great day." She turned, heading back down the hall of the building where his temporary apartment was. It was small and cramped and smelled like new paint and old carpet, but it did the job.

He couldn't wait to get home to his wife and his dog and his house that smelled more like the former than the latter, thank heavens. He couldn't wait to get back to Jak and Harper and little Eddie, the family that had adopted them—or maybe it'd been Mark and Laurie who had adopted Jak, Harper, and Eddie. And now they would soon add a fourth to their little family. Or maybe they'd all collectively gathered each other and become a unit who had all lost and then gained and understood each other in ways others never could.

And he might get his wish in the next day or so, because so far, there had been no break in the case. The news driveled on and on about what had happened at Deercroft Academy, doing more to divide than anything, each "side" using the loss of life to further their own agenda long before the bodies had even been placed in the ground. Screeching and blaming and generally getting nowhere helpful. Typical.

He brought the package to the writing desk near the window that overlooked an alley and pushed his laptop aside. Inside the envelope were a few thumb drives that had the camera footage from all surveillance in the area of Deercroft Academy from the two hours before and after the shooting. He'd already looked through some of it, and the computer forensics team at the NYPD had looked at more than that, but so far, they hadn't come up with anything on the white-haired man or the woman in the coral sweater.

They had, however, found the shooter on video and had been able to track him from one of the subway stations to the school. They'd attempted to map his travel to the subway station as well but had lost him. Of course, they didn't really need to map him considering they had already identified the man and knew where he lived, but Mark would have liked to have had that information anyway, more for his own reasons than anything.

He chose one of the thumb drives based on the time frame—directly after the shooting had occurred—and inserted it into the side of his computer. The drive contained a list of videos, and Mark began going through them again, this time more closely.

He'd gone through half of the footage by noon. Mark rubbed his eyes and got up to make a second pot of coffee in the tiny kitchen. Again, he sat, poring over the images that moved from this angle to that one, disorienting sometimes. Often, he had to pause and figure out where he was looking, only to realize he was looking at the same spot he'd stared at a moment before but this time from a different vantage point. He was almost ready to throw in the towel for the time being and seek out some lunch when he paused, his hand on the mouse, about to click to the next video.

There. He leaned in slightly. A tall head above the crowd, wearing a baseball cap with a few wisps of silvery hair barely showing at the nape of his neck. There for a second and then gone. The man wasn't just tall, he was markedly tall. Just like Ms. Maples's description. Mark clicked back through the videos right before and after. He thought he got a glimpse of the man here and there, but it was as if…as if he was walking down the street in a way that would evade the cameras.

Interesting.

Unfortunately, once the streets that led to the academy became more residential, the cameras all but disappeared. If the man *was* evading city street cameras, he wouldn't have had to once he turned off the main drag.

Mark sat back, considering for a moment, and then he put a different thumb drive in, this time from directly after the shooting.

There again.

Only this time, the very tall man in the ball cap appeared to be walking with a woman.

Mark clicked through a few images, his heart giving a small jump. It had to be.

The woman wasn't wearing a sweater, but…she might have taken it off. The couple were leaning into each other as if they were having an intimate conversation.

Or as if she was supporting him.

He clicked through the rest, this time with more focus and excitement, the feeling that he'd found something that might lead somewhere else boosting his energy.

Unfortunately, that hope crashed when the couple turned a corner onto a street that, as far as he knew, had no available footage.

Damn.

But before they turned, Mark saw the man trip slightly, a small stagger that made the woman stumble too before they both righted themselves and continued on.

"Who are you?" Mark muttered.

He clicked through a few more cameras on different streets, moving through time, but the couple didn't appear on any other footage.

Double damn.

He sat there for a minute, drumming his fingers on the desk. He felt as if he'd just discovered something that had changed the case. He just needed to figure out how to move it forward even more.

The girl. He had more information about what she looked like now. Or...mostly. She had dark, wavy hair that was half clipped back. About five foot five he'd estimate, average weight. It was more than he'd had to work with until right that minute.

It took him about thirty minutes to find the same girl on the footage in the time frame before the shooting. And this time, she was wearing a bulky, coral-colored sweater. He used the videos to follow along behind her, much more easily than he'd followed the tall man in the ball cap. But it appeared...it appeared almost as if she was following that man. He rewound and rewatched until he was almost certain that was what she'd been doing. She *knew* him. But they hadn't arrived together. And whether the man realized he was being followed, Mark couldn't say.

What is this all about?

He picked up the phone and called the district where the detectives working the case were stationed. Mark made his request, and an hour and a half later, another delivery person arrived with a second package.

Mark thanked the young man, tipped him, and shut the door, and despite his tired eyes, he was eager to get started poring through more video.

"Where did you come from?" he murmured to the unknown girl, rewinding through time, going farther outside the radius, tracking her to the moment it appeared that she spotted the tall man, jerked to a halt as though in shock, and then raced across the street and followed his path. *She didn't plan to be at that school. She was only there because of him.*

Back…back…she'd been walking briskly, looking over her shoulder frequently as though she expected to see someone behind her. *Did you think you were being followed?*

All his hackles were raised.

"Come on. Bring me somewhere helpful." *Somewhere that will help me learn your name.*

He paused the video. There she was, exiting a building. He zoomed in. The Department of Social Services?

"Okay, okay, now we might have something." He was talking to himself the way he did when there was a possible break in a case. If Laurie had been there, he'd have looked up to see her smiling at him. She knew his tells.

He used a search engine to find the number to the department and then dialed it and waited on hold. He identified himself to the receptionist, who put him through to someone else and then someone else. It was a big department, and lots of people had been working that day...he got the same hopeless answer once, twice, three times. Finally, the fourth person he was transferred to suggested that he speak to a social worker named Chantelle who was a manager and definitely would have been in the office as she didn't go out on calls.

When the woman named Chantelle answered in a clipped greeting, he once again gave his spiel, with much less enthusiasm than when he'd first given it twenty-five minutes before.

"Hold on, what time?" the social worker asked.

"A few minutes after one."

"Oh. Yes." She sighed. "That would have been Autumn Clancy. I'm not sure what you're calling about, but if it has anything to do with the fact that she stole my files—"

"Hold on, please." His heart drummed. "You said her name is Autumn Clancy?"

"Yeah. She's been a thorn in my side for years. But she's never outright stolen from me. I was surprised, honestly. She's a pest, but she's never been a thief."

"Is Ms. Clancy a client?"

"She was one of my cases for several years. She was put into the system at birth. I took over her case when she was fourteen and placed in a foster home and later adopted."

The system. Faint alarm bells started ringing. Mark Gallagher was very familiar with *the system* and the myriad ways children could be victimized, whether by those inside or out.

"She was an ADHM baby," Chantelle was going on. "And she was raised at a hospital just outside the city."

"ADHM baby," he murmured.

"Mm-hmm. You're familiar with ADHM kids, right?"

"I am." Mark knew as much as the average person did, he supposed. It had been a terrible, tragic time when so many babies were being diagnosed and subsequently passing away from what turned out to be cancer. It was almost too much to watch unfold on the evening news. Of course, the kids affected were children born of addicts, most of whom became wards of the state, so few people who didn't also live that lifestyle knew anyone personally affected. In short, it was not a suburban problem, so if you lived in the suburbs, you were mostly removed, for good or for bad. Good for obvious though perhaps selfish reasons. Bad because those with the most means to help weren't helping as much as they might if they'd been confronted by the very real human cost day after day. At first, people were afraid to touch the ADHM kids, even medical workers. Afraid they were contagious. There was one public service announcement after another, especially when a few of the kids survived. Apparently, Autumn Clancy was one, because the woman he'd followed down the street using dozens of cameras looked to be in her early twenties. Which would exactly coincide with when the first reports of ADHM babies being born had occurred.

He hadn't thought there were very many ADHM survivors left, if any at all.

The system.

Had the tragedy been used to victimize children already suffering?

How is this linked to your case, Autumn Clancy? To the lost? The children he'd been searching for for years who'd been sold into cruel experiments for profit, the "profit" taking any number of diabolical forms. Mark didn't know for sure if there was a link to the program here because there was no way ADHM kids could ever be expected to do the work they sponsored.

Even so, he had a deep feeling there was a connection that he currently couldn't see.

"Ms. Rogers, I very much need to speak with you. Can you meet me now?"

"Now, well—"

"I would greatly appreciate it."

"Sure. If you get here in the next fifteen minutes, I can give you a half hour of my time."

"I'm leaving now."

Mark jumped out of his chair and raced from the building.

Her name. He had her name. *Autumn Clancy.*

CHAPTER TWENTY-TWO

Autumn and Sam ate outside every night that week. They sat at the wooden picnic table on the deck at the back of the house that overlooked the lake. It was a relatively small lake, and only a few cottages dotted the slip of shore. Autumn told him that a man named Stan Burroughs had built the cozy cottage with his own two hands back in the sixties, and when he passed away, it went to his son, who had become a lawyer and moved to New York City. His son put it up for sale, and Bill had bought it after his wife, Allie, died.

She told him about her adoption and all about Bill, and he saw the way her eyes became soft and her lips tipped whenever she talked about him. Although he was overjoyed that she'd found a family to love her, it made him feel lonely too. He felt again like he was sitting on that fence, looking in.

The weather had grown cool. The trees were trying to hold their last remaining leaves, the forest floor a carpet of red and gold. Sam watched as they fluttered and floated to the ground. He thought about the apple trees and how they must be almost bare as well.

Things are always changing, Sam. Life is moving all around us, even when we don't realize it.

Was that what Adam had meant? A leaf got picked up by a slight breeze, dipping and rising and somersaulting through the air. Sam felt that way too lately, his thoughts flipping and sailing, traveling to places his mind had never been. He pictured himself walking down that city street toward the school where he'd learned Amon had an assignment. He pictured Autumn as she caught sight of him and then followed him to the school. Their paths, somehow, had miraculously *converged*. Against all odds and defying every probability. Weeks, maybe even months before, Autumn had planned to be there on that day. Even while Sam was avoiding killing himself, while he was working on that apple farm and sitting on fences alone, life was moving toward that very moment, and he hadn't even realized it. Couldn't have known. *Have faith.*

The same way she'd entered his life so many years ago and then left the journal behind that had kept him sane in more ways than one. It hadn't always seemed like a blessing, truthfully. And just recently, he'd wished for the escape he imagined in madness. But then again, he couldn't have known she'd come *back* into this life, and he'd be grateful he had retained a mostly sound mind. How would he have enjoyed her if he hadn't?

You're a fool. And you'll be worse off when you're parted again.

Yes, well, at least it would be permanent.

He looked over at Autumn, wrapped in a thick sweater, a book in her hand. She read a lot of books. Bill must too, because it was his cottage, and there was a whole shelf of them inside. Sam could tell she was preoccupied though sometimes, because she'd tap her bookmark and look away from the pages, staring unseeingly beyond her novel, a troubled look on her face. If she wasn't here with him, she'd probably be researching or calling or doing who knew what toward finding answers about what he'd shared with her. It made him nervous, and it made him ever conscious of their limited time together. As soon as he was able, he'd have to leave. Then she could research to her heart's content, but she'd never find anything concrete—the program would have covered their every track.

Now though…now, for this waning pause of time, it was just her and him and the dwindling canopy of leaves surrounding the small cottage where they waited things out.

It was a nice evening, and they'd remained outside, sitting and watching the water after they'd eaten the ravioli from a can. Every time she opened one of those cans, she looked apologetic and said things like, "Well, this will have to do," like he might have complained about it.

But Sam didn't care about food. He'd eaten hospital fare most of his life, and then he'd had to eat lots of things worse than that when food was scarce and you ate whatever you could find that was halfway edible during missions.

He was perfectly happy with canned ravioli.

Especially if he could look at her while he ate it.

Sam stretched one arm, opening and closing his fist as he flexed his fingers. He was getting stronger by the hour. He'd dressed his own wounds that morning. He was still walking stiffly and carefully, but he *was* walking. He'd even taken several slow strolls through the woods alone.

He closed his eyes and raised his face to the fading sun and felt the bare brush of warmth upon his skin.

A pen was on the table in front of her, and every few minutes, she'd reach for it without looking up from the page and then underline something in her book. That went on for a while, and though he liked watching her when she was unaware, he found he wanted her attention.

He cleared his throat, but she didn't look up. He'd been busy for the last several days filling in the pages on the pad of white paper. But he liked to work on it while she was sleeping so she wouldn't ask what he was doing. The book she was reading must be riveting. He didn't like that book. Whatever it was.

As the sunset brightened, she brought the book higher to block out its glare. Sam reached out slowly and slid the pen quickly across the table and under his hip.

He waited, and when she reached for it a few minutes later, he watched from his peripheral vision as she lowered her book, a confused frown on her face. She set the book down and then bent, looking under the table. She huffed. "What in the world?" she murmured. "Sam, did you see my pen?"

"Maybe it blew away."

She sat up. "A pen? Blow away? I don't think so. Plus, there's hardly any wind."

"Maybe it walked away."

"Walk—what?" She peered at him more closely, her eyes narrowing.

He liked the feel of her attention focused his way. It was the very best thing that had ever happened to him.

"Sam."

"Autumn."

"Do you have my pen?"

"Can you describe it?"

She paused. "It's, oh, yea high," she said, bringing her hands up and approximating its size. "And yea wide. It's made of plastic, and it contains *ink*."

"What color ink?"

She let out a small laugh that melted into a clearing of her throat. She put her hand out, tapped her foot, and Sam pulled the pen out from under his thigh and handed it over.

"Sneaky," she said, rapping the pen against her wrist. "Huh."

A smile tugged at Sam's mouth. "You had it coming. You *tripped* me once."

"I did, didn't I?" She grinned suddenly. "You fell right on your face."

"I didn't fall on my face. I fell on top of you."

She blinked, her smile melting into memory. "Yes," she said, and her voice sounded breathy. "Yes, I remember."

Their eyes met and held, and there was something there, but Sam didn't know what to call it. He *felt* it though. It had weight. Whatever it was felt crushing in a way nothing ever had. It felt both heavy and like it might float from his grasp if he tried to hold on too tight.

"It was the last time I felt human," he said, pressing his lips together after he said it. He didn't know why he'd admitted such a thing except that it was true, and he'd be leaving soon anyway. He had nothing to give her. He'd only taken—stolen—but it felt like something to tell her she'd made him feel human once. She'd given him hope for the first and the last time in his miserable life.

"You asked me that when you were mostly unconscious," she said. "You asked me to tell you that you're human. Why don't you feel human, Sam? Is it because of the surgeries?"

He shrugged. Maybe it was mostly to do with the metal

under his skin or the fact that he'd been built by doctors, but he felt it more deeply than that sometimes too, and he wasn't sure why. "What do you think makes a person human?" he asked her.

She chewed on the tip of the pen, and the sight of her pink tongue made a spark of arousal light inside him. He let himself enjoy it, just for a moment, before he breathed it away. She was quiet for quite a long time as though she was thinking very hard about how to answer his question. It made him feel important in a way he'd never felt before. Especially because it was *her,* and he knew he would love the words she said even before she said them.

"I think a better question is, what feels true?"

He hadn't expected that answer. He wrinkled his brow, confused. "True?"

"Yes. Because only things that are true satisfy the human soul."

"Truth hurts sometimes," he said. *More often than not from my experience.*

"Yes. But it's better to know, because then you can base your decisions on truth instead of lies. And then you have a chance at peace, because what is untrue feels jarring and abrasive. It doesn't ever quite settle, no matter how hard you try to swallow it down. It keeps you in a constant state of agitation. So you have to search for that which is *true,* because those are the things that make your soul sing. And when your soul sings, you know without a doubt that you're human."

"My soul doesn't sing," he said dejectedly. The only sound he'd ever heard rising inside him had been the howl of a beast.

But she smiled, and it was soft. "Sure it does. Maybe you haven't been listening."

He paused, considering her for a moment. *She* was his truth. His North Star. The only thing he'd ever counted on to lead him to places that felt good and right. And she was even more beautiful—her skin and her soul—than he'd realized. How was that even possible? "Is that why you keep searching? For the truth about your past?" *Even though it hurts? Even though it'd be easier to let it go?*

She looked over at him and paused as though he'd surprised her with the question. "Yes," she said. "Yes, that's exactly why."

"Hello?"

The sound of a man's deep voice startled Sam, and he stood quickly, moving his body in front of Autumn's.

"It's Bill," she said, moving around Sam and heading for the back door that led inside the house. "Come on."

Sam followed warily. Autumn had told him that her adoptive father, Bill, had retrieved the medical supplies for her and brought them to the cottage so she could help Sam. He'd also dropped off a phone, some food, and the clothes Sam was wearing when Sam had been unconscious. He seemed to be helping them, but still, Sam remained cautious. The man obviously cared for Autumn, and it wasn't good for Autumn to be helping Sam. He knew that and wouldn't blame her father if he reported Sam to get his daughter away from him.

Autumn was giving the man a hug as Sam stepped inside, and she quickly let go and stepped back. "Sam, this is Bill. Bill, Sam." She looked sort of nervous but also excited, as though she was showing her father something she wasn't sure he'd approve of but hoped he would.

Bill stepped forward; his forehead creased with worry. He held out his hand.

Sam knew what a handshake was of course. But he didn't think anyone—not one single soul—had ever offered. He reached his hand out and took the other man's in his.

"Sam," Bill said very seriously. "I'm glad to see you looking well."

"Bill," he said. "Thank you for the pants."

Bill gave a short laugh that turned into a cough, but he nodded. "Well, they're not mine. We're not exactly the same size. I picked them up at the... Oh anyway, I'm glad I could help." He glanced at Autumn. "I trust my girl, Sam, but you have to know how dangerous this is for her. The police have to be looking for you."

"What is the news saying?" Sam asked.

"They're saying witnesses described a Good Samaritan who stepped in to help. They say you saved a lot of children." Bill peered at Sam for a moment, assessing. "But they also think you're involved and may have known that man. Some are wondering if you went there together, and you changed your mind while he didn't."

"That's not true," he muttered.

"You might want to consider contacting the authorities and letting them know."

"No," Sam said. "I can't do that." He paused. "Was there a...description put out of me?" If so, someone in the program would put two and two together. How many scarred, six foot six, muscular young men with white hair and tan skin were there in the world?

Bill's gaze moved to Sam's hair as if he was considering the same thing. "No," he said. "Whoever reported your actions apparently didn't get a very good look at you."

Sam frowned, wondering how that was possible. His hat had come off, he remembered that. And he couldn't have hidden his size no matter what he'd done. But maybe the person who saw him had been too traumatized by the scene at large to recall any specifics. A knot of tension loosened inside him. If they didn't have more details on his appearance, then maybe he had a chance of disappearing again without worrying every day of his life that he'd be spotted. Reported. Imprisoned. *Killed*.

And that meant Autumn was probably safe too. There was nothing to connect them. "I'm leaving soon," he murmured. "And then Autumn can get back to her life."

"Well...okay. All right. Where will you go?"

Sam shrugged. He didn't know, but even if he did, it was better that he not tell Autumn or Bill. "What is the news saying about Autumn?"

"Nothing. They reported a woman who may have witnessed the shooting but nothing more than that. No description. Nothing. They don't seem to think *she* was involved, only that she may have seen something that might help investigators."

Sam let out a breath of relief.

"So there's no way for them to have traced Sam here?" Autumn asked.

"I don't think so," Bill answered. "Unless you don't own that red truck and the owner reported it missing."

"I don't own it," Sam told them. "It belongs to the man I was working for."

"Even so," Autumn cut in. "I don't think the truck could be connected to the shooting in any way. It was parked pretty far away."

That was true. Of course, Adam might have reported it stolen, but police would just think the old man was naive for trusting an unknown vagabond with his truck. Others would tell them Adam had a long history of being too trusting.

"What about the shooter?" Autumn asked, her eyes darting quickly to Sam and then away. "Have they identified him?"

"Oh yes. They know who he is. It was obvious he was planning the shooting."

For a moment, Sam wondered who Amon had died as. Who had given his life so they could pin the crime on him? The question made his guts twist.

Bill looked at Autumn. "Have you thought any more about telling Sheriff Monroe about this? He might be able to help—"

"No," she said. "No, I won't put Ralph in that position. And I don't think there's anything he can do. We're still talking things over, but I've been thinking about next steps, and I might have some leads."

"Leads?" Sam asked. "What leads?"

"There was something in my chart. It's about me, not you, but it's something I want to look into."

"Now's not the time to—"

"I know, Bill," Autumn said, laying her hand on his arm. "I will lie low for a while, I promise. There's not much I can do out here anyway. At least until Sam gets well and we're certain no one's looking for either of us. I told the clinic your great-aunt Hortense had a medical emergency and I'm caring for her."

"*Hortense*? Who would ever care for that hateful old witch?"

"*I* would," Autumn said. "Apparently." Autumn looked at Sam. "Will you be okay in here for a few minutes while I talk to Bill outside?"

Sam nodded. He was feeling sore anyway and needed to

lie down and rest. Autumn and Bill headed outside, and as Sam reclined on the bed, he could hear their voices floating to him through the glass. They were speaking low, and he could only make out snippets of what they were saying. He thought Autumn was giving Bill instructions on…visiting people? Her patients?

"She'll tell you to go, but be persistent. She doesn't mean it," he thought he heard her say. And "…encourage him, but if he resists you, lay off or he'll get annoyed and go out of his way to…"

He had no idea what any of that meant except that whatever it was she was instructing Bill to do, it was because she couldn't do it herself. Because of Sam. He also thought Autumn and Bill might be arguing a little, and it made him feel bad that he was causing trouble for her. It was the last thing he wanted.

Sam dozed off for a while, and he woke to the sound of the door closing and Autumn's footsteps as she came inside. "Is everything okay?"

She nodded, looking slightly troubled. "It's a relief to hear that the authorities don't have a description of us," she said, though that worried look remained. "But…the program covered for the shooter, didn't they?"

"Yes," Sam said.

Her shoulders dropped. "They're very powerful," she murmured, obviously considering what a cover-up of that magnitude would take.

"What about Dr. Heathrow, Sam? I keep thinking about him. You sounded…grateful to him for healing you, but he's part of this too. The program. The treatments. He knew about what was happening to us in the woods. He stayed silent about that at the very least."

Sam stared at the wall. Yes, Sam knew that the doctor was caught up in the web of lies and cover-ups too, just like Sam himself was. He knew Dr. Heathrow had done wrong and looked away when he shouldn't have. But he'd also healed Sam and so many others. He'd *fathered* him in the only sense of the word Sam understood. Loyalty rose up in Sam for the only person who'd known who he was and been on his side. Before now anyway. "He was used for his skills by the program too," Sam said woodenly.

She looked away worriedly and chewed on her lip for a moment before her gaze came to rest on him again. "I've decided something, Sam."

"What?"

She raised her chin. "You keep saying you're going to leave when you get better, but I'm not going to let you."

He felt a tug at his mouth. "You're not going to let me?" How would she stop him? Maybe in his current condition, she'd have a slim chance. But once his strength was back, she'd have no way to stop him from leaving. Or doing whatever he wanted to do for that matter.

"No. I'm not going to let you." She sat on the side of the bed and took his hand in both of hers. "We need to team up. You and me. Once it's safe to leave, we need to find answers. I'm asking you. Please stay with me, Sam."

Oh. So that was how she was going to stop him. She was going to look at him with her beautiful dark eyes and ask.

And Sam was completely helpless to deny her request. Completely helpless to deny her anything she wanted. Anything at all.

Autumn didn't belong to him, but Sam belonged to her. He had for a long, long time.

CHAPTER TWENTY-THREE

Morana watched the screen and then glanced at the one next to it, numbers and letters scrolling by that indicated the back-and-forth chatter about Sam. It was somewhat incomplete, but Morana knew the language enough to understand the gist: the program was hunting Sam.

Had Sam not realized that he wore a tracking device under his skin? Perhaps most of them didn't consider it; after all, they'd been trained to be obedient. What reason would they need to be tracked? They posed little to no risk of disappearing, and if captured, they understood well they wouldn't be rescued lest it put the program in jeopardy. Maybe they believed their phones and other devices provided any tracking they might require as it related to communication.

But Morana knew. And she also knew that though they'd known Sam hadn't completed his final mission, they'd allowed him to bide his time on an apple farm, postponing the inevitable. They'd have stepped in and taken over where Sam had failed when they deemed his time was up.

It was difficult for them, she figured, destroying that which they'd spent so much time and money on. In many ways—though obviously not all—Sam was the living embodiment of their vast intelligence and tremendous superiority. Their egos had gotten in the way of their best interests, however, because the pause had given Sam time to commit the cardinal sin of interrupting a mission and potentially exposing the program. To Morana's knowledge, nothing like it had ever happened before.

Not only had Sam interrupted a mission, but he had also gone and gotten himself shot to pieces, apparently damaging his tracking device so that it was ineffective. Lucky, Sam. Only for those of them in the program, luck could only hold out so long.

Her cell phone dinged with a message, and Morana knew what it would say even before she opened it. They wanted her help locating Sam. She typed a quick response and then turned back to the computer. Yes, Sam's luck wouldn't last. It might take her a while, but in this day and age of computers and cameras and backdoor entries into every digital system under the sun, no one could stay hidden for long.

CHAPTER TWENTY-FOUR

Autumn kicked the cottage door closed behind her, her arms full of the chopped logs she'd gathered from the pile near the shed outside. She halted, spotting Sam standing near the table, his hands behind his back. There were two bowls of what appeared to be mac and cheese on the table, steam rising in the air. Autumn smiled, turning to the fireplace and squatting as she set the logs down on the hearth. "You made dinner?" She'd stayed outside longer than it took to collect the firewood, just gazing out at the lake and thinking about their complicated predicament, thoughts that had turned to hopeful daydreams of how this all might turn out well. The first star had appeared in the sky, and she'd closed her eyes and turned her dream into a wish. "Thank you, Sam."

Sam gave what looked like a forced smile, his hands still behind his back.

"Are you okay?" Her gaze went to the mac and cheese. Was he nervous he'd messed up dinner somehow? It was almost foolproof. The three-step directions were right on the box.

Sam brought his hands from behind his back, set down the pad of paper he'd asked for the week before, and stepped away as though it might bite him. As if it was best that he distance himself from it.

Autumn took off her gloves slowly. It appeared that he couldn't look at her, his eyes glued to the table.

"I wanted to thank you," he finally mumbled. His cheeks were flushed. Was he *blushing?* "For taking care of me. For helping. And for staying too. For not leaving me here alone."

"You already thanked me for caring for you," she said with a smile. "And I wouldn't have left you alone." She threw her gloves aside and then shrugged off her oversize sweater and tossed that onto the back of the couch. She took in his nervous expression, and tenderness took hold. What a sweetheart he could be. So uncertain. Looking so hard for acceptance. "But I appreciate a nice dinner. Thank you, Sam," she said again, this time with more meaning as she sat down. "That was very thoughtful of you."

"I would've, ah, made you something…better for dinner, except…"

Oh my gosh, the guy looks utterly lost and completely flustered. She wanted to laugh, and she wanted to hug him.

"Don't be silly. Mac and cheese is my absolute favorite."

He released a breath and took a seat too and then picked up the pad of paper and handed it to her. "I…did this for you. Made it. Copied it." His blush deepened, his cheekbones tinged a deep shade of pink. "For you, to give it back. I shouldn't have taken it. I tried to figure out a way that I could give your journal back to you. Even though it's just…

not as good." He pushed the pad of paper across the table and then withdrew his hand quickly.

Autumn tilted her head, confused as she picked up the pad. She turned back the cover, her heart giving a small gallop. It was her name and her birth date, written in precise all-caps printing.

She brought a hand to the silver necklace at her throat that Bill had given her on the day her adoption had become legal, the one she never took off. Something clogged her throat, and she swallowed around it as she turned the first page, and then another and another, her heart beating ever more swiftly.

"You rewrote my journal," she whispered. She raised her gaze, meeting his. His face was still flushed, eyes wide as he waited for her reaction. It looked like he was holding his breath. Scared. *Oh, he cares so very, very much.* Autumn stood, rounded the table, and wrapped her arms around his neck. "Oh, Sam, thank you. I can't believe you did this." He'd had it memorized. All these years. The entire thing. And she couldn't begin to understand how or why, but he did, and he'd rewritten every single word.

It was a moment before she realized how tense he was and that his breath had turned to small, almost-silent staggered pants. She unwrapped her arms and leaned back slowly. She'd noticed before that he seemed to tense each time she touched him, but she'd thought it was due to his injuries.

Now she realized how averse he was to being touched at all, and her heart pinched.

She brought her hands gently to his golden stubbled cheeks, cupping her hands in their shape, though only brushing his skin. Their eyes met, and there was a world of raw need in his. Autumn remembered what it was like to crave touch, something that was rare when she was younger. She'd become such a tactile person as a result, so it hurt seeing what touch did to Sam. He was an ADHM baby too, motherless just like her. Had he *ever* been held or caressed or simply cared for gently?

"Thank you, Sam," she whispered again. She returned to her chair and sat down across from him once again. "Will you tell me why you memorized it?"

He blinked, looked away, ran a hand over his short hair. "Your words...the way they made me feel. I'd never felt that way before." He paused and met her eyes. "Repeating them made things easier. The surgeries...the pain."

She pulled in a shaky breath. She felt honored and overwhelmed. She gave him another smile, and he smiled back, this one appearing more natural as his broad shoulders lowered.

She kept the journal on the table but used one hand to thumb through it, catching passages, poems, word combinations she'd liked, descriptions, poorly drawn sketches—one of him. Her boy made of moonlight. A smile skittered across her face as she remembered the girl she'd been then. "These were my thoughts during that time," she said. "This was who I was."

He watched her so intently. "What do you mean? Who you were?"

She closed the book and picked up her fork, taking a mouthful of macaroni. "Well, we're different during different phases of our lives, don't you think?"

"How so?"

The question appeared to startle him, maybe trouble him slightly too. She was beginning to understand his facial expressions and body movements. He hadn't told her nearly enough about himself, and she felt strongly he was holding quite a bit back, but even so, she'd begun to *know* him, to understand him, even if his "tells" were subtle, his mannerisms extremely reticent, his personality almost…muted.

He was rough around the edges, introverted, often withdrawn, but there was a world of tenderness that lived inside him too. He protected it, and she understood that he had great reason to do so. Those who had "raised" him had not valued that quality, nor encouraged it. If anything, the opposite was true. So the fact that he'd managed to protect it anyway spoke to his strength of heart and his iron will.

She also knew he didn't see it that way.

He was so deeply complicated, and some part of her wondered if she'd ever *really* know him, even if he allowed her in. Because she sensed that he didn't fully understand himself. His own thoughts. His own feelings. What she did know was that despite his rough exterior, no one who didn't possess a tender soul would have given her the gift he had.

She thought about his question. "Don't you think you were different when you were in the hospital than you are right this minute?"

He took a bite, chewed, looked thoughtful. "I know more now. I've had different experiences."

"Right. And those things change you. They alter your views of the world, of people. Your tastes change and expand."

He looked thoughtful again. "Experiences change your mind, but do they change your soul?"

It felt like something clanged inside her, dull and echoing. "No, but souls don't need changing. All souls are good. The minds are what get warped."

"Maybe. But souls can be ruined too." He said it so matter-of-factly, in a way that made her heart thump hollowly, similar to the way she'd felt when he told her his soul never sang.

"Do you think your soul is ruined, Sam?"

"Sometimes." But his expression told her more. His expression said, *All the time.* He gave her an unpracticed smile. "But this is supposed to be a nice dinner, so let's talk about happier things."

She watched him for a moment, taking in his golden lashes and his full lips, that square jaw, and the matching scars at his temples where metal plates had been embedded under his skin. He'd told her that the doctors had healed him and then been forced to use metals in place of body parts that had been damaged by the pharmaceuticals. But what could have possibly been damaged at his temples? How did medicine ruin ribs? Or knees?

Something was terribly off.

And not just about him. About her own experience too. She sensed something deeply sinister, even beyond being left in the woods so that "trainees" could practice hunting with real prey. *Her.*

But he was right. As many challenges as they faced, they also needed moments of lightness in order to deal with the things weighing them down. She gave him a secretive smile. "There's a box of cake mix in that cabinet," she said, gesturing behind Sam. "We can make dessert too."

He looked surprised. "Cake?"

"Sure. We'll eat the whole thing and make up for all the birthdays we spent in a hospital." She took a bite and swallowed. "When is your birthday, Sam?"

"I don't know."

"They never told you?" They never sang? Never gathered in the lunchroom—not for cake, their systems couldn't handle that, but for applesauce or sugar-free pudding—as they had in her area of Mercy? That seemed very odd. And terribly cruel.

He shook his head, but he didn't seem upset about it, not like her.

"Well then, we'll definitely make that cake," she said.

Sam smiled and nodded, and then they did talk about happier, more mundane topics. A little about the town she'd grown up in, her schooling, the career she loved, and about the apple farm he'd worked on, doing odd jobs for the blind man named Adam. When they were done with dinner, Sam cleared the table as Autumn stoked the fire.

She kneeled in front of it, staring into the flames, enjoying the moment of peace and safety, the sounds of water and dishes clicking behind her. She glanced back at him, and the vision held an absurdity that made her want to giggle. Sam. Doing dishes. The man belonged emblazoned across the pages of a comic book, fighting for peace and equality, not standing in a quaint cottage kitchen doing *dishes*. His back was so broad, his waist so narrow. Her eyes went lower, and a flare of heat arced up her spine. Speaking of things that should be emblazoned across pages of just about anything…

She turned back to the fire before he could catch her ogling his ass.

Very professional, Nurse Clancy.

Except she wasn't only his nurse. Not even close, and she knew it. Their connection, even barring any ass ogling, went far beyond professional.

He cleared his throat behind her, and she startled, a blush

moving up her neck as if he'd caught her thinking about him. *Stop being ridiculous.* She turned.

"I'm going to go take a shower," he said. "I haven't yet today, and I...need one."

"You don't have to explain your reasons for wanting to shower," she teased him.

He seemed confused for a moment but then smiled awkwardly. "Okay. Well." Then he turned stiffly and walked to the bathroom.

To take a shower without hot water. She assumed.

We didn't have hot water in the hospital. I guess I'm just used to it.

She stood and walked back to the table where she sat down and opened the recreated journal again so she could look through it more closely. Reading the words made her feel so emotional, so sad for the girl she'd been. Sick. Confused. Searching for love.

In some ways, she'd been relieved to leave this girl behind. To cast her off. Forget her. Because it had been a hard, lonely time. The girl in the pages of this journal had thought her days were numbered, and she'd lived in a constant state of fear, waiting for another friend to die.

But...

Reading these words, the questions, the phrases, made Autumn remember that she'd been a fighter too, despite all she had going against her, despite the fact that she barely had the energy to walk a flight of steps. She'd fought hard and she'd loved hard, and Autumn felt proud of her younger self for how she'd conducted her limited life even in the midst of sickness and pain and loss. Her eyes filled with tears. Sam had carried that girl in his heart and his mind even when Autumn herself had not.

What a gift he'd given her. She suddenly felt even more overwhelmed than she had when she first realized what he'd done.

The sound of the shower drummed behind the bathroom door.

That sweet, wounded, brave, sensitive man should not shower under frigid water.

It wasn't right.

The injustice couldn't stand.

Autumn closed the journal, and then with a deep intake of breath, she stood, heading toward the bathroom. Heading toward Sam.

CHAPTER TWENTY-FIVE

Mark knocked on the door of the duplex, the shouts and laughter of children playing ringing through the air from the park across the street. Something savory was cooking in one of the units, and the smell wafted to him below.

The door opened a crack, and a tiny face peeked out, a little boy with dark skin and a short-cropped Afro staring curiously up at him.

Mark smiled. "Hi. Is your mom home?"

The little boy shook his head, not offering more.

"Your grandma?" The woman he was there to see was in her fifties, plenty old enough to be a grandma, though from the woman's name, he'd assumed she was Middle Eastern. "Is there an adult here?" Mark finally tried.

The little boy nodded.

"Can I talk to him or her?"

The little boy nodded again and then closed the door. Mark was hopeful the boy was going to get this unknown adult, though he couldn't be sure. A moment later though, the door was pulled open again, and an older woman with dark swept-back hair laced with gray stood there, wearing a similar curious expression to the one the little boy had given him.

"Salma Ibrahim?" he asked, taking his badge from his pocket and holding it up for her. "Agent Mark Gallagher." This was one of the people Autumn Clancy's social worker, Chantelle, had been able to tell him Autumn had been searching for. The woman who, as far as Chantelle knew, Autumn had never found.

She frowned, her eyes on his badge. "Yes," she confirmed. "I'm Salma. Agent? What can I do for you?"

"There's not a problem," he assured her and saw her shoulders drop a fraction. "I just have some questions about a case, if I might take a few minutes of your time?"

"A case..." She glanced behind her, and Mark heard not just one child's voice but several, coming from a room beyond. "Yes, yes, of course. Come in."

She opened the door wider, and Mark stepped inside.

Salma closed the door and gestured to him to follow her. "I run an in-home day care," she said. "Let me just get the children set up with a show." She waved her hand at a sofa in the front room she'd led him to. "Have a seat, and I'll be right back."

Mark sat down, glancing around the room. It was clean and neat, but the furniture was obviously older. It might not be stylish, per se—even if Mark couldn't exactly define *stylish* other than what he'd seen on the covers of the Pottery Barn catalogs his wife received in the mail—but the space felt cozy and welcoming, with neatly folded throw blankets and a whole slew of family photos on a table in front of the window.

Salma came back into the room, apologizing for the wait, though she'd only been gone three or four minutes, and took a seat in the chair across from Mark. "What is this about, Agent…"

"Gallagher," he said. "But please, call me Mark. I'm working on a case, and the name of a woman who may or may not be involved came to light. Autumn Clancy. You would have known her as Autumn Sterling."

Salma brought her hand to her mouth as her eyes widened. "Autumn?" she breathed. "Oh my goodness. She's alive, isn't she?"

"She is. Did you think she was deceased, Ms. Ibrahim?"

"Salma," she murmured, turning her head and staring out the window for a moment. "No, not really." She turned her attention back to Mark. "Autumn was an ADHM baby. She lived at the hospital I worked at, nine years ago now."

"Yes. ADHM babies didn't generally have a good prognosis."

"No," Salma said sadly. "It was all but a death sentence. Thank the good Lord that time is past. How is Autumn?"

"I don't know. I haven't met her." He'd called her place of employment though and found that she had taken a short leave of absence. *Curious timing.* Only he was all but certain that it wasn't curious at all.

"Oh. I see."

"Like I said, her name's come up in the course of an investigation."

"What kind of investigation?"

"I'm afraid I can't disclose the details."

"How did you connect her to me?"

"I talked to the woman who was once her social worker, or at least inherited her case. Autumn was adopted out when she was fourteen. Her social worker told me that among the other reasons Autumn has been contacting her for years is that she was looking for you."

Again, Salma's hand came to her mouth as tears formed. "Oh, oh dear. Oh, sweet Autumn." She closed her eyes, and it appeared she was in pain.

"You knew her well then?"

"Very well. I was her nurse at Mercy Hospital. I'd cared for her since she was a toddler." She paused for a moment, obviously gathering her thoughts. "I was dismissed, and they didn't even give me the opportunity to say goodbye to any of my patients. I've always wondered how that affected them... I've wondered so many things..."

"Can you tell me about the reason for your dismissal?"

Something fiery came into her eyes. "They feared me. So they terminated my employment and made sure I was reported to the board and stripped of my license. They made sure I could never work as a nurse again." The fire was still there in her eyes, but so was an edge of what he could only call grief. She'd obviously mourned the loss of the children she'd cared for and her career. Her calling, perhaps.

"What did they fear, Salma?"

A small child came into the room, scampering to Salma. "Jamal no nice," she declared.

"Jamal wasn't nice to you?" Salma asked, opening her arms wide. "I'll talk to him. Come here, pumpkin."

The little girl hurried into Salma's arms, and she lifted the tiny girl and sat her on her lap. The child had a pacifier around her neck, and she popped it into her mouth, lying back on Salma's chest. Salma stroked the little girl's hair distractedly. Mark had a vision of his own daughter when she was that age. She'd had a pacifier too...they'd had a bear of a time getting her to give it up...

"What they feared," Salma said, picking up the conversation where it'd left off and bringing Mark back into the present, "was that I was going to expose them. And I tried. Believe me. They sent a whole fleet of lawyers to my door to threaten me. Then they accused me of stealing, said I was a liar who was trying to stir up trouble to hide my own crimes. I tried to go public, but no one wanted to stand with me against a hospital administration and a pharmaceutical company. I fought. I really did. But in the end, they won. I had no career, no money, and my reputation was ruined. It took such a toll on my marriage that that ended too." Her mouth set as she looked away. "I started using my maiden name and opened an in-home day care. Thank goodness my friends and neighbors stuck by me for the most part. And I've been taking care of their little ones ever since." She smiled though it appeared sad, her arms tightening around the child in her arms. "I get to love these children, but I didn't help the others."

Mark sat back, looking at the little girl in Salma's lap, eyes half-closed, expression sleepy as she snuggled into the woman. "What did you see? What did you try to expose?"

She took a deep breath, her hand still smoothing the child's bangs off her forehead. "I got a look at Autumn's chart. Not the one we were allowed to see but the one Dr. Heathrow kept. He left it in Autumn's room after one of his visits, and he was back lickety-split for it, but not before I'd opened it and read what it said. I already suspected...like I said, I'd cared for her for a long time."

"Suspected?"

"That she wasn't born with ADHM in her system at all.

I just didn't know that they knew it. I hadn't considered that level of evil. Until I looked at his file."

"I...see." Mark frowned. "So you believe they lied about her medical status? To what end?"

She met his eyes, her hand stilling on the toddler's head. The little girl had surrendered to sleep. "So that they could experiment on her."

Mark's shoulders bunched.

Salma huffed out a small breath, her shoulders going back. "I know it's difficult to believe these types of things happen—"

"You'd be surprised how open I am to the possibility," Mark murmured as he willed his muscles to relax. "Can you tell me more about how you concluded that the hospital was experimenting on her?"

"And others. Not just her, but I didn't get a look at anyone else's file." She chewed at the inside of her mouth for a moment. "Some of them, *most of them*, were legitimately sick. They had tumors so large you could see them right under their skin. But there were others, the lucky ones, they said, who hadn't yet shown signs of the disease. Only... Autumn, she was *healthy*. It was the damn medication that was making her sick."

"At the time, did you think that was what was making her well? Or at least keeping her that way as long as possible?"

"Yes, because that's what they said." She speared him with her intense gaze again. "But she went off the medication, didn't she? And if she's alive, I'm assuming she's well. *Miraculously* cured." The sarcasm in her voice was clear. Before he could ask another question, she went on. "I never told anyone this because I didn't want Autumn to be targeted, but I suppose that's no longer a concern. I was the one who suggested she go off the medication."

"You mean…while she was in the hospital? While she was being treated?"

"*Yes.* I knew it was that damn cocktail Dr. Heathrow brewed in his lab. I knew it was. No ADHM diagnosis was keeping that baby girl sick. It was his medication and *only* his medication. I'm a nurse. Or…I was. But I'm also a mother. And a mother knows when her children are naturally sick… and when they're being poisoned."

Mark's brain was on hyper speed. This was…a lot. And nothing he'd expected. But…damn if it didn't start to make this whole case tie in even more. "Dr. Heathrow," he repeated. "He was the administrator of the hospital?"

"He was the head scientist and lead of the ADHM treatment protocol. He helped manufacture the drug cocktail all ADHM babies were put on at birth. Nasty stuff. Caused awful, debilitating side effects."

Mark remembered something about it. They'd hoped to use it for patients with other kinds of cancer as well, but it hadn't ended up being approved. Although from what he recalled, the drug had been lauded as a great success as far as ADHM kids, a real boon to the poor suffering children who, because of it, had received more years than they would have otherwise gotten. He imagined it'd been a boon to the pharmaceutical company as well. For a time anyway. "So Autumn took your advice and…went off it on her own? Wouldn't that have been discovered?"

"I don't know if she did. Like I said, I just suggested it. And not in so many words. She understood what I was saying though. She was a bright little one." She looked out the window again. "If they did discover it, maybe that's the reason she was suddenly miraculously cured and sent away. She would have been useless to their research study. Not only would she have disrupted it by going off the cocktail, but she'd have far too many questions."

Research study. He knew all about research studies involving innocent children who were completely alone in the world. *Too much.* He needed to speak to Autumn Clancy as soon as possible. He'd been biding his time, getting to know all he could about her in an effort to make sure he wasn't barking up the wrong tree. But now...well, this changed things dramatically.

A smile played on Salma's lips. "She's been looking for me? All this time?"

"Apparently so, yes."

"I had no idea. Like I said, they wouldn't let me contact my patients at the hospital. Then later...I thought maybe they were all gone, and if they were, hearing it definitively would be too hard to bear."

"I understand."

There was a small ruckus of voices and what sounded like toys being dumped from a bin in the back of the house. "Oh dear," Salma said.

"I know you've gotta get back," Mark said, "but is there anything else you can tell me before I go?"

Salma stood slowly, shifting the little girl in her arms. She seemed torn. What had she seen that she'd had to hold back all these years? Mark waited. "I worked second shift, one to nine. I tucked my babies into bed, and I went home. But...I suspected something was going on at night after I left, but what it was, I couldn't say."

"What did you suspect?"

Her gaze flitted away. "I don't know, only that those children sometimes woke up with scratches and bruises on them that couldn't be accounted for. And it seemed to happen on the same night about once a month."

"What could it have been?"

She shifted the child, and the small girl murmured in her sleep. "Honestly, after what I experienced and the lengths they went to shut me up, I wouldn't put anything past them." She sighed, and Mark heard her sorrow in the sound. "There was something else too." She seemed to gather her thoughts. Or perhaps talk herself into saying whatever she was about to say. "Those vivid dreams that they said were a side effect of the medication seemed to be especially prevalent on that one night. And it wasn't *only* scratches and bruises they woke with. On more than one occasion—and always during a full moon—a child I'd thought would live for at least another six months passed overnight."

Mark took that in. "Are you saying the full moon had something to do with their death?" That sounded...mystical. Mark was many things, but a mystic was not one of them. He dealt best with cold, hard facts.

But Salma shook her head. "I don't think the moon had a thing to do with it. But what *did*, I couldn't say."

"Miss Salma!" came a small voice from the back of the house.

Salma turned her head, obviously trying not to wake the girl in her arms when she quietly called back, "Coming!" She walked Mark to the door, and he thanked her for her time. Just before she shut it behind him, she said, "Mark, if you talk to Autumn, please, give her my contact information and tell her I'd love to see her."

"I will."

He jogged down the stairs, inhaling another breath of the delicious food cooking in the apartment above Salma's. *I wouldn't put anything past them.* Salma's words rang in his ears. Mark had thought once that children were off the table when it came to evil deeds for profit, but he'd learned that that was emphatically not the case.

Jak Fairbanks and the fact that he'd been left in the woods as a helpless child and subjected to brutal experiments had been his introduction to the vicious acts men were willing to do to innocents when there was incentive involved.

Oh yes, children weren't only profitable, they were especially so.

CHAPTER TWENTY-SIX

She opened the door quietly, slipping in and taking a deep breath to calm her nerves. *What are you doing, Autumn?* Only she knew very well what she was doing, and though she was anxious, beneath that beat the wings of a long-caged bird who knew it was about to fly.

Somehow, someway, this moment had been building for many years. She'd carried her boy made of moonlight in her heart all this time, the driving force that kept her searching, kept her looking for answers even when they seemed impossible to attain.

And he'd carried her with him as well.

Two virtual strangers who were anything but, living separate lives, each possessing a piece of the other.

She didn't completely comprehend what he'd endured, and she had a feeling he was glossing over the worst of it or maybe even leaving it out. All she knew was that his body was a map of scars, he cringed away from human touch, and he'd been taught to deny himself even the most basic of creature comforts.

Like hot water.

The shower curtain was closed, the bathroom very small, but no steam filled the air. He was standing under a frigid spray because someone had made sure he was used to it. Or worse, *someone* had made him believe the momentary comfort of a hot shower was a luxury he shouldn't allow himself.

He's only ever known discomfort, pain. Maybe even brutality, though I wonder if he'd classify it that way. I wonder if he even realizes the extent to which he's suffered.

If I want him to know gentleness, I'm going to have to teach him.

It was suddenly very clear. He'd saved her once, and she'd saved him right back, but there were more ways for a human being to be saved, and she sensed he needed several.

She shrugged out of the robe she'd put on, goose bumps erupting on her skin, nipples pebbling. In this back room, away from the warmth of the fire, the air was chilly.

She said his name softly, pulling the curtain open slowly, the metal rings grating on the curtain rod.

Sam turned, wiping water from his eyes, rivulets streaming down his skin. *Oh.* Her eyes did a quick sweep of his naked body, her mouth going dry. He had waterproof bandages just over his stitches, but other than those small, covered areas, she could see every glorious inch of him.

Oh, good Lord, he was sublime.

Amazing.

A wounded god. An immortal superhero. Part man, part monster, or so he thought. But what a glorious monster he was.

His brutal beauty was staggering, yet at the same time,

she almost wanted to laugh at the comical sight of such a large man in *such* a small shower.

Still, she was planning on joining him.

"Autumn?"

Those nerves fluttered wildly in her stomach. Nervous. Excited. *Certain*.

She met his eyes, turned the faucet to warm, and then stepped behind him into the stall. It appeared he'd stopped breathing for a moment when a large gust released, his eyes widening as he took the smallest—and only one he could—step back, making room for her. "Autumn."

"Sam."

"What are you doing?"

"Joining you."

"Oh."

"Is that okay?"

The water had heated, steam beginning to swirl around them.

His lips parted—those beautiful soft lips—and though no words emerged, he nodded, blinking. She saw his strong throat move as he swallowed and sensed his nervousness. And his excitement at her nearness.

His expression gave him away, his *body* gave him away, and he sucked in a breath when his erection grazed her hip. She didn't dare look down. If she did, she'd lose all nerve completely.

This was for him. But it was more about making him feel comfortable with her touch, and oh, she hoped it was about helping him realize he deserved pleasure. No matter how small.

"If you think you need to thank me for the journal—"

Her surprised laugh interrupted him. *Oh, Sam*. "No.

I'm grateful for the journal. Moved beyond words. But… no, I'm not in the habit of getting naked to thank anyone for anything."

"Oh." He searched her face. "That's a good…rule of thumb. I'm glad to hear that."

She almost laughed again because he was so damned adorable, and he had no idea whatsoever.

"Turn around," she commanded.

He did—slowly—though he glanced furtively over one wide shoulder like he preferred to keep an eye on her to know what was coming.

She smiled. "I'll tell you before I touch you."

He turned all the way around then, his head dropping forward as he put a palm on the wall. She thought he murmured her name again but if he did, it was a bare whisper above the spray of the water. Numerous scars marred the skin of his back, ones she hadn't yet seen. Muscles upon muscles, sleek yet scarred. He leaned forward, ducking enough to put his head under the stream. A small moan escaped him, and the sound reverberated through Autumn.

"How does that feel?" she asked.

"Good," he answered. "Very good."

"Cold showers are for the birds," she said, and his answering laugh sounded pained. She reached forward and turned the faucet just a hair so that the water was even warmer, just bordering on hot. "I'd like to give you your first hot shower experience in the hope that you never again choose differently." To Autumn, the moment seemed dreamy, almost unreal. In a way, it felt like the forest where she'd once run from him, only minus the fear.

There was none of that here, and she wasn't running from him now. Quite the opposite.

For Sam, however, she sensed that half of him wanted to escape. This shower. This moment. And she'd let him go if he decided it was too much. But she desperately hoped he wouldn't.

"Can I touch you, Sam?"

He made a grunting noise that sounded pained, and she saw his body tense, but again he nodded. Autumn soaped up a washcloth hanging on the bar behind her and brought it to his skin. He let out another soft moan—a sound that was both pleasure and pain—as she ran it over his scarred back. They were more surgical scars, and she wondered what metal had been inserted beneath this skin. It made her want to weep to know not just the depth of pain he'd experienced but the scope. How many years did he spend recovering from one surgery or another? She'd been sick for fourteen years of her life, but she hadn't been sliced into repeatedly. What had he done to survive? In what ways had he disassociated from his own skin? Because he'd have to, right? Tenderness engulfed her as thoroughly as the steam swirling around her limbs and penetrating her pores. She wanted to make things better for him in any way she could.

She cupped her hand and filled it with water and then trickled that over his back, rinsing the soap. "Okay?" she asked softly.

"Yes, okay," he said, the tortured tone receding slightly.

Her lips tipped. She'd take it.

"I'm going to touch your backside now, Sam," she said, and even she could hear the throaty desire in her voice. She found his form, his size, incredibly sexy. And his ass. *Jeez*. She'd thought it was nice clothed. But naked...it was a work of art. If she were a sculptor, she'd have sculpted his ass and taken it everywhere she went.

Which would be very odd and creepy, but she might not care.

She pressed her lips together to stifle her own nervous laughter.

She brought the soapy cloth to the muscled globes. He let out a small gasp, lowering his head farther. He was still hard, she was sure of it, though she couldn't see from where she stood. She imagined it though, and a surge of moisture pooled between her thighs.

"Is that okay?" she asked again.

"Yes," he said. "Yes, please don't…don't stop."

There we go. She felt a sense of deep compassion but also one of victory. He was letting his guard down, and she understood his struggle. She did not take it for granted. She dropped the cloth, using her hands this time to soap up his skin, her fingers feathering over his back, down over that beautiful backside again, and then again, her index finger running along the puckered surgical lines. Whoever had stitched him up hadn't cared that he would scar. No plastic surgeon had tended to these wounds. It was as though he'd been to war and been operated on in some foreign battlefield.

Yet she knew that wasn't the case.

"Dr. Heathrow said anything more than temporary desire was weakness," Sam said, the string of words surprising her.

Dr. Heathrow. She'd only had brief interactions with the man. He preferred to be in his lab. In the building where Sam lived. But to this day, when she thought of Dr. Heathrow, she got a bad taste in her mouth.

"Desire isn't weakness, Sam," she said, leaning forward and kissing his skin. He shuddered, and it ended in a sigh. "Yearning is human. And you're human."

He paused for a moment as she splayed her hands over

his skin, moving up, down, up, down. He seemed to have relaxed, the tension from his muscles drained. He seemed to have become used to her hands on his skin. He was trusting her.

"I still don't know if that's true," he said.

Oh, Sam. It hurt her to know he struggled so profoundly with his own humanity. He'd mentioned it more than once, and it brought her such deep sadness.

"I know it's true, Sam. And I also know that you, as much as anyone, deserve what every human wants: love. You want to be loved, don't you, Sam?"

He was quiet for several minutes as she soaped his shoulders and his arms. She liked that he was obviously thinking while her hands were on him. It meant that he had let down his guard enough not to be hyperfocused on the sensations she was causing. It meant he might actually enjoy it one of these days. "I don't know," he finally said.

"Why don't you know?"

"I don't think there's anything about me that's lovable."

Her hands stilled. Her heart cracked. And though they were both naked, in what felt like a warm, intimate cocoon, the tenderness she felt for this terribly wounded man suddenly eclipsed her desire. "Does that feel true, Sam?" she said, leaning forward and kissing his back.

"I don't know. All I know is that if desire is weakness, then I'm weak. My desire for you goes on and on. It has no end," he finished quietly.

Oh.

She leaned forward and kissed his shoulder. "Sam," she said.

He turned around slowly in the small space, and she gazed upon his unguarded expression. Beautiful. Raw. A gift he'd given her. She raised her fingertips and ran one along his bottom lip. He let out a pained sigh. She wanted so badly for him to kiss her.

"And yet," he said, his voice raspy, "it can't matter. I can't let it. And you don't want me to."

"I don't?"

"You shouldn't."

He reached behind him, turned off the shower, and pulled back the curtain, stepping from the small space that had felt like a sanctuary for a brief moment. He picked up a towel and attempted to wrap it around his waist to the same result as before while also clearly struggling to keep his eyes averted from her body. After a moment, he gave up on the towel and started walking from the bathroom nude.

Despite the situation, she suppressed a smile. She was tempted to feel rejected, but she also had a feeling Sam had rarely, if ever, let anyone as close to him as he had just done, had never allowed his heart to show in his eyes the way he had earlier. So she decided to feel lucky instead.

Autumn stepped from the shower and grabbed a towel.

When Sam got to the door, he turned halfway. "Do you still want to make a cake?"

"Damn straight I do."

She saw the corner of his lip twitch before he walked out of the room.

As she wrapped the towel around her body, she decided to take heart. He'd allowed her to touch him, and he hadn't flinched away. He desired her. Clearly. And he wanted to experience closeness, she could tell he did. He just had no idea how to let another person in, even though desire usually made that part easy.

Nothing was easy about Sam.

But Autumn cared about him.
She desired him too.
And she'd always liked a good challenge.
"Watch out, moonlight boy," she murmured under her breath. *Because my desire for you goes on and on as well.*

CHAPTER TWENTY-SEVEN

Mark opened a search engine, typing Dr. Heathrow's name in the browser window. A list of hits came up, and Mark scrolled, reading one title after the next, opening one article, quickly reading the copy, and then opening another. It only took him about twenty minutes to get a more complete picture of the man who, as Salma had already told him, had worked as the head scientist and lead physician of the ADHM treatment protocol that had started twenty-five years before when the first ADHM babies were born. In article after article, the doctor was lauded for his research on pioneering drug protocols and surgical innovations that had helped ADHM kids live longer lives.

Mark tapped his fingers very lightly on the keyboard as he considered what he'd just read. So the doctor was a scientist *and* a surgeon. He heard Salma Ibrahim's voice in his head: *He helped manufacture the drug cocktail all ADHM babies were put on at birth. Nasty stuff. Caused awful, debilitating side effects.*

Okay, so it seemed Dr. Heathrow had been in charge of all facets of ADHM care. He'd carried out the actual work at Mercy Hospital in New York, but he'd come up with the protocol used at all care facilities nationwide. Dr. Heathrow had invented the drugs used to treat all ADHM kids, and he also outlined and performed the surgical procedures they'd undergone. That was a lot of responsibility given to one man. *Power.* Mark felt a buzz of unease, the old quote from Lord Acton running through his mind: *Absolute power corrupts absolutely.* How many examples of that had he seen in his lifetime, not only in his work but elsewhere? He tapped on the keyboard lightly again. The doctor couldn't have done it completely alone. If he'd helped manufacture the drug cocktail, he'd done it in conjunction with a pharmaceutical company.

Mark opened a second browser page and did some more digging. The information wasn't difficult to find. "Tycor Labs," he muttered, typing in the company name and reading through the available data. He'd heard of the company, of course, as they were a manufacturing giant. He scrolled through the list of their pharmaceutical products, noting the majority of them were cancer treatments. So it made sense, he thought, that they would have manufactured and sold the experimental drug that treated ADHM babies and children riddled with cancerous tumors. The medication had been subsequently taken off the market after it failed to pass long-term safety protocols, but it was still praised for its use with ADHM kids. *Why though?* Mark wondered. If it couldn't pass safety testing, how did they know it'd helped ADHM kids at all?

Perhaps a better question was how would they ever prove whether it did or did not? Most of the ADHM kids were already dead.

To put it bluntly, the ADHM kids had been guinea pigs for the drug that, in the end, had never gone to market because of its adverse side effects. Of course, its experimental use had been justified by the fact that they were dying anyway. The risk-reward ratio was one that favored *trying anything*. Risking anything. Giving them any possible chance. But what if it hadn't really helped them at all? What if it had only made things worse?

What if there were some who knew in fact that it did but considered those children of such little value that they continued to give it to them in the name of their experiment anyway?

I'm a nurse. Or...I was. But I'm also a mother. And a mother knows when her children are naturally sick...and when they're being poisoned.

Salma's words again. And a reminder that it was possible not only were sick children being made *sicker*, but healthy children were being made ill as well.

Mark sat back, rubbing his temples, suddenly feeling ill himself, as though thinking too hard about those phantom children who may have been put in more pain than they already suffered was bringing on a sympathy headache.

He stretched his neck from side to side, intent on getting as full a picture as possible before postulating any further.

Mark went back to the page of articles featuring Dr. Heathrow's work with ADHM kids, scrolling down the page and then clicking on to the second. More articles about ADHM...interviews...a dinner where Dr. Heathrow had been the guest of honor and recipient of a humanitarian award. Mark paused in his scrolling, something of interest catching his eye. He clicked on it and read the first couple of paragraphs. His stomach dipped, that feeling of disquiet he'd had moments before ratcheting up. It seemed in his early career, before ADHM or drug protocols, or Tycor Lab, Dr. Heathrow had authored several studies on human augmentation.

Mark performed another search, clicking until he came to a PDF file. "Bingo," he said, opening the document authored by the doctor himself.

He leaned toward the screen, reading through it quickly, just enough to digest the gist. He'd print it out and read through it more closely later. The paper went into proposed methods of adapting technology and materials only previously used in bone fusion and limb amputation to revolutionize and drastically enhance human performance.

Why did Mark have the feeling many of these buzz phrases that read like scientific marvels stood for ideas that were decidedly much darker?

There were diagrams of limbs, torsos, and other body parts that Mark only briefly examined. It was all out of his area of expertise, but he got the idea. In essence, the doctor had proposed ways to make super soldiers.

"Jesus," Mark breathed. This was not a coincidence. Mark could feel it.

He scrolled to the end of the paper and then went back through it, looking for the part that discussed ethical concerns with such technology, but no discussion existed. Sadly, he wasn't surprised. Angry, yes. Surprised, no.

Mark spent another twenty minutes looking for more information on Dr. Heathrow's continuation of research into enhanced human performance, otherwise known as genetic engineering. The man had attempted to obtain grants but was unsuccessful. After that, Mark could find no further proof that he'd pursued the field. Evidently his interest in that area of study had diminished and he'd turned to other endeavors.

Or had he?

Had he given up on engineering humans because of a lack of financial backers? Or had he figured out another way? Or perhaps been approached by others who'd expanded his funding options? And more chilling, expanded his potential client base: sick children with no parental oversight.

The deep chill that snaked down Mark's back had nothing to do with the wind that suddenly gusted in the window, lifting the curtain next to his chair and then dropping it back into place.

CHAPTER TWENTY-EIGHT

Another week passed by, and the weather grew cooler. Sam continued to heal. Autumn was encouraged by the fact that he continually scratched at his stitches. "Tap them," she reminded him. "I don't want you to tear them open. But if they're itching, it means they're healing well."

"Yes, I know," he answered.

She studied him as he closed his eyes, laying his head back. Yes, of course he knew. He had likely healed more times than almost any other human.

Autumn passed the time by reading and by adding to the back of the journal Sam had made her—lists of avenues she wanted to go down as far as researching the program Sam had told her about, including Dr. Heathrow himself. Sam seemed both protective of the man and troubled when she brought him up, quick to move the conversation to other places. She could understand why, she supposed. The doctor had healed Sam, but he'd also hurt him. And others too. There was a cloud of mystery surrounding the man, and whenever Autumn recalled him, a shiver of disquiet scurried down her spine.

Bill stopped by and brought more groceries, asking her covertly how everything was going, the look in his eyes telling her he continued to worry. She smiled and reassured him that they were both doing well and keeping themselves occupied. But she only had another week and a half off work. She needed to decide what to do, not only with herself but with Sam.

She quizzed Bill about what was going on in the outside world as related to the crime they'd been involved in. Bill told her that the news reports were dying down, which simultaneously caused her relief and made a knot form in her stomach. No one should ever stop talking about those little kids who were targeted and suffered injuries, a few physical but all of them emotional. Not ever.

There would be people who didn't though, even if the world moved on. Their families, their friends...the community. It was their collective job now to love and comfort those children as well as they were able.

However, to know that even the mention of a mysterious "Good Samaritan" was no longer front and center in Americans' minds would soon begin to open up their options.

Ever since Sam's first hot shower, tension had been swirling in the air like the steam that had enveloped their naked bodies. They watched each other now, lingering looks and furtive glances. Autumn's breath would catch and her heart would stall when she looked up and caught him staring at her, a primal look on his face that Sam quickly blinked away. His expression was often first surprised, then remorseful, melting into dejection as if he was busy disciplining himself for whatever he'd been thinking.

He'd lived a strict life of discipline, Autumn knew. Of denying himself. But oh, she wanted to *know* what brought on that heated look, the one that made his eyes grow lazy and fierce all at once.

She desperately wanted him to kiss her. Truthfully, she'd been waiting since she was fourteen years old.

But she was pretty darn certain that he was not going to make the first move. She'd given him the opportunity.

If you want this, you're going to have to take charge, plain and simple. Sam is not a man who will sweep you off your feet.

Yet in his own way, he'd done exactly that.

Autumn had once struggled with her own physical identity. As someone who had been sick for so many years, she was extremely careful with her body, and it'd taken her quite some time to feel comfortable in her skin. She'd had one serious boyfriend in high school, but they'd run their course once graduation came along and he'd gone to college in another state. She'd realized then that he'd been more of a friend than anything and that she hadn't felt *passion* for him so much as that he made her feel *safe*. Which, at the time, she supposed, was what she'd needed.

Sam didn't make her feel safe. In some ways, just the opposite. But Autumn finally knew what the scalding wash of passion felt like whooshing through her veins and muddling her mind.

And he hadn't even *kissed* her yet.

So okay then, she'd be brave. She'd help him remember that he was too. And that she was worth the risk.

They walked together, she read as he rested, and they both cooked meals and gathered firewood. In some ways, the complication—the size and scope and overarching ramifications—of their situation melted into sweet simplicity in that small cottage by the lake. Yet Autumn was all too aware that it could not last.

One night after dinner, Autumn asked, "What do you say to bundling up and taking a walk? Do you feel up to it?"

"Sure."

"Okay, great."

They finished their meal, and then Autumn put her sweater and gloves back on, also grabbing a beanie this time. She tossed Sam a zip-up sweatshirt lined in fleece from the closet, and then they stepped out into the clear, chilly evening as the sun began to dip below the water.

She led him to the path that meandered between the trees at the edge of the lake, just wide enough for two, and Autumn found that she felt strangely shy walking so close to him like this, the plumes of their breath meeting in the air in front of them. "I made a wish out here last week," she told him.

He glanced down at her. He was so tall, so masculine, and she could feel the heat of his body even though they weren't touching. "What did you wish?"

"For answers," she said.

He looked away as they walked, out to the water, golden and rippling under the lowering sun.

"But also," she went on, "for you to heal." *In every way.*

"I'm already almost healed."

"I'm not totally convinced of that," she said, giving him a sidelong look. "But I know a way to test it."

He frowned. "How?"

"If you can catch me! Don't trip this time!" she called as she took off running.

She heard an incredulous laugh behind her and ducked between two trees, not running very fast, not really trying to get away from him at all. His stitches were healed nicely, and she didn't fear that he'd tear them, but she wasn't going to risk it.

She could hear Sam behind her, and something about being pursued by him made excitement thrum through her veins. How very different from how their story began. Only then, she'd thought it was a bad dream. *Then*, she hadn't known who was in pursuit. She laughed out loud as he caught up to her, his staggered breath and the crunch of his heavy footsteps directly at her back. He touched her and she laughed again, tripping over a root and pitching forward. Sam reached out and caught her around the waist, steadying her, but she went to her knees in a bed of pine needles and then rolled to her back, laughing up at the canopy of trees above. Sam dropped down beside her, rolling to his back as well.

For a moment, they lay there as they both caught their breath, the last rays of sun filtering through the dimming woods. *Beautiful. Peaceful.*

"You're healed," she declared.

He let out an agreeable grunt. "I know."

He'd said he would leave when he was healed, and Autumn had asked him to stay. He'd given her a half-hearted yes, but she was afraid that he wouldn't honor it. And in all honesty, she didn't exactly know what to do with him once they left this temporary home. Would she take him to her small house? Leave him there while she went to work every day? It was all so up in the air, and it made her feel slightly desperate and very unsure. Because although she had no plan, her heart—her heart didn't want to let him go. And in many ways, she knew even trying would be an impossibility.

Autumn turned, going up on one elbow and gazing at

Sam, her eyes moving to those soft, soft lips of his. They'd been this close once before, their faces nearly touching. And even though she knew now it'd been reality, sometimes that long-ago moment still felt like a dream. "You almost kissed me once," she murmured.

He turned his head, his expression surprised as their gazes met.

"In the woods, when I tripped you," she said, as though he might not remember. And maybe he didn't. But she had a feeling he did. "Do you ever think about what it would have been like?"

"All the time," he answered. "Every day of my life."

Oh. Sometimes he could be so incredibly *honest* that it stole her breath. She hadn't expected that, and it made her pulse jump, her heart pick up speed, her blood moving more swiftly through her veins than when she'd been running.

Autumn reached out and laid her hand over his heart and felt the strong pulse under her palm. He was growing used to her touch now, and he no longer flinched. But that was all brand new, and she couldn't help wonder… "Have you ever been with a woman, Sam?"

He turned his face away from her, looking back to the gap between the trees where the sky had turned dusty rose.

Part of her didn't want that answer as she didn't want to picture Sam with any other woman. She was also surprised by the fleeting wish that she hadn't been with anyone and that Sam might be her first. But either way, she knew it would be good to verbalize this between them. "Have you had relationships?"

"No, but I know pleasure," he said in answer. But the bleak look on his face told her differently. Of course he knew the mechanics like nearly every other adult human and brief, blissful relief. But judging by his expression, it was one that quickly melted into melancholy, a dissatisfaction he might not be aware of or know how to explain. That wasn't true pleasure.

"It's different when someone else gives it to you," she said. From what she now understood, he'd only ever known another's touch to bring pain and anguish. He didn't know how to let his guard down. And what she wanted was suddenly as clear as day to her. She wanted to teach him. She'd teach him what gentleness felt like but also sexual pleasure. She understood what it was like to believe that bodies were mostly made for misery, for your bones to feel like prison bars. She'd been released from that terrible hell, and her heart's desire was to break him free too.

Why?

Why do you want that?

Was it selfish? Partly. There was the undeniable fact that she was attracted to him and also that it would bring her joy to see him happy. But there was a selfless element involved too, because she sensed that freeing him from one cage might mean he left her, even though she'd asked him to stay. And that would bring her pain. Yet even still, she wanted to see him learn to receive.

She leaned over and kissed him lightly on his cheek, feathering her lips along his jaw. Then she leaned back, watching him. He'd tensed, but his breath had picked up, his chest rising and falling more quickly. "Was that okay?"

"Yes," he said, his voice cracking on the one word.

Her heart sped and her breath grew short. The tense set of his jaw, the way she could feel his heartbeat pumping along with hers. The masculine scent of him. They all served to make her feel both woozy and alive. "Can I do it again?"

"Yes." Almost a sigh.

So Autumn leaned over, and this time, Sam turned his head so that he was facing her. Their lips met, so very gently, eyes still open. When she pulled back slowly, she said, "I think you're beautiful, Sam." She lifted her hand and ran a finger over his cheekbone and then used her thumb to smooth his brow. He looked at her as though she'd just spoken a different language, using words he didn't understand. "And I want you to trust me enough to touch you... everywhere. Will you try?"

His lips parted, eyelids lowering, and he nodded, and this time, it was Sam who leaned in for a kiss.

Their lips brushed and then held, and Autumn waited a moment before she used her tongue to run along the seam of his mouth, his lips parting on a small gasp of breath. His tongue met hers so very tentatively, a moan that sounded like pain vibrating from his chest. But he didn't pull away, and after a moment, his tongue ventured deeper, finally, *finally* dancing and twisting more fully with hers.

With a guttural groan, he turned his body and pressed closer, their kiss catching fire as he tilted his mouth and took control. A thrill raced through her, electrifying her nerve endings.

She could feel that he was hard, his sizable erection pressing against her thigh. She wanted to let her hand wander. She wanted to wrap her fist around him and hear him groan. She wanted to part her legs and bring his hardness to the place between her thighs tingling with need.

Her pebbled nipples brushed against his chest, and she barely withheld a groan, their tongues still twisting, Sam licking into her mouth with ever mounting intensity. He tasted so good. Those lips were just as soft as she'd known they would be. She imagined what it would feel like to have that unpracticed mouth on her body, to feel him press down on her from above, to fill her. Would it hurt at first as he stretched her? God, she didn't care. She was so wet and needy, practically on the verge of orgasm from his kiss alone, yet even so, she took care to go as slow as he obviously needed to go. To let him set the pace.

It was torturous bliss. It was the sweetest moment of her life.

No hands. Just mouths. Just breath and this tortured man's surrender. To her.

She felt powerful and scared. Invincible and as though she held the most precious of treasures in her shaky, undeserving hands.

Please don't let me drop it.

She knew what this kiss meant to him. He'd laid down his armor at her feet. He'd taken his beating heart from his chest and placed it before her.

And she would treat it with the reverence it deserved. *Sam. My Sam.*

"Sweet," he said breathlessly when their mouths parted and they came up for air. His lips brushed the side of her mouth. "You taste so sweet."

"So do you," she whispered, finally bringing one hand up and running it over his short hair. It'd grown out since they'd first arrived at the cottage, but it was still little more than a choppy buzz cut. It was another part of him that was such a strange mystery. She'd wanted to ask him about his coloring, but she sensed that he was insecure about the way he looked, and now was definitely not the time to make him feel unsure about himself. Like her, she doubted he'd know much of his parentage. His family history. How often had she mourned not knowing where she came from and who her people might have been? Now was not the time for mourning.

"When I said earlier that I'd thought about the moment we almost kissed," he said, his gaze searching hers, "I didn't tell you that, some years, it's the moment that kept me breathing. The one true, good thing that happened in my life."

"Oh, Sam," she said, leaning her forehead against his. She didn't know what else to say. What miseries had he experienced that the one happy moment he brought forth had happened almost a decade before? And again, she felt deeply honored. Humbled and undeserving.

But none of that was the reason excitement shimmered through her system. That was simple chemistry, and it could be neither manufactured nor destroyed. She found this hulking, complex, distinct sweetheart of a savior extremely attractive, and that was that.

She leaned forward and kissed him again, tasting his lips and his tongue and then whispering against his mouth, "Let's make better memories than that one. A whole slew of them. Life is unpredictable and sometimes shorter than we realize. And I don't think either of us, *especially us*, should waste a moment of it."

"You've already given me a whole slew of them," he said. "Just being here with you is enough to last me a lifetime."

But she didn't think he knew the half of it, not really, so she sat up, came to her feet, and reached her hand out for his. He looked at it for a beat, then two, and finally grasped it and stood. She tipped her head back, and they stared at each other for a moment in the last light creeping through the trees. There was an understanding in that look. And a promise of what was about to happen between them.

Sam took her hand in his, and they began walking back home.

CHAPTER TWENTY-NINE

The cottage felt like a completely different place than it'd been when he'd very first woken up in it, when he'd thought he'd lost all sanity and wanted to stay in the haze of madness because that was where she was. The furniture was the same. The walls were still made of logs. The same pictures remained on the walls, and the bed still held the same blankets he'd slept under the night before.

But everything was different. Because *he* was different. And now it wasn't simply a cottage. It was the place where Autumn had healed him, where she'd pressed her naked skin against his as steam had filled the air, and when he looked out the window, he could see the woods where she'd kissed him and he'd kissed her back.

He could die now, he realized. He could die happy.

Yet now, more than ever, he didn't want to die at all.

He wanted to live. And breathe. And look at her and talk to her and kiss her again and again and again.

But he was scared too. He was scared because he'd never

allowed himself to be with a woman. Not because he didn't crave it; he did. But because he'd been trained and conditioned to hurt, to conquer, to make women scream and beg and cry.

He'd been taught that sex was about dominance and that men like him should take, whether it was offered or not. They'd given him drugs and then sat him before a screen where he'd watched movie after movie. Reality and fantasy had melded together. He'd become desensitized to the screams and the blood. He was built to be a monster, and that was what he'd become.

Sometimes those visions still came to mind. So he gave himself pleasure when he had the need, and he didn't allow the possibility that he'd lose control and even come close to making a woman plead for mercy.

But now Autumn was standing by the bed, looking at him with both heat and expectation in her eyes. He was amazed, the same way he'd been all week, every time he thought of how she'd touched his wet skin under the warm swirling steam. But he was scared. He wanted her so desperately he was shaking with it, but he was afraid he'd hurt her, and that mattered more to him than satisfying his raging lust.

She held out her hand and he went to her, unable to resist. He couldn't figure out how he'd arrived in this place. Not this house but with her, looking at him with desire, wanting him. "Is this a dream?" he asked.

She laughed softly. She was so beautiful. The woman standing before him was poetry itself, as though that journal had birthed her and not the other way around. He smiled because of his rambling thoughts, the way his brain was tripping all over itself.

"No," she answered. "Not a dream." She stepped back

slightly and pulled her shirt off and then unbuttoned her jeans and pushed them to the floor. "I want to touch you in a way that clears the shadows that appear when I've touched you before today. I want you to feel pleasure that lingers, that makes you feel like the man you are. Will you let me?"

Sam's mouth was dry, but he managed a nod. He reached out and took her hand. He could hardly bear to look at her. He wanted her. He yearned for her touch. But still his fear remained. "Autumn," he gasped. "I need for you to tie me up."

She ceased moving completely, confusion coming over her face. "Tie you up?" She looked stricken. "I told you I'd never do that."

"This is different."

"Sam, I trust you."

"I don't trust me, Autumn. Please. Please. I beg you."

She searched his eyes for several seconds, and he didn't blink. He needed this. Not just for her but for himself. He had never let anyone other than his doctors touch his body, and at the end, he hadn't even allowed that. They simply hadn't cared. They'd defeated him with straps and needles, and he'd woken confused and in agony. Alone. He didn't know what he might do if he lost control, but she wanted this, and he did too. She'd *awakened* something in him when she'd willingly touched his naked skin, so he was willing to try.

But only with safeguards.

"Tie me up," he repeated. It was hard to say the words. He'd been tied up before, and it'd led to terrible things.

This is different.

Trust her.

Yes, he did. He trusted no one else, not a single soul in

the whole wide world. But he trusted her because he knew her heart. It was etched upon his skin, unseen but as real as the scars he wore.

Autumn gave a small nod, so small that if he'd blinked, he would have missed it. She walked into the bedroom, and his hungry eyes watched her as she moved, her bare hips swaying, as his body shook with need.

When she emerged, she had something in her hands. *Socks. They're long knee socks.* Those would work as well as anything. His heart jumped, from both trepidation and lust. He was vibrating with desire. But he knew the bonds were necessary. He was a monster, and monsters were unpredictable, especially when need was pumping through their veins.

"First," Autumn said softly, "I'm going to undress you."

He supposed that was necessary. He couldn't speak. It was almost too much for him. *Her. This.*

Autumn's cheeks were flushed, her eyes shining with some unnamed emotion, but her hands were steady as she unbuttoned his shirt, spreading it open and then laying her palms on his pecs. She leaned her head back, her lips slightly parted, her delicate throat moving as she swallowed. "Everything about you is so beautiful, Sam," she said.

A sound vibrated in his throat. Sam had heard himself make all sorts of noises before, some automatic, unbidden, but he'd never heard himself make a sound like that.

She trailed her finger down the scar that ran from his throat to his navel. He'd received that one when he was very young. He didn't even remember what it'd been from. And he didn't care. He'd always hated his scars, hated what they represented. But he was suddenly grateful that particular scar was especially long and gave Autumn something to run her finger over for several breathless moments. He'd never look at it the same again. Autumn leaned forward and grazed her lips lightly over the puckered skin, and he shuddered, his breath emerging in staggered pants. "Autumn," he breathed. *An urgent plea. A desperate prayer.*

She leaned away, pushing his shirt over his shoulders and letting it drop to the floor. For a moment, she simply gazed at him, her eyes roaming over his shoulders, his chest, and down to his navel. He felt the way he did when she'd first stared at him after the shower when his towel had fallen. He buzzed with electricity, with *life*, with some magic he couldn't define but knew was in her and somehow was leaving its traces on him as well. She hooked her thumbs in the waistband of his sweatpants and brought them down his hips and over his straining erection, and those too dropped to the floor. He stepped out of them and kicked them aside.

She stared at his manhood, and impossibly, he swelled larger, throbbing with what was both pleasure and pain. Autumn swallowed again and let out a small nervous laugh. "I'm skeptical this is going to fit," she said.

Fit. She meant to put him inside her. *Oh God.*

"Tie me up now," he grated, lying down on the bed and lifting his hands to the wooden bedposts. "Make them tight."

She straddled him, leaning forward and tying his wrists one by one.

"My feet too," he said.

She met his eyes. "Sam—"

"Please," he begged.

She paused but then got off the bed, walking to the footboard and tying each ankle in turn. She looked at his feet for a moment, tracing the scars at his ankles, her pretty lips dipping into a frown momentarily. She returned to the bedside and then climbed up and straddled him once again.

She grazed his erection, and he hissed, a zap of bliss causing him to arch his back, his body seeking more. He felt an urgency to take and pound and possess, and even while he instinctively tugged at his bindings, he was simultaneously grateful she'd tied them tight.

Autumn leaned forward, feathering her open mouth over his, using her tongue to trace his lips. He groaned, his hips coming off the bed, seeking. "Madagascar," he sighed. He couldn't think. He only had his senses. And she tasted like her scent. Vanilla beans. Flowers. Sunrises. Snowfalls. All things sweet and clean and wonderful. Moments he'd been in so briefly and never wanted to leave.

He wanted to weep with the beauty of her, the intensity of this moment, unlike anything he'd ever experienced or ever thought he would. Even in his wildest dreams.

Autumn smiled against his skin, moving lower, licking slowly around his nipple as his nerves lit on fire and burned like a thousand sticks of dynamite, flaring toward some unknown end, not just a climax of his body but of his heart. *Sparking. Buzzing.* She kissed over his scars, rubbing her lips and her tongue and her hair over his skin, causing him to groan and writhe and beg, words and phrases spilling from his lips between harsh pants of breath. He couldn't even hear himself over the blood whooshing in his ears and rushing through his body.

A strangled gasp burst from him when she wrapped her hand around his cock, sliding down slowly and then coming back up. She was right, it was different when someone else gave you pleasure. He wanted to laugh—with joy, with disbelief, with wonder—but he didn't think he was capable.

"Sam," she whispered, "you're very large, and I think it's best if I..." And then the heat of her body was gone as she got up, and he made a strangled sound of dismay, lifting his head as a smile played on her lips.

She removed her underwear and tossed it aside, and then she unhooked her bra and let it slide to the floor. She stood before him, naked, and this time, he let himself look. *Beautiful. Perfect.* Every inch of her. Her round breasts. Her small brown nipples, hard and tight. Her slim waist and beautifully round hips. And the short patch of dark hair at the apex of her thighs.

Images invaded his mind. Pumping hips and monstrous growls of possession. He swallowed, gasped, shut it out. He was tied down, tamed, and she was in charge. Not him.

Trust.

She climbed back up and swung her leg over his hips. "I think it's best if I come," she said, reaching between her thighs and using a finger to outline her lips.

He groaned. He couldn't watch or he'd come too, and then it'd be over, and he wouldn't let that happen. *Not yet.*

But he also *had* to watch. He couldn't look away. So he gritted his teeth and watched as her finger moved on her body.

She was causing his cock to bounce on his stomach, and even that slight contact was sweet torture.

"I'm pretending this is your hand, Sam. I want this to be you touching me. Promise me it will be soon." Her mouth parted as she arched her back, her nipples puckering tightly.

He grunted, his vision going hazy as he stared at her ever-quickening movements. He was so tense his muscles ached, and his veins protruded from his skin, rushing hotly with blood. He memorized the way she moved her finger as she brought herself pleasure and wrote another page to her journal, storing that too inside himself with all her beautiful words and pieces of poetry. It was colored with the secret hues of her body and the private sounds bursting from her lips. It was another part of her he never expected to receive, and he would cherish it just as he did with every other precious part of this woman.

Her soft skin was glistening, and Sam was sweating too, desperate with need and a hundred other feelings he'd never had before. She gasped. "I'm so close, Sam," she said. "It won't take long, and then...oh," she moaned. Her head went back as her movements quickened, and less than a minute later, she tensed, crying out, shuddering as Sam held himself as still as possible and willed himself not to join her. He was a master at denying himself, yet he'd never come closer to failing.

Her head fell forward, and for a moment, she simply breathed before raising her face to his and kissing him. This kiss was as slow as the one in the forest but even deeper, and again his hips began to circle, to reach. Every inch of him was electrified, including his mind, his heart.

"Are you okay?" she asked when they came up for air.

"No," he said honestly, and despite the answer, whatever was on his face made her smile.

"Ready?" she asked, and he sensed she was asking herself as much as him.

"Yes," he answered. *No. This might leave the worst scar of all.* Yet he'd beg her if she stopped.

She took him in her hand and brought the head of him to her opening, meeting his eyes as she began lowering herself. *Oh, dear God. Oh.* He never imagined pleasure like this. Never. She was so hot and soft and wet, and his body shuddered yet again at the way her body enveloped the tip of him. She adjusted herself just a little, blinking, focusing as she lowered herself just a bit more. She was right, he was large, and she was not, and though he shook and struggled not to plunge up into her, he was worried he'd lose the battle.

"Autumn," he panted, and whatever she heard in his voice made her press down harder, a small cry falling from her lips until he was all the way in.

Oh God oh God oh God.

She released a breath, and he felt her body relax. Her lips tipped in a smile as she closed her eyes and began to move. "Mmm," she moaned. "God, you feel good. We don't seem to fit, but we do, don't we, Sam? Perfectly."

"Autumn," he said again. It was the only word he was capable of. The only word ever created. The only one that mattered in all the world.

"Hold on, just a minute," she said. "I want to feel you. I want to…oh." She moved more quickly, back, forth, back, forth, until he couldn't hold out any longer. He lifted his hips, and with one upward plunge, he came with a roar, spilling into her, the pleasure so dizzyingly powerful, he swore he lost consciousness for a minute. The bliss exploded and then sizzled through his veins, like the dying sparkles of those fireworks, dripping and cascading its last glittery light into every corner of his broken body.

Only in that moment, he didn't feel broken.

He didn't feel scarred or ruined.

He felt *alive*. He felt powerful, but not in any way he'd ever experienced power before. He wasn't even sure that was the right word, but he didn't have another.

Her hair was tickling his shoulder, the slight weight of her body covering his own. He wanted to hold her. He wanted to run his hands along her spine, to feel each bump and curve of her perfect creation. But he was still shaking, still coming down from the wild cascade of feelings and emotions, and he still didn't quite trust himself.

Autumn sighed, holding him instead but gently, as though she knew he couldn't take much more than that. He'd just experienced sensory overload on a scale he never had before. And though it'd been the most amazing experience of his life, he needed to process, to come down off the high, to relive it again and again, but only in his mind.

For now.

The pleasure he'd just experienced had rearranged him.

Maybe she'd be willing to do this again. But even if she wasn't, he could live in the memory of this moment for the remainder of his days, even if only a handful existed.

Autumn remained still, seeming to know he needed it. Her. His angel. Her breath ghosted over his skin as she whispered, "I made a boy of moonlight." She paused, kissing his cheek lightly, so lightly. "And he turned me into the burning sun."

CHAPTER THIRTY

The sun crested the lake, the molten water sparkling gold. The world was once again coming alive.

Autumn brought the coffee cup to her lips, taking a small sip of the hot liquid and adjusting the blanket around her shoulders. She heard the soft pad of feet and glanced over her shoulder to see Sam, white hair mussed, eyes sleepy.

She felt a small zing in her belly at the sight of him, at the memory of what they'd done the night before. It had been…well, frankly, it'd been *hot*. And amazing.

Things were already complicated. And she hadn't figured out exactly how the night before changed things, but it certainly had. She'd gotten up with the sunrise to think about that, but each time she pondered it, all she wanted to do was relive it all over again.

So yeah, no insight had been gained.

"Good morning," he said, his gritty voice rolling over her nerve endings and causing them to tingle.

"Good morning."

He took a seat beside her, and she offered him some blanket. He took it, scooting in next to her so that half went over his shoulder, and half went over hers. She took another sip of her coffee. She'd noticed he didn't drink coffee either and thought about whether she should try to introduce it to him like she'd done with hot showers and decided that she didn't want him to feel like she was trying to take control of every aspect of his life. If he wanted coffee, he could ask for some.

"There's a heart on that squirrel's fur," he noted.

She followed his gaze to where a squirrel sat busily gnawing on a nut, one eye trained on them. It had darker markings near its hip, and Autumn could see that those markings were indeed in the shape of a heart. She watched the squirrel for a moment as it watched them. She glanced at Sam, taking in his now-familiar profile. She wondered how a man who had endured a lifetime of lessons in brutality would notice a heart on the side of a squirrel. She wondered at how a sensitivity like that hadn't broken him.

"Once," he said, still watching as the squirrel scampered up a pine tree and disappeared into its branches, "I went into a tiny bookshop in Bangalore."

She watched him, curious and mesmerized, wondering where he was going and why he'd thought of it. She stayed still, as though to make a movement might snap him from his sleepy reverie. And because she sensed that he was allowing her a peek into the heart of him, she waited with bated breath for him to continue.

"It smelled like tea and old paper," he said, drawing in a breath as though he could smell it still. "I sat in the back, and I looked at the pictures in this book about how to cut paper into art using a scalpel and removing so much of it that when you held it up, you could see right through it." He nodded to the place where the squirrel was rustling the tree branches. "Squirrels...flowers, feathers, all sorts of things."

"That sounds amazing," she whispered.

"It took me two hours to look through the book cover to cover. I wondered why someone would want to cut paper into pictures. To put such meticulous, time-consuming work into something that would only sit on a shelf or hang on a wall? I thought about it for a long time. The old woman who ran the shop didn't tell me to go. She let me sit there most of the day. She offered me tea and cookies that tasted like spice."

"What did you decide?" Autumn asked. "About the reason someone would cut paper into art?"

"That there wasn't a reason at all, except that it was beautiful."

Her eyes hung on him, his sharp angles, the scar that ran down his cheek. "Did that seem silly to you?" she asked. This man obviously had so little beauty in his life.

"Silly?"

"To do something merely to enjoy it. To create only for beauty's sake?"

He speared her with those deep cobalt eyes. "No," he said. "Because I'd read your journal, and I knew that beauty serves a purpose. Beauty...saves."

Oh God. This man was going to break her heart. He was precious to her. *He* was beauty, and he was strength. Not just of body but of heart, and she admired him beyond all words. How could she not? "Sam," she whispered, laying her head on his shoulder and then reaching out and taking his hand in hers and lacing their fingers together, loving that she finally could. His hand was large and calloused, but it held no scars.

She turned her hand over so she could see his better, the smooth skin of his knuckles, just a sparse dusting of gold hair—almost the same hue as his skin—long, strong fingers with short, blunt fingernails.

She twisted slightly toward him and raised her other hand, using a finger to smooth the tiny golden hairs, enthralled with his odd coloring.

"It wasn't always like that," he said.

"Wasn't always like what?" she asked, bringing her head from his shoulder so she could look at him.

"The color." He moved his eyes upward. "My hair was dark once. Almost black."

She frowned. "How did it…I mean…"

"It happened after a treatment and never went back to the way it was. I was thirteen, I think. Or fourteen." He gave his head a small shake. "I don't know. Those years blend together." And by the expression on his face, she could clearly see he meant it in a negative sense.

"What kind of…treatment?"

But Sam shrugged. "I don't know. At first, I thought it would grow out…or change back…but the years went by, and it never did." He let out a sigh, gazing back out to the lake, shimmering under the morning sun.

She looked up at his white hair, remembering the first time she'd seen him, how magical and beautiful he'd seemed to her. And though she knew now he was no dream, she still thought him beautiful, and though perhaps not magical per se, he was extraordinary. On the whole of the earth, there was only one man like Sam.

And while Autumn didn't think the world would be worse off with more men just like Sam, she was glad she got the only one.

But he's not yours. Not really.

Only…yes, he was. Perhaps not to keep. She had no idea what a life with Sam in it would look like or how they could make that a reality. They faced roadblocks and challenges that she'd pushed to the side because there was nothing else to be done. But…she wanted it. She wanted Sam in her life. Not temporarily. Not a dream. Not a *memory*. But for keeps.

Fear trilled, echoing along her nerves. *Don't think about that. Don't even consider it. At least not right now. There is still too much to overcome.*

But we have this moment. For whatever reason, we've been given this moment.

She brought his hand to her lips and kissed it. Sam looked her way, letting out a soft growl, almost a purr, and there was an answering sound deep inside her that caused no outward noise.

She stood and pulled him to his feet, and Sam followed her back into the house. Back to bed.

They spent several delicious hours there, even though Sam insisted that she tie him up. "What are you worried about?" she asked him.

"Hurting you."

"You won't," she sighed between kisses.

"I might. It's better this way."

But was it? She wanted his hands on her too. But she also couldn't deny that his fear made her nervous as well. So she did as he asked, enjoying him in the ways he allowed.

Autumn stretched and yawned before sitting up and rolling her neck on her shoulders. She was getting used to waking up in this bed, even though the expected someone wasn't currently sleeping beside her.

Outside the window, the sun had already risen. How late had she slept? She was generally an early bird. Well, she had performed quite the workout the night before. She swung her legs over the bed, feeling that now-familiar ache between her thighs. She started to smile but pressed her lips together instead. This temporary life they were living in this cottage by the lake was not meant to be enjoyed, not really. They were hiding out, passing time, on the run so to speak, and yet…and yet Autumn was also falling in love.

The smile she'd worked to suppress melted into a frown.

Oh, Autumn. Oh, you are a very stupid girl.

Her heart dropped and then floated and then settled somewhere near the place it was supposed to be. She let out a small huff of breath, feeling strangely winded.

Oh, this was terrible. Horrible.

Wonderful.

She loved him. She did. Strange, curious, beautiful, broody Sam.

And there was no fathomable way this was going to work.

She clenched her eyes shut, too many warring emotions to deal with here, where there was nothing to do but wait.

Except…she only had a short time before she had to return to work, and perhaps there was one errand—one bit of research—that could be done safely and discreetly, with little risk. And she needed to talk to Sam about it.

She pulled her sweats on and then left the bedroom, spotting him outside on the deck, looking out over the water like he seemed to love to do. The silky white strands of his hair caught the muted sunlight and glinted both silver and gold. Metallic. Just like much of him.

Autumn pulled on her boots and jacket and went outside.

He must have heard her approaching, but he didn't turn. She put her arms around his shoulders, nuzzling his neck and kissing his cheek.

He smiled, leaning into her touch, enjoying. *Allowing* where once he'd all but shrunk away. "You shouldn't have let me sleep so late."

"I didn't *let* you sleep. You were snoring. What was I supposed to do?" He smiled as she took the seat next to him and faked a moment of outrage.

"I don't *snore*."

He started to laugh, then cut it off. "Oh. No, you definitely don't. That must have been a plane flying overhead." He squinted up at the silvery sky, pearly rays splitting the clouds.

She laughed and gave him a teasing swat. Sometimes, like now, he surprised her with his sense of humor. It was as if he wanted to laugh, he just hadn't known how.

Before.

Before this.

Before her maybe? Although she hesitated to take credit for Sam's personal growth. That was all his to own.

She swore she saw him stretching though, taking tentative steps outside the box he'd put himself in, testing the solidity of the new ground beneath him.

For a few minutes, they simply sat in companionable silence, enjoying the crisp air and the gauzy sunlight sparkling on the water's surface. It would be wonderful to go inside and stoke the fire, let it warm their chilled skin. She'd like to spend the rest of the day there with him…just…exploring.

God, she couldn't get enough of Sam. But she also knew there were important answers that might be waiting.

"Sam, I have to go somewhere."

He looked over at her, his eyes worried, body still. "Okay. Where?"

She took a deep breath and told Sam about the files she'd stolen, about the portion of her own file that listed her as a "suspected ADHM" baby.

His brows lowered. "What does that mean?"

"I don't know. Maybe nothing. But maybe...something." *Maybe something very big.* She paused for a moment. "I found my mother. The day of the...shooting," she said, glancing at him and then back to the lake. God, that day was such a blur. Meeting her mother had been...well, eventful to say the least. *Traumatic.* At any other point in her life, it would have been the most momentous thing that had happened to her.

"She, my birth mother, told me that she'd never taken the drug. She said she was about to but was...interrupted."

"So why were you in the hospital?"

"That's what I'm trying to figure out." She paused for a moment, gathering her thoughts. "It's possible my birth mother was lying or just plain forgot. It's also possible the hospital made a mistake or an assumption. But...it's also possible someone lied."

Sam's face was troubled. "Why would they do that?"

"I don't know exactly. But when I took my file, I also took a few more that were part of the stack. I looked through those as well, and another boy's file says the same thing as mine. Suspected ADHM."

"So you want to see if you can find him?"

"Yes. I might not even be able to locate him. But if I

do, and if he'll see me right away, I'd only be half a day, no more."

"Was he adopted like you?"

"His file says he left the hospital when his aunt adopted him and continued his treatment at home. At that point, his case with the foster care system was closed, so there's no further information." *I need to compare our stories.*

"He might be dead now," Sam said, still not looking at her.

"He might be. But I have his name and his last known address, which was just outside New York City. It's about two hours from here. I can't do an internet search from the cottage. But I was going to take my car still parked at my house. It should be safe enough. No one has my name, my description from the shooting is basic at best, and the story is dying down anyway."

They were both quiet for a few minutes before Sam said, "Your mother...was she a...good person?"

Autumn pondered that a moment. She thought about how Sam had told her that not only minds but souls could be ruined. Twisted. Killed even, so that something darker rose in their place. She still wasn't sure that was true. She'd seen how a loving and kind mother could act toward her own child and someone else's in Veronica Monroe and, to some extent, the nurses at Mercy, especially Salma. Veronica had accepted Autumn into her home and heart instantly, and her love had been a much-needed balm throughout the last nine years. But her birth mother? She hadn't been evil to her necessarily, but she had certainly been no mother. And she definitely wasn't good to herself. "Maybe she was good once, a long time ago, but not anymore, no."

"I'm sorry," Sam said, turning his head and looking at her. "I know you wished for her to be."

Their gazes held, and Autumn's heart gave a kick. Yes, he did know. No one else knew the way she'd longed for her like Sam did. The way she'd wondered and hoped. He'd read her most personal words and dreams.

Autumn was glad he had. Glad he knew. She was honored he'd treated her thoughts—her feelings put to words—with such reverence.

She tipped her chin, opening her mouth to speak, when something wet and cold hit her cheek. She tilted her head back farther, watching as tiny white flakes drifted from above. "It's snowing," she said wondrously. "Oh my goodness." She stood, and so did he, Autumn laughing as the wind picked up, the breeze swirling with white.

Sam smiled as he watched her spin around once, raising her arms. She stopped, laughing. They wouldn't be able to stay out here too long. It was getting colder by the moment, and she didn't think there was any snow gear in the cottage.

Sam tipped his head, catching a few snowflakes on his tongue, laughing as one hit him in the eye. He squinted. Time slowed. Autumn watched him as he raised his face again, crystals glittering in his golden lashes. His tan cheeks were flushed with cold, his lips a deeper shade of pink, and the joy on his face was innocent and guileless. *Look at the light within him. Radiant.* It socked her in the gut. It felt like, for just a second, he'd opened his chest and shown her his hidden heart. It stopped her breath, and for the barest instant, everything was right in the world. Every single thing.

There was no past to get mired in. No remembered pain or shattering injustice that might never be made right. No anger or resentment, no doubt, no fear. Nothing at all to overcome.

And loving him was as simple as drawing in air.

Just a beautiful moment, as pure and shimmery as the

snowflakes that fell. The future was theirs, anything they dared to dream. Anything at all.

And even when it passed, when the moment moved on and became a different one, a part of her stayed there and remembered what perfect had felt like. And she knew that any version of heaven she experienced from that day forward wouldn't be quite right without him.

I love you.

She didn't say it. He wasn't ready to hear it. But she did. Oh, she did.

He brought his face forward, his eyes sparkling, that smile still playing on his mouth. The snowflakes on his face were melting into droplets of water. *He's glorious.*

His smile faded. "Are you okay?"

She realized she was standing completely still, staring at him, and she laughed, nodding, not quite able to find her voice just yet.

He watched her for a moment, questions in his eyes. "Should we...go inside?"

She nodded again, laughed again. "Yes. Let's go inside."

They returned to the warm cottage and took off their boots by the door. Sam turned to her to say something when they heard the sound of a car pulling up in front of the cottage. Autumn's heart jumped, and she rushed across the room to the front door, Sam right behind her. *Please be Bill.* But he'd just brought groceries a few days before. *Who else?*

She peeked out the window, breath rushing from her lips. "It's Sheriff Monroe," she said to Sam. "I know him. He's a good man. He'd never hurt either of us."

Sam was tense but didn't attempt to stop her as she pulled the door open.

"Autumn," the sheriff said. "What the hell is going on?"

CHAPTER THIRTY-ONE

Sam's arm shot out, and he stepped between Autumn and the older man in the sheriff's uniform.

"It's okay, Sam," Autumn said, ducking from beneath his arm. "I know him."

The sheriff shut the front door and walked toward them, glancing at the makeshift hospital bed near the window, his eyes lingering on the table covered by medical supplies. "I knew something was up when I kindly offered to drive out here and check the pipes Bill mentioned were making strange noises a few months ago and he nearly shit a brick falling all over himself saying he'd already done it. That man's a terrible liar. And wouldn't know a water pipe from a pipe cleaner. Then Peggy Lou at the secondhand store mentioned Bill came in last week and picked up a few pairs of pants in a size that definitely wasn't his." He looked Sam up and down, clearly assessing his size and coming to the correct conclusion.

"Damn Peggy Lou and her mouth," Autumn murmured.

The sheriff eyed Sam. "This is the sick aunt, I presume?"

Autumn let out a nervous tinkling laugh, glancing up at Sam and then back to the sheriff. "Well, see, it's sort of a long story."

"I've got time."

Sam took a step closer to Autumn, quickly considering his options. He'd already sized the sheriff up, judged his weight and his strength. He could take this man, gun or not. He could outrun him too. But then he'd have to leave Autumn behind. His mind raced. His options were poor.

The program had drummed into them that the lack of connections was important for survival, and now Sam knew exactly why. If you *cared*, your options became fewer. And they also became confusing. They made you question the *why*.

Of course, he'd already learned that lesson once in Macau, but this was *Autumn*, so the lesson hit even closer to home.

Before he could make a move, the sheriff put his hand up. "Take it down a notch, big fellow. I'm going to assume you're a decent sort if Autumn approves of you." He looked at her. "I oughta wring your neck. Oh, step back. It's a figure of speech," he said to Sam, who relaxed his stance and swallowed back the growl that was rising in his throat. He hadn't even realized he'd moved.

Autumn took a deep breath, looking between the sheriff and Sam. "Do you…er…"

"Yeah, I recognize him," the sheriff said, scratching his cheek and again giving Sam the once-over. "Damn if you aren't exactly what she said you were."

Sam's eyebrows shot up. Autumn had *described* him to this man?

"He's not a *what*, Sheriff. He's a *he*."

"I can see that."

"I'm also gonna assume he's the unknown Good Samaritan from the news out of New York City, and you're the possible witness."

Autumn gaped at him for a minute. "How'd you piece that together?"

"It occurred the day before you supposedly up and left your beloved patients without a mere check-in, racing out of town to care for the old cantankerous bitch you referred to as Satan's bride when she visited town six years ago. Didn't exactly add up."

Autumn shifted on her feet. "Oh."

The sheriff's gaze landed on Sam again, continuing to size him up, and strangely, Sam didn't feel judged harshly under the scrutiny. The sheriff looked more thoughtful than anything.

"You're not going to turn us in, are you?" Autumn asked quietly.

He thinned his lips. "You're putting me in a predicament here, Autumn Clancy."

"I tried not to. *Bill* tried not to."

The man sighed. "Yeah. I know. I know." He turned his scrutiny on Autumn. "You had to go and be *tireless*, didn't you?"

"In my search for answers?" She nodded. "*Yes.* I had to be tireless. I don't know another way to be."

"Don't I know it." He sighed yet again. "And that tireless search led you to him. You do know I mostly thought you were suffering from some delusion."

Autumn smiled, and it was soft, like a feather, the way she sometimes smiled at him. "Mostly."

The sheriff walked to the couch and sat down. "I'm going to need to hear all the details. And while I do, I'm going to need a drink. If I remember correctly, there's some whiskey in the lower right cabinet there," he said, pointing into the kitchen.

"It's still morning. And you're on duty," Autumn said, but then she grinned, and Sam could see that her shoulders had relaxed.

"Yeah," the sheriff said. "I'm bending a lot of rules today."

The sheriff listened as Autumn told the story of the day the shooting had happened. He didn't say a word, just nodded and sipped his coffee with a splash of whiskey. When she was done, his mug was empty, and he looked both troubled and resigned.

"You do realize that I could lose my position if it's found out I helped harbor a criminal."

"He's not a criminal. And neither am I."

"You're both wanted for questioning."

Autumn's eyes slid to Sam. "I know. But there's something bigger going on here. We don't know exactly what, but we need time to find out. Sam might be in danger if he's taken into custody."

"What kind of danger?"

"I was in a program at the hospital. Those people will want me back." Which wasn't exactly true. After all, they'd dismissed him. But they definitely wanted him dead.

"That's a pretty cryptic answer, Sam."

"I'm sorry. It's the only one I can give right now."

The sheriff studied him for another moment. "You sure do have quite a few scars, Sam. Did you serve?"

"Yes." He *had* served, just not in the way the sheriff meant.

"I'm asking you to trust us," Autumn said.

"Us, huh?" The sheriff glanced away. "I was never here," he said. "Wash the mug. Put it away. After I drive off, make sure you brush away my tire tracks."

Autumn grinned, jumping up and throwing her arms around his neck, even though he was still sitting. She kissed him on his cheek. "Thank you," she said, standing and moving back so he could stand too.

The sheriff seemed to be considering saying something to Sam but then simply nodded and closed the door behind him. A minute later, they heard his car start up and drive away.

Half an hour after that, Sam used the red truck to drive Autumn to her car. Sam dropped her off in front of the small house, and when she put her hands on his face and gazed into his eyes, Sam got the impression that she wanted to say something but didn't. What did she want to tell him? That she might not come back? The hairs stood up on the back of his neck. Sam had done all kinds of dangerous things, but he'd never felt fear like he felt when he considered not seeing Autumn again.

But then she murmured, "I'll see you soon," against his lips, and Sam was able to pull in a full breath as she hopped out of the truck and headed toward her car.

Sam returned to the lake, following the back road directions Autumn had written out, even though he could have done it without those. He'd been trained to make note of landmarks, escape routes, and other directional details.

When he walked inside, the cottage felt strange. Empty. And for a while, Sam simply sat on the couch, melancholy creeping over his skin, familiar yet unwanted. He hadn't even realized that he'd ceased carrying it until it was back.

Sam went out to the deck and sat there for a while too, watching the movement of the water and the clouds. Loneliness. He'd always felt lonely, but it'd never been this piercing.

This is what it will be like when you're alone again.

Yes, of course it would. He hadn't lied to himself about that.

He'd considered it worth the risk.

But here he was now, after less than an hour away from her, and he was drowning in it as sure as if he'd submerged himself in the frigid lake stretching in front of him.

She'd asked him if he'd ever thought about kissing her in all the years they'd been parted. *Yes*, he'd told her. *It was the last time I felt truly alive.* But he hadn't known the half of it. He hadn't realized that those few stolen moments with her so many years ago barely scratched the surface of what it felt like to *feel alive*. She was the one who'd provided the experience, then and now, but this time it was intensified beyond any words Sam had to describe it. If *this* was life—laughing with her, looking at her, being inside her body as she stared down at him with pleasure-filled eyes, hearing her speak, seeing her lips tip with happiness that he'd given—then he fully understood why people clung to it, fought for it, and feared its end. For the first time in Sam's life, he understood what it felt like to *belong. To want and receive.*

And it was wonderful. And terrifying.

She'd been right about pleasure being different when someone else gave it to you. He'd treated pleasure like food. Essential and enjoyable, as long as you didn't overindulge. But Sam *wanted* to overindulge with her. And the ideas of how to do that didn't disturb him like the videos they'd watched at the hospital.

But Sam didn't want to think about the hospital or anything else. If he sat here all day, staring out at the lake, all he was going to *do* was think. Torture himself. He couldn't bear it.

So he went into the house and prepared himself for what he'd decided needed to be done.

Fifteen minutes later, Sam was pulling onto the road again in the old red truck, the license plate splashed with mud since he figured Adam had reported it stolen. Then again, maybe the old man was still waiting for Sam to return it, having faith that he'd just gotten hung up somewhere and would be back anytime. Sam sighed as he watched the landscape streak by.

He followed the signs that pointed the way to New York City, veering toward the town where the apple orchards stretched. He felt a moment of apprehension when he pulled onto the one-lane road that led to the old man's farm. He would be there and gone before anyone could call any authorities, however. And even if someone attempted to detain him, well…he was well prepared for that too, though it wasn't his wish to fight anyone. He simply wanted to return what wasn't his.

But when he drove through the gates of the farm, his blood cooled in his veins, making his body feel rigid. There was a For Sale sign near the front gate, and the place looked abandoned. Shock and alarm descended. This was the last thing Sam had expected. It hadn't even been a month since he'd been here. *What happened?*

There was one other vehicle in the open space near the house where seasonal workers used to park, and Sam pulled in next to it and then turned off the engine. He stepped down, the closing of the door echoing in the silent space. No sounds of machines. No animal noises. No music or laughter coming from the white house nearby. Sam moved slowly and cautiously toward the car, and when he peered inside, he saw a briefcase and what looked like real estate flyers.

Had something happened to the old man? Why else would he sell his farm? Something was very off.

Do you see me as a lucky man?

Adam loved this place.

Sam steeled his spine, experiencing the same eerie sense of *wrongness* he'd felt in Macau.

His head pivoted as he walked slowly to the barn and entered the small room where he'd slept. His skin prickled with the sense that someone had been here looking for him, someone who knew very well who he was. His duffel bag was still there, though it'd been moved, and the zipper was halfway open. And when he did a quick search of his belongings, he found that nothing was missing, furthering his suspicion that the person who'd rifled through his things, did so more for identification than theft.

Sam knelt near the cot where he'd slept and pried up the floorboard and removed the weapon he'd hidden there.

That was when he saw the shoe print in the dust on the floor. Much larger than the average man's. One very close to Sam's own size but with a different tread. His stomach clenched as he stood and secured the gun in the waistband at the back of his pants. Yes then, one of *them* had been here. How had he fooled himself into thinking they wouldn't catch up with him eventually?

He heard the man's footsteps just as he'd stepped from

the dim interior of the barn out into the light of day. *One seventy-five at most judging from the sound of his feet, five ten from the shadow on the ground.* Sam sized the man up before he'd even come into view, relieved it wasn't one of *them*. Whoever it was, Sam could take a man of that size easily, but still, he pressed his body against the side of the barn, hoping a physical altercation wouldn't be necessary.

"Hello? Who's there?"

Sam's breath released slowly, shoulders lowering as he moved away from the barn.

"Holy shit!" the man said, coming up short when Sam appeared. His gaze flickered over Sam, and he took a slight step back. "Hi. I thought I heard a vehicle." He held his hand out. "I'm Joe. I'm the agent for this property." He glanced down at the camera hanging around his neck. "I'm just taking a few pictures."

Sam lifted his duffel bag. "I used to work here. I came back for this. Why is the farm for sale?"

Joe shook his head and gave a small grimace. "Sorry to have to tell you, but the owner of the farm was murdered." He shook his head as a buzz took up under Sam's skin, the word echoing: *murdered, murdered, murdered*. "Awful thing. Tied up and then shot point-blank. Apparently, he employed a lot of riffraff so—" The man's eyes widened as he obviously remembered that Sam had just identified himself as the hired riffraff. "But anyway, the police suspect one of them but don't have any leads. The deceased owner's family is local but weren't interested in running a farm, so it's up for sale at a real bargain. Just moved the animals out yesterday to their new homes, but the equipment is all still here. Don't suppose you're in the market for an apple farm, are you?" Joe attempted a grin, but it quickly faded when Sam simply stared, mouth pressed into a firm line, the monster inside him rumbling and rising and rattling his chains.

Someone had killed Adam. Tied him up and assassinated him.

Someone with a size fourteen or fifteen boot who Sam suspected had been looking for him.

"When did this happen?" he asked, forcing his voice through his lips.

Joe scratched the side of his neck. "Oh, the same day as that school shooting in New York City. I don't remember the date, but I remember thinking, damn, it was a violent day. What in the hell is wrong in the world?"

Sam held the howl back with increasing effort. It wouldn't do for Sam to scare Joe so that he reported him. "I'm sorry to hear that," he forced himself to say. "He was a decent man." And it was because of Sam that he was dead. He pointed in the direction where he'd parked the truck. "The truck belonged to Adam. I got held up returning it, but there it is."

Sam turned away as Joe said, "Oh. Okay. I'll tell his family. Er, have a good day!" he called.

Sam walked off the farm in the direction of those woods where he'd spent weeks living off the land and then first come upon the old blind man.

Things are always changing, Sam. Life is moving all around us, even when it seems to be standing still.

But sometimes, that moving, swirling fate brought assassins to your door.

Sam first began jogging and then moved into a full out sprint, crashing through the brush and weaving between the trees before he fell to his knees, finally allowing the monster within to bellow at the sky. *My fault, my fault, my fault.*

CHAPTER THIRTY-TWO

The muted doorbell echoed inside the white, two-story house with the small front porch. Autumn's gaze went to the freshly painted dark green shutters and then to the flowered wreath hanging on the door. The occupants obviously took pride in their home.

The door was pulled open, and a man about her age stood there, wearing jeans and a button-down shirt. "Autumn."

She smiled, stepping back as he pushed the screen door toward her to allow her entrance. "Hi, Kaden."

He smiled in return. "I almost feel like I should hug you or something. Would that be weird?"

She laughed. She felt the same way, and she had since the minute she'd heard his voice on the phone, and he'd confirmed who he was. An immediate connection. It'd been surprisingly easy to find him since he still lived at the address in his file. A quick Google search at the library she'd stopped at that morning, and she had him on the phone ten minutes later.

They hugged quickly, and when they stepped back, Kaden said, "There are other ADHM survivors, I know that, but you're the first one I've met in person. Please come in."

Autumn stepped inside. It smelled like some sort of toffee candle, and she could hear a child's voice coming from upstairs, followed by a woman's. "Thanks," she said. "Your house is lovely."

"That's all my wife. Ashtyn. She's putting our daughter down for a nap, but she'll be down in a few to meet you. Come on in here," he said, leading her to a living room that featured a large tan sectional and baskets near the windows filled with toys. Autumn sat down at one corner, and Kaden sat near the middle, turning to face her. "I'm so glad you called me. I went online once a few years ago to see if there was a message board or somewhere I could connect to other kids like us, but…"

He didn't have to finish that sentence. "They've mostly passed," she said. "The few of us who remained are scattered." She bit at her lip momentarily. "Or they don't choose to revisit that time. There's a stigma."

"There is." Kaden ran a hand through his short brown hair. "They did so many public service campaigns and put out so much information about the disease, yet the idea that ADHM babies are contagious or…"

"Dirty."

Kaden gave a quick nod. "Damaged."

"I know. I've experienced some of it. I think it's disturbing to a lot of people. You know, just the whole idea of tumor-riddled babies. I also think there's this fear that the disease will somehow be passed down to our kids if we have them." Her eyes widened slightly, going quickly to the baskets of toys and then back to him. "I mean—"

"You can speak completely freely here," he said. "And you're a hundred percent right. I think those are the main fears. Even Ashtyn's mom, who is the nicest woman you'll ever meet, took her aside before we married and asked if there were tests that could be done to ensure no concerning genetic material would be passed to our kids." He paused. "I mean, the truth is there really isn't any guarantee, you know? The oldest survivors are just a few years older than you and me. The group of us are just beginning to have kids."

She nodded, her brow dipping. She'd had regular check-ups even after she'd been declared healthy. There had never been anything unusual on any of her tests but...Kaden was right, there was no guarantee. Above and beyond that though, she might never have had it in her system at all. *Suspected ADHM.*

"I still have effects," Kaden went on, "but my doctor says it's likely more to do with the medication. And they're mostly mild: joint issues, some tinnitus, stuff like that. I accept those trade-offs happily though considering it's what saved my life. What about you? Any lingering effects?"

"No, thankfully. But that's actually part of the reason I wanted to meet with you."

A pretty brunette woman walked in the room. "Hi, Autumn? I'm Ashtyn." The woman bent down, gathering her in a quick hug the same way her husband had. "I feel like you're already family. Joined by such a rare and miraculous circumstance. Did Kaden offer you something to drink?"

"Oh shit," he said. "Shoot. No." Ashtyn swatted at him jokingly, and he gave a self-deprecating shrug. "See, she's the one with all the social graces. When she's not around, I'm useless."

"Oh, you have your good points too. Autumn, would

you like a glass of water? Iced tea? We have plenty of snacks too if you're hungry. They're mostly things appealing to a picky two-year-old, but let's be honest, no one knows good snacks like a toddler."

Autumn smiled. "No, I'm good, but thank you."

Ashtyn took a seat next to her husband. "You said you got Kaden's name through a contact at social services. I didn't know they'd give that kind of information out. I wish we'd known." She glanced at her husband. "We'd have asked ages ago. Like I said, in a way, you're family simply because of that shared experience."

"I feel the same way," Autumn said. She felt slightly nervous about disclosing how she'd come by Kaden's name. In actuality, she'd put off deciding whether she was going to admit to having stolen his file, even if accidentally, until she'd met him. But now that she had, she felt safe doing so. "And actually, social workers *won't* give out that kind of information. At least not the ones I've spoken to." *Begged. Cajoled. Over years and years. To no avail.*

Ashtyn and Kaden wore matching expressions of concern. "So then…how…"

"I found my birth mother," Autumn said, the picture of that dank room appearing front and center in her mind for a moment before she shoved it forcefully away. When would *that* image cease to bring on an immediate depression? "She told me she'd never taken the drug."

Kaden and Ashtyn glanced at each other.

"I know what you're thinking," Autumn said before they had to figure out a diplomatic way to suggest her mother was being less than truthful to absolve herself from blame or regret. It wasn't an off-base assumption. Autumn had strongly considered it too. Until…*suspected ADHM*. "She could have been lying. She could have forgotten or been wrong. But then I stole my case file from a social worker."

Their eyes widened. It really was almost comical how in sync they were. Autumn told them about taking the file from Chantelle's file cabinet, how several others had come with it, and how she hadn't had time to put the others back.

One of which was Kaden's.

"I'm sorry that I invaded your privacy," Autumn said. "But it's been like pulling teeth to get answers. Even so...I wouldn't have stolen anyone else's file on purpose, but... well, I'm hoping maybe we can work together to try to come up with some answers."

"I'm glad you're here, however that happened," Kaden said. "But what do you need help answering?"

She reached in her purse on the floor next to her and removed her file and his, then flipped hers open on the coffee table in front of them. "Well, here"—she pointed to the place where the words were written—"it says suspected ADHM."

Kaden leaned forward, looking at the place she'd indicated. "So they thought you were born positive but weren't sure?"

"Maybe. I don't know." Autumn pulled Kaden's file from beneath hers and flipped it open. "The other files I took list a positive ADHM diagnosis. But yours says the same thing as mine. Suspected ADHM."

Kaden's frown deepened as he sat back. "Suspected ADHM," he repeated.

She watched him process that for a moment. "Is there any indication your mother never actually took the drug?" she asked gently.

"I don't know. I mean, I never heard that that was a

possibility." His gaze shifted for a moment, obviously thinking. "I was only at Mercy for six years before my aunt came for me. She'd had her issues too, but she got her life together and petitioned the court to adopt me even though she knew how sick I was. It was a bit of a battle, from what I know, but she prevailed, and I came here to live with her." Kaden glanced at his wife, the worry lines on his forehead growing deeper. "Tammy, that's my aunt, had turned into sort of a homeopath. She credited herbs and detoxes and who knows what else for helping her kick drugs."

"She took you off the medication," Autumn whispered.

"Yeah. She did. And I immediately felt *human*."

Oh God. At the news, Autumn barely managed to hold herself upright. Her stomach clenched. She knew exactly what he meant because she'd experienced the same thing. *My special, beautiful girl. Grow strong. Oh, Salma.* For all intents and purposes, someone had "taken" her off the medication too. *Thank you, Salma. Oh, thank you.* If Salma hadn't put the idea in her mind, she wouldn't have done it. And then she wouldn't have been released, wouldn't have gone to live with Bill… She couldn't consider it. She blinked away the tears suddenly burning the backs of her eyes.

Kaden had paused, but now he continued. "I started thriving. I gained weight. I could eat. I could sleep without more meds. I could focus at school."

"Did you tell anyone?"

He glanced at his wife. "Not for a while. I was young and I trusted my aunt, or maybe I just felt so good I didn't want to question it, but in any case, she suggested I don't mention it to my doctor, so it was a good year before he realized why I was doing so well. He said we were being reckless and insisted I go back on the medication."

"Did you?"

"No. Tammy fought it. She was a fighter, and I think she'd lost enough times that she simply wasn't afraid to toss it all on the line. For herself. For me. For anyone she loved."

"God rest her soul," Ashtyn said softly, and Kaden gave her hand a squeeze.

"Anyway, I hadn't developed any tumors. I was feeling great and doing well in school. The doctors were amazed. They ran test after test." He paused for a moment. "Then Dr. Heathrow came to the house to see me."

"Dr. Heathrow?" That surprised Autumn. Why would Dr. Heathrow want to be involved in the treatment of a boy who was no longer at his hospital?

"Yeah. He talked to my aunt, asked for an exact account of side effects I'd experienced and how those had lessened or gone away entirely." He frowned. "I remember him patting my head like a dog and saying, 'I wanted to see the miracle boy,' which sounded kind of nice, but the look on his face was something else. He didn't look happy at all. I remember his expression as barely contained anger."

A shiver went down Autumn's spine as she pictured the man, his face still clear in her mind though she hadn't seen him for almost a decade.

Kaden went on, "Anyway, the next day, I got called into my doctor's office and was declared healed. No more tests, no nothing. That was it. Thinking back, it was abrupt. Strange. But again, I was ten."

Autumn nodded slowly. She was disturbed, still confused, the pieces coming together in a way she wasn't sure she was ready to acknowledge just yet. "My story is similar, at least as far as the abrupt declaration that I was healed. I'd gone off my medication on my own."

Kaden raised his brows. "At the hospital? You must have had to sneak."

"I did. The hospital staff never said that they knew I was no longer taking the drug cocktail." But now she wondered. Had they suspected? Had they caught her on camera sneaking around the other facility as she'd once believed? Both? In simple terms, was she suddenly more trouble than she was worth? "Kaden, did you ever have dreams of being in the woods?"

He looked briefly confused. "What woods? The woods surrounding the hospital?"

"Yes. Or…general woods. Any woods."

"No. I did experience the very vivid dreams that felt real. Those were all the drugs though, because I don't have those now."

"Yes, I experienced those too," she murmured. They sat there for a moment, both quiet, going over their own thoughts.

"Okay, I'm just going to come out and say what I know we're all considering," Ashtyn said. She glanced at her husband and then looked at Autumn. "Is it possible they knew you didn't have ADHM but put you on the medication anyway?"

Kaden looked at her, his face draining of color. "Why would they do that?"

"Because they needed a control group," Autumn said, voicing what had been slithering through her mind but that she'd only put into words right that moment.

"That can't be true," Kaden said, but Autumn heard the note of doubt in his voice. "That would be pure evil."

Yes, yes, it would be. But so would being left alone and defenseless in the woods so children could practice being monsters.

CHAPTER THIRTY-THREE

The sheriff's office looked like any other small-town sheriff's office and, Mark thought as he entered the building, smelled like one. A somehow pleasant mixture of stale coffee and Xerox paper. Or maybe it was just pleasant to Mark because he'd worked in buildings like this all his career. To him, they smelled like *purpose*.

"Agent Mark Gallagher here to see Sheriff Monroe," he told the receptionist when he stepped up to the desk.

"Is he expecting you, Agent Gallagher?"

"No. But if you'll let him know it's official business about an important ongoing case, that would be appreciated."

"Absolutely, sir." The young girl picked up the phone and spoke on it as Mark wandered to the bulletin board hung near the door, perusing the myriad notices common to small towns: missing pets, community meetings, a kid named Timothy advertising his lawn mowing business. "He asks that I send you back," the receptionist said, and Mark turned back to her. "His office is just around the corner, first door on the right."

"Great. Thank you." Mark followed the instructions, and when he turned the corner, the sheriff was already standing in his doorway.

He held out his hand as Mark approached. "Agent Gallagher? This is a surprise. We don't usually deal much with the feds. Come on in. Have a seat," he said, gesturing to a chair in front of his desk.

Mark sat. "Thank you for seeing me without an appointment. A lead pointed me here this morning, and there wasn't time to call." Truthfully, there had been plenty of time to call, but Mark had wanted to see the sheriff's reactions without any advanced preparation.

"It's no problem. A lead you say? What can I help you with?"

"There was a school shooting in New York City about a month ago. I'm sure you heard about it."

The sheriff linked his hands on the desk in front of him, expression grim. "Real tragedy. They always are." The sheriff's gaze was direct, but his body had gone still. He'd grown cautious suddenly. "What about that situation brings you here?"

"I have reason to believe Autumn Clancy witnessed the shooting."

"Autumn?" He leaned back. "What makes you think so?"

"I can't get into that, Sheriff. But being as she works with the department, I thought it might be helpful to talk to you about her."

The sheriff looked away. "Autumn Clancy is one of the most decent, honest people I know, Agent Gallagher. Truth is I think of her as a daughter. Lots of folks in town do." He paused. "She was adopted by one of the locals when she was a teenager. She had a real rough beginning, and somehow, it didn't stop her from showing genuine love to every single person she meets. If Autumn was anywhere near that terrible crime, I can guarantee she was not involved, nor would she cover for anyone who was."

Mark watched the man for a moment. *Nor would she cover for anyone who was.* He knew. He knew where Autumn was, and he knew where the white-haired man she'd helped leave the scene was too. Mark would bet his bottom dollar on it. The sheriff obviously cared very deeply for Autumn Clancy, and he would also wager that if the man was going to share her current whereabouts with Mark, Mark was going to have to give him a good reason to, beyond professional threats.

"I have no reason to believe she was involved in the shooting, Sheriff. However, she's with someone who might have knowledge of the shooter."

The sheriff frowned. "The shooter? I thought he died by suicide."

"He did. It's complicated, but I have reason to believe the shooter was not identified properly."

"I'm not following."

Mark took in a deep breath. The last few days had been full of following up leads about who the identified suspect had been, who Autumn Clancy was, even talking to two different doctors and asking them how the white-haired man might have survived being shot so many times at such close range—questions that had only been met with confusion and halting guesses. And now he needed to learn more about Autumn Clancy and her connection to the man who seemingly had some kind of superpower. He'd needed a few minutes to size the sheriff up, to get a feel for him as a professional and as a personal acquaintance of Autumn Clancy. Now that he had, he decided to trust him with at least some of the truth. "I used to work for the Montana Department of Justice," he said. "But several years ago, I began working for a small undercover task force."

"I see. What sort of task force?"

"Did you hear about the case of the foster care children who were being put in experimental training camps for various reasons?"

"Yeah. Yeah, of course. Who didn't? The news went on about that for months. We received bulletins here, were asked to keep our eyes peeled for anything suspicious that might be related. I believe there's still the flyer with the tip line out on the bulletin board. Of course, that thing needs a good organizing. Anyway, one of those kids survived growing up in the woods, didn't he? Out in Montana?"

Jak. "That's right. However, Dr. Swift, the man who conceptualized and began this social experiment, hasn't been brought to justice. He remains wanted." And Mark would spend the remainder of his days hunting that man who used and horrifically abused unwanted children for his own malignant purposes. And, to Mark's knowledge, continued to head the program to do so, though each one was an individual offshoot, which made Mark's job especially challenging.

"Okay. But the program is no longer operational, correct?"

"On the contrary. We believe it's grown. We've even located a few of the program locations, though all the details haven't been made public because we've tried to protect the privacy of the individuals we've rescued. It's a difficult journey for them. So far, none have managed to assimilate into society." That was the worst part. And he couldn't help but feel at least some personal responsibility. *I didn't find them soon enough.* "Some of them are too damaged."

"Too damaged," the sheriff repeated, a troubled look coming into his eyes.

"Yes. They've been trained as assassins, killers, put through torturous programs that break them in ways most people can't imagine. If we were able to rescue them in time, perhaps there would be a chance…but because we haven't—"

"They're a danger to society."

"Yes. Exactly. Or they might be." It killed Mark that the ones they'd located so far were so incredibly damaged—if that was even the right word—beyond repair. Jak had survived—*was now thriving, thank God*—and Mark refused to give up the hope that others could too. If there was just one thing or one *someone* that made them question the message. Something or someone that had saved their mind. Their soul. Like Jak with Harper's mother's teaching notes. Maybe it would be an instructor or even a fellow program member whose kindness was greater than the things used to break them. Even so, Mark knew that all of them would be broken in some way or another. And that they all would require healing.

"If I may ask, why is this task force of yours such a secret? I work in law enforcement, and I thought that whole case had disappeared."

"The task force operates independently because we're all but certain there are plants within the three-letter agencies. There's no way an operation of the magnitude of Dr. Swift's works without that aspect." No way bodies disappeared, convenient "holdups" happened consistently, and cases were closed without any investigation whatsoever, to only mention a short list of things Mark had seen. "There's money involved," he told the sheriff. "Big money. Governments and multimillionaires use the services of these men and women. A vast cover-up could be easily bought and paid for."

The sheriff looked slightly shell-shocked as he took in a breath.

Mark understood. It was chilling and overwhelming, and he'd had plenty of time to accept the scope of it all.

"Wow." The sheriff stared at the wall for a moment, obviously thinking. After a minute, he met Mark's eyes. "What does this all have to do with Autumn Clancy potentially being at the school shooting in New York City?"

"I think she helped the man who acted as a Good Samaritan leave the scene of the crime. I think that man might know more about what happened that day. What really happened."

"Is he one of the trained assassins, Agent?"

"He might be."

The sheriff swore under his breath.

"I was told Ms. Clancy has taken a leave of absence from work to care for a sick relative," Mark said. "And I'd wait for her to return, but I think the matter is more urgent than that."

The sheriff swore again, this time more a hiss than a word. "She's not caring for a sick relative."

"I didn't think so, Sheriff. Can you tell me where she is?"

CHAPTER THIRTY-FOUR

"Sam?" Autumn called, flinging the cottage door open and rushing inside. "Sam?" The red truck wasn't parked out front as she'd expected it to be, but maybe he'd parked it on the far side of the house that was obscured by trees. She removed her jacket and tossed it on the back of the couch. *Where are you?*

It was freezing in the house, and she rubbed her hands together as she walked to the kitchen, expecting to see him through the window, sitting on the deck in his usual chair, having let the fire die down while he stared out at the lake, but he wasn't there either.

Her stomach tightened, and the first buzz of panic skated along her spine. She went to the bedroom, the panic notching higher when she saw that the bed was neatly made and his jacket and hat were gone. In the bathroom, she found the razor and toothbrush he'd been using, but that didn't give her much consolation.

Did you leave? Without saying goodbye? He had seemed

tense and oddly quiet—even for Sam—when he dropped her off. She'd assumed he was just worried about her and not relishing their parting, but she hadn't even considered that he'd been planning to leave while she was gone.

A lump formed in her throat, and she swallowed it down. *No, no, he wouldn't.* He wouldn't have left. But if he *had*, she didn't have a clue where to begin looking for him.

She stood there in the cold, empty cottage where they'd spent so many wondrous moments, and a sob rose inside, a gasp of pure fear that he was lost to her when she'd only just found him.

When she'd just begun to love him.

So when she caught a glimpse of movement out the front window and tossed the curtain aside to see Sam walking toward the cottage, she let out a small cry as she flung the door open and rushed outside.

She ran the short distance and launched herself into his arms. He let out a sound that was half grunt, half *oomph* as he caught her, dropping the duffel bag that had been in his hand and wrapping her in his arms.

She sensed his distress by the way he held his body even before she'd gotten a good look at his expression, so she pulled back, her gaze moving over his face, taking in his forlorn eyes.

"Where did you go?" She noted his cleanly shaven face. She couldn't see even a wisp of hair beneath his ball cap. She reached up and removed his cap, looking at his buzz cut, the same one he'd had when she'd first brought him to the cottage, the one easily hidden by a hat. He had also had his sweatshirt hood pulled up over the hat when he'd walked toward her up the dirt road, likely to hide the scar on the side of his face so he could travel as incognito as possible out into the world.

"To return the truck to Adam. It wasn't mine."

Adam. The old man he'd worked for on the apple farm. She glanced behind him in the direction of the main road. "How did you get back?"

"I hitched a ride on the back of a flatbed. They dropped me off a few miles from here."

His voice. It was lacking all emotion. "Did it not go well? What happened, Sam?"

"They killed Adam," he said, voice so even it sent a shiver down her spine as much as the words he'd uttered.

"What?" She took a small step back. "Why? Who?"

"The program," he said. "They tracked me somehow. Maybe using the truck or…public cameras. I…don't know. Maybe they questioned Adam, and he didn't cooperate in the way they wanted him to. Maybe…"

He stared off past her, his expression so bleak it broke her heart. He hadn't mentioned it to her, but the fact that he'd unintentionally stolen something from someone had been bothering him all this time. But not just any someone… He cared about the old man. She had heard it in his voice when he'd spoken of him and described the place where he'd worked. He cared what he thought of him. *Sam. Sweet Sam.* He'd taken a risk to do what was right and found that the man had been killed. *Oh God*. And clearly, he blamed himself.

And it scared her too. If they had tracked him there… could they track him here too? Even if they hadn't yet, could they eventually? "Let's go inside," she said, her eyes moving from tree to tree as though, even now, there were snipers positioned to take them both down.

"I'll be in in a minute," Sam said. "I want to check the property. Lock the door."

"Do you think… they know where you are?"

"If they did, we'd know. But I still want to look around."

Autumn swallowed, her fear growing now that she knew Sam was concerned about their safety here too. She gave a quick nod and then moved swiftly to the cottage and locked the door behind her.

Autumn sat on the couch as she waited for him. She felt sad, like she'd come down off a mountain and needed time to adjust to the air pressure down below. She mourned for the old man Sam had cared for and for Sam's obvious grief and self-blame. And she acknowledged that because of what they now knew—that Sam was being tracked—they wouldn't be able to stay here for long, this beautiful refuge that they'd found. She'd known that anyway, but she hadn't expected their time here to be cut quite so short.

For the past month, she'd been focused on staying out of the public eye, keeping Sam hidden so he could heal. But she'd known that at some point very soon, they would have to reenter society. Autumn was expected back at work, and Sam…well, Sam couldn't stay locked away somewhere, whether that place be a remote cottage or her small, one-bedroom house.

But now, even that murky plan had been destroyed by Sam's discovery. It was probably best that they leave in the morning. But to where?

What are we going to do?

A few minutes later, Sam called her name from the front porch, and she let him in. "Everything good?"

He gave a nod and then moved to the fireplace where he went about building a fire, and Autumn made a pot of coffee.

When she'd poured herself a cup, she returned to the

living room. Sam was sitting on the rug in front of the roaring fire, staring into the flames. She set the steaming mug on the heavy trunk used as a coffee table and pulled a couple throw pillows from the couch, tossed them on the floor, and joined him. Then she leaned forward, wrapping her arms around Sam again and resting her head on his chest, listening to the steady beat of his heart, absorbing his warmth. "I'm sorry, Sam. So sorry. We're going to have to talk about what's next."

"Did you find him?" Sam asked. "The boy from the file?"

She pulled back and then propped a pillow against the trunk and rested her back on it. She let her eyes move over Sam. He was obviously ignoring her comment, deeply troubled, overwhelmed, perhaps in a bit of shock, and maybe he needed the distraction of hearing what she'd found out. "Yes." She told him about Kaden and Ashtyn, about Kaden's experience being taken off the medication.

"Just like you," Sam said, turning his gaze back to the fire.

"Yes," she murmured, recalling Ashtyn's question, and Kaden's answer at the end of their conversation. She picked up the mug and took a sip of the hot coffee, letting it warm her insides.

They needed a control group. Babies and kids they knew didn't have the disease.

She told Sam about that too, which caused the worry lines between his brows to grow deeper.

"I don't know what to do," Autumn said. "I'm in possession of more information now, but it almost doesn't matter. Whichever route I go, they're all going to say the same thing again. Only now it won't just be me. It will be Kaden too. We experienced hallucinations. We had medication-induced fever dreams. We should enjoy our lives, blah, blah, blah. And I mean, I do. I *do*. But it doesn't change the fact that I—*we*—were also robbed of years and years when we would have been healthy, *normal* kids. We were *lied* to, and I want to know why."

Autumn watched a small muscle in Sam's jaw as it clenched and unclenched. She leaned forward and put her hand on his arm, and he turned his face to her.

"I know you helping us is a risk, Sam, now more than ever. I know you're afraid the authorities will take you into custody to question you about the shooting. But you can corroborate what I've reported about the woods. And we can't run forever. Those people killed someone you cared for. If we report what we know...there must be *someone* who can help us, who will give us the protection of...whistleblowers or...something. Sam?"

He had turned his face back to the fire. "I've done illegal things, Autumn. Things that would not be overlooked by law enforcement," he said stoically.

"I...well, I mean...I figured you were sent to do things that soldiers do, but you were part of a program. Sam... whatever you've done, you did because other people directed you."

"I still *did* those things."

Will you tell me about it, Sam? The words were on the tip of her tongue, but she bit them back, fear swirling in her belly. Maybe now wasn't the time. Perhaps they were already dealing with enough as it was.

Sam watched her, then looked away, lowering his shoulders as though trying to make himself smaller. Autumn reached out her hand to him. She sensed she was letting him down in some very important way, and though she wanted to fix it, she was so incredibly torn. *I'm not loving him right. But I'm scared too. How do I do this?*

The situation was so complicated, so uncharted, so terrifying, and Autumn was equal parts frustrated, afraid, and just downright sad. She was desperate to help him, to find justice for them and so many others, and to figure out a way to move forward and find safety.

Because she loved him. *There must be a way to figure this out.*

"I almost didn't return today. I'm a safety risk to you, Autumn. But I couldn't…" He let out a gust of breath.

"What?" She gripped his arm. "No. Sam, you have to promise me, no matter what, that you won't leave without telling me. I couldn't bear that. I couldn't bear wondering if you're okay."

"You can bear more than you think. You're the strongest person I know."

"Sam, please—"

Before she could say another word, the sound of a vehicle met her ears, and they both turned toward the front door.

Autumn's eyes flew to Sam's, fear jolting her. "Whoever it is isn't trying to sneak up on us. It's probably Bill." Bill had told her he was meeting with clients today. She'd planned to update him on her trip to Kaden's tomorrow. But maybe his schedule had changed.

But Sam had gone to his duffel bag and pulled out a weapon. Autumn gasped at the sight of it as he took her arm and positioned himself in front of her next to the door. It happened in an instant, his movements those of someone trained to expect untold definitions of "trouble."

The knock came then, and neither of them moved.

"Autumn Clancy?" came the voice of a man.

She met Sam's eyes, and he brought a finger to his lips.

"My name is Agent Mark Gallagher. Sheriff Monroe sent me," the man called, his voice muffled through the wooden wall.

Sheriff Monroe sent an agent here?

As if the agent outside had heard her internal question, he said, "The sheriff told me to use the password Boston cream doughnuts. He said that's how you'd know I could be trusted."

Autumn's breath gusted from her mouth. "Let him in," she told Sam. Sam looked at her suspiciously, but she tipped her chin. "The first day I came to live with Bill, he took me out to dinner in town and told me I should order whatever I wanted. I ordered Boston cream doughnuts. Only people who've known me since I was fourteen know that. Plus," she added, "if the guy on the other side of the door wanted to harm us, would he really be waiting for us to open this rickety door instead of merely kicking it in?" She'd whispered all that, and Sam squinted as he listened. She implored him with her eyes. They'd just been wrestling with what came next, and now this man was here—this agent—sent by someone she trusted more than almost anyone in the world. And he was offering them help through the door as if he'd shown up in answer to their call.

He glanced to the rickety door and then back to her, his shoulders lowering, apparently conceding at least that point.

"We need help, Sam. Maybe he can offer some."

"And if he can't?"

"He leaves, and then we do too."

His eyes moved over her face, and something resolute came into his expression. She saw his muscles loosen, and then he stuffed his weapon in the back waistband of his jeans and walked to the door.

When he opened it, a good-looking older man stood on the other side, his mostly gray hair cut short, wearing jeans and a fleece-lined canvas jacket. His eyes went to Sam, his expression registering no surprise, as though he'd expected to see the very large, white-haired man standing next to Autumn.

"I'm only here to offer help. I'm not a threat, I promise. I know you both were at Deercroft that day, and I know you're both innocent," the agent said.

Next to her, Sam was very still. And she had no doubt that should it become necessary, he would use the weapon in his waistband or fight this man. But though she had no idea who this agent was or how he'd found them, her gut told her he wasn't a threat. At least not physically. And at least not yet. She looked past him. He'd come alone.

"How...how did you find us?" Autumn asked.

"I located you after watching hours of street camera footage. I retraced your steps to your social worker. She was able to give me your name."

Fear continued to creep through her system. Would this agent ask them to come with him? What was Sam going to do? He'd made it clear to her he would not be taken into custody. *I've done illegal things.*

"May I please come in?" the agent asked. "I'd like to explain more about who I am and the agency I work for. And I think we can all help each other quite a bit."

CHAPTER THIRTY-FIVE

Mark rubbed his hands together, the warmth of the fire easing the cold from his bones. He looked across at where Autumn and the man she'd introduced as simply Sam sat staring at him cautiously.

How familiar this was. Yet how apprehensive he still felt. He'd experienced a buzz of excitement driving here, knowing he was likely about to meet one of *them*. But he never knew how one of *them* was going to react. Or behave. Or...accept.

Sam. His name was Sam. And he was tall and big and muscular just like all of them were. Only Sam's looks had surprised him. While most of them shared the same linebacker build—at least thus far—Sam was different. His hair was an unlikely shade of white, while his skin was tan and his eyes almost black. His coloring was very unusual to say the least. Something had been done to him, and though curiosity drummed within, so did dread. Mark almost didn't want to guess at what had been used to achieve such a thing or the justification behind it.

"First, I want you to know, I'm not here to arrest you, detain you, or anything of the sort. I'm hoping for your cooperation because I'm looking for the truth, but I'm also here to offer you the help I believe you need."

"Help us?" Autumn asked. Sam simply stared.

"Yes. I'm prepared to give you temporary housing and any protection you might need while we sort all this out."

"Even though we didn't come forward after the shooting?" Autumn glanced at Sam. She was obviously choosing her words carefully, though Mark sensed she was more concerned about him.

Autumn leaned infinitesimally closer to Sam. Mark wondered if she even knew she'd done it. And it eased his worry, because from what he knew of this girl, she was rational, and she was beloved. It had to mean she had more than a modicum of good judgment. And she'd obviously deemed this man worthy of her affection, if not more.

It wasn't a guarantee, but it was a good start. And far better than he'd had with the others. Excluding Jak, of course, who had had Harper. And it'd made all the difference. Maybe it would in this case too.

The muscular man sitting next to her looked as taut as a wire. And Mark could see that if he threatened Autumn in any way—not that Mark was planning on that, quite the contrary—Sam would react swiftly and probably violently.

They were all wired differently. From each other but especially from other, more average humans. Yes, Mark knew Sam would fight if he had to. After all, he'd been trained to do so.

"I understand why you didn't come forward. And before I ask you to trust me, to be honest with me, I want to be honest with you. I work for a task force dedicated to finding those who have been unwillingly and sometimes unknowingly enrolled in a program that seeks to create...super soldiers for lack of a better description."

Mark saw Sam draw back slightly right before he caught himself, stilling completely. Yes, that had gotten his attention. Autumn glanced at Sam and then back to Mark. She wasn't overly surprised either. Sam had already confided in her—at least some of it. *Good*.

"Unwillingly..." Autumn murmured.

"Meaning it's done when they're babies...or children. The first man I found in this program is named Jak. I'll tell you a little more about him later. Since Jak was rescued, the task force has located two additional groups. There were only five survivors, all of whom...didn't adjust well to outside life and have subsequently been institutionalized." He looked back and forth between Autumn's and Sam's rapt expressions, thinking about those poor souls he'd just mentioned. *Didn't adjust well*. There was a whole world included in that description, but he didn't have time to go into it now. He could tell by the way Sam's eyes had widened when he'd said it though that the man had some concept of what he alluded to.

Mark had left his weapon in the car so as not to pose any threat. But Sam likely had one somewhere close by that he would use at a moment's notice and with the skill of a trained professional if it even became remotely necessary. But he was digesting Mark's words, and he was obviously attached to the woman sitting next to him. Both extremely positive signs. There had been one success story, and God, but he hoped for a second.

"How did you find them?" Autumn asked.

"I became interested in a series of crimes where each

perpetrator had several of the same defining qualities as the men in these programs. To simplify, they were all large, strong men who appeared more like athletes or soldiers than the typical criminal element. Flimsy evidence at first, I realize, but the more I looked into the situations and the accused, the more I became convinced these men were who I thought they were. Eventually, they led back to the groups I mentioned."

"What sorts of crimes did they commit?" Autumn asked, suspicion creeping into her tone.

Mark looked at Sam, who remained still and silent. Mark had the impression he already knew the answers to the questions Autumn was asking. He appeared neither surprised nor curious, simply stoic.

"They varied," Mark said. "Mostly shootings. A stabbing. The other thing that made the crimes similar was that they occurred during a time that was extremely advantageous to someone who was facing a major scandal in the news cycle."

"There's always a major scandal in the news cycle," Autumn noted.

"Seemingly so. But not all are willing to pay the price to change public focus."

A flare of surprise widened Sam's eyes before his shoulders sank as if with understanding. He leaned back slowly against the couch cushions. Autumn glanced at him, worrying her lip again as she focused back on Mark. "Willing to pay..." Autumn all but whispered. "Are you saying someone instructed the men in these programs to commit crimes in order to take the spotlight off them?"

"That's exactly what I'm saying."

"Oh," Autumn breathed. She paused, giving Sam another worried glance, but he remained staring straight ahead. "So...you think the school shooter was...hired to do that? To...distract from whatever else was in the news?"

"Or was about to be in the news," Mark said. "Something that would ruin a career or many careers. It typically works. At least to turn the focus away long enough that the person or persons can come up with a lie or take the pressure off for various reasons." *To scrub a database, hide evidence.* The list went on. "Is it possible, Sam? That the man who shot those kids that day was used as a false flag operation?" He wouldn't ask Sam about his own involvement in any program, not yet. He'd let Sam come at this from a safer angle, if he even chose to do that.

Sam's big shoulders rose as he took in a breath and then fell. He looked at Autumn for several long moments, and whatever decision he was making was obviously based on her. When he looked back at Mark, his expression was stark, stony. "Yes...it's possible. I didn't know the why."

Mark let out a deep, slow exhale of tension. In answering that question, Sam had just answered a few more. Mark could see very well that Sam knew that too. He might be a singularly focused thinker in some ways—they had to be by design. But this man was also very obviously intelligent. However he'd come to the decision, Sam had decided to be honest with him, to accept the help. Likely to offer the woman sitting next to him some protection. *Thank God*.

Mark let out a deep breath as he went back over Sam's words. The men and women in the program weren't told the why of their missions, just the how. They'd been trained not to ask questions. *They were training you the way they train suicide bombers,* he wanted to tell Sam. With conviction and to believe that their purpose was righteous. And he would tell Sam this when the time was right. But information overload, especially of this magnitude, had to be doled out slowly. Carefully.

He didn't know what Sam had already realized on his own and what he had not.

"What was the shooter's real name?" Mark asked. "I believe the man whose identity they used was a patsy. A man with few contacts who worked from home. He likely had an undiagnosed disorder that made him extremely averse to social interaction. That's been a similarity in these cases too." The killer in each false flag operation thus far had died at the scene, but their "identity" hadn't held up. And eventually, after following several related leads, Mark's task force had located the two groups he'd spoken of. While there hadn't been any happy endings, he took comfort in the fact that the people he'd rescued were now safe, as was society from whatever crimes they would have been sent to perpetrate.

"Wait, are you telling me the body they took from the crime scene was not the shooter?" Autumn asked, massaging her temple.

"Not necessarily, but I think his identity is false. They likely killed the real Jason Leads. Whether the body in the morgue is the actual shooter's or was switched out is anyone's guess. It's a vast enough network that I'm sure they could pull off something like that. It's a cartel of sorts. There are copious amounts of money involved and many levels of participation. As far as the members themselves, they are people who believe they're working for a greater good. There's little they won't do."

Autumn blinked rapidly a few times, then looked at Sam. She opened her mouth as though about to ask a question but then shut it, looking helplessly at Mark.

"If it was the shooter's body in the morgue, you would

know it. He had surgeries like me, but far fewer. His name was Amon," Sam offered sullenly. "I don't know his last name. If we had real ones, we never used them."

"Who, Sam? Who kept your last name from you? Who trained you?" Mark held his breath as he waited for Sam to give him the name of just one person involved in this evil, just one. Or refuse.

"Dr. Heathrow was in charge of our medical treatment and our training." An expression of deep despair crossed Sam's features before he quickly added, "He tried to help us though too. My organs were tumor riddled. My bones were brittle."

Dr. Heathrow. The same man in charge of Autumn's medical treatment. The same man Mark had read about online. The one who'd been so interested in human augmentation. Another buzz of dread moved through Mark, his eyes moving from Sam's peculiar white hair to the scars on his temples.

Mark's gaze moved to the scar that started at the base of Sam's throat, wondering how many surgeries he'd had and for what exactly. And though that information would help Mark form a more complete picture, it was still private, so for now, he'd take what Sam offered and no more. "The surgeries…they were experimental then?" he asked.

"Of course, Agent Gallagher. But it was worth the risk," Sam said.

The statement sounded rehearsed, but Mark let it go. If Sam was lying for the man who'd essentially spearheaded his brainwashing, it wouldn't be a surprise. And maybe the surgeries were worth the risk. Sam was obviously healthy and strong, even if his coloring was strange and he sported a concerning and unusual number of surgical scars.

Mark could see Sam was becoming slightly agitated with questions about Dr. Heathrow, so they'd come back to that later. "Why were you at Deercroft that day?"

"I went to the apartment, the one the program kept in the city. Amon was there. He seemed off, and I caught sight of an address where he was heading. Something wasn't right, and I…" He shook his head. "I don't know why. I just did."

"Do you know the address of the apartment?"

Sam nodded, and he gave it to Mark. Mark texted it to one of his trusted associates in New York City. Surprisingly, the text sent, even though he only had one bar on his phone. He wasn't expecting much to come from it though. If experience with the way this whole operation worked told him anything, the place would have been cleared out after the man named Amon completed his job, especially one that included such heavy police involvement. Likely, they'd rented another one somewhere else already, but Sam wouldn't know where that was. Sam wouldn't be trusted with anything regarding the program ever again.

Mark considered the man, sitting there still and silent. He was obviously struggling, and Mark felt a wave of compassion. In answering Mark's questions, Sam was going against everything he'd been trained to protect. In essence, Mark was pushing in the wrong direction toward a mental and emotional magnet. *He's strong.* Not of body, though that was certainly the case too, but of spirit. He doubted Sam knew it, but Mark did. And Jak would too. "The program can't be happy with you for involving yourself in another member's mission. For taking bullets for those who were supposed to increase the casualties." Innocent children.

"No, but that was already the case. I was kicked out of the program weeks before that."

"By Dr. Swift?" Mark asked.

Sam's eyes flew to him, obviously surprised that he knew the man's name. His features evened out, and he nodded. "He gave the order to Dr. Heathrow."

"Why?" Mark asked.

"Because I didn't follow an order," Sam said, looking away.

Mark studied him. He was being evasive. *That's okay. We have time. I'll earn your trust, Sam.*

"Do you know where Dr. Swift lives, Sam?" Mark asked, though he mostly knew that Dr. Swift didn't have permanent dwellings. And the others had already told him that no one knew of his whereabouts for more than an hour at a time and never in advance. It was wiser that he stayed on the move. But unfortunate for Mark and the others attempting to hunt the evil bastard down.

"No. I never met with him in person," Sam said woodenly, confirming what Mark already knew.

"I don't suppose you still have the phone given to you by the program?"

"No. It was confiscated when I was…dismissed."

"They expected you to commit suicide, didn't they, Sam?"

Autumn sucked in a small breath, looking at Sam with equal parts shock and dismay.

Mark knew enough to know that if you were dismissed from the program, you were removed in shame. The final mission was to take your own life. And thus far, from what he knew, all of them had obeyed. But these people were brainwashed and terrorized in countless ways. *Tread carefully,* he reminded himself. *Triggers abound with men such as Sam.* How could they not?

"Yes," Sam said. "I was going to… I kept meaning to…"

"Sam," Autumn whispered, her knuckles turning white as she squeezed his hand.

"What stopped you?" Mark asked.

Sam looked at Autumn with the same worshipful look Mark remembered Jak giving Harper so many years ago, not to mention the last time he'd seen them. "She did," Sam answered.

"I see." He studied them, noted the way they continued to lean into each other. "So you two met at the hospital? That's how you know each other?" That was one part of the puzzle he hadn't been able to figure out until now. Until Sam had told him he too had been under Dr. Heathrow's care. Although knowing what he knew, *care* likely wasn't the appropriate term. But there was still lots of digging to do concerning that.

Autumn confirmed, telling him about the newer building she'd lived in next to the lab, which had also been Sam's home. Her eyes cast to the side as though she wasn't giving him the complete story, but again, now was not the right time to push. Mark was holding a few things back too.

The lab. Mark had a million questions about the lab, and he wanted to start volleying them at Sam right that minute. But he knew from experience that patience must reign.

"We have a lot to talk about and a lot to try to work through," Mark said. "I sense you need a team. And I'd like to be part of that, if you'll trust me." He looked between the two of them again. So young. So deeply uneasy. *Autumn hopeful, Sam guarded*. Mark was hopeful too, and in anticipation of this meeting, he'd made a few arrangements that he knew would make things easier. "I called and asked Jak, the man I told you about, the first one rescued, and his wife,

Harper, to meet us at a house on the river. It's only a thirty-minute drive from the town you live in, Autumn. Will you both come with me? We can all figure out what to do from here."

Sam glanced at Autumn. "You can keep her safe? No matter…what happens?"

Mark paused. *No matter what happens.* What he meant, Mark surmised, was if Sam was harmed or chose to leave. Mark would not lie to this deeply distrustful man, not when trust was so tentative. "From what I've gathered, Autumn's identity isn't known. Law enforcement doesn't have her name or a photo of her." He looked over at her and then back at Sam. "We're dealing with very dangerous people, Sam, but I have no reason to believe anyone except you might be a target. And this safe house we'd head to isn't listed in any official databases. We wouldn't stay long—just long enough to gather more information and figure out next steps."

Mark saw Sam's expression settle into resolve. Autumn and Sam shared a look, and then Sam turned to face Mark, appearing somehow both certain and defeated. Autumn's safety was obviously essential to him. His own mattered much less.

"Yes, we'll come with you." Sam hadn't said he'd trust him, but Mark hadn't expected him to.

That's okay, Sam. I don't mind working for that.

CHAPTER THIRTY-SIX

The beautiful vacation home was situated on the edge of an inlet, the water only separated from the house by a small, sloped lawn. Sam and Autumn stepped onto the deck, looking out at the bare trees and the icy water. There'd been a deck overlooking water at the cottage where they'd stayed for weeks, but this one felt world's different, and not only because this one was expensive and multilevel.

Because everything's changed, Autumn thought, glancing at Sam. He hadn't said much on the journey there, and he was still silent. Sullen. They'd stopped once after Mark had asked them if he could test a small vial of each of their blood. It could wait, he had told them. If they were averse to being poked by even one needle, he would let them choose, but it would help to provide some answers. So they'd both agreed and stopped at a clinic where they'd had blood drawn, two vials that Mark had sent to a lab he trusted. Autumn hadn't asked what precisely he was looking for, but she welcomed any answers he might be able to give. She'd been looking for answers for a long, long time.

She'd called Bill and told him they were leaving the cottage and why, but not the details of where they were headed. Then she'd called Sheriff Monroe as well, who sounded relieved, which made her glad of their decision to trust Agent Gallagher.

When they'd pulled up to the house, her lungs had expanded slightly. Perhaps in the back of her mind, she'd held out in giving Agent Gallagher her complete trust until the moment he delivered them to the place he'd described.

She sensed in her gut he was a good and decent man, but she was also in a situation she'd never expected to be in, one that was changing and morphing into something different by the moment. She was struggling to keep up, having trouble categorizing her thoughts and feelings, so she simply held tight to Sam's hand. Her anchor. She vowed to be one for him as well.

"I put your bags in the room right there," Agent Gallagher—Mark as he'd asked them to call him—said, pointing to the room that overlooked the river.

"Thank you, Mark." Autumn gave him a small smile. They hadn't had much. Just the things Bill had brought for them, Sam's duffel bag, which looked practically empty, and the few medical supplies Sam still required. Although required wasn't the right word, at least not as it related to Sam. He would heal on his own now. The supplies were *her* way of continuing to care for him in a tangible way.

There was the sound of a vehicle arriving at the front of the house, and Mark headed in that direction. "That'll be Jak and Harper," he murmured. "I'll be back."

Autumn walked to where Sam was standing at the edge of the deck, looking out over the lawn and the few barren trees. The water beyond was gray, reflecting the bruised sky overhead. She leaned against him. "You okay?" She wanted to talk about so much with him. About the program, about what he was thinking regarding what Mark had told them about the others, about the fact that they were involved in an ongoing investigation but shockingly not the one they thought they were.

"Yes," he said simply, even if there were a thousand other words in his eyes. *Later. We'll be alone later.*

As voices and footsteps approached, they turned to see a man Autumn could only describe as...well, *strapping* was the first word that came to mind when he stepped through the door. He was built like Sam, tall and broad, though not quite as muscular. The woman behind him was petite and pretty and very pregnant. She stepped through the sliding glass doors onto the deck, Mark behind her, a little boy in his arms. The boy was midsentence, something about a frog or a dog or a hog?

"Shush for a minute, Eddie," the woman said, moving in front of the strapping man. "We're going to completely overwhelm them."

Sam stepped closer to Autumn and just slightly in front of her, positioning himself as a guard dog might.

The brunette woman smiled warmly at Autumn and then at Sam as she approached. "I'm Harper," she said. Her gaze moved from Autumn to where Sam stood, her eyes softening as she took them both in before turning. "And this is my husband, Jak."

The man named Jak studied them carefully too, his gaze lingering on Sam.

"And this sweet little terror is Eddie," she said as Mark set the little boy on his feet.

Eddie went immediately to his mother's side, leaned

against her leg, and peered up at Sam. His eyes were wide, his mouth opened slightly. Sam peered down at him, one eyebrow raised.

"Are you a *wizard*?" Eddie asked, his expression utterly awestruck.

"No," Sam answered, regarding the child warily as though he too was unsure exactly what this strange creature was.

"An *alien*?"

"Eddie!" Harper said, bringing her hand down and then patting his cheek in an attempt to quiet the boy.

Autumn had the urge to laugh, and the sensation made something ease inside her. If her sense of humor was still intact, she was going to be okay. The child's honest innocence was just the balm she'd needed, even if Sam was still staring suspiciously at him.

"No," he answered again, though with less certainty.

"Well, I—" Harper began.

"A superhero!" Eddie exclaimed, taking a step closer to Sam, the awe in his gaze increasing.

"Er—"

"I can run fast!" Eddie said, turning and racing as fast as his little legs could carry him to the edge of the deck and then back to where they all stood. "See?"

"You're not fast at all," Sam noted, causing Autumn to stifle what was sure to emerge as the mixture of a laugh and a groan. Clearly, Sam had rarely if ever encountered a young child.

"Am too!" Eddie declared, the honest insult obviously not fazing him one bit.

"Your legs are too short to be fast."

Eddie appeared to consider that, his eyes moving from

Sam's feet to his white hair. "My dad says I'm going to be a giant like him someday," he finally said.

Sam opened his mouth to respond.

"Giants live at the top of beanstalks and eat kids for dinner!" Eddie declared.

"Uh—"

"Why don't I show you where you'll be sleeping tonight, giant-to-be?" Mark said, taking Eddie's hand. "It's a loft bed, taller than me. You have to use a ladder to get into it."

Eddie's eyes widened, but he looked torn, his gaze moving between the unusual superhero and the man who had just promised a bed with a ladder. "I'll be back!" he told Sam, taking Mark's hand.

Judging by Sam's expression, he considered that a threat.

"Autumn," Harper said, shooting a quick look at her husband, "I'd love to stretch my legs a bit after traveling all day. Would you like to join me for a walk?"

"Um." Autumn caught Sam's eyes, and he gave her a nod that told her he'd be okay. "Sure," she said.

When she looked back at Harper, she noticed that the woman was watching them, a gentle smile on her lips. Autumn followed her to the set of steps off the deck that led to the yard. They crossed through the winter grass and went out the gate that led to a path that traveled along the shore.

"When are you due?" Autumn asked.

"Eight more weeks." Harper smiled. "It feels like a lifetime at this point. And like I should savor the time before I'm juggling two." But she smiled again, bringing her hand to her swollen stomach. She obviously loved motherhood.

A longing rose up in Autumn, the hope that someday she'd have a family as beautiful as Harper's. Harper and Jak had obviously found a way to make it work, even though she had to assume Jak had faced many of the same emotional and mental challenges that Sam did.

You're getting ahead of yourself, thinking of a potential future with Sam when you haven't figured out the present.

"It hasn't all been smooth sailing," Harper said, "Jak's adjustment."

Autumn was surprised that Harper had seemingly read her mind.

Harper offered a knowing smile. "I was once right where you are. Or…close enough anyway." She paused. "They're very much like wounded warriors. The adjustment to a more normal life is almost the easy part," she said. "It's the grief and the anger, the fear…those things are the real battles. But if Sam has come this far and retained his sanity and a heart that holds any amount of kindness, then there's great hope that he'll recover."

Sanity. Kindness. Yes, he possessed both of those. And his heart didn't just hold a small amount of kindness, it overflowed with it, whether he knew that or not. Whether he *wanted* that or not.

He's a walking miracle, Autumn was constantly reminded. And so was this woman's husband. She suddenly felt an overwhelming wave of gratitude for having been brought together with Harper. *I'm not alone.*

"Will you tell me about your husband?"

Another smile tilted Harper's lips, this one almost dreamy. But then it faded, a small crease forming between her brows. "He grew up alone, in the woods. He was forced to survive starvation and cold, things no human, much less a child, should endure. He was studied, watched, but never helped."

Autumn's blood chilled at the mere idea of a small child braving winter alone in a forest. "Oh God," she whispered.

What kind of evil had to run through a person's veins to watch something like that and not be compelled to help?

And it made her wonder about Sam. He'd said he was cured with a medication that harmed him. That the medication made the surgeries he'd endured necessary. But he'd also been trained as a sort of super soldier to fight and to kill. But what had that training consisted of? Had Sam been tortured in ways he didn't speak about? What had he experienced that Autumn still didn't understand? Another chill went through her, this one born of fear at what she might not know. Knowledge she'd be faced with that would hurt.

But Sam will have been the one who experienced it. It's not about you. Still, she felt herself bracing for what might be to come.

Harper had paused, but now she went on. "The loneliness was the worst, I think. And knowing that others could have helped him but didn't."

Autumn nodded. She understood that, even if she didn't yet have all the pieces of her own puzzle. But to know that hospital staff possibly stood by as she was lied to and hurt made her heart crack under the weight of the betrayal. To know that others might not have considered her worth saving, even strangers, hurt in a way that was difficult to articulate. Someone had decided her life meant nothing. It had to take someone so viciously soulless to be able to watch a child endure horrific circumstances and not step in. "Did those people come to justice?" she asked.

Harper paused. "Yes. I'd say so. Except for the man who heads the program," she murmured, her brow furrowing as she pulled her coat more tightly around her.

"Dr. Swift," Autumn said.

"Yes, that's him," Harper said. "If any human being

deserves to burn in the fiery pits of hell, it's that man. And until he's caught, this network will continue."

"He's the head of the snake," Autumn murmured.

"Exactly."

"Does Jak have a role in this task force that Agent Gallagher runs?"

"He consults with Mark, yes. We're also able to provide part of the funding in the form of private donations when necessary. Jak's grandfather left him a rather large inheritance when he died." They rounded a bend in the river and walked in silence for a moment before Harper stopped. "Should we turn around?"

Autumn halted too. "Oh, yes, I'm sorry. You're probably tired." They turned and began heading back to the house that was a mere speck now. Autumn could barely make out the two figures standing at the deck, talking about who knew what.

Harper smiled. "I'm fine, but Sam will be looking for you, and I don't want to walk out of sight. He'll want to see where you are, even if you're not right next to him." She gave Autumn a smile that was both teasing and knowing. "You're obviously very close."

Autumn felt Harper's questioning gaze on her but felt warmed by her curiosity. She had an ally, someone who understood something few others would.

"Yes," Autumn said. She gave her a brief description of how they'd met, glossing over most of the details the way Harper had with Jak's story. She knew they both understood the magnitude of what was beneath the surface. Autumn had a feeling she and this woman were going to be friends, not only because of their shared experience but because she seemed like a lovely person and was already easy to talk to.

There was a relatively short stone wall separating the property they were staying on and the one next to it, and Harper gestured to it and then hoisted herself up, letting out a small laugh at what Autumn assumed she saw as a lack of grace. Autumn took a seat next to her, glancing up at the deck where both Sam and Jak were still conversing, both men leaning on the rail, their gazes fixed on the spot where Autumn and Harper sat. Autumn moved her gaze to the water where Harper was also looking, and for a moment, they sat in companionable silence.

After a minute, Harper said, "You love him."

Was it that obvious? "Yes," Autumn admitted, and something about admitting it to another person made it feel all the more real. She picked at a thread on the hem of her wool coat. There were so many issues, so many questions to resolve, healing that had to happen. But it seemed to Autumn that all that would come much more easily if she could help Sam through it. With love. The same way that Bill and the town had helped her. Day by day. But while the town and Bill loved her, she was *in love* with Sam, and that, perhaps, added a level of complication. "How do I love him right?"

"Accept him," Harper said immediately. "Honor his choices. Don't presume what's right for him. He's had a lifetime of that."

A leaf floated by on the water, caught in an eddy, swirling in front of where they sat and then moving on. "Don't treat him like a child," Autumn clarified.

"Right. And that can be tempting because men who have grown up the way Jak and Sam have didn't get a childhood. In some respects, they're incredibly innocent. And in others, they're very, very jaded."

Yes, that was an apt way to describe Sam. He was very literal too, which Autumn found charming yet frustrating. That innocence Harper spoke of.

"Even more than that, Autumn, you have to love *all* of him. You have to let him know you love and accept every part of who he is. Not everything he's done—others choreographed that, manipulated, and coerced in horrific ways. But he's forever changed because of it. And you have to assure him you love him—you want him—for every aspect of himself. He can't fear you secretly hate a part of who he is, no matter how small, no matter if he'd rid himself of it if he could. It's there, and you have to love him for it."

Wow. Autumn took a moment to let Harper's words penetrate. She sensed deeply the truth in what she'd said. And she could only imagine the things Jak had struggled to accept about how he'd lived, perhaps what he'd done to survive, and how important Harper's acceptance was to him. Yet while Sam and Jak were similar, the difference was that Jak had grown up almost completely alone. "How did Jak survive the loneliness?" she asked, because while hearing it earlier had broken her heart, she was still amazed that he'd come out of it emotionally intact.

"He found my mother's teaching notes," Harper said, shooting Autumn a smile. "It's a long story that I'll happily tell you later, but when I was a child, we were in a car crash in the wilderness where Jak grew up. The authorities never found the vehicle, but Jak did. My mother's notes were in it, and they sustained him in so many important ways." And though it'd obviously been many years since she'd discovered this fact, her expression still spoke of amazement. *Her mother's teaching notes.*

"Sam found my journal when we were only teens,"

Autumn murmured. When Harper looked over at her curiously, Autumn explained, "It was just a book of poems and musings. Some drawings..." She shrugged. "Thoughts and dreams. He memorized it though. Every word. It was taken from him, so he rewrote it for me," she said, and even she could hear the awe in her voice. *Still*. It still awed her that he'd read it so many times he'd committed it to memory.

"That was the thing," Harper murmured, and there was awe in her tone as well.

"The thing?"

"The thing that saved. There has to be a *thing*, Mark says. Or a person. Just one. And he's right. A miracle." She grabbed Autumn's hand and squeezed it. "Your journal kept him sane," she said. "And it kept him human. It made him ask questions and showed him an alternative to what he was being taught. It opened his heart, and when the heart awakens, the mind will follow. They thought they caged his mind, Autumn, but your journal was an open window. The others didn't have that. In some ways, you are a god to him. You are the voice in the dark. You are his angel. You are *hope*."

"Oh...no, that can't be true." *I'm so imperfect. Not nearly worthy of that. Not nearly able.* "But if it is, I don't know if I can be that for someone forever."

"You can't be," Harper said. "He has to find his *own* voice, or he won't survive."

"How do I help him do that?"

"You already have. Now all you can do is be there for him as he navigates the rest. Jak did, and I'm placing my bets that Sam will as well."

Autumn turned Harper's words over in her mind. They simultaneously filled her with hope and apprehension. They brought insecurity too. "Do you think my journal...the words he used to sustain himself...well, that's why he..."

"Is hungry for you?" Harper laughed. "Anyone can see it in a glance. Men like Jak and Sam are very...forthright in that way. They don't hide it. They can't." She shot Autumn a grin. "No. I'm sure he feels some gratitude and respect for what your mind created that was strong enough to hang on to through whatever suffering he endured. But...you very obviously appeal to him for...other reasons as well. Reasons I don't think have anything to do with your poetry."

She grinned again, and Autumn couldn't help her answering smile.

After a moment though, Harper's smile dwindled. "He's hungry for you. And that scares him."

"Should it scare me too?"

Harper shrugged. "Maybe. You'll have to decide that. But if you decide it does, you have to let him go."

Autumn blew out a slow breath. Yes, that truth had been skating at the edge of her mind, and she hadn't yet acknowledged it because she hadn't wanted to. But she felt it in her bones. Yet even the *thought* of letting him go made her *ache* inside.

They were both quiet for another moment, Harper obviously letting her mull that over. It felt like something Autumn needed to do in private though, somewhere she could listen closely to her own heart, so she changed the subject. "You're obviously close to Agent Gallagher," she said. "Can we trust him?"

Harper smiled warmly. "Implicitly. We do. He proved himself to us many years ago when he helped rescue Jak and helped him find his place in the world. And he's been a part of our lives ever since. He's a grandfather to our son, and"—she patted her stomach—"to this one. And he's a father figure to us both. He's a good man, through and through. Trust him. I promise. You will not find a better team member."

Team member. "Thank you. It's been hard. Only us, facing so much uncertainty alone." And it'd been wonderful too, in some ways, but Autumn was so incredibly grateful that they had a team to walk with into whatever might be coming next.

"You're not alone anymore," Harper said, resting her hand on her shoulder. "We're only here for a short time, helping you and Sam settle in, offering whatever we can. And then we'll head back to Montana. But I hope you'll consider us family and call on us whenever you need to. And if at any point, you want to stay with us, we have more than enough room."

Relief flowed through Autumn, a feeling of community that she'd felt when she'd first moved in with Bill and met the people of her town. Only she'd been so young then, slower to trust, slower to listen to her gut, skittish in ways she wasn't now. She stood, reaching out her hand for Harper, who took it and stepped down from the wall, offering the same self-deprecating laugh she had when she'd climbed onto it. "Thank you, Harper. You have no idea how much I needed a friend."

Harper linked her arm with Autumn's as they started to walk. "Oh, but I do. I know very well."

Autumn conceded the point with a smile as they headed back up the stairs toward their men.

CHAPTER THIRTY-SEVEN

Sam stood in the doorway for a moment, watching suspiciously as Jak and Eddie wrestled on the floor. The child let out shrieks of laughter, attacking his father with all his strength, which was to say barely any. His father laughed, easily holding him at bay with a single extended arm. Sam couldn't understand it. He didn't understand play that didn't involve one opponent winning. But this clearly didn't, since if they were playing to win, Jak would have effortlessly overcome the small child who might someday be a giant but definitely wasn't one now.

It's how dogs play, he thought, remembering back to watching a mutt behave in the same way with her puppies on a street in Mexico City. He'd sat in the shade of a tree as he'd waited for a signal to come through on his phone about his target and watched her for a good long while. It'd interested him in the same way the sight before him did now. He'd thought then that the mutt was teaching her young how to fight, and maybe that was what Jak was doing too. But it surprised him, and he wasn't sure exactly why. Possibly because Sam had learned to fight, to be strong, in a much different way. There had been no laughter, no fun. There had only been images of violence and blood and carnage. And later...Autumn's pale, weak body lying prone for him to do with as he pleased. A deep shiver snaked down his spine, and he forced his mind back to where his gaze still lingered on Jak and his boy, tussling like wolves.

Then again, Jak had practically *been* a wolf for much of his life. He'd told Sam some of it. He'd told Sam to think of him as a brother.

Sam and Jak were the same yet so very different.

Sam didn't romp or laugh or play. He wouldn't even know how. When he tried to imagine it, it made him want to laugh and, strangely, to cry.

Harper, sitting on the couch nearby, using large needles that clicked and clacked to weave together a piece of yellow string, laughed when Jak growled at Eddie, flipping him over and putting his palm underneath the boy's head so that it didn't hit the floor. Eddie shrieked with apparent glee again, and Sam turned away, feeling inexplicably sullen about the whole scene.

Perhaps seeing Jak, who had endured similar trials, enjoying his life should have made Sam hopeful he could have that too. But it only did the opposite. To survive, he'd had to kill, but it hadn't been his sole purpose. They hadn't pumped darkness into Jak the way they had with Sam. Black tar still coated his mind, causing images to rise unbidden.

Autumn was sitting on a window seat in the eating area, a direct view to where Sam had just stood, watching Jak and Eddie play. She smiled, patting the seat next to her. Sam sat down, slumping against the pillows and staring morosely out at the gray water. This house was impressive, but he missed their cottage. He missed the way he'd felt there. He missed sitting on the rickety deck gazing at the forest, watching the way the water reflected the sky. Hearing birds chatter and squirrels squabble over nuts. It'd made him laugh. There was a deck here too, but it didn't feel the same.

Something inside him was different too, and he couldn't seem to focus on the sky or the birds or whatever small creatures might come along and amuse him. Mostly, he missed being alone with Autumn and feeling almost human. He'd just begun getting used to her touch, not just tolerating it but *craving* it, and now she didn't touch him as much because there were others around. And he didn't know how to do that either, be *around* people. Interact. Converse. They seemed to enjoy it, but it only brought him anxiety and made him more aware of his *otherness*.

"Kids are funny," she said, laying the magazine she'd been reading down. "And that Eddie is a little handful." She laughed, obvious affection dancing in her dark eyes. He could tell she liked the kid by the way she constantly smiled when he was around.

"I can't have any kids," he said, his tone matter-of-fact.

Autumn looked slightly stricken, and he immediately regretted the way he'd said it. "Oh. I'm sorry, Sam." She looked away, biting at her lip. She was upset, and it made Sam feel upset too. "Um, maybe we should have talked about that…at the cottage…when we…but, I'm on the pill. I've missed a few now but that shouldn't…well, you know." Her eyes moved over his features, staring at him like she needed rescuing.

Sam wanted to rescue her. It was all he wanted to do.

It was a burning flame inside him. Only Sam didn't know what to rescue her *from*, except possibly himself, so he simply stared back, helpless.

She lowered her eyes. "They almost took that from me too," she said. "The ability to have my own children." Her lips tipped down. "I've thought about that. I was so close," she murmured. "What if...well..." She blinked, bringing her gaze back to his and shaking her head, as if she wanted to take back what she'd said.

What if.

What if they had made her like him? Taken from her in the same way they'd taken from him?

He'd never really cared about not being able to have kids before. Never cared that they'd pumped him full of so many chemicals that they'd killed any chance of that. The thought of Sam with a child was ridiculous. But suddenly, the acknowledgment scratched slightly, like someone was picking at a scab that had almost healed. Not particularly painful, just...bothersome. *Why?* One more reminder of what he'd never be? Then again, what they'd done to Adam was a reminder as well. He felt stuck, confused, tormented, afraid to stay and afraid to go.

But you should go. You should. Agent Gallagher can keep Autumn safe. You're a risk to everyone.

Autumn reached out and took his hand, and for some reason, it made a needy wail rise in him. He pushed it down. He'd never heard that sound before, and it made him want to run away. He wanted to grab on to her, claw at her, pull her close, meld himself with her. To fuck her and fuck her until he finally felt *relief.*

He stood, her hand dropping, her expression startled. "I'm going outside," he said, the sentence streaming together into one long, mostly unintelligible word. Before she could reply, he turned and walked to the sliding glass doors and then out onto the deck.

He leaned against the railing, the same way he and Jak had done the day before, staring out, mostly unseeing, into the choppy water. It had rained earlier, and the air was still misty, dew sparkling on the midmorning grass. That same wail rose inside, turning into a growl. He was a monster, and though he'd stuffed the most fearsome part of his dark soul down, it wanted out. It wanted free.

He focused on his breath, in, out, lowering his heart rate as he'd been taught to do. *Calm. Steady. One operates best when one is in control of one's functions. Sharp. Deadly. Unaffected.*

The words that wound through his mind had been given to him, but he needed them now to restrain his roiling emotions.

He caught sight of a bird and watched as it landed at the side of a puddle, flapping its wings as droplets flew out into the air. *She was right to bring you to nature to heal,* Jak had told him when he'd described the fishing cottage and the way he'd sat on the deck and walked in the woods. *Nature reminds us of our place on the earth. It reminds us of what it means to be human.*

Maybe.

But Sam still didn't know if he was human. Maybe all the chemicals, all the metal and plastic and who knew what else had altered his very DNA to such a degree that he was more machine than man. Jak had been talking about a different sort of healing than bullet holes or stitched-up skin. But Sam didn't know how to measure any other type of healing than that.

The sliding glass door behind him opened, and he turned

to see a blur of dark hair barreling toward him, Superman cape flying out behind his miniature body.

Before Sam could brace for impact, the little thing latched onto Sam's leg, wrapping his arms and legs around him like a monkey on a tree. Sam frowned down at him, waiting. For what, he wasn't sure. The little monkey's grip grew tighter. Sam lifted his leg, giving it a shake to see if he could dislodge the thing. A peal of muffled laughter rose from the place where the kid's face was planted just above Sam's knee. If Sam bent his leg and kneed the kid, it would injure him. His knee was made of steel. He gave his leg another small shake. This time, the peal of laughter was louder as Eddie leaned his head back, gazing gleefully up at Sam.

Sam's confusion increased. *What does this kid want?*

He shook his leg harder, and Eddie shrieked with delight. Something loosened in Sam, that monster wail fading. *He wants to play.*

Sam felt lost. He didn't know how to play. He began walking, and Eddie's giggles rang out, unceasing. Sam had the urge to laugh too at the blatant ridiculousness of this. There was a small boy clinging to his leg.

Harper came out the door. "Oh, Sam, I'm sorry. Eddie—"

"Eddie?" Sam cut in. "No, I haven't seen Eddie. Maybe he's inside." Muffled laughter against his knee.

Harper's eyes danced. "That's so weird, because I didn't see him inside. You're sure you haven't seen him?"

"Nope. I have no idea where he might be. It's just me out here. Me and the growth on my leg."

"Oh. Yes, that's quite the situation there. Does it bother you?"

"Only when I'm trying to sleep," he said. His belly felt

warm. Maybe he *could* be like Jak. Sort of. At least a little. And that was better than nothing, right?

"Okay then," she said, taking a seat on one of the chairs that flanked a dining table, under a large tree whose branches overhung the deck. "I guess I'll just wait here and see if he shows up."

"Sounds good," Sam said, pacing the edge of the deck once and then again, the muffled laughter continuing. He suddenly didn't feel like such a monster, but even so, he acted as if he was one, holding his arms out, and walking with a staggering gait, groaning hideously. Back and forth he walked, his groan turning into a smile. The little boy laughed so hard, he lost his grip, slipping down Sam's leg and falling to the deck.

Sam bent down and picked him up, delivering him to his mother where she sat laughing too, one hand on her pregnant belly. Sam glanced to his left where Autumn sat watching through the window, a dreamy smile on her face, her eyes swimming with tears.

His stomach dropped, misery descending, at the pure joy on her face.

Joy for what she obviously wanted. Something she could only get from a different man. *One who was fully human and not mostly monster.*

Joy for what she'd never have. Not if she hung her hopes on him.

And really, all that was the least of their problems.

He muttered something to Harper, turning and descending the stairs quickly, hurrying through the yard and onto the path that meandered along the water, walking until his lungs burned, but his breath came easier.

CHAPTER THIRTY-EIGHT

The full moon outside the bedroom window glowed, casting a pale silvery glimmer through the opaque curtains. Autumn hadn't pulled the shades. There was no house directly across the way from which they might want privacy, and she preferred to wake with the sun.

And gaze at the moon.

She turned, her moonlight boy's hair as silver as the moonglow. She reached over and ran a finger over his silken hair and down his scratchy cheek. He murmured in his sleep, something unintelligible, and her heart squeezed with love. *Sweet, broken man.* His emotions seemed to exist on a roller coaster. Almost content one moment and then deeply distressed the next. Autumn wondered if he realized that part of his turmoil was that he was grieving for the old man named Adam. And of course, that emotion was only compounded by his guilt and his self-hatred. Thank God for Harper, there to give her an encouraging nod when Sam suddenly bolted, disappearing for hours and then returning, sweaty and morose.

Autumn wanted so badly to help him, but she could only love him. And she'd do that fiercely.

As long as he'd let her.

He murmured the word Macau again. He'd said that same word in his sleep before. Was it a place? A person? His murmuring became louder. He sounded so upset, his expression distraught. She wanted to let him sleep, but she also so badly wanted to comfort him. "Sam," she whispered, laying her hand on his shoulder.

He whimpered, thrashing his head, suddenly bolting up and turning toward her, his hands rising as though he was fending off an attack.

"Sam," she said again, a note of fear in her hushed voice this time. "Sam, it's me."

He let out a groan, collapsing back to the pillow, his forehead glistening with perspiration. "Autumn," he said. "I'm sorry."

She turned to him, bringing her palm to his cheek. "You have nothing to be sorry for, Sam. Nothing." For several moments, she simply soothed him, running her hand along his cheek, his damp forehead, over his hair. She leaned over and kissed his shoulder, wrapping her arm around him and holding him close. "Tell me about Macau," she said softly.

If she hadn't felt his muscles tighten, she might have thought he didn't hear her. But they had, so she waited for him to speak.

The curtains rustled in the light breeze coming through the slip of the open window. It was cold outside but warm under the heavy blankets, and Sam was like a personal heater, warmth emanating from his large body. The house was quiet around them, only the distant hoot of an owl and the soft sounds of the water kissing the shore beyond. The room felt dreamy, intimate, almost unreal. And maybe because of it, Sam would find it safe to open up to her about the things that haunted his dreams.

"I was sent to kill a man in Macau," he said very quietly.

A shiver of dread moved through her. He'd been sent to take a life. Just like Amon. "Who?" she whispered.

"I didn't know his name. All I knew was where he lived and that he was powerful. I don't know in what capacity. It mattered to someone but not to me. I cased this man's house. I gathered what information I could from the locals. I heard people saying that his daughter was dying."

"Dying from what?"

"I didn't know." He sighed softly, and she sensed how hard this was for him as he gathered the words to describe something that still haunted his dreams. "I heard a woman who worked in his home say his daughter was disabled and considered a...burden. I got the impression she'd been left to die."

"A burden?" Autumn breathed, her heart constricting. *Oh God*. That description hit Autumn particularly hard. It was exactly what Mercy Hospital had represented—a place where the unwanted, the burdensome, the children society preferred not to see were sent to die.

Sam was silent for a moment, perhaps to let her digest that, perhaps to gather his words. "I didn't think much about it. I didn't even know if it was true or just gossip. I entered the property, prepared to complete my mission."

"To kill this unnamed man."

"Yes." She saw by the set of his jaw in the dim room that he was struggling.

"But?"

"But I saw...her."

"Who?"

"The child. The little girl. I entered through the back of the house. I passed a door, and I heard…I heard a tiny voice, a moan. I almost kept going. I told myself to keep going. But…but I didn't. I opened the door. I went inside."

She continued to hold him. It was all she could do.

"She was so small. Her legs were atrophied. But her eyes…her eyes were like yours. Large and dark and…they contained a whole world. They reminded me…" He let out a gusty breath. "Her body was mostly dead…" He made a sound, something between a choke and a moan, and Autumn ached for this tenderhearted man. "But her eyes were beautiful. Her eyes…"

"What did you do, Sam?"

"It wasn't any of my business. To do anything other than kill the man I'd been sent to kill meant failure."

"Did you leave her there?"

"No. Sometimes I wish I had."

"Do you?"

He scrubbed his face with his palm. "I don't know."

Autumn pictured it then, though it hurt. The tiny, emaciated girl, alone in a room, left there for God knew how long to suffer and die because she was considered a burden. Useless. And Sam's hulking body, a shadow at first, drawing nearer. Had she been afraid? Had she thought he was death himself? Or had she seen him as the savior he'd been?

"I picked her up. She weighed nothing. She felt like a rag doll in my arms. I tried to leave the same way I came in, but I couldn't because I was carrying her. I was spotted by the man's security, and they chased me. Us. I was able to get back to my vehicle, and I put her in the front seat. I laid her head on my lap, and I drove. They followed. It was a bumpy ride. I tried to keep her head still. But…"

His words dwindled as though he'd gotten lost in that far-off land where he'd been sent to take a life but instead followed his soul's direction to save. After a moment, Autumn prompted him. "But?" she whispered.

He jolted slightly as though traveling swiftly to the present. To her arms. And she liked to think that was the thing that made him continue. "I finally evaded them. I got to a location where I could ditch the vehicle. I went to pick her up, to carry her, but she had died. She was already dead."

Oh, Sam. Her throat felt clogged. She felt his heartbreak, his deep confusion, as if it was her own. That was the reason he'd been dismissed from the program he'd been unwillingly enrolled in. He'd failed in their eyes, but he'd been a blazing success in hers. *They* were the ones who'd failed, because they couldn't suppress his humanity, his inborn need to answer the call of the helpless, no matter the cost. Her love for him was a living, breathing thing that felt too big, too overwhelming for her heart to contain. "She died being rescued," she said when she found her voice.

"But she still died."

"I'm sorry, Sam. I'm so sorry."

She squeezed him tighter, bringing her lips to his skin, kissing and soothing, whispering words of love. She felt his body loosen, his breath come easier. The owl outside hooted again, nearer this time, and the curtains stirred, a shiver of moonlight making the room sparkle, but only for a moment. He turned to her, his gaze moving over her face. In this low light and with the shifting shadows, Sam looked like any man. His scar was gone, his coloring blended. She only saw the angles and dips of his face, the soft swell of his lips.

They'd taken so much from him. So much. Yet he'd retained a gentle heart. A miracle. *Her* miracle. Her love.

The curtain lifted, a filmy shaft of moonlight falling over Sam momentarily and exposing him to her in all his myriad differences. Her heart warmed. There he was, her Sam, the real version she preferred. The version built from pain and struggle and strength and fortitude. And though she was deeply sorry he had been made to experience those things, he was *him* because of them.

She felt him respond to her touch, not just in acceptance but with need, so she let her lips linger on his neck, her hand exploring the contradictions of this man's body. The landscape of Sam. *I could spend the rest of my life charting you.* Velvety smooth in one spot and raised and rough in another. Muscle to knead in one area and the resistance of a metal plate somewhere else. He groaned softly, a masculine sound of arousal that her body immediately responded to, softening where Sam was growing hard. "Every inch of you is beautiful," she told him, meaning it down to her marrow.

He made a grunt of disagreement, a note of bewilderment under the gruff sound.

I'm going to make you believe it, Sam. Someday.

She laced her fingers with his, bringing them up and gazing at her small hand in his large one. She remembered thinking, so long ago, in that forest where she'd first cast eyes upon him, that he could crush her beneath him if he wanted. Yet in some metaphorical way, she felt like she was holding *him* in her hand, that only she was the one capable of crushing. His heart, his view of himself. Again, she felt that edge of fear, that unworthiness, but she breathed it away. He was counting on her, so she would be brave. "Touch me," she whispered.

"After that?" he breathed.

After that. After he'd told her what happened in that distant land where he'd tried to save a little girl and, to his mind, failed.

But not to hers.

"Especially after that," she said.

His breath hitched. "Tie me up."

She raised herself up and leaned over him, her gaze meeting his in the shadowy room. "No. I want to feel your hands on me. I want to feel you over me. Because I trust you. Because I love you."

He blinked, his soul shining in his gaze, his lips parting in a surprised O. He took her face in his hands, cradling it gently, and she tilted her head, smiling, nuzzling her cheek against his palm. He brought his mouth to hers, kissing her softly, slowly, as she lay back on her pillow and he leaned over her, his large body above hers for the very first time. She relished the moment, the feel of his lips pressing down on her, the heat of his naked skin mere inches from hers. Despite being at his mercy, she'd never felt more protected. She whispered his name between kisses. There was no fear, no trepidation. She knew he would never hurt her. She always had. He'd learned to receive, but she realized now that maybe it was even more important that he learned how to trust himself enough to give.

Their kisses grew deeper, his skin hotter, the press of his arousal probing her hip. She shivered with delight, with anticipation, growing wetter between her legs with each stroke of his tongue. "Undress me, Sam," she said between kisses.

He hesitated for only a moment, leaning back and helping her lift her tank top over her head. The mechanics of undressing, of removing her underwear, his boxers, was awkward in the close quarters of their double bed, yet there was something dreamy about it too, something magical and secret, and they laughed softly, that laughter dissolving into moans as naked skin touched naked skin and again, he brought his mouth to hers.

"Please," she whispered, taking his hand to her breast, sighing when his rough palm grazed her nipple.

He raised his head, watching her face as he explored, running a thumb over her nipple as she moaned his name. His hips thrust, an instinctive seeking, and as if he'd heard her silent asking, he brought his mouth to the place his fingers had just been. She gasped, pressing her breast to his mouth, fireworks of pleasure bursting between her thighs when he gently pulled.

He spent several minutes going between her breasts, kissing, exploring, and though there was a dreamy quality to their interlude, for Autumn, it was also bright and vivid. Not the room or the outside world but them, their bodies, as they sought and gave, pleasure flowing from one to the other. As if she'd fallen asleep and been swept into an electrical storm.

He trailed his hands down her stomach, touching, feathering, seemingly rapt, intent on knowing every inch of her. Autumn gloried in his slow exploration. He was also driving her insane with desire. "I need you so much, Sam," she said, lifting her hips, her own desperate seeking, the raw need to be filled and stretched, to feel the way her body so naturally accepted him. To experience the welcome invasion of every part of her all at once: her body, her heart, and her soul.

She almost expected him to hesitate or even resist, when he didn't, when he first brought his hand between her legs, stroking, she almost wept with the bliss but also the relief. He was as caught up as she was, even if not as certain. She could still see the vulnerability in his heavy-lidded eyes, still feel the unpracticed nature of his movements. It made her craving for him rise higher. She was vibrating with it. She'd known sex could be more than she'd experienced it in the past, but she'd never realized passion could be like this. Like burning hunger. Like sweet insanity.

His finger dipped inside her, and she cried out softly, her hips bucking. He let out a low growl, doing it again and then using his finger to mimic the movements she'd made with her own hand when she'd made herself come. She'd told him there was something infinitely better about having someone else give you pleasure, and she hadn't been wrong. "Oh, Sam, Sam, Sam," she moaned. It was so good. His finger sped up, gliding easily through her drenched folds. She was only delicious sensation and breath and the booming echo of her own heart. Her body sang, and so did her soul, each note calling his name. "Please," she panted, and he covered her body with his, replacing his finger with the blunt tip of his erection. Their eyes met. His body quivered. He was shaking with need, with some measure of fear perhaps too. "I love you," she breathed again, right before he began pressing slowly inside, her arousal easing the way, her body remembering him, ecstatic at his return.

He panted, groaned, gasping her name as he began to move, slowly at first, pausing before each deliberate press that brought his flat stomach to hers. She spun higher, the electrical storm sparking around her, glowing brighter, carrying her away so that she could only wrap her legs around his hips and hold on tight.

His movements sped up as he relinquished some control,

and she let out a strangled gasp of joyful bliss, his hips thrusting ever faster. She wanted to scream with the pleasure, but she knew she couldn't do that, not here, so she turned her head to the side, squeezing her eyes shut as the first wave of release crashed over her, making her gasp and thrash. It went on and on, one crest after the other until she was mindless, boneless, and sobbing his name.

He came with a gasp and a groan, pressing his face into her neck as he shuddered, pressed, and poured into her, eventually slowing, their stilted breath merging with the gentle breeze making the curtains lift and sway. She ran her fingers over his back, up his arms, the beauty of what they'd just experienced still sparkling through her cells.

At some point, they fell asleep, though it was hard to remember the difference between reality and slumber. She woke slowly, her body remembering the night before her mind brought it forth. She reached for him, but his side of the bed was empty. She leaned up to see a note on the bedside table, telling her in his blunt, all-caps writing that he'd gone for a walk. She placed it back down and then hugged her pillow, a dreamy smile tilting her lips, the beauty of the night still filling her with wonder.

CHAPTER THIRTY-NINE

"Do you have a minute to chat?" Mark asked as he came into the kitchen.

Autumn placed her almost-empty coffee cup down, looking up at the agent who, in only a few short days, had begun to become a trusted friend. His expression was troubled, and a tremble of trepidation made the hair on her neck rise. "Of course. Is everything okay?"

"I'd like to tell you and Sam about what I've found regarding—ah, here he comes now," Mark said, nodding out the window behind Autumn.

She turned to see Sam walking across the yard from the path along the water, a hood pulled up over his head, shoulders hunched.

He came through the door a moment later, taking down his hood. Their eyes lingered, memories of the night before flowing between them, adding an invisible shimmer to the air. Her heart quickened, and she had the inane temptation to giggle, despite her worry about why Mark was calling a meeting with them. "Good morning," she said instead. "Mark wants to tell us something."

Sam looked at Mark. "Okay."

"Let's go into the living room," he said, leading the way.

When they got there, Jak was already seated near the fireplace. Harper had told Autumn she was taking Eddie into town for some groceries, and Autumn had assumed Jak was going with them too, so the sight of him surprised and concerned her.

It was clear that Mark had wanted him there for a purpose.

The knowledge made her concern climb higher.

She and Sam sat down on the couch, and Mark took the other seat flanking the fireplace.

"I got the results back from the lab my task force works with that I overnighted your blood samples to," he said, diving right in. "Neither of you were ever exposed to ADHM."

It felt as if a bomb detonated between Autumn's ribs. She looked over at Sam, who was staring at Mark, his expression stunned. "How is that… I mean, I suspected it about myself, but Sam…" She was at a loss for words. She reached out, taking Sam's hand in hers. It was cold from his walk, and it sat limply in her own. "Sam was never exposed either? That must be a mistake because…" Her gaze flew over him. His knees, his ribs, his shoulders, temples. *Oh God*. Then *why*?

She looked back at Mark. Both his gaze and Jak's were on Sam, both men watching him closely as though he might blow at any moment. Her fingers tightened on his.

"No," Mark confirmed. "It's not a mistake. Sam, are there any questions I might answer that will make this easier for you?"

"Say anything you want, Sam," Jak encouraged. "We're

all here. To share this. Yell if you want to, flip a table. We'll clean it up."

Sam's body had grown still. He sat silent and morose now, but his eyes...his eyes were shimmering with what looked like rage and confusion. Grief. "I was sick with something else then," he said, still obviously trying to find a better explanation than the one he'd just been given, but Autumn heard the uncertainty in his voice. "That's why I had the surgeries. The surgeries that made me..." His words cut off with a small, choked noise. *Oh, Sam. Sam.*

"No, Sam. You weren't sick," Mark said very gently. "You were never sick."

"Why did they think I was?"

"They couldn't have," Mark said, and Autumn appreciated the directness. "They would have known you were not. We can do more testing to show—"

"No, never again," Sam growled. "No more tests. No more." His voice was a strangled yell, and a sob moved up Autumn's throat. *What did they do to you? Oh, Sam.*

"Okay, Sam. No more," Mark said, the same gentleness in his voice, the tone a father would use.

She didn't blame Sam for his grief, his obvious pain and confusion. She herself had felt similarly when she'd read the words in her folder: suspected ADHM. But Autumn had also been cut free of her incorrect diagnosis—if that was all it was, a big, giant *if*—many, many years before. Sam's had gone on and on and to a much more invasive extent.

"If neither of us were ever sick," Autumn said, "then *why*?"

Mark sat back. "I located the nurse you were looking for. Salma Ibrahim."

Autumn drew in a breath. "Salma?" Just the woman's

name on her lips was a soul balm at just the moment she needed one. "Where? How?"

"I have a few more resources than you," he said, offering a small smile. "She had her license taken from her. She's working as an in-home day care provider. She's well, and she misses you. I'll give you her information."

"Yes, please."

"Salma had seen evidence that caused her to question things at Mercy. They fired her before she could copy that evidence or do anything with it. Then they destroyed her reputation and her credibility until she had no choice but to give up and attempt to rebuild her life."

"Oh my God," Autumn said.

Oh, Salma. She'd helped her when no one else had. To know the woman had suffered for it made Autumn ache. *Without you, Salma, I never would have known I was well.* She shuddered inside to think of it. To imagine what would have happened to her had she *not* gone off her medication.

Sam hadn't said a word, but she sensed his tumultuous emotions as they rose inside him, his hand growing ever warmer by the moment as, inside perhaps, his blood boiled. "She suspected the truth, that I never had ADHM," she guessed.

"Yes. And more so that you and several of the others were being used as a control group for the cocktail of medications they had you on, specifically the Mesmivir."

She blew out a breath. To have it confirmed… God, it hurt. And it fanned a flame of anger, one that was just beginning to flicker. They'd stolen years from her. *Years.* And double that of Sam's.

"Your blood tests confirmed Salma's suspicions," Mark said. "I'm attempting to pull files that will provide more information, but a lot is sealed. And I assume much has been destroyed."

"*How?*" she asked.

"That's always the biggest question," Jak said. "And I don't know that I've come to a reason that brings me any peace." He looked at Sam. "But maybe that's a good thing, because there should never be peace when it comes to hurting children. So here's my best guess: greed, weakness, fear, pure evil in some cases, though I think that's rarer." He paused for a moment. "I've spent a lot of time considering their reasons, but I think it's time better spent working to rescue those still suffering. You're not nearly there yet, Sam, but you will be. If I can offer you any hope right now, it's that you will be."

Autumn hoped to God Jak's words were penetrating, though from the look on Sam's face, too much pain was radiating inside him for any words to make much difference.

Autumn's anger and grief were a flickering flame, but Sam's were a raging inferno, and rightly so. They'd experimented on both of them. But what they'd done to Sam had destroyed his belief that he was capable of being a human being. *Of deserving love.* Her eyes moved over his visible scars, and she pictured the many others. So many others. But it was the deeper scarring that she now feared the most. The ones that had scraped away at his soul. Jak had mentioned pure evil was rare, but if anything should be defined as such, it was this.

"If some of us were the control group, then others really were sick," she said as she voiced her thoughts. "But were they made *sicker* by the medication?" The very idea was making her nauseous, her head pounding.

"I don't have the answer to that," Mark said. "Not yet."

Not yet. Autumn reached up and massaged her temples, alleviating the ache in her head if not in her heart. She had tried to dig up answers; Salma had attempted to do so too and been destroyed. But if she had any hope, it was that Agent Mark Gallagher had the weight of the government behind him.

Or was the government involved in what had been done to them? Mark had said he worked for a classified task force under the cover of one more public. So in essence, they worked in secret. How far up did this go? She swallowed, the world swaying. It was too much to consider, much less ask about. She gripped Sam's hand tighter, his fingers finally curling around hers.

They'd *both* been betrayed. Deeply. "They put us in the woods," she said. "To be hunted." She hadn't mentioned it yet because she saw the misery in Sam's expression each time they spoke of it. But Mark needed to know the depth and breadth of the evil so he could hold the right people responsible. "They told us our memories were dreams." Sam looked away, and she squeezed his hand more tightly.

I won't let you go. This is not your shame to carry.

Jak's brows raised, and Mark blinked. "Salma mentioned the dreams that seemed to coincide with the full moon," he murmured.

"It's how we met," Autumn said. "The part of the hospital where Sam was raised was off-limits to us." She told them about the dreams that weren't dreams, about Sam protecting her, about the dirt under her fingernail, her suspicions, Salma's instruction, the silver hair she'd put under her tongue, the only hiding spot she could think of, guessing they might clean her body before she woke.

"They," Mark said. "Who do you think *they* were?"

"The staff, I imagine. Or at least a few members of the staff. It couldn't have happened without their cooperation, even though it only took place once a month. For whatever reason, they chose the full moon. Maybe it was just a marker. I don't know."

Mark blew out a long breath. She had the feeling that little shocked this man, but what she'd just told him had. Mark and Jak shot each other looks full of the same shattered surprise. For reasons she couldn't quite explain right then, it made her feel better that they both still felt horror at what was horrible. They weren't hardened, though if anyone had a right to be, it was men who rescued brainwashed and tormented human beings.

Did the other nurses know too? Did they even suspect? Did even one other fight like Salma, or did they all look away?

"Sam," Jak said. "What were you told was the purpose of those nights?"

"Training. Training to be killers." He looked absolutely distraught, and a faraway look came into his expression, as if the dark forest he spoke of was appearing within his mind. "Some didn't run," Sam said, still looking away, his eyes focused on the trees outside the window. "Some hid or lay still." He paused, and they all waited. The weight of their collective despair in the room was palpable. "We could do whatever we wanted to them. There weren't any rules, except to make it quick. Making them scream more than once was discouraged."

She held back the tears that were threatening to fall. *I will not cry, not now.* It would kill Sam.

He went on, his tone wooden, expression distant as he continued to stare past her. "They were weak and sick. If we didn't practice…if we didn't hunt them, their dying would be prolonged. Their pain would be prolonged. We were only questioned if we usurped another hunter's choice or got in his way. That was the only rule."

Jak stood and then grabbed a wooden chair from the writing desk near the door and set it next to Sam. He put his hand on his shoulder and gripped. "I understand your pain and your guilt, Sam. I was set up too. To hurt. To kill. It's not your fault," he said. "And more than that, you disobeyed their orders, Sam. She's here," he said, nodding at Autumn. "She's here because you protected her."

Sam breathed out, dropping his head and bringing his hands to his face. In so doing, Jak's hand was jolted away, and Autumn's hand was dropped. "Did you watch violent films? Play bloody video games, over and over and over? Were you punished if you refused? Rewarded if you did not?"

Jak shot Mark a look, and Mark's face fell. "No," Jak said. "I overcame other things but not that, Sam."

Sam scrubbed his hands down his face, standing with a low growl and stalking out of the room.

With a small cry of distress, Autumn stood to follow him, but Jak stopped her with a gentle hand on her arm. "He needs time," he said.

She sank back down onto the couch. "What did he mean about films and games?" she asked weakly.

"He means they used mind control on him," Mark murmured, giving his head a shake, his eyes filled with worry. "They attempted to rewire his brain."

Brainwashing. They'd tried to make him violent. But they'd failed. Sam was gentle. If anyone could attest to that, she could. "How much time should I give him?" she asked Jak.

Jak appeared deeply troubled. He looked in the direction

Sam had gone for a long moment, then at Mark and finally back to Autumn. "Most likely quite a bit. His entire life has just been pulled out from under him." He paused. "Those walks he keeps going on are good for him. He notices everything, and spending time in nature is important because it will help him remember who he is, his role on this earth. It might sound silly, but I assure you it's not. He considers himself half monster, half machine. His body ceased to be his long, long ago." A shadow passed over Jak's handsome features before he continued. "But I believe he held on to enough of his mind that he can still find his way back. With your help, and when he's ready. It might be a bumpy road, but he knows your voice, Autumn. He's depended on it for a long, long time. It's what he will use to find his way home."

CHAPTER FORTY

The monster inside was screaming again. Bellowing. Violent visions swept through his head, the ones they had shown him over and over and over for years on end. Only now, *their* faces were the faces of the wrecked and wounded. The nurses, the doctors, the ones who had hurt and used him. And Autumn. The ones who had looked away, who had kept quiet, who had allowed such brutality to occur and sounded no alarm at all. Nothing. They'd done *nothing*.

He wanted to rip and tear and *destroy*.

But that was who they'd trained him to be. So he wouldn't. Not here.

Sam stared at himself in the mirror, water droplets rolling down his skin. *Cold* water droplets, the ones he'd become accustomed to, the temperature that offered a strange sense of comfort. He had never been sick. He'd been born healthy. The monstrous howl rose, his hands fisting, his features twisting. They'd taught him to kill, and it hadn't come naturally. He'd done it anyway because he'd been convinced it was right. But he'd *gladly* kill now with no persuasion whatsoever. He'd hack and stab and maim all of them if given the chance.

Every. Last. One.

They hadn't *healed* him as he'd been told. They hadn't *helped* him. They'd sliced into him. They'd replaced his body parts with metal. They'd removed what was his. They'd *stolen* from him. The rising moan could be held back no longer, and it rushed from his mouth as he leaned forward, bracing himself with his hands on the sink, attempting to calm his pounding heart.

I was normal once.

He'd believed that the doctors had healed him, had performed necessary surgeries that not only repaired his ruined body but made him stronger, more powerful. Better. *Valuable.* They'd been healed for a purpose. Made *strong* for a purpose. They'd told him that he and the others would be an elite fighting force who would be sent on righteous missions for governments and special forces. And though he'd eventually begun to suspect that the missions were not what they'd been told, at least he could say that they had saved his life. Even if they hadn't used it for anything good. But that too had been a lie. Every bit of it. The surgeries were merely experiments using his flesh. There was no righteousness in their work. They weren't making the world better. They were merely pawns for rich people to use to distract from their sins, to commit atrocities that served others' greed for power. Disposable. Subhuman.

Unnatural.

All the violence that had been funneled into his brain had been used to groom him to do anything…anything they wanted him to do, no matter how violent, no matter how gruesome. Without remorse. He'd been born completely human.

And now...now...

His brain was as ruined as his body. He gripped his head, using his fingers to squeeze until it hurt. He wanted *out* of his own skin. It didn't belong to him. Nothing did. They'd taken it all.

He stepped to the wall and knocked his forehead against it once and then again, harder, harder, again and again until his breath came easier and his heart slowed. He stood there for many minutes, his head throbbing as he breathed, the monster quieting. *For now.*

He'd fooled himself into thinking there was a way forward, but that wasn't true. He'd lingered here too long, even knowing his presence only risked her safety and in more ways than she realized.

He dressed and left the bathroom, heading toward the bedroom he shared with Autumn. As he passed the window, he caught a glimpse of all of them on the back deck, Eddie using a big wand to blow bubbles. One exploded in his face, and he laughed, causing the rest of them to laugh as well. Sam's gaze moved to Autumn, her beautiful, smiling face watching Eddie, her eyes then moving to Harper, who said something Sam couldn't hear, her hand running over her pregnant belly. Autumn's eyes held sadness, but her smile grew, her pretty teeth showing. He saw the way she looked at them. He saw the longing in her eyes.

They almost took that from me too.

Even if both their safety could be assured...even if he managed to contain the monster inside him...how fair would it be that Autumn almost had her ability to have children—a family—taken away once, only to have it taken away again?

Where was the justice in that?

And if there was no future for them, then why put her in any further jeopardy? He'd done enough of that.

He stood there watching her as she laughed. She was so beautiful, it pained him. So full of life, with so much love to give. *I love her.*

Sam hadn't been built for love. He'd been built for pain and mayhem. Nothing more.

Sam turned away from the window and walked to the bedroom. He had nothing to offer her. Nothing at all. His limbs felt as heavy as the other parts of him made from metal. He was nothing more than a walking machine. *Do machines feel this much pain?* He didn't know, but maybe there was one person who could answer his questions, who could offer a *reason why* that would help rid him of this terrible anguish he carried.

His duffel bag, with the few items he owned, was on the floor, though *owned* might not be the right word, considering most of the items now inside were things Autumn's father had given to him. He no longer had the weapon that had been in it when Agent Gallagher had shown up. He'd thrown it in the river the first day they'd arrived. The more he thought about it, the more he worried that there was a tracking device of some kind on it. Maybe that was how they'd located the apple farm where he'd lived for a time. He hadn't been able to find one, but he'd tossed it anyway. They were surrounded by two strong men who would fight for them if need be, and both had several weapons as well. He'd killed for the program with that gun, and he didn't want it anymore.

He picked up the bag and set it on the bed and then put the toothbrush and razor he'd carried from the bathroom into a side pocket.

The door behind him opened and then shut. He didn't turn.

"Sam? What are you doing?"

"Packing."

She came up beside him and placed her fingers on the side of his jaw, turning his face to hers. Her gaze went to the red spot on his forehead where he'd banged it against the wall. There was so much concern in her eyes. Fear. "Why, Sam?"

He turned back to the bag and zipped it closed. "I'm only risking your safety being here."

"I'll take that risk, Sam, in order to stand beside you."

"That's ridiculous. There's no reason to take any risk for me."

Her hand dropped, and she opened her mouth to speak, but he interrupted her.

"There's no place for me here, Autumn. I'm not like Jak. Jak isn't a freak of nature. Jak can blend in. Jak isn't reminded every time he looks in the mirror who he is."

"Who he is?" she asked. "Who are you, Sam? Who do you think you are?"

I'm nobody. I'm a monster. I don't know. I don't know. "I'm a murderer, that's who I am," he said. It was one thing he knew for sure and something she couldn't deny. And Autumn, beautiful, precious, miraculous Autumn, deserved better than that.

"You're not. You're a savior. You saved me, and you saved that helpless little girl."

"I didn't save her. She died." The picture of her frail, sore-ridden body filled his mind, and a red cloud of rage blossomed in his brain. He'd just gotten control of the monster within, and now it was *back,* and he didn't want that. Autumn didn't understand the world. She didn't know how ugly and brutal it was. She didn't *see* him for who he really was because she insisted on viewing him and the world through rose colored glasses. "That girl died because the very people who were supposed to protect her with their lives left her to die a horrible, miserable death. They let her suffer, Autumn. They were her family, and they let her suffer. They must have heard her, calling for help. And they didn't answer."

He'd expected her to look taken aback by his harsh words, but she didn't. She took a step closer, her eyes so soft he wanted to fall into them. He turned away but felt her hand on his arm. "Did you feel that way too, Sam? All those surgeries, all that pain, did you call for someone who never came? I did."

He attempted a laugh, but it came out half growl, half some sound he couldn't describe. "But no one did, did they?" He turned to her, meeting her eyes. Those eyes, those eyes. "You might as well have called into a void," he told her. It was cruel, yet it was true.

"I wasn't calling into a void," she said evenly. "Because you answered. *You* came. You rescued me just like you rescued that little girl."

"She's *dead*."

"There's nothing you could have done about that. I think she waited for you, Sam. She waited until she wasn't alone. Because of you, she didn't die in a back room, alone."

Autumn, Autumn, Autumn. He wanted to wail her name, collapse in her arms, take from her until she had no more left to give. He hated himself for it. "You have a way with words. Only words are meaningless in a world like the one we live in." He pulled in a breath. "Maybe I saved that little girl or tried anyway. But I didn't always *save*. Mostly I didn't. If you…" He released a ragged breath. His lungs felt so damn tight. "If you knew all of what I did, if you pictured it, you'd feel differently about me."

"No, I wouldn't. I'm sorry I ever gave you that impression. I'm sorry I was ever stupidly scared, even for an instant. I failed you. I was a hypocrite because *I* was the one who told you truth mattered above all else and then I was afraid to hear yours."

He almost let out a disbelieving laugh. *She* was apologizing to *him*? Did she even hear what he was telling her? He was describing all the ways in which he was monstrous.

"I want you to feel safe with me, Sam, even your darkest parts. Because I want to share your burden." She put her hand on his arm, her touch gentle, loving, just like her, and it almost killed him. It almost stole his resolve. "Because I realize now that there's nothing you could do of your own free will that would make me turn away."

She was wrong though. She had no idea. Some truths were simply too terrible to carry, and he wouldn't ask her to. He wouldn't. He steeled himself. He knew how. He'd forced himself to do things he hadn't wanted to do for all his existence. He shook her hand away. "What does free will mean when it comes to taking a life? The things I did, I knew they were wrong. I knew." He'd completed many "successful" missions. He'd killed, in ways both bloody and not. He'd looked in men's eyes and seen their life drain away. He'd been the assassin, maybe even killing men like Adam. Decent men who had families and apple farms and generosity in their hearts. Either way, innocent or corrupt, those faces lived inside his head along with the images of violence. They'd never leave, not as long as he lived. No wonder the program directed them to kill themselves. It was best really, for everyone, especially for them. A small, surprising mercy. There was no life after what they'd become.

She chewed at her lip, seeming to consider what he'd said. "You had limits, Sam. I don't know that you ever defined them for yourself. But you found a way to follow your conscience, maybe not every time but more than they expected. Do you know how strong you had to be to do that?"

She thought he was strong? Not even close. He was the weakest man on earth. "Oh Jesus, Autumn," he said. Her continued faith in him *hurt*. It wasn't his to keep, and to see a glimpse of it and have to let it go was more painful than all his surgeries and procedures combined. It made him feel desperate and angry. He didn't want to give it up. He wanted to keep it, to keep her. But he couldn't, he couldn't, and he lashed out with the hurt, the unfairness of who he was, who he'd been made to be. "You romanticize everything," he growled. "It's fucking stupid because life is not romantic. Life is ugly and awful more often than it's not. And people are evil. They kill children and they laugh about it. They lie and they cheat and they steal, and they feel no remorse at all, or if they do, they justify it anyway."

His growl became fiercer, but her eyes grew softer as if she didn't hear. Okay then, he'd *make* her hear.

"You should know that better than anyone because *you* were used. You meant *nothing* to them, less than nothing. No mother. No father. No one to protect you. So you were simply a body to test their drugs on, no better than a lab animal. They wouldn't have cared if you died, except that they'd have to find another nothing to replace you with. They would have let you be raped and murdered, and then they would have lied about it and covered it up because you. Meant. Nothing."

They stood there, toe-to-toe, him breathing harshly, pain etched in her face but fire blazing in her eyes. That same fire that had warmed him—not his body but his heart—so long ago in a cold forest where she'd been left to die. Oh God, he loved her. He loved her so fiercely he wanted to fall to his knees and beg her to forget the cruel words he'd said.

"I'm sorry," he breathed, turning his head.

"Don't be," she said, surprising him. Always surprising him, his Autumn. He turned his gaze to her again. "You told the truth. I did mean nothing to them. At least nothing more than cells and bones and systems they could test their products on in order to become rich and powerful. They *did* leave me to die. And yet..."

She tilted her head, regarding him. He hung on her words. He always had. He supposed he always would.

"And yet you didn't let me be raped. Or murdered. You stepped in, and you protected me when it might have cost you. Even when you'd been trained to do differently. I might have meant nothing to a soulless group of evil people looking to profit off the backs of the weak and the helpless. But I meant something to you, and that's what matters to me. That's *all* that matters to me."

He released a gust of breath. That pain again. The hollow one. The one that stirred his need, made it swirl inside, a bottomless tornado of longing that would only unleash destruction. On him. On her. He stepped back, turned away, looking out the window at the cloud-covered sun. He had to let her go. It was the only way to love her in the way she deserved to be loved. "Your words meant so much to me," he said. "Every one of them. But they were a child's words. I should have treated them with the weight of any silly child's thoughts. You should grow up, Autumn. You should realize that the world is far different than you envisioned it once. Dreams based on impossibilities don't ever come true."

There was silence behind him for a moment. He'd succeeded in hurting her. It made him miserable. "Who's to say what's impossible?" she finally said quietly. "When there's love?"

Love. Oh God. He wanted to scream and howl. And rejoice. And grieve. "I'm a ticking time bomb." She shouldn't trust him. He couldn't even trust himself. And she certainly shouldn't love a dormant grenade. "My training didn't just consist of chasing you through the woods. They installed violence into our brains. It lies there in wait."

Sam startled, his head whipping in the direction of the other room where Eddie shrieked with glee or surprise or outrage or one of the many other things Eddie shrieked about.

"Is that why you're pushing me away like this?" she asked. "I know you need time to accept the information you've been given today. That's only natural, Sam. And I'll give you all the time you need. Years if that's what it takes. But let me help you." She moved closer. "Help me understand. Are you worried you're going to mentally blow up someday? Are you worried they planted things so deeply in your mind that they might rise to the surface when you're unaware because of a smoke alarm or…a shrieking child? Please don't push me away because you fear what might light some latent fuse—"

"I can't have children!" he shouted, taking a step toward her, looming. Attempting to scare her, not because he wanted to but because she needed to be scared, and he had to make her see *why*. She arched her back but stood her ground.

"I'm sorry they took that from you without your permission. There are other ways to create families if we decide—"

"If we decide? There's nothing for us to decide." He stepped away from her, grabbed his duffel bag, and then moved toward the door. "Let me go, Autumn. You deserve far more than what I have to offer." *Nothing. You deserve far more than nothing.*

He heard his name fall from her lips, pleading, as he stormed out the door, and his stomach muscles clenched in agony. But he kept walking anyway, because Sam had saved her once, and he intended on doing it again, only this time would be far more permanent. This time, Sam would save her from himself.

CHAPTER FORTY-ONE

There was only one possible person to turn to now, and he stood in front of the man's house, staring bleakly at it, the last glimmer of hope barely glowing in his chest.

Sam had nothing except a few items in a duffel bag. But Dr. Heathrow would help him, wouldn't he? He was the only father Sam had ever known. Maybe it was Dr. Swift and others like him who pulled all the strings. Maybe Dr. Heathrow was like Autumn's Salma, caught up in an endeavor he thought was good and just and was tricked like Sam. Like all of them. *Please, please, please.*

Despite the sense of desperation, he managed to keep putting one foot in front of the other. The doctor would help him find a place to go at least. Sam hadn't asked him for help when he'd dismissed him from the program, because he'd planned on ending his life. But that had been delayed and then delayed again. He'd probably go through with it now in one manner or another. Perhaps it was time. All their programming hadn't compelled him to do it, but his weakness, the probability that he would never be able to fully let Autumn go, might very well be the reason he needed. The monster inside would always claw for her, reaching, reaching, and he simply couldn't let it happen. Refused to hurt her more than he already had. Didn't want to live a life of never-ending misery.

Let me go. The words had come from his mouth, but inside he'd been screaming, *Keep me.* And maybe she would, for a time, but not forever, and that would kill him just as much as a bullet to the head or a knife to the heart, only *worse.* He'd left so he wouldn't suffer more than he already had. And because he loved her and he wanted her to have her dreams. Because he'd left, now she was safe.

He walked slowly up the steps. The house was massive, with a white brick facade and black shutters, the landscaping as groomed and pristine as the hospital gardens. Not a leaf dotted the expanse of fall-faded lawn.

He pressed his finger to the doorbell and heard that distant chime within. Footsteps sounded, and a moment later, the door was pulled open. Dr. Heathrow stood there, the color draining from his face as he stumbled back. A small gasp emerged, and his hand came up as though warding Sam away.

Sam stepped inside, reaching out to the doctor who continued backward. "Please," Sam said. "I need help."

Dr. Heathrow stumbled into the room next to the foyer, pointing a finger at the phone and then back at Sam. "Stay back, monster!" he said, tripping on a chair leg, almost falling but catching himself. He came to stand against a wall, cowering, as Sam advanced.

Sam's throat closed. Devastation. The thing he'd known but hadn't wanted to confront was staring him dead in the eyes. This man had not been tricked or mislead by a pharmaceutical company or by others who had misdiagnosed Sam and then asked the doctor to perform surgeries he didn't know were unnecessary. He'd done it all knowingly and then profited from the missions he sent his creations on. *You created me. You made me what I am.*

Sam stopped, that hollow feeling inside opening impossibly wider. He stood for a moment, staring blankly at the man he'd once thought…loved him? No, no, he hadn't felt that. But he'd thought he cared. He'd thought he *tried*. He'd thought he'd felt sadness to see Sam go.

"You knew," he said. "You knew I was never sick. Were any of us?"

Dr. Heathrow's gaze darted around the room and then back to Sam. He swallowed, straightening. "Not in the traditional sense of the word. But you needed saving."

Sam's blood slowed, a part of him dying, though he couldn't say what. "Saving," he repeated.

"Saving from an existence of uselessness," Dr. Heathrow spit out. The man stood taller, as though remembering his own importance. He straightened his shirt. "I did that. I made you what you are. I gave you purpose, an ability to *provide* something to the world few others can. What would you have been otherwise, Sam? A bottom-feeder. A drain on society just like your mother and your father. *Nothing.*"

"I would have been free," Sam said, and his voice sounded as dead as his soul. *My body would have been mine.*

"Free? Ha! Like your mother who was probably a slave to drugs? Just another whore who spread her legs for pocket change? Like your father who must have begged strangers for any measly scraps they were generous enough to throw his way? Free like *that*? All you damaged mistakes born from low-IQ addicts and thieves. I shouldn't have expected more from you, Sam, but I did. I did."

"You had no right," he said, and his voice sounded less dead this time, his breath a mingled growl. The monster was coming to life. "No one gave you permission to do what you did to me."

"Who had a right then? Who was going to give permission? Your parents? They couldn't have cared less that you were alive. Your mother threw you in a dumpster! Did you know that, Sam? Some bum found you naked in a reeking pile of trash! She didn't even put a blanket around you."

Dr. Heathrow laughed then, high-pitched and dripping with cruelty, and Sam withered inside. He'd never let himself hope that his mother had loved him, or he hadn't thought he had. But in that moment, he knew that he'd lied to himself. Because deep inside, he'd held the silent, secret wish that someone out there loved him from afar. *Remembered him*. He knew the hope had existed because he felt it shatter, and he suffered as the shards of the dying dream cut his inner flesh.

How many more of his own lies, his own miscalculations would he have to confront? It was too painful to consider.

"The program rescued you. Do you have any idea how much money was put into you? Each surgery, even the ones we thought would surely fail, you survived. You were made stronger. You should be grateful! What a disappointment you are. You couldn't be trained. Always daydreaming. Seldom paying attention." Dr. Heathrow made a sound of disgust in his throat. His face was regaining color as though his own righteousness was boosting his vigor. "Even so, we put you in the field, ever hopeful you'd take to the work once you got your feet wet." That same sound of utter disdain. "But you proved a disaster. Even worse, here you are, having failed your final command. The one drilled into you since birth."

The part of Sam that might have kept control bent and surrendered to the reeling, spinning, sickness and rage swirling inside him. It was the monster, and it was clawing for release. Everyone, all his life, had *lied* to him. Vicious, unthinkable lies. And then they'd stolen his body and twisted his soul. He was a freak and a monster. Because of them. A growl emanated in his chest, rising. He took a step toward the doctor, then two. Dr. Heathrow had grown confident with his words, but now he faltered, his eyes flashing fear.

"Whatever you're thinking, I'd tread carefully," the doctor ordered, attempting to sound commanding and failing miserably. "We gave you some time. But your time is up. We know where you've been. There was a tracking device on one of your ribs. It was damaged in the shooting, but even you should know we have methods of finding anyone, Sam."

There was a tracking device on one of your ribs. The news hit him like a blow. They'd known where he was all along, every moment of his life, even the places he'd found a moment of freedom—or so he'd thought. But that too had been a lie. They'd tracked him like a dog. They could have swooped in and killed him at any moment. And they probably would have if he hadn't disappeared—into New York City first and then to the cottage with Autumn.

"We know where you're living, Sam," the doctor said, his voice high-pitched and squeaky. "And we know with whom."

With whom.

Autumn.

No!

They'd used those methods and tracked him to the house on the river? Had they been casing the area, and he hadn't even known? Sam's chest rumbled as his jaw clenched, the growl bursting from his mouth. The doctor let out a squeal, ducking and cowering, attempting to slink along the wall.

Red-hot rage incinerated Sam's blood, hot enough to melt the metal he was made from. The monster rose from the molten river of what had once been Sam, reforming himself from fire. And Sam surrendered.

He picked up a chair, throwing it with all his might against the wall. The doctor screamed as it crashed, splintering to pieces. Sam roared. He'd murdered for this man. He'd done terrible, violent things for this scalpel-wielding demon. He picked up a glass table and threw that too, and it rained shards. Sam thundered and smashed and threw, demolishing his way through the doctor's house to his office as the man screeched and rolled into a tiny ball in the corner, the evidence of the monster's presence lying in a heap of broken glass and shattered furniture all around him.

"You're all but dead!" the doctor screamed. "They're coming for you, Sam. You and the woman too. Is that why you're here? It won't matter. They'll find you anyway. You should know that!" He flailed his arm, his finger pointing at his desk.

You and the woman too. Sam pivoted toward the desk that held a laptop and swooped it up, the word ELIMINATE flashing on the screen. Sam's breath exploded, the yell on his lips faltering as he looked closer at the image next to the word. *No, not just one image. Photos of me and Autumn.* His breath sawed in and out of his chest, the fiery fiend within glowing hotter. Dr. Heathrow had ordered a hit on Sam.

And on Autumn. He thought Sam knew. He believed that was why he was here.

His living, breathing rage turned, shoulders hunching, hands rising. Dr. Heathrow's eyes widened. There were tears on his cheeks, and he was quaking with terror. He raised his hands, a defensive gesture as Sam advanced on him.

CHAPTER FORTY-TWO

Mark's foot eased off the accelerator as he rounded the corner, taking the exit as the GPS instructed. Sam had left, not just for one of his walks, the ones Jak called mini pilgrimages, but for good. At least that was what Autumn's impression had been as she'd tearfully explained what he'd said.

They'd tried their best to ease Sam into the knowledge, the magnitude, of what had been done to him. But even Mark hadn't realized the extent of the evil. It was no wonder Sam was reeling. And he'd be looking for any solid footing that would help him hold on, any possibility that his entire life hadn't been a terrible, ghastly lie.

The other two groups Mark had found had been brainwashed as well, but they hadn't been mutilated and pieced back together. Sam had been tortured, experimented on, horribly abused, and brainwashed to become part of a mindless cult. Men and women for hire who would do anything, kill anyone, follow any order no matter how violent or immoral.

Mark thought he knew where Sam would look for any possible stability first. Because he would hold on to a final sliver of hope. And that final sliver was Dr. Heathrow. The man Sam had made excuses for, the man Mark had seen him struggle to label a villain. His father in a sense, and Mark's gut churned to think of it.

He pulled into the driveway of the grand, white brick colonial. He'd been pulling information on the man since he'd first heard his name from Salma Ibrahim. By anyone's measure, he was a vastly wealthy man. *Blood money.* Mark would bet his life on it. There was no way a doctor could have believed the people he'd operated on had needed the surgeries Autumn had described. Sam had been told his bones were brittle, his organs diseased. But they hadn't been. They'd cut into his healthy body and done whatever they'd wanted in the name of who knew what. An unthinkable horror. How many hadn't made it? How many had died on the operating table or soon thereafter?

How many hadn't had Sam's incredible strength?

Mark jogged up the steps, slowing when he saw that the door was open, a centimeter of gleaming marble showing but nothing more. His internal alarm bells rang. He stepped to the side and then pressed the bell, leaning forward only slightly as he listened. *A muffled crash.* Mark removed the firearm holstered under his coat and used his foot to push the door open.

Slowly, he went inside. "Agent Mark Gallagher," he called. "Hello?"

There was broken glass on the marble foyer floor at the open doorway to Mark's right, and he hurried toward it, his weapon preceding him. The room was destroyed. His eyes flew from one corner to the other. *Jesus.* Had Sam done this?

The sound of something falling to his right had him whirling around, his gun aimed at...a cat. He let out a harsh breath, lowering his weapon as the feline scampered away.

Mark left the room and then did a quick search of both floors as he announced his presence. It appeared no one was home. In the master bedroom, Mark noted the closet door was open, a few shirts and hangers littering the floor, and on a shelf of suitcases, one spot was empty. Obviously, someone had packed in a hurry, not even bothering to fully shut the front door. Or using a different exit, the garage perhaps.

He descended the curved staircase and returned to the study with the broken furniture. Someone had thrown the pieces against the walls, which showed large dents and torn wallpaper. Pictures that had once hung there were now in shards on the floor. Perhaps the doctor himself had done this, but...Mark was almost certain it'd been Sam. The dents on the walls were deep.

What did he say to you, Sam?

Whatever it was, it'd broken him.

Whatever it was had brought out an explosion of violence. But Mark saw no blood, no evidence that a human had been hurt. The furniture and artwork had been the victims here.

In the corner, a mahogany file cabinet lay on its side, the top drawer smashed open, a pile of folders spilled out onto the floor. *The doctor's files.* He knelt and picked up the open folder at the top of the stack. It didn't list a name, but he recognized the picture. *Sam.*

Oh Jesus.

He opened it and flipped through, reading quickly the extensive list of surgeries and treatments, a lump filling his throat at the sheer number of them. Sam's first operation had been when he was nine months old. It was a miracle he was still alive.

He glanced at the stack of files he'd set next to himself. Many of them featured red stickers on the front that said simply *Deceased*.

All these victims had been taken from the system under the guise that they were ADHM babies. They weren't. From what he could tell, not one of them had actually tested positive for the disease. One of the files had fallen open, and the photo of a toddler met his eyes, a black-haired girl whose skin was mottled and blistered by whatever was done to her. Vomit threatened. Mark steeled his spine. *Take in the information. React to it later.*

He couldn't take these files with him. He'd need to go to a judge immediately and get a warrant if they were going to be used as evidence. But he had to know what had been done to Sam, the others, to understand fully what he was dealing with here. The pure, undiluted evil. And he wanted to give Sam his history when he was ready. The man had been tortured. He deserved that much. Mark used his cell phone to take photos of each page, flipping quickly.

He slowed for a moment when he saw the report done on the experiment to his hair. An attempt to permanently lighten his coloring had been deemed a failure for the unusual color they'd achieved, more silver than blond. Mark could only guess at the reason for researching the ability to change the appearance of foster babies at birth… *Dear Jesus,* it was too sick and evil to comprehend. He felt empty. So empty. It reminded him of the cold, ruthless Nazi doctor Josef Mengele, who never received punishment for his heinous acts of brutality. Only he would have been proud of Heathrow's work and even greatly outdone by these villains.

Mark's hands rarely shook, but they did now as he returned the files to the drawer, leaving the file cabinet where it lay, another piece of broken furniture in a room full of destruction.

As he moved toward the door, his foot hit the edge of an open laptop obscured under a pile of loose papers. Mark picked it up and pressed the keypad. The home screen lit up, displaying an open email message. He began to scroll down to what looked like the top of a photo, but right before his eyes, the message blinked out, disappearing, just before the entire screen appeared to digitally melt. Had someone just remotely scrubbed the computer? *Holy hell.* Mark set the piece of equipment on the desk. Maybe computer techs would find something on it later, but he had a feeling it had been rendered useless.

CHAPTER FORTY-THREE

Autumn stood at the window, staring dispassionately—and mostly unseeing—out at the bleak, gray sky. Her mood reflected the weather. *I miss you. Where are you?*

Jak and Harper had taken Eddie for a walk on the shore to hunt sea creatures (per Eddie), and they'd be gone for a while. She had a feeling they'd left as much to hunt for the elusive Loch Ness Monster as to give Autumn some time alone, and she appreciated it.

She'd failed to convince Sam to stay and let her—and Jak, Harper, and Mark—help him. She'd tripped all over her words, grown desperate, gotten ahead of herself, pressured instead of relieved. She clenched her eyes shut, wishing she could go back in time and do better, say the things that would have brought him comfort, hope, instead of making him flee.

She pulled in a big breath and let it out slowly.

Regardless of whether Mark was able to find Sam or if he appeared on his own, it was time for Autumn to figure out her own life and whether she could return to it.

Which brought both happy anticipation and immense pain. Because she'd likely be returning without him.

He thinks he's a monster. But he wasn't a monster. Far from it. What had been done to him was monstrous.

He was a human being. Deserving of the same love, the same respect, the same personal liberty as anyone else, regardless of whether he had someone there to advocate for him when he was born and immediately cast aside. And he'd been treated as no more than a *thing*. She didn't know how to help him accept that level of betrayal. She was still attempting to accept her own. And she had love, family, and community. He'd never had anyone. Not a single soul.

You have me, Sam. Please remember you have me.

She saw movement at the sliding glass door, a massive figure, and for the whisper of a moment, the thought that he had returned made her gasp with joy, taking a step in that direction.

But it wasn't Sam. The beefy man who stood there smiled, his flat face breaking into a menacing grin. A flood of adrenaline made her body jerk. Autumn screamed, turning again and running through the house, grabbing Jak's keys from the kitchen counter. She headed for the front door just as the window next to it shattered, a hand reaching in to turn the lock. *The alarm. Why is the alarm not sounding?* She'd set it herself after Jak and Harper left. They'd disabled it, but how?

She skidded to a stop, letting out another scream as she pivoted and then ran to the back room. She heard more glass shatter as another window broke. *Oh God, oh God.* Sobs rose in her chest.

She slammed the door to the bedroom she and Sam had shared and rushed to the half-open window. Another man was approaching, and she let out a yelp as she flung herself forward, attempting to shut it before he could grab the edge. But she wasn't fast enough, and his meaty arms shot out, and though the window slammed down on his hands, he simply grinned, pushing and opening it once more.

Autumn stumbled backward. She heard heavy footsteps in the hall, her head whipping back and forth between the locked door and the window where the man's head was now coming through. She sobbed, backing up, plastering herself against the wall as the door handle jiggled. The man's shoulders appeared in the open window as he gripped the sill, ready to hoist himself through.

Please don't kill me. Please don't kill me. But she had a feeling that was a given.

She thought of Sam and Bill and Ralph, Veronica, and Caitlin and all the people she loved so much, the ones that had brightened her life in ways big and small. She opened her eyes, staring at the large man who was going to kill her, her vision blurring, but she blinked the tears away. *I'll fight with my fists and my teeth.* But like once before, either way, she vowed to go with her eyes wide open.

But suddenly, the man was pulled backward, a grunt falling from his mouth as his chest hit the sill. His eyes widened, face registering shock, as he fell out the window. She jerked with surprise, panting as she leaned forward to see what had—

"*Sam.*" The word was a breath and a sob, mingled as one, and she ran forward just as the door behind her splintered, rattling in its frame. She ducked, and Sam grabbed her under her arms and pulled her forward. The man who had been coming in the window lay on the ground, a spray of blood around him. "Sam, Sam," she sobbed. "You came back for me."

He took no time to greet her, simply grabbed her hand and led her around the side of the house where another man's body lay on the ground, blood pooled around his head.

Vomit moved up Autumn's throat, but she swallowed it down, taking Jak's keys from her pocket and handing them to Sam. "Jak's car," she said. He pulled her in that direction, both of them ducking as they ran behind a row of hedges to the street and then to Jak's vehicle.

Please don't come back, Jak and Harper. Stay gone.

They're not interested in them though.

But she had thought they weren't interested in her either, only Sam.

Behind them, down the hill, a man emerged through the front door of the house, shouting at someone behind him as he headed their way.

Sam pressed the unlock button, and they both jumped inside. Autumn strapped on her seat belt as Sam fired up the engine and then peeled away from the curb. She turned her body to see three brutish men coming out of the house.

"You're here," she said, the last word ending on a sob. She could hardly believe it. She'd been preparing to die. She'd be dead. If not for him, she'd be dead.

"Of course," he said, gripping the wheel. His hands were cut, knuckles bruised, and she stared at them for a moment. She wanted to ask him where he'd gone, what he'd done, and who had sent killers after them, but they were in a race for their lives, and she'd hear all the details of *why* later.

"Head toward the town limit," she said. "Sheriff Monroe will help us." *God, she didn't even have her phone.* But she had her life. They both did. At least for now.

He glanced at her and gave a short nod before turning

onto the road that curved around the water, a steep drop on one side, a wall of rock on the other.

She looked over her shoulder at the winding road behind them, spotting a black truck, advancing quickly. "It's them," she breathed.

Sam's eyes went quickly to the rearview mirror and then back to the road. His knuckles were bloodless where he gripped the wheel, bruises standing out in sharp contrast.

The roar of the truck grew louder, and Autumn held back a scream, grabbing the handle above the door and holding on for dear life. She wanted to cry with terror, but she didn't dare distract or startle Sam.

The truck hit their car with a screeching jolt and then fell immediately back. Sam lost momentary control of the car, and it skidded precariously close to the edge of the cliff. Adrenaline poured through Autumn's system, her breath coming in pants. She gripped the handle, crying silently as Sam got control of the car, punching on the gas and speeding around a bend.

They turned onto a straighter portion of road, and the truck advanced on them again, jolting their car, a sickening crunch of metal as the steering wheel shook and Sam worked to keep the car on the road.

Again, Autumn looked over her shoulder to see the truck advancing on them. *Not again. Please not again.* It was so much bigger and more powerful. There was no way to outrun it, and they still had miles to go. *OhGodohGodohGod.*

One of these hits was going to drive them over the edge of the road to the river below. A moan burst from Autumn's lips. She braced for another impact as the truck came right up to their bumper, but instead of hitting them, it made a sudden swerve, coming up next to Sam's window.

"Duck!" he yelled, and she did as he said, putting her head on her knees, more tears tracking down her face as she quaked with fear. Sam took his foot off the accelerator, immediately dropping back, and Autumn sat up, her eyes wild as she looked for the truck.

The truck slammed on its brakes, and Sam swerved by them, punching the accelerator again as they came to another bend in the road. Again, Autumn gripped the handle and squeezed her eyes shut, just waiting for their car to tip. But it didn't. It raced around the curve just as the truck did too.

"Fuck," Sam hissed, and when she looked up, she saw why. There was another black truck, stopped, blocking both lanes just up ahead. The truck behind was slowing down. She and Sam were trapped. There was nowhere to go unless they went over the edge.

Two men stepped from the truck ahead, and Sam slowed to a crawl. "There are too many of them. I can't fight them all off, not for long anyway. We're going to have to run. When I come to a stop, jump out and follow me down the bluff."

"Okay, okay, okay," she sobbed. She was trembling violently with terror, but she knew as well as he did that they had no other choice.

The truck behind them was coming toward them slowly. They knew they had them boxed in. Sam slammed the brakes, the car coming to an abrupt stop, and pulled the emergency brake. "Now," he said, and they both jumped from the car.

Autumn ran around the front to where Sam was holding out his hand for her. Another shot of adrenaline gave her the strength she needed to race beside him, hand in hand, as they heard shouts from either direction.

"Here!" Sam yelled as he ducked into the foliage at the edge of the road, Autumn directly in his wake.

The slope here was steep, but there was plenty of brush to hide behind, and Sam led her, more quickly than carefully. She heard shouts from above over her staggered breath and the blood whooshing in her ears.

Sam stopped, crouched, and pulled her with him. She went to her knees in the dirt, holding on to the trunk of a skinny tree. Their eyes met and held, chests rising and falling as they took a moment to catch their breath.

They'd been here before, hadn't they? Hiding behind trees from monsters. Only then, she'd thought him one of them. Now, she knew he was anything but.

She brought his abraded knuckles to her lips and kissed them, murmuring his name. "I love you," she said. "I love you, Sam."

"Autumn," he said, his voice filled with gravel. He brought his hand to the back of her neck and laid his forehead against hers. "I love you too. I've loved you all my life. I'm sorry—"

Before he could finish that sentence, the sound of sliding gravel met their ears, the brush shaking at the very top of the incline directly above where they hid. *Oh God.* They'd found them. Sam yanked her to her feet as she let out a tiny gasp. He craned his neck, looking up, and she followed his gaze, seeing that foliage shook in each direction. They'd spread out and were moving downward simultaneously.

They jumped to the rock-covered ground, now fully exposed, Sam's head whipping in both directions. "Fuck," he swore under his breath. The slope where the monsters descended was behind them, the choppy river in front.

There was one outlet that appeared to have access to another bluff, but it was far away, across the slippery rocks.

"You have to run," Sam said.

"Run? Without you? No!"

"Yes. Go while you still can. I'll hold them off as long as possible. Run. Get help."

"Sam, no, I—"

"Run!" he hissed, baring his teeth and startling her.

On a small, choked sob, she backed up, their eyes holding. A goodbye. His were fierce, but within the fierceness, she saw the love. And the grief. She reached out, and he reached back, their fingers brushing, just as the first man broke through the brush and began heading toward them. *Oh God. Oh no. Sam, Sam, Sam.*

Autumn turned and began making her way as fast as she dared across the slippery rocks toward the exit beyond while, behind her, Sam faced down an army of monsters.

CHAPTER FORTY-FOUR

The beasts appeared through the mist, approaching from all sides. Sam turned slowly, watching them draw closer. *Five, there are five.* And only one of him. His feet were wet. The tide had risen in the last few minutes, and it washed over the rocks and onto the shore. *Hurry, Autumn. Move quickly.* Thank God she'd gone when she had. The rocks were only getting more slippery and harder to cross. He had to hope that even when they made it past him, the conditions would slow them down. He'd hold them off as long as he could, though he had no illusions that he could overcome so many. Eventually one or more would get past him, and they would go after her. *Please let her head start be enough.* He knew what their order was. They weren't failures, not like him. They'd carry it out unflinchingly, spurred not only by their training but by pack mentality. They were always most dangerous together, a need to outdo each other in their brutality.

He heard their growls, smelled the bloodlust swirling in the vapor rising from the ground. He crouched, his muscles primed. *Autumn. Autumn.* He would not make this easy for them. He'd make them work to take his life. He would not go quietly. Too much had been stolen from him already. And though they might take his life, here today, they would not take away his fight. That belonged to him and only him. Until the final moment.

They moved closer. He knew them, these monsters. They'd been children together, had trained and studied side by side. In another life, they might have been called brothers. But not in this one.

The man on the right was Corbyn, and he was the first to withdraw his weapon. A knife, long and curved.

Sam had expected to take a bullet and wondered why they hadn't yet gone for a shot. Now it was clear. They planned to cut him. His heart gave a thump. He'd been cut so many times before, he didn't relish it. But for Autumn, to give her the extra minutes she needed to escape with her life, he'd let them slice him limb from limb. *Take your time, devils. Give her all she needs to get away.*

Corbyn took three steps forward, and the others did too, withdrawing various knives. Sam pivoted toward one, then another, anticipating which of them he'd take on first. Corbyn's jaw clenched, and he let out a yell, rushing forward, and Sam leaned his shoulder in the man's direction, adrenaline pumping, preparing for impact.

But suddenly, Corbyn came up short, his twisted face registering surprise as he looked at his wrist. One by one, the rest of them did the same, checking the device, responding to the small vibration only detectable to the wearer. An emergency had just been called. *Stop. Wherever you are, whatever you're doing. Halt.* Sam was familiar. He'd received messages similarly as well, though generally not in the middle of a mission. They all stopped, looking around at each other, appearing surprised, then angry, then resigned. One by one, they turned and walked back toward the rocks, ascending the cliff through the brush in the direction of their vehicles.

Sam watched, confused, his heart racing. Were they going to attempt to catch up with Autumn instead? But no, the road traveled in an alternate direction. The road would not intercept her escape.

And though Autumn was a target, he knew his own death would be more important to the program. So why had they turned away?

Sam stood alone on the small slip of shore, breathing harshly, still poised to fight, confused and suddenly unsteady as he watched them get in their trucks and turn back the way they'd come, their engines roaring and then disappearing completely. Movement above as a lone figure climbed slowly down the incline, his confusion increasing, though not his fear. "Morana," he said when she'd made it to him.

She moved toward him, her leg dragging slightly, and he watched her warily.

"Don't make me hurt you," he said. He could, and he would, but he had no desire to do it.

"I'm not here to threaten you, Sam." She let out a small laugh. "I'm well aware of my physical limitations."

He looked up again, listening for the sound of engines coming back. He didn't understand.

But apparently reading his mind, Morana said, "They fortified your body, Sam, but they fortified my mind. I never let them know how much, but between you and me, I'm smarter than all of them." She glanced at the road above. "I intercepted the order once I received the alert that it had been sent. I'm sorry they got as close to you as they did. The text the members just got told them the target has changed. It isn't you. Or Autumn Clancy."

His brain buzzed with confusion. He was still primed to fight, prepared to die, and though his heart was slowing, his muscles were still held tight. "Who? What target?"

Morana just smiled, stopping a few feet from where he stood. "You won't have to worry anymore, Sam. You're scrubbed from all databases pertaining to the program. There's no record that you were ever born."

He struggled to understand. Morana had...deleted his existence? From the computers where his files were kept? "Dr. Swift knows I exist," he said.

"He only knows your number, Sam, and your particular skills. Dr. Swift has been notified you're dead. You followed the final command."

He stared at her, confused. "Dr. Heathrow knows I'm not dead." The man he'd once considered a father had put out the hit on him. And Autumn. He'd seen the email acknowledging receipt of the order. "Plus, he has paper files."

She waved her hands. "Let the police find them. Let them see what they did to you. To us. There's no way to attach that file to you, Samael. You are only subject number 1043."

"Autumn—"

"When he learned you were with her, Dr. Heathrow took her betrayal personally. He wanted you both dead. She has nothing to worry about anymore either. The program doesn't care about her. She was Dr. Heathrow's subject, but she wasn't one of theirs. Only you were."

Subject. It was only Dr. Heathrow who'd wanted Autumn dead? Because it was his experiment she'd compromised. He'd considered her his property, and she'd proven herself ungovernable by him. She'd kept digging and digging, finding answers, finding Sam. It was coming together for him, piece by piece. But if all this was true, Dr. Heathrow had reason to try again, even if Morana had intercepted his order this time. "Dr. Heathrow—" he started again.

"Sam. Trust me." She took a step closer, then another. A bird trilled somewhere close by, and Morana's gaze moved in that direction and then back to Sam. She looked sad suddenly. Lost.

Her expression startled him because he'd never seen that depth of emotion on Morana's face. He saw that she was pretty even despite the pallor of her skin and the way her left eye drooped just slightly. They'd done that to her when she was a teenager with some type of brain surgery or another. Sam remembered now. She gazed at him with something that almost looked like longing. But for what?

"I wanted things too, Sam, just like you. They made me a monster as well."

He studied her. Yes, she would have been normal, just like he would have been. They'd stolen her body from her, her life, turned her into what she was, yet she too had managed to somehow hang on to some humanity despite their best efforts.

Morana reached in her pocket and brought out a handgun. Sam startled, bracing. But Morana brought it to her own head, the same way Amon had done in that schoolyard as he'd carried out the final command. She gave him a sad smile. "I used to think maybe we'd been made for each other. The two of us, cooked up in a lab. But…see, Sam, I'm not made for anyone. And though I broke the rules for you, I won't break the final command."

Sam raised his hands in a stop gesture, imploring her

to listen to him. "No, Morana. Don't. You don't have to. Please." His mind scrambled. He wasn't good with words. But she'd given him some, and he understood now what she'd meant though he hadn't before. "You know that other version of yourself that you mentioned? At the apartment that day?"

She watched him stoically, not lowering the gun.

"I thought about that," Sam said. "I know what you meant. You were talking about the life you would have lived if they hadn't changed you. If they hadn't filled your mind with things you didn't want or agree to. If your body had belonged to you. I know now what you meant." Sam struggled to choose the right words that would penetrate the darkness inside, the same way Autumn's had done for him. "But, Morana...I think we can live that life. I think if we try really hard, every day, we can be that alternate person, because that person is still in there, deep inside, just covered in all the junk they heaped on us."

He'd realized that. Standing over Dr. Heathrow, *one* with the monster inside. Fully merged. He could have killed him, savaged him, but he hadn't. Because *he'd* been the one in control. *Sam*. Whoever *that* was. But he wanted to find out. He wanted to know him. All along, he was stronger than the monster. It'd taken freeing it to realize. The doctor had wanted him dead. The program had wanted him dead. So Sam would live. He didn't know what that meant, not yet, but he would try. It was all he could do.

"You're stronger too, Morana. You defeated them today. Please."

He exhaled harshly and took a step closer, reaching for the weapon.

Her gaze remained on him. "They won't break the final

command either," she murmured, completely disregarding what he'd said.

They? Who is they?

"I've given it. It's kinder. There's no place for them." A resoluteness came into her expression, and Sam's pulse jumped. "But you, Sam...I hope there is another life for you out there, and I hope you live it."

She fired the gun, blood exploding from the other side of her head.

Sam yelled her name as he leaped forward, catching her body before it hit the ground. For the breath of a moment, her eyes met his right before they glossed over, the life draining out of her as she went completely limp. And in that moment, he saw only peace.

Sam fell to his knees in the water, holding her lifeless body as her hair swirled in the rising tide. A bird trilled again, clear and somehow triumphant. Sam lifted his head, watching as it soared into the sky and out over the water.

CHAPTER FORTY-FIVE

Doctor Jeffrey Heathrow woke slowly, groggily. His eyes came open, and he blinked up at trees. The bare gray branches stretched toward him, and he had the strange thought that they looked like skeletal hands…reaching. His head pounded and his body ached. He groaned in pain as he attempted to sit up but fell back onto the prickly ground. *Where am I?* He attempted to orient himself, to remember how he'd gotten *here* in the cold woods.

Sam.

Sam's face appeared in his memory, teeth bared, eyes wild. He'd destroyed his study. He'd thought he was going to kill him. But then something had come into Sam's eyes, something the doctor could not discern. He'd appeared stunned and then…victorious. He'd backed away, turned, and left him there. Headed to Autumn Clancy no doubt. Good. He'd given the order that both of them be taken out. It would only make things more expedient if they were together. Regardless, the men sent to kill them would not fail. He could count on them.

With effort, the doctor pulled himself to a sitting position, bringing his hand to his throbbing head. He'd run upstairs, packed a bag. He'd thought it safer to head to his yacht, the one the program had purchased in a different name, until word came in that Sam and Autumn Clancy were dead. He'd headed for his car when...

He'd seen Morana in the reflection of his shiny Mercedes. He'd started to turn...

The doctor brought his hand to his scalp, feeling the large lump under his sparse hair. She'd hit him over the head.

The wind picked up, whipping sharply and causing him to shiver. He looked around, fear enveloping him now. It was *her* who had rendered him unconscious and somehow delivered him here. How long had he been unconscious? What the hell was going on?

He stood slowly, bracing himself against the trunk of a tree. The sky was dim. How long had he been out? He felt drugged. The doctor turned his arm over and then pushed his sweater up and peered down at the bruised needle prick. Yes, he'd been knocked over the head and then drugged. Anger mixed with fear.

Morana and whoever else had assisted her would pay a hefty price.

They'd forgotten themselves. The doctor had an army of soldiers at his command. It didn't matter that two or three had gone rogue. There were plenty more, and they were loyal. Despite the dizziness, the reminder of his superiority boosted his strength.

He whipped his head toward the sound of something moving toward him through the woods. Something large. And it wasn't attempting to hide its approach.

"Hello?" he said, and though he attempted a commanding tone, his voice sounded frail.

No one answered. But now there was movement to his right and his left as well.

The doctor turned and stumbled forward, falling and picking himself up off the ground. "Name yourself!" he demanded.

A growl to his left. Low laughter to his right.

Fear rose higher, and he turned once again, running this time, though slowly. Too slowly. His limbs were weighted, head foggy with whatever had been injected into him.

He tripped and then pulled himself to his feet. He ran again, weaving through the forest he'd been left in alone.

Exhaustion quickly overcame him as he huffed and stumbled and tried to pull his body forward, but it was as if he were running through molasses. He let out an enraged grunt. Who had *dared* do this to him?

The things behind him were crashing through the woods now, though he had the impression they were merely walking, footsteps heavy but unhurried as he struggled and sweated.

He tripped again, yelping, just as the first of them appeared through the trees, the others mere seconds behind. His monsters. *His* creations. They surrounded him.

"Stop now!" he ordered.

They continued forward as though they didn't recognize him at all.

"I demand you stop now. Do you know who I am?" he screeched.

There were eight of them, no, ten. All the ones who had survived the surgeries and were still alive, except Sam and Morana. He knew who they were, each one of them.

He'd named them after all—after monsters and fiends. He'd opened them up with scalpels and saws. He'd administered pharmaceuticals, both experimental and not. He'd charted and observed and compared and calculated data about their bodies and their minds. He *controlled* them. So why weren't they listening? He looked from one face to the next, expressions blank. They had no emotions. He'd made sure they did not. All machine, no humanity left.

Again, they advanced, a few of them stretching their hands as they drew nearer. He shook with terror. Who knew better than he did what they were capable of?

"It was for the greater good," he screamed. "You should be grateful to me. I made you! Stop now! Cease!"

A menacing growl. A grunt. He saw the savagery in their eyes. They meant to tear him apart with their bare hands.

"Please!" he begged. He put his palms together in the praying position, tears running down his face. But he had not taught these monsters about prayers or pleas.

A hand wrapped around his throat, squeezing, lifting him off the ground as though he weighed no more than a feather. He shuddered, a gargled cry coming from his throat as the rest of them descended.

"Make it quick," he begged.

But they didn't make it quick. They'd been ordered to drag it out for hours, and they were eager to oblige.

And when it was over, when their bloodlust had been satiated and the doctor was nothing but a pile of ruined flesh and broken bones, they too followed the final command they'd been given.

CHAPTER FORTY-SIX

The official story was that patient 1043, a male, and patient 1201, a female, both died on the rocky portion of shore of the Hudson River that day. The woman's body had been recovered, though the man's had been dragged into the water by the rising tide and likely swept into the ocean. They'd been thoroughly brainwashed, fed a lifetime of lies that led to the follow-through of that final command.

But before she'd died, patient 1201 had collected ten terabytes of classified files from Mercy Hospital for Children, working in conjunction with Tycor Labs, information that painted an appalling and gruesome picture of experimentation on the most helpless patients possible: indigent orphans. Abandoned by their parents, victimized, and horrendously abused by the state. They'd been used as science experiments to enrich others, their innocence exploited, their humanity disregarded.

Patient 1201 had forwarded the proof of the widespread corruption to media outlets both small and large, independent journalists, to the whole of Congress, among many others. Some might have ignored it or hidden the information on their own—after all, the corruption ran far deeper than anyone knew—but it had been too widely distributed for that. The genie was out of the bottle.

A genie that raised its trumpet and blasted the heinous tale of crimes against humanity.

A bevy of human rights lawyers had descended, offering their services pro bono to the remaining ADHM kids, of which there were far too few. A handful. Most had succumbed to the disease itself or more specifically the tumors it caused. Others had surely died of the medication or a diabolical mix of the two. Likely it would never be proven either way.

Tycor Labs negotiated a settlement with claimants, and then the company filed for bankruptcy, though the owners were still worth billions.

Autumn was asked to testify before Congress, and she did, but then she returned to her sleepy little town in the mountains, the one where the townspeople protected her from the news cameras that attempted to disrupt her requested privacy. And her grief.

It hadn't only been doctors and pharmaceutical executives who'd known of the lies and abuses and done nothing, it'd been nurses and administrators, too afraid to put their careers or pensions on the line, too fearful to stand alone in the face of giants.

The extent of the experimentation done on the children later sent out into the world as hired assassins, false flag operators, and agents provocateurs was mostly kept classified. After all, the crimes they'd committed, though driven by years of mental, physical, and psychological torture, were only slowly being uncovered. Jak had been meant to be one of those assassins before his grandfather essentially ended the experiment. Sam had not been so lucky. Neither had the rest of them, some of whom were surely still out there, doing their captors' bidding and believing they worked toward some form of greater good they did not care about nor question.

While the global conversation regarding the ADHM babies and those who'd been falsely diagnosed as such mainly surrounded medical ethics and pharmaceutical corruption, the greater story, to Mark and the small group of men and women he worked with, was about the mastermind who continued to evade capture. Dr. Swift, who preyed on innocence and sniffed out other morally empty individuals looking to enrich themselves on the backs of children, remained at large. And with him, the names of those who were malevolent enough to purchase their services.

Autumn paid attention to some of the coverage, but mostly she didn't. After all, she'd lived it. Instead, she focused on her patients, her family, her friends, and the small garden she'd planted at the back of her house.

Most mornings, she woke slowly, a memory, a *knowing*, skirting through the rooms of her mind, telling her *something* was wrong but not exactly what. An inborn coping mechanism, that brief delay. A biological kindness. *Brace*, it whispered. *Brace*. And then reality came flooding in, like the tide she imagined had delivered his body to the bottom of the ocean.

He was gone.

Only…she had another feeling too—one she couldn't shake. One she didn't want to. He was gone, yes, only he wasn't dead. She was sure of it. Somewhere out there, he picked apples or plowed fields or unloaded cargo. Some days as she knelt in her garden, she'd picture him. She'd close her eyes and turn her face to the sun, and she'd *feel* him, just as sure as she felt the kiss of warmth on her skin. Not beside her or down the street but *somewhere.* Somewhere. Still alive, still breathing, still holding her heart carefully in his large, calloused hands.

But it wasn't until six months later that she received the proof that confirmed her feeling. It was a picture of the Grand Canyon, and when she turned it over, she saw his handwriting, which she knew well from her recreated journal. Her breath caught, and she let out a small gasp, tears springing to her eyes. Her hand came to her mouth as she read:

Answer: With others. Anything done in love is never finished. It goes on and on, handed from one generation to the next. So all we can do is put our whole heart into the small corner that is ours.

She leaned back against the counter, bringing the card to her chest, shaking with both laughter and tears. He was alive. He was alive. And it suddenly clicked into place what his message meant. He'd answered her question from so long ago. *How do you build a temple that takes a hundred years to build?*

The next postcard came from Monument Valley, and it said:

A: By not wishing it forward or regretting what is already gone.

Autumn grinned, her heart rejoicing. "How do you conquer time?" she whispered. *Indeed,* Sam. He was answering her unanswerable questions, one by one as he overlooked a sunlit canyon or sat beneath the dappled shade of a tree or gazed at a waterfall at dawn.

"He's on a pilgrimage," Harper said, the sound of baby Faye's happy coos in the background making Autumn smile. "It's necessary, Autumn, but I know it's hard. Hey, what would you think about coming out to Montana for a long weekend this month?"

She only needed a moment to think about it. "Yes," she said. "That sounds wonderful."

Later, she looked up the definition of a pilgrimage: *a journey, often into an unknown or foreign place, where the person goes in search of new or expanded meaning about their self.* Her heart squeezed tightly. He was rebuilding himself. And she was overcome by his strength and his sensitivity, two things no one could take from him or cut from him or exchange for steel. Untouchable. *Oh, Sam. If only you knew how hard I'm rooting for you.*

He'd thought himself a monster. Or a machine, perhaps. Metal. Screws. More parts made in some factory rather than flesh and bone and blood. But he wasn't. He was strength and love and power beyond evil.

Hamilton Pool, Texas.

A: Look to Autumn. Her bravery overcame their plans.

"How do you overcome death?" Autumn said out loud, smiling as she walked from her mailbox to her door. "Look to Sam as well," she added.

Blue Ridge Parkway, North Carolina.

A: The deep brown of her eyes, the glints of red in her hair, the pink of her lips after she's been kissed.

Autumn grinned, her heart expanding. *What is the color of love?*

Then the postcards stopped for a while, and Autumn grew worried, her mind whirling with concern.

"It's okay," Harper told her. "Pilgrimages provide insight,

but they also bring up more questions, some of which will be hard to answer. Give him time."

"I don't have much of that," Autumn murmured. She missed him. She missed him so badly it was its own distinct pain. But God, was she grateful for Harper and Jak, who were there for her any time she needed them, just a FaceTime call away. She had Bill, who she sat with often in the evenings on his porch, rocking and speaking of her hopes and fears. And she had her friends, her community, but no one else on earth understood what she was going through like Harper and Jak did. And maybe more importantly, no one could give input on what Sam was likely going through than them.

In July, she received another postcard, this one from New River Gorge, West Virginia. And just as Harper had told her, instead of answering her questions, he'd posed one of his own.

How do I become worthy of her?

"You already are," she whispered. She looked at the postcard again. If he'd traveled across the country and was slowly making his way back to her, he was almost there. *Hurry, Sam. Please, please hurry.*

CHAPTER FORTY-SEVEN

The small house was quiet, the surrounding street still other than the whispering leaves and the hush of the summertime breeze. Sam stood in front of the tree near the white picket fence, taking it in, gathering his nerve. He inhaled a breath of rose-scented air. Somewhere there was a bush nearby, though he couldn't see it from where he stood in the gloomy dusk.

Sam looked up at the full moon. It'd been his final sign. He'd seen it on the calendar, only a week away, and known it was time to head to Autumn. They'd met under it once, and so they would again.

A wispy light flickered through the window, just beyond a gauzy curtain. A candle? The glimpse of light called to him like a tiny beacon, and he pushed off the tree, moving toward the gate.

"Stop right there."

Sam froze, his eyes moving to the side as the barrel of a shotgun poked through the trees. His heart slowed, then picked up speed. *Ba-boom, ba-boom*. Autumn. He started to turn, his muscles primed to grab the gun, to jerk the person holding it from the cover of foliage, to—

"Oh geez, is that you, Sam?"

His breath released in a gush, his muscles unclenching as the person holding the weapon stepped from the cover of the trees. It was an old woman, and she *grinned*.

"Aren't you supposed to be some sort of trained assassin?" she asked, lowering the weapon.

A trained assassin? He supposed he was. Though he'd hoped to put that training far behind him. "Do you *know* me?"

"'Course I know you. You're all she talks about. Kinda sick of hearing about you, truth be told." But her grin widened, and she gave him a once-over before she slapped her denim-clad knee. "A trained assassin, and I woulda had ya!" She laughed, and Sam let out a self-deprecating chuckle.

"I wasn't exactly expecting a sharpshooter to be waiting here in the bushes," he muttered. *And I was distracted. Autumn's within a few feet of me right this second.*

"Yeah, I suppose not." She glanced toward the house. "I'm Ms. Hastings, by the way."

"Nice to meet you, Ms. Hastings. But, ah, what are you doing out here?" Sudden worry jolted him. "Has there been some kind of trouble?"

"No, no. But a few of us are sitting out back playing cards, and I saw your shadow looming around the corner of the house. Autumn's taken care of all of us in one way or another. And it was important she feel extra safe tonight."

"Tonight? Why? What's wrong?" His muscles tightened again as he primed himself to sprint toward the house. Toward Autumn.

"No need to be alarmed," Ms. Hastings said. But her gaze slid away. "I suppose you should go in. She'll be glad to see you. Here, I'll walk you to the door."

No need to be alarmed? What was going on? They made it to the blue front door, and Ms. Hastings turned the knob, letting the door swing open. Sam hesitated, his nerve endings twisting in a different way than they had when he'd first walked up toward Autumn's house, the one he'd dropped her off at so long ago in that old red truck.

"Don't be offended if she doesn't give you much of a greeting," Ms. Hastings said before she stepped back and closed the door behind him.

What did that mean?

He stood in the quiet foyer, uncertain. *Afraid.* His heart quickened again, pounding in his chest, his ears. He moved forward as if in a dream. As if he'd walked back in time to that misty forest, creeping through the trees, nervous, yet a thrill of excitement trilling through him. He was about to see her.

Movement out a back window caught his attention. He saw three or four people sitting on the patio at a table, playing cards as Ms. Hastings had said. He recognized the sheriff. *What are they doing out there? And why isn't Autumn with them?*

The soft sound of music hit his ears, something slow and sweet. Violins, he thought, a piano. It rose, triumphant, and then dipped into melancholy as he moved forward over the wooden floors, through the dimly lit house.

He barely took in the surroundings, only that there were rugs and throw pillows, cascading plants, and artwork on the walls. She'd made it beautiful. Her home. And though he wanted to stop and look around, he wanted to see her more.

Something was happening in that back room, and he didn't know what, only that he both wanted to run toward it and away.

As he approached the doorway where the flickering light came from, he heard a moan of pain, the splash of water. He smelled the scent of lavender. His heart jumped, fear spiking, breath stalling as he put his palm on the door and pushed it open. For a moment, he simply stood there, trying to make sense of the scene before him as he caught his breath. His feet began moving before he'd directed them to. Toward *her*.

Autumn. Autumn. Autumn.

His heart rejoiced at the sight of her even as confusion gripped him in a vise.

She was lying in a large tub of water at the end of the bed, and there was a woman kneeling next to her, her back to Sam.

He approached slowly, his gaze roaming Autumn, moving from her hair to her closed eyes to the black bra she was wearing to…

Her hugely pregnant belly.

The kneeling woman was murmuring something to her, something soft and reassuring. Autumn's eyes opened, meeting Sam's. Widening. Her lips fell open, and she let out a small sound of shock, which morphed into a grimace and a grunt of pain as she leaned forward, putting her hand on her swollen stomach.

The woman next to Autumn looked behind her, spotting Sam. Autumn lay back, blowing out several breaths and reaching out to Sam. He all but ran to her, going to his knees on the other side of the tub and taking her hand.

"Oh, Sam." She started to cry, tears tracking down her flushed cheeks. "You're here. You made it."

"I'll give you two a moment," the woman said, standing and offering Sam a gentle smile. "She has a little bit of time before the real work begins."

Autumn gripped his hand, the tears continuing to fall as she whispered his name again and again. He leaned forward, using his other hand to touch her cheek. "Autumn. You're..." He looked helplessly at her stomach, eyes widening when he saw it moving with the life within.

She let out a small, strangled laugh. "The word you're looking for is pregnant," she said, the laughing melting into a grimace as she shut her eyes and breathed through another contraction. "You're going to see your baby born, Sam," she said once the pain had passed. "You're here," she repeated as though she was still convincing herself it was real.

Dizziness overcame him. The room spun, and he stood, a sound of distress falling from his lips as he gripped his head. This was... He stumbled back. He had the vision of Autumn's wide, watchful eyes just before he turned and hurried from the room, bursting out the door and all but plastering his body to the first empty wall he came upon. Someone moved past him, back into the room. The birthing room. *Autumn's giving birth.* He was pretty sure it was the woman who'd left them alone. The nurse or the midwife or whoever she was.

Oh Christ Almighty.

How did he come to terms with this?

You're going to see your baby born.

His *baby?*

Wait...he couldn't...except apparently, he *had*. *They* had. He pressed harder against the wall, bringing his hands up and gripping his head. Someone clapped him on the shoulder, and he startled, his arms dropping.

Bill stood there, looking at him solemnly. "I don't suppose this is what you expected to return to," he stated.

Sam couldn't yet form words. The sound that came from his chest spoke of his confusion and distress and something much different lurking just under those two emotions, but one Sam couldn't quite identify just yet over the buzz of shock.

Bill nodded as if the sound he'd made told him all he needed to know. "Yeah," he said, and though he nodded somewhat gravely, his lips tipped at the corners. "This is it, Sam. The end of one journey and the start of another. Take a minute. Let it settle. This is where you choose to go away again or accept the miracle you've been given. Miracles don't always come in the form of a gentle, guiding light. Sometimes miracles zap you right on your ass. I know a thing or two about that, believe me." His smile grew as Sam simply stared. "Anyway, it's your choice, no one else's. If you need me, I'll be in the kitchen drinking and waiting to become a grandpa." With that, he walked away, whistling.

Sam exhaled, taking that minute that Bill suggested. Letting it settle, though that might take longer than a minute. That might very well take a lifetime. All these months, Autumn was pregnant. And now she was giving birth. *You don't have a lifetime, Sam. Get it together.*

He pushed off the wall, rushing back into the dim, herb-scented room.

"You need to be in a hospital," he declared, standing over the tub Autumn was immersed in.

She opened her eyes and gazed at him with such calm in her expression. She reached her hand out, and he took it and then fell to his knees beside her once again.

"No, Sam, no hospital."

The older woman on the other side of the tub assisting Autumn smiled at Sam as well. "Hi, Sam," she said. "I'm Jackie. I've heard a lot about you, and I'm glad you're here. Autumn has had a low-risk pregnancy and is right where she wants to be. Birth is rarely a medical emergency and I have every confidence that Autumn won't require either equipment or medication. Birth is the most beautiful, natural thing a woman's body ever does."

Sam took a deep breath, his muscles relaxing as he gripped Autumn's hand more tightly in his. Of course she hadn't wanted a hospital. Not the smell or the memories. She wasn't sick. She was welcoming new life. They both were. That other emotion, the one that had sat just beneath the shock and the fear, emerged, stronger, mightier than the others. It was *joy*.

"Water," Autumn murmured, closing her eyes again and leaning her head against the side of the tub.

Jackie gestured to a cup with a straw sitting on the table next to him, and he brought it to Autumn's lips.

"I can't have... I didn't think..."

Autumn let out a small breathy laugh though her eyes remained closed. "Apparently you were misinformed."

He gazed at her, his eyes roaming her beautiful face, the one he'd pictured every day for the last eight and a half months. But even though he'd kept the vision front and center in his mind, it didn't compare to the real one before him now. She was the only woman who existed on God's green earth. "I love you," he said. The words came easily. They were simple because they were true.

Her eyes did open then, but only for a moment. "I love you too," she whispered, the last word turning into a moan as she gritted her teeth and squeezed his hand. After a minute, she relaxed again, leaning back. "Did you know more babies are born during full moons?" she asked him.

"I didn't know that."

She smiled. "Well, now you do. Tell me about where you've been, Sam."

So he did. He told her about the red-hued cliffs of Arizona and the rainbow-sheened springs. He described the majestic mountains of Colorado rising over lush fields of wildflowers. He told her of the ranch he'd worked on and then the supply room of the general store, moving from place to place, learning things about himself he'd never known.

He told her about the roar that had always come from inside him, the one he'd feared all his life. Finally, he'd closed his eyes, and he'd *listened,* realizing that what he'd thought was the monster rising within was the howling song of his soul. And though it was a song of sorrow, a wail of longing and loneliness and long-endured misery, it was a song all the same. It was the expression of his humanity, an undeniable truth, the yearning for love and the hope that what was sorrowful now might someday be joy. He'd hung his head, and he'd let it sing, tears coursing down his cheeks as the monster faded and the man emerged.

And he'd known it was time to go home.

Time to figure out what to do with the rest of his life—something using his hands, something that connected him to the earth. And time—apparently—to be a father and a husband if she'd have him.

She smiled, though her eyes remained closed as she focused on the growing pressure, and then she reached for him and laced her fingers with his.

Jackie left them alone as Autumn's contractions drew

closer together, and Sam blotted her skin with a cold washcloth, telling her how much he loved her and what a warrior she was. And she gripped his hand and murmured that he was a warrior too, and their baby would be as well.

Jackie returned to guide Autumn as she began to push, and Sam watched wide-eyed and breathless. Finally, with a mighty yell, she pushed their baby out, reaching into the water and bringing the small body to her chest.

Autumn sobbed, her cry filled with relief and victory, and a moment later, the baby joined her, its wail filling the candlelit room.

"It's a girl," Jackie said with a grin, rubbing her back and encouraging her lusty cries.

A girl. A daughter. *I have a daughter.*

Jackie cut her cord and then bundled her up and placed her in Sam's arms before helping a shaking Autumn from the tub and then leading her to the bed. *Sometimes miracles zap you right on your ass.*

Sam let out a disbelieving breath, marveling at the tiny miracle in his arms. His daughter stared up at him, trusting. Perfect. A beautiful, perfect girl. *Life.* "I will protect you forever," Sam vowed, protectiveness moving through him as he kissed his child's head. She had Autumn's eyes and Sam's lips. He couldn't believe she was real.

He walked to the bed where Autumn sat, propped up on pillows. He sat next to her and carefully handed her the baby. "Hi," she breathed, bringing her lips to the baby's cheek and then running her finger along it. "My girl of fire and moonlight."

Sam wrapped his arms around her, encircling them both. *Them.* His treasure, more precious than gold.

"What will we call her?" he asked.

"I thought Estella," Autumn said, meeting his eyes. "It means star."

"It's perfect," Sam said as they both returned their gazes to the baby.

This is it, Sam. The end of one journey and the start of another. Bill's sage words struck him again. And right then, he had all the faith in the world that their journey would be a wondrous one, filled with hope, challenges, adventure, and love. And that sometimes, even the monster got a happily ever after.

Steamy, addictive and emotional ...

Available now from

PIATKUS

Do you love contemporary romance?

Want the chance to hear news about your favourite authors (and the chance to win free books)?

Kristen Ashley
Ashley Herring Blake
Meg Cabot
Olivia Dade
Rosie Danan
J. Daniels
Farah Heron
Talia Hibbert
Sarah Hogle
Helena Hunting
Abby Jimenez
Elle Kennedy
Christina Lauren
Alisha Rai
Sally Thorne
Lacie Waldon
Denise Williams
Meryl Wilsner
Samantha Young

Then visit the Piatkus website
www.yourswithlove.co.uk

And follow us on Facebook and Instagram
www.facebook.com/yourswithlovex | @yourswithlovex

PIATKUS